GIFT OF THE ALUIEN

THRICE BORN

By Summer Hanford

Martin Sisters Publishing

Published by

SkyVine Books, a division of Martin Sisters Publishing, LLC

www. martinsisterspublishing. com

ISBN: 978-1-937273-65-1
Cover Art By: Summer Hanford & Justin Girard
Science Fiction/Fantasy
Printed in the United States of America
Martin Sisters Publishing, LLC

DEDICATION

In loving dedication to my grandmother, Shirley Watson Buecheler. Thank you for being an intelligent, capable, beautiful woman and setting the stage for all of us who follow.

To Neil,
Enjoy reading about Ari's big adventure!
Merry Christmas!
Summer Hanford
11-16-13

An imprint of Martin Sisters Publishing, LLC

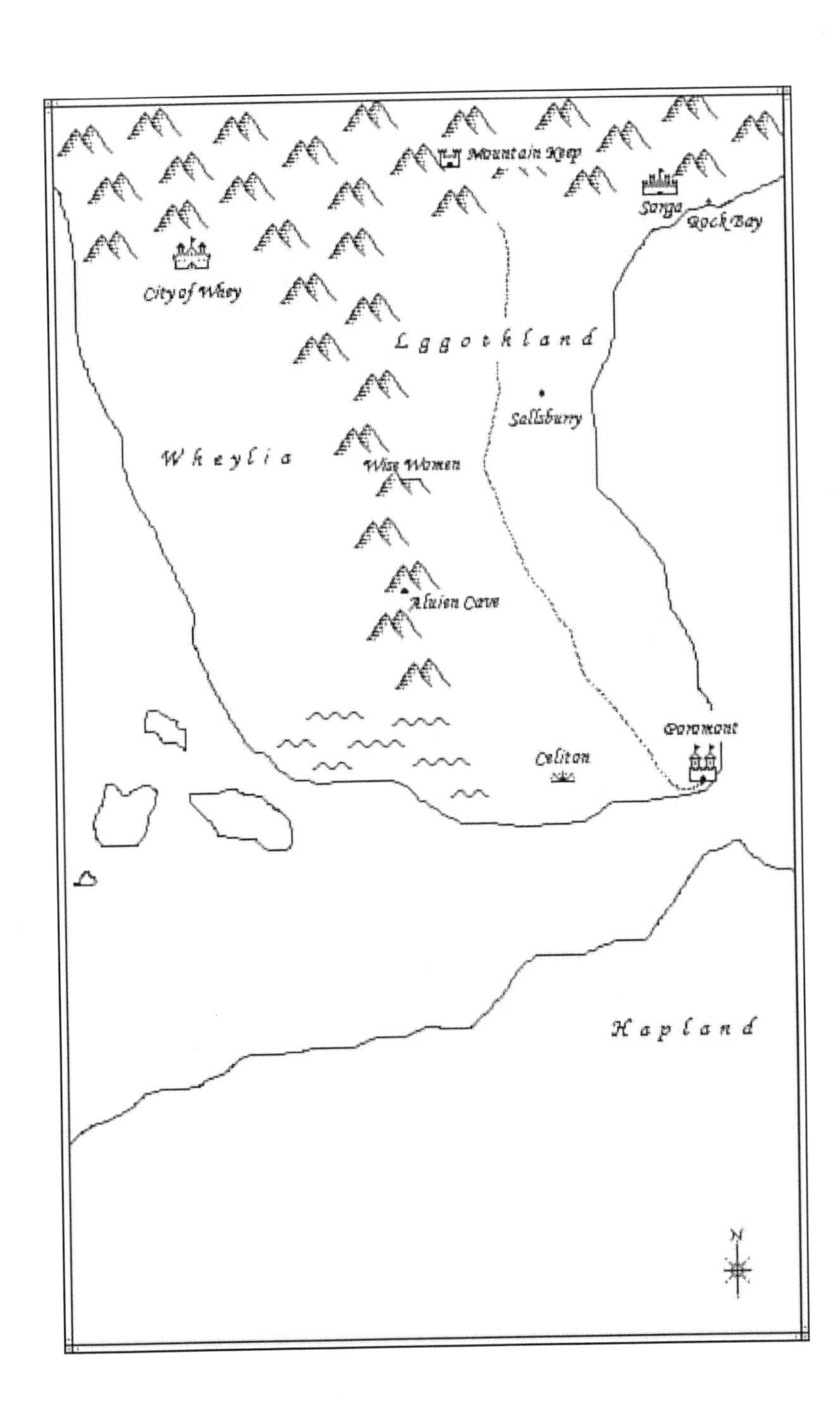

Mountain Keep
Sorga
Rock Bay
City of Whey
Lggothland
Sallsbury
Wheylia
Wise Women
Aluien Cave
Goromont
Celiton
Hapland
N

Chapter One

Ari walked down the aisle in front of the stalls. Dust motes swirled around him in the light streaming through the stable doors. He checked the horses, making sure they had plenty of water and fodder for the evening. For almost five years, since he turned ten, taking care of the horses at his uncle's inn was Ari's job. Before that, when he was little, he helped his older cousin, Mactus.

Ari's other cousin, Jare, was supposed to help too, but Jare's idea of helping was usually to threaten Ari with a beating and sneak off for a nap. Ari didn't mind. Whenever Jare did help, Ari had to go behind him and redo everything. Ari worked hard to take good care of the guests' horses because he hoped to be a stable hand for a great lord someday, or maybe even get to drive a coach. He wanted to see more of the world than his Uncle Jocep's inn in Sallsburry.

"Good night," Ari told the horses. They watched him with liquid brown eyes as he swung shut the stable doors, the smell of cut hay wafting out. Across the inn yard, Ari could hear music and laughter spilling from the common room. The other doorway leading into the walled yard, the one from his aunt's kitchen, was already shut for the night, as was the gate that closed off the inn yard from the street.

Ari looked between the gate and the common room. Another good thing about Jare not helping was there was no one to tell on Ari when he snuck away. It was a perfect spring night, and although his uncle told him many times not to do it, Ari couldn't resist the forest beyond their small village. It would be alive with the sounds and smells of spring, and when the sun finally fell below the horizon, the full moon would be nearly as bright as day. Ari loved it in the woods.

He crossed the hard packed earth of the inn yard to the gate. With a quick look around, he slid one side open and slipped through. He knew his uncle would come out later to latch it for the night, but there was an old apple tree leaning against the outside of the wall, its branches draped in blossoms, and Ari had long since discovered he could climb it and use its strong limbs to get over the wall and back into the yard.

He paused in the alley outside, listening for any sign his departure had been observed. When no voice was raised to call him back, he snuck onward, through the dirt streets of the small town and into the fields beyond. Ari kept to the edges of the fields, following the low walls made by years of stones pulled from the rich earth each spring and piled to the sides.

The last flickering orange glow of the sun left the sky just as Ari entered the forest, making it doubly dark. He paused, the coldness of the spring evening and his sudden lack of vision running a shudder through him. For a brief moment, he considered going back, his uncle's oft-repeated warnings about how dangerous wandering alone in the forest could be running through his mind.

Ari shook himself, shrugging off such childish fears. He would be fifteen that summer. He was practically a man. The woods were not scary.

Ari was usually obedient. His aunt and uncle were kind, and he worked hard at the inn for them. They took him in when his parents died, when he was very small, and Ari was always grateful for that. He had a good life at the inn, even if his cousin Jare made Ari do both their work, but he just couldn't seem to stay out of the woods that spring. The mystery of it, always looming beyond the neat fields surrounding the village, the space under the trees looking so dark and impenetrable, called out for exploration. All that past winter, Ari had felt something growing in him, and when spring came, the draw of the forest was more than he could resist.

He stood still for a long moment, breathing in the combined smells of last fall's rotting leaves and spring's new growth, until his eyes adjusted. The moon rose early, so it wanted only the fading of daylight for the world to be bathed in its silver glow. Once he could see well enough not to walk headlong into a tree, Ari started forward. It was not bright enough to make navigation under the trees easy, but he knew his path, having a destination in mind. There was a clearing not far from where he was, where he would be able to sit and look up at the stars and listen to the cacophony of noises the spring forest made.

Ari was almost to the clearing when a strange light flickered at the corner of his vision. He stopped, turning. Even though the moonlight was bright and the leaves on the trees still bundled into tight little balls, waiting to open, he couldn't see far. Trunks and branches seemed to bind together into impenetrable darkness. Try as he might, he couldn't see anything moving. His heart seemed to stumble in his chest, and he shook himself again, reminding himself there was nothing to be afraid of. Feeling foolish, he resumed his way toward the clearing.

He could see the clearing from farther away than he expected, the moonlight glowing unnaturally bright inside it, making the journey seem strangely tedious. But as he neared, he saw the light inside the clearing was moving. Coming bright from the left, then flickering off to the right. Fear spread skeletal claws through him once more, pulling his skin taut and shortening his breath. Glowing creatures flowed through the empty space before him, running one after the other.

Entranced, Ari crept to the edge of the trees, his fear fading as he took in the creatures' beauty. He stared in wonder as one after another, luminous beings flittered across the clearing. They were manlike but bleached of color and radiating light fit to rival the moon. Ari crouched low among the still-dormant bramble, barely daring to breathe, lest he catch the attention of the beautiful creatures before him and startle them away. Here was surely something magical. Something far beyond the realm of Ari's life at the inn.

But one of the beings stumbled, falling to its knee. Ari half rose, nearly crying out, startled to see that fluid grace halted. The being looked around, and Ari saw fear and pain mar its glowing face. It turned to him, somehow sensing him, eyes picking Ari out among the brush. Its glow dimmed to reveal a seemingly normal man, clothed in loose-fitting white trousers and a long tunic slit up the sides for ease of movement. It clutched its side, as if wounded.

"Go back to the inn, boy," it called in a musical voice. "Danger runs alongside the Aluiens in the forest tonight."

Ari opened his mouth to answer, but his words were stolen by the undulating darkness that rose up behind the glowing being. Evil as palpable as the stench of decay radiated from that darkness. Terror shot through Ari, and he fell backward, barely aware of the confusion on the glowing being's face. From the darkness, a black-coated knife rose. Ari cried out, pointing.

The glowing being turned, springing away just in time to avoid the fast-descending knife. In a flicker, it was gone, and Ari was alone with the darkness.

Eyes that burned with anger came to rest on him. Ari's first instinct was to get up, to run away, but his body wouldn't obey him. The darkness coalesced, revealing the form of a man. Ari tried to force himself to crawl backward, but he remained where he was, at the edge of the clearing, watching in terror as the dark came for him.

"You shouldn't have done that, boy." The man's voice was slippery smooth, soothing. Ari felt the will to run melting from him. "I had plans for that Aluien, and now they're ruined. Why would you ruin my plans, boy?"

Ari's body went limp on the cold damp earth. He could barely focus on the words. He blinked, feeling almost as if sleep would overtake him.

"Do you know what I was going to do to him?" He knelt on the ground beside Ari, leaning over him. A pale man with hard, dark eyes. "I will show you."

Deep in Ari's mind, fear cried out, screamed and thrashed, but none of it could latch onto his will. He lay there, transfixed and unmoving, as the man lifted his knife.

"I was going to do this," he said, viciousness filling his tone. His arm slashed out, raking the knife across Ari's throat. Hot blood welled out to spill down either side of Ari's neck, pooling on the rain-saturated forest floor. Darkness and pain rolled through him, sweeping away thought and reason. In moments, there was nothing left of Ari but pain and a sinking feeling, sinking toward death.

In the last instant, the last moment before death overtook him, the man with the knife jerked away, and a bright light replaced him. A beautiful light, shining fit to outdo the moon.

Chapter Two

Ari burst from the forest just as the edge of the glaring red sun crested the horizon. He ran headlong across a field full of wheat toward the village. He couldn't believe he had woken to find himself in the woods. He'd meant to spend only a short time there before returning to his uncle's inn. He must have fallen asleep, and now it was morning, and he was almost sure to be caught out. He careened into the village, tendrils of fog swirling in his wake. Darting to his left, he ran down a narrow alley along the side of his uncle's inn. To his relief, all looked quiet within the sprawling two-story structure.

He fell into a more careful pace, for if those inside yet slept, stealth was a greater ally than speed. He edged along the wall of the inn, peering around the corner. A quick glance revealed the narrow street behind the inn was empty. Ari ran to the ancient apple tree leaning against the outer wall of the inn yard and shimmied up the rough trunk, his leather-clad feet readily finding purchase. Wincing as a piece of bark jammed its way into one hand, he paused for a moment on an outstretched branch, peering through the thick foliage. He rubbed his palm, listening to the sounds in the courtyard below.

He didn't hear any signs of wakefulness, or smell the warm smell of fresh bread. Maybe they were all still asleep.

Ari was usually the first up, waking before the sun cleared the surrounding buildings to tend the visitors' horses. His aunt would rise shortly thereafter to begin baking for the day. He would only be caught if by some bad luck, a guest decided to leave before dawn. Ari grimaced. Then he would not only have a reprimand from his uncle for sneaking out to the woods again, but a beating from Jare as well. There was only one thing Jare hated more than being roused from bed to fetch Ari, and that was finding Ari gone and having to tend the horses himself.

Carefully, Ari slid along the branch and lowered himself into the courtyard. As the tips of his toes touched the cold, packed earth, the door to the common room swung open. For a frantic moment, Ari's muscles bunched with the intent of launching himself back onto the branch, but experience told him he couldn't make the jump and reason reasserted itself. Instead, he stepped back, fading into the thick shadows that still draped the walls.

A bulky shape filled the rectangle of light spilling into the inn yard, and Ari could see his uncle holding aloft a lantern inside the still-dark inn, lighting the way for a guest. As the stranger stepped into the yard, a pale warhorse trotted forward from where it had stood in silent vigil beside the stable.

Chagrin filled Ari at his inattentiveness. How could he miss a saddled horse waiting by the stables? Let alone a horse of that size and caliber? A knight's horse, he realized, a thrill of excitement running through him. To be a knight's page must be even more exciting than driving a coach. Ari's gaze darted around the inn yard, searching for the lucky page who must be nearby, because a knight always traveled with one. He noticed a second horse followed the first, laden with packs.

"I see you have the horses ready." The knight's voice rolled from him like a river of boulders down a hill. A large hand reached out to pat the destrier on the neck.

“Yes, my lord, just as you requested, my lord.”

Ari’s lips twisted at the deference his uncle showed the knight. He always found it amusing to hear his uncle humble a voice so well accustomed to bellowing over a crowded taproom or shouting at disobedient boys.

“Good, good.”

As the knight checked over his tack, his cloak swung back to reveal the glint of metal and a blue tabard. Ari inched forward to see better.

“Now, about that boy of yours,” the knight said. “I’ll give you five gold crowns to compensate for the loss of his services.”

“My lord, you must understand.” The innkeep’s voice took on a strained note. “Mactus is a boy no longer. He's seen seventeen summers and is to be wed this very fall!”

Mac was engaged? Ari’s brows rose in surprise. He’d missed a lot by sneaking out the previous night: the arrival of this strange lord and his older cousin’s engagement.

“Don’t think you can foist your younger son off on me. That lout wouldn’t last a day in my services,” the knight said, his voice rumbling threateningly as he swung back to face Ari’s uncle. One mail-clad hand rested lightly on the destrier’s neck.

“No, my lord, it’s not that, my lord, it’s just—” Ari’s uncle floundered, raising his arms in a gesture of helplessness. Looking about as if seeking a source of aid, his gaze fell upon Ari, who stood near a wall that, at that moment, lost its shadows in the growing light of a new day. The innkeep’s eyes flew wide.

“What’s this!” With the quickness of a man who lives only as his opponents die, the knight swung round, one hand reaching for the hilt of the broad-bladed sword hanging at his side. He focused immediately on Ari as the source of the innkeep’s startled gaze.

“Ari?” his uncle gasped weakly, the lantern dangling forgotten in his hand. It was hard to tell in the early morning light, but Ari thought his uncle’s face lost all color.

"So you thought to hide the best of them from me!" roared the knight. "Come here, boy."

This last was delivered as a crisp command, and Ari jumped forward, coming to stand before the blue and silver-clad knight. Looking up into the man's grizzled face, Ari felt the world start to careen about him.

It was a face out of tales. The drooping mustache, now gray with age. The broad forehead with thick bushy eyebrows turned down over a dented, crooked nose and a single narrow scar above the right eye. Rosy cheeks worn rough by the elements. Ari realized the true meaning of the blue and silver embroidered surcoat. This was Sir Cadwel, the king's own champion and the greatest knight of the realm.

"Not that I can blame you," Sir Cadwel said. "This one is by far superior to the others. Yes, he'll do nicely."

"Ari?" the innkeep croaked again, invoking Sir Cadwel's scowl. "But, Ari, wh—"

"What I offer would compensate a noble, let alone a peasant," Sir Cadwel barked. "Turn around, boy, so I can take measure of you."

As if the knight's impatient gesture released him from a spell, Ari's legs buckled and he found himself kneeling in front of Sir Cadwel. All he could do was stare in astonishment at the ground on which the knight's metal sollerets rested. Sir Cadwel, here, at their inn, asking, asking . . . Ari looked up in amazement, hazel eyes blinking.

"Me? Me, my lord, to be your page?" Ari wasn't even embarrassed at the unmanly squeak in his voice. He was too astonished to care. A vision galloped through Ari's mind of himself on his own giant destrier, clad in the king's silver and blue, pennon snapping atop his lance.

"As long as you have no deficiency that causes you to fall to the ground like that." Sir Cadwel smiled slightly, gesturing for Ari to stand.

Shaking, he complied.

"But Ari—" the innkeep began.

"Let us away before yon innkeep can find means to spirit you into hiding again, boy," Sir Cadwel said, shooting Ari's uncle a repressive glare. "Come, help me to mount." The knight nonchalantly tossed a clinking sack to Ari's uncle before turning to his horse. For all his dumbfounded demeanor, the innkeep caught the coin with his usual agility. Ari scrambled to lengthen a stirrup for the knight, not wanting to fail in his first task. Hands shaking, he readjusted the stirrup and took up the reins of the packhorse. So awed was he at his strange deliverance, he never thought to look back as he obediently followed the knight down the road. He, Aridian, was now page to the most valiant knight in the realm, the king's champion, Sir Cadwel.

***

Ten days and an equal number of taverns later, Ari did look back, but by then, his uncle's inn was relegated unalterably to the past. Ari gazed sullenly at the broad iron-clad back of Sir Cadwel where he bestrode his destrier, Goldwin. As he walked, Goldwin kicked up clouds of dust that settled over Ari, who trailed behind, leading the pack animal. The past week had been an endless succession of trudging down dusty lanes all day and sitting in soot-filled taverns all evening.

At first, Ari plunged into his duties eagerly, finding them an interesting change from his usual chore of tending the inn's horses. Of course, he had Goldwin and the packhorse to care for, but Ari soon developed a rapport with them, and this duty was pleasant. Helping Sir Cadwel to mount and dismount was a minor task, but helping him to put on his armor every morning and remove it every night proved much more arduous. Ari began to wonder precisely why one needed to wear armor every day while traveling through the center of the kingdom. Sir Cadwel didn't seem to appreciate there were six buckles to be fastened on one arm alone.

Ari asked why the knight went armed, but he received different answers depending on Sir Cadwel's mood. In the morning, as they set out, Sir Cadwel lectured on the necessity of keeping both body and mind disciplined. In the evening, as Ari undressed an inebriated and uncooperative king's champion, Sir Cadwel muttered darkly about enemies. Apparently, being the most renowned warrior in the realm involved a lot of fights, and fights made enemies. Ari privately decided that if he were ever in any fights, he would be sure to kill everyone involved to keep them from stalking him later.

"Of course, it wouldn't be chivalrous to kill women and children," he said quietly to the packhorse as they trudged through a profuse cloud of dust. But male children grew up, and women made more children. Still, killing them seemed unnecessarily brutal and not at all noble.

"I spy a town ahead," Sir Cadwel said, interrupting Ari's moral dilemma. "We shall see if it boasts an inn."

Ari rolled his eyes. Sir Cadwel hadn't risen until nearly noon and, although they were on the road only a few short hours, Ari knew they would stop as soon as they came to a town with a tavern, were it near dark or no. It seemed to be the knight's intention to be falling down drunk by the end of every evening.

Maybe all heroes do that, Ari mused. He didn't think heroes spent so much time in taverns, though. He always thought they would sleep on the ground or on rocks.

Indeed, there was a fair-sized tent among the items on the pack animal as well as plenty of food to be eaten on the trail. Ari wanted to venture into the forests lining the road. He noticed the leaves were very full for so early in spring, and he was curious if their variety differed from at home, although they had not yet traveled far. Certainly, camping would be better than yet another tavern. Yanking on the reins, he drew the packhorse alongside Goldwin.

"How many days does it take to get to the capital, my lord?" he asked.

"As many as possible, lad," replied Sir Cadwel, scowling as he rode. "As many as possible."

Ari sighed, letting himself and the packhorse fall behind again. He knew Sir Cadwel paid his uncle for Ari's services. He wondered if there was any sort of law about him running away.

They continued down the dusty road to discover that what lay ahead was not a town and had no inn. What the knight spotted with his keen long-sight was a cluster of farmhouses and barns. Ari's relief was short-lived, for Sir Cadwel's arrival to the small community sparked off a spontaneous gathering which expanded to include a leisurely supper, and while the farmers didn't have ale, they did have an elderberry wine the old knight found more than satisfactory.

At least the air is nice out here, Ari thought. He sat at the edge of the firelight on a low wall constructed of bulging grain sacks, watching Sir Cadwel and the farmers drinking and laughing.

It wasn't that he minded taverns so much. He'd been raised in one, after all, but he now knew that his aunt and uncle kept a clean tavern, as far as such things went. But clean or no, it was always more pleasant to be out of doors. Here, he could smell the earth and apples. Even the scent of animals wafting up from the pastures was not so bad, compared to the smell of stale beer and vomit that infested some of the less savory taverns he'd recently had occasion to visit.

Ari frowned. Could there be apples so soon after winter?

"May I sit here?" a girl's voice intruded softly.

Bare feet and the worn hem of a light blue dress appeared between Ari's gaze and the patch of dirt he was scrutinizing.

"Umm." The skirt was attached to a trim young woman, perhaps all of fourteen, near Ari's own age, and was topped by a wave of long blonde hair and a bright smile. "Yes?" he asked her. Grimacing, he tried again. "I mean, yes, of course," he amended, trying to steady his voice, even though it didn't tend to squeak much lately. He slid over slightly to give her room, but she ended up sitting quite close to him.

"It must be an honor, being a page to such a great man." The girl smiled winsomely at him.

"It must be." Ari winced at his own lack of conviction. "I mean, it is." He looked away, trying to force down an unmanly blush. He didn't think any of the girls in his village had hair quite so blonde, or so long. Not that he had much time to associate with his peers in town as he was usually kept busy at the inn, except when he snuck out at night to the woods. He did know what all the girls in town looked like, though, and none of them had such pretty hair. He wondered if it was as soft as it looked, and he felt his face start to heat again.

Sneaking out at night. His mind prodded the idea, reaching for a memory. There were apple blossoms on the trees that last night at home. How could there be blossoms at home but apples here already?

"And such a horse! I've never seen such a beautiful horse." She looked up at him through long lashes, scattering his thoughts. "Can I pet him?"

"Oh, uh, of course. He's in the barn." He supposed she felt obliged to ask.

"I know that." She leaned closer. "I was hoping you would show me. I'm a little afraid of him."

Ari shrugged and stood up. He almost fell over when he felt her warm palm against his own. Hand in hand, they tiptoed toward the barn. For some reason beyond his comprehension, Ari agreed with her decision to go in stealth.

It's not as if I'm not allowed to pet Goldwin, he thought, but he crept alongside her nonetheless, trying to be inconspicuous.

She opened the stable door and slid through, pulling him in behind her. "Shut the door," she whispered.

He did, quietly as he could, and they slipped into the empty stall next to Goldwin's, finding their way in the flickering light from the now distant bonfire that filtered through cracks in the rough wood walls.

"Oh, he's so handsome!" the girl exclaimed, squeezing Ari's hand. "Pick me up so I can reach over the stall!"

She turned her back to him. Feeling clumsy, Ari clasped her slender waist with both hands, lifting her as high as he could. Reaching out, she patted the horse on the back. Goldwin ignored her.

Squirming, she turned to face Ari as he managed to put her down gently, which he counted as quite a feat since he was sure he was going to drop her and make a fool of himself. She wasn't at all heavy, but he wasn't accustomed to having his hands around the middle of a pretty girl, or on any other part of one, for that matter.

"You're handsome too," she breathed, and he realized he still had his hands clamped firmly on her.

She moved forward as if to kiss him, lifting one hand to touch his dusty brown hair, and Ari took a half step back, unbalancing them both. She gave a little laugh as they fell into the straw, her eyes glinting with mischief and a cunning that caused him to feel leery of the whole situation. For the life of him, Ari couldn't figure out how he ended up on top of her when he was the one who fell backward.

"And you can bed down in here," a deep voice said suddenly, lamplight spilling into the barn as the door opened wide.

"Daddy!" the girl squealed, drawing all eyes to them.

Ari gasped, looking down at her in consternation. She met his stunned gaze with a fiendishly amused look, which the others couldn't see, raising one eyebrow slightly with a little shrug.

"What are you doing with my daughter?" the man roared in a manner that was almost convincing.

"Daddy! I didn't want to! He said he wanted to show me the horsie!" Tears sprang from her eyes like a spring storm.

Ari scrambled off her, leaping to his feet.

"But I—" he said.

"But nothing!" The man charged up to Ari, stopping just shy of trampling him. Behind the irate farmer, Ari caught a glimpse of Sir Cadwel, who was for some reason grinning hugely, looking too drunk to be of any help.

"You've sullied my daughter's honor! You noblemen's sons are all alike! You come through here, accept our hospitality, and then you try to corrupt our innocent children!"

The girl ran to her father, sobbing. He put an arm around her and swung about to glare accusingly at Sir Cadwel.

"We will be compensated for this! I demand this young man do what is right!" the farmer said.

Ari looked about frantically. The man couldn't mean marriage? Even though Ari was certain the man's anger was all an act, he didn't have any way to prove it. Ari eyed the distance back to Goldwin's stall. He was pretty sure he could get himself atop Goldwin and escape before anyone could stop him. Sir Cadwel cleared his throat, his face casting itself into grave look. Ari realized the knight was not so intoxicated as he seemed.

"Yes, what is right," Sir Cadwel said in his rumbling voice. "I believe the law of the land claims a tenth of a man's worth if he's caught in the act of defiling a young—" He glanced at the weeping girl. "—virgin, and therefore spoiling her chances of a happy marriage and leaving her to burden her parents for all time."

"That is the King's Law!" The farmer's angry facade lost its fervor in the face of what seemed like capitulation from the knight.

"I take it, then, there is no doubt in your mind that your daughter has been befouled beyond repair?" Sir Cadwel asked.

"None! Did you see how he lay atop her? We practically caught them in the midst of the act instead of just after. Oh, but if only I was a moment sooner!" the man said, raising one hand dramatically to his forehead.

"A moment sooner and I wouldn't be a part of this charade," Ari muttered under his breath.

"So it was after? I'm glad we've cleared that up," Sir Cadwel said, holding up his hand when Ari opened his mouth to protest.

Ari's mouth snapped shut. He shrugged, scowling. He couldn't believe Sir Cadwel was going along with this. The farmer looked momentarily confused, seeming to gather his thoughts, probably trying to remember where he was in their script. The girl stepped in.

"It was awful, Daddy! He pulled up my dress and, and—" She burst once more into inconsolable tears.

"Ah, yes. No need to go into any details, my dear," Sir Cadwel said. He looked over his shoulder at the growing crowd of farm folk. Some looked amused; some glowered. Whether the anger emanating from the latter was at the farmer and his scheme, or directed toward Ari and Sir Cadwel, Ari didn't know.

"Take this, then." Sir Cadwel reached into his belt pouch and brought out five shiny coins.

The farmer's eyes bulged in anger. "Five pieces of silver?" he roared. "You place the worth of a nobleman's seed at such a price? Do you think to cheat me?"

Ari was sure the man's eyes were going to fly from his head at any moment, which promised to be an interesting diversion when it occurred. Sir Cadwel laughed.

"No, but I consider it more than fair for the orphaned nephew of an innkeep in Sallsburry!" The knight chuckled, tossing the money at the man and turning to walk toward his bedroll.

Surely they must fly out now, Ari thought, watching the farmer as the whites of his eyes bulged to an impossible distance from their sockets. The man's jaw hung open for a moment, then he shot his daughter a look that promised she would pay for the way all their neighbors were laughing.

"Common trash!" the girl spat, offering Ari a swift slap across the cheek. With a toss of her head, she stormed off in a swirl of very pretty hair.

Scowling and cursing profusely, the farmer scrounged in the heavy chaff that covered the barn floor, picking out the coins before stomping away too.

Rubbing his cheek, Ari walked over to help Sir Cadwel with his armor. The knight was still chuckling. Ari hadn't seen him so clearheaded and high-spirited on any eve thus far. Sir Cadwel put a hand on Ari's shoulder, sobering.

"Let that be a lesson to you, lad," Sir Cadwel said. Shaking his head, he went back to unbuckling his breastplate. Though Sir Cadwel generally insisted on being fully armored as he traveled, that night he had taken supper in his breastplate and mail only. It still looked very uncomfortable to Ari.

"Not to trust farmers?" Ari asked, confused.

"No, lad, not to trust women!" The knight chuckled once more, obviously finding his joke amusing.

"What would you have done if he didn't believe I'm a commoner? I mean, I am your page, after all." Ari strove to salvage some dignity from the incident.

"I would have insisted he keep his side of the law." Sir Cadwel's face took on a hard look that Ari had already learned to recognize as the knight considering strategies for dealing with an enemy.

"His side of the law?" Ari frowned, having never heard of either side of the law before.

"Aye," Sir Cadwel said. "The king is not such as fool as to have only the one side of the law. Else what would prevent people from the type of abuse you saw here tonight?" Ari felt a stab of relief. It meant much to him to know Sir Cadwel realized he was not in the wrong. "If the woman accepts payment for the crime, she is to be branded on her left cheek so all know she is not fit to be taken to wife. It is a harsh law, and not generally enforced, but I could have invoked it if I chose. I am the justice of the king."

This last declaration was made with his deep and gravelly voice full of a stern coldness, all hint of laughter gone. Sir Cadwel fell back into his usual brooding silence, leaving Ari to unbuckle and remove the rest of his armor unaided, the knight almost as unresponsive as when he was stone drunk.

Chapter Three

Two days later, they reached the King's Way. Ari had heard tales of this great road all his life from travelers at the inn, and now that he finally set eyes on it, he wasn't disappointed. The highway ran from the mountainous northernmost end of the kingdom to the great seaside capital in the south. It was guarded by the king's men, ensuring free and safe passage from end to end of the country. This, Ari had heard, was good for trade as well as for the keeping of the peace.

The road was broad enough for four carts to travel abreast. It cut through wood, field and hill indiscriminately, letting nothing bar its clear, straight path. Spaced out over a day's easy travel were inns manned by people local to the region, but which also housed the king's men who guarded that stretch of highway. This meant the inns were cleaner, larger and more orderly than was common. Ari always heard the king tried to assign people in a road garrison near their place of origin so they would have more pride in and love for what they guarded.

Ari straightened his shoulders. This was what being a page should be like. They journeyed along the King's Way, one of the most amazing feats of engineering in the kingdom. The sun was bright. The road was full of fellow travelers and lined with apple and pear trees, and it resounded with music.

Music?

Ari looked back to see the minstrel who had performed at the inn they'd stayed in the previous night strolling down the road, strumming out a cheerful tune on his lute.

"Good day, me lad!" the tall well-favored man called, seeing Ari looking back.

Ari smiled and waved over his shoulder. Within moments, the man came abreast Ari and the packhorse, his long legs propelling him forward with ease.

"And good day to you, my noble Lord Cadwel!" The blond man addressed the back of Sir Cadwel's head where he rode before them on his giant dun-colored horse. The minstrel folded into a graceful bow, strumming some very noble-sounding notes, all somehow without breaking stride.

Sir Cadwel grunted, not looking back.

"How great it must be to be beholden to so grand a master." Bright blue eyes peered around, then looked down at Ari. "Why, the ballads I could compose if only you would let me accompany ye on your next wondrous deed!"

"What name do you go by, bard?" Sir Cadwel asked without turning, his tone sour.

Ari had noticed the knight showed a perverse dislike for compliments or reminders of his past acts of valor, discovering early on that if he asked Sir Cadwel to tell him about any of his oft-recounted accomplishments, the knight would fall instantly into his darkest mood.

"Why, Larke, me lord, and none other," replied the brightly clad man, executing a quick series of dance steps as they walked.

"A presumptuous name, bard," Sir Cadwel said.

"Aye, me lord, but one to which I have the rights of skill and look," Larke said.

Sir Cadwel twisted in his saddle, scrutinizing the bard. Ari knew, were that look directed at him, his knees would have started to shake, but the bard just smiled amiably, his fingers plucking out a foreboding chord on his lute.

"You do bear some passing resemblance to the legendary bard Larkesong," Sir Cadwel said, turning back. "As for skill, I cannot say it was such that I took note last night."

Ari blinked in surprise. He thought Sir Cadwel had been too drunk to notice the bard's performance by the time Larke had wandered into the inn the night before.

"Perhaps this night I will find truer song and better please your lordship," Larke said with deference. "Assuming ye be sober enough to notice," the bard said in an undertone only Ari could hear.

Ari stifled an unmanly giggle, but even if Larke had yelled out those words, Ari doubted Sir Cadwel would have responded. Looking up the King's Way in the direction of the capital, Sir Cadwel sank back into his typical brooding silence. Ari shrugged and turned his attention to the bard, realizing here he might get the answer to a question which was troubling him.

"Minstrel Larke," Ari said, "how is it that apples grow so early in the spring south of Sallsburry? In my home, they were but buds when I left, yet as we travel, I've seen many near full fruit."

"Spring?" The bard chuckled. "Have not your fun with me, lad, for I know as well as you that the time of year is late summer, nearly fall." With laughter in his voice, the bard launched into a gay travel song, not seeming to mind he had to carry both body and chorus. Ari looked around himself in a dazed fashion, blinking repeatedly.

***

That night, Ari lay on a straw-filled mattress, which did little to keep the hardness of the floor below it at bay, staring at the ceiling in confusion. He had, trying to seem as sane as possible while doing it, asked several people what time of year it was, and all agreed it was nearly fall. While that explained the apples, it did nothing to ease Ari's mind.

It had been early spring when he snuck out of the inn and spent the night in the woods. Yet it must be late summer now, as people said. Once his eyes were open to it, there were so many indications that time had passed and of the season. The full leaves on the trees. The heavy summer air. How tall he suddenly was. The way his clothes fit so poorly. How his voice rarely cracked these days.

If it's late summer, then I'm fifteen, he realized. *Surely I would recall my fifteenth birthday?*

Yet he didn't. Lying there on the floor, he listened to Sir Cadwel and Larke breathing, both deeply asleep. The bard took his lodgings with them, insisting he would follow Sir Cadwel until he had the makings of a great ballad. Sir Cadwel seemed too despondent to care one way or another. Ari gathered from the almost complete depression Sir Cadwel traveled in that they must be nearing the capital.

Closing his eyes tightly, Ari tried to recall the night he'd last snuck out of his uncle's inn. At first, he remembered only the forest full of noise and life and himself wandering happily through it, free from the torment of his cousin Jare and away from the crowd and noise of the inn.

He just walked, as usual, then lay down in a glade to stare at the stars. That must have been when he fell asleep.

No, that wasn't right. Ari's mind pressed at the memories, chipping away the quiet vision of stargazing and sleep to get at the turmoil beneath. He remembered hiding. He went to the glade to look up at the stars, but something was amiss. Concentrating, Ari dredged up a memory of crouching in the brush. He recalled that clearly, memories darting to the surface of his mind like carp finding the first hole in the ice in spring. The memory of glowing white beings running through the forest bubbled to the surface.

Aluien. The strange word whispered in his mind.

One of the glowing beings, the Aluien, stumbled into the clearing, falling to one knee, sword still clutched in his hand, although he looked as if he had not the strength to lift it. What a beautiful creature the Aluien was. Sculpted, with light softer and paler than moon glow emanating from him. Raising his head, he spied Ari and called to him from where he knelt, panting, left hand clutched over a wound in his side. Then the darkness crept up on the Aluien from behind, black-bladed knife raised to strike. Ari cried a warning. The Aluien sprang to his feet, speeding away.

Ari gasped, sitting bolt upright on his cot. His hand went to his throat, feeling the pain of what had happened next. Sir Cadwel snorted and rolled over, but he didn't wake. A long-fingered hand reached to lay itself on Ari's forehead.

"Shh," Larke's melodious voice said. "Forget, young Aridian. You aren't to know these things. Forget, me lad," he whispered, and Ari did forget, falling into a dreamless sleep.

***

"So part of a page's training is sword work?" Ari asked Larke for the eighth time since leaving the inn that morning, this time speaking very loudly.

Sir Cadwel gave no indication he heard. They were very near the capital, and the graying knight was not even maintaining the pretense of civility. Ari sighed. He was rather fond of the idea of learning to use a sword.

"Minstrel Larke," Ari whispered to the buoyant man walking at his side. "Why doesn't he want to go to the capital? He's the king's champion."

Larke opened his mouth to reply.

"So it's swordplay you want," Sir Cadwel bellowed, wheeling Goldwin to face them.

Ari jumped, shooting the bard an accusatory glance, as if Larke had started the conspiratorial whispering. "Yes, sir?" Ari said.

"Well then, I see our irrepressible minstrel wears a blade. Perhaps we can give you a demonstration." Sir Cadwel dismounted with a speed and agility that belied both his age and the amount he had drunk the night before, his sword whistling from its sheath.

"My good Lord Cadwel," Larke said, holding empty hands out before him.

"Do not call me lord," Sir Cadwel growled.

"Good sir knight," the bard said, his eyes pleading. "This blade at my side is but for show! Part of my costume and nothing more. So slender 'tis that one meeting with your great sword would cast it in twain."

The fierceness drained from Sir Cadwel's face. Ari let out a small sigh of disappointment. It wasn't that he wanted anything to happen to Larke, but the prospect of a duel was exciting and he hadn't before seen Sir Cadwel so animated.

"Still, you are correct, sir," Sir Cadwel said, his eyes taking in the nearby woods and the sun's height in the sky. "We've come far enough today, boy. Let us make camp and find some stout saplings. I'll give you an exercise in defending yourself."

Ari struggled to contain an undisciplined whoop of joy. They would sleep in the forest, and he would learn swordsmanship from Sir Cadwel. Worried the knight might change his mind, Ari began flinging possessions from the packhorse.

"We don't want to make camp in the middle of the road, boy," Sir Cadwel said. "Set up back there a ways." The knight pointed to the tall grass, well back from the road, where the first trees stood.

Selecting a small axe from the pack mule, Sir Cadwel waded through the grass to the edge of the forest and began hacking down saplings.

"I shall procure us some wood for the fire," Larke said, an indecipherable smile tugging at the corners of his mouth. Humming, the bard disappeared into the forest, leaving Ari alone to wrestle with the large canvas tent.

***

Later that evening, Ari lay on his thin blanket on the hard ground and wondered how everything that seemed lucky to him could turn out to be so dismal. He was sure he had never before known such pain. Certainly not when his uncle punished him or when he and Jare scuffled. Learning to use a sword seemed so glorious, but so far, it amounted to a series of beatings administered by a stick-wielding, strangely joyful Sir Cadwel.

There was a time, though, he thought. *A time when I was in such terrible pain.* His hand went to his throat, but the skin there was smooth. He half-expected to find some terrible scar.

Before he could focus on that thought, a soothing hand was laid upon his forehead, and he drifted into a deep and dreamless sleep.

***

The following morning, Ari didn't feel that bad at all. He realized he must have exaggerated his own misery, so that evening, determined to become a knight, he doggedly pursued the idea of learning swordsmanship. Sir Cadwel seemed impressed with Ari's tenacity and ordered him to fashion their original branches into padded practice blades with hilts. All in all, Ari felt practice went much better the second night.

By their third day of practice, Sir Cadwel had undergone a noticeable change. Most drastically, for the past two nights they traveled past the evenly spaced inns, stopping in clearings near the road. Sleeping in the out of doors without the aid of mead caused the knight to rise far earlier, and much like at his uncle's inn, Ari had to wake just the dark side of dawn. Not that he minded. They traveled no farther than before each day, but now in the evenings, Ari was learning how to use a sword.

Sir Cadwel, perhaps sensing Ari's momentary preoccupation with his thoughts, swung a hard blow right at Ari's head. Ari got his padded sword up just in time to block it, managing to halt the momentum of the big man's weapon just shy of his nose.

"Hold a moment," Sir Cadwel said. "Come here, boy." Sir Cadwel pointed at the ground in front of him.

Ari lowered his sword, frowning. He thought he was doing quite well, taking fewer hits from the knight's practice sword than usual. True, he'd let his thoughts wander for a moment and had almost suffered a broken nose as a result, but he had stopped Sir Cadwel's blade in time.

"Not bulky like that lout of a cousin," Sir Cadwel said, reaching out to grasp Ari's shoulders and turn him from side to side. "I don't know where you get your strength, boy."

"Must be that wiry sort of strength," Larke said from where he sat, cleaning his lute with a well-worn scrap of cloth.

"Must be," Sir Cadwel said. "Still, I've never seen anyone learn so fast. At this rate, he'll be good as any knight in a year. Better than many."

"Me? Good enough to be a knight?" Ari couldn't believe his ears. His thoughts raced with the idea. Visions of himself riding a giant warhorse just like Goldwin filled his mind.

"A knight?" Sir Cadwel shook his head, his eyes taking on a sad, contemplative look. "I'm afraid that's out of the question."

"But you just said," Ari said.

"I know what I said, boy, but it's impossible." Sorrow colored the knight's tone, adding to Ari's confusion.

"But—" Ari began again, his vision throwing him off the back of the warhorse as it galloped away without him to find itself a real knight.

"You see, me lad," Larke said. "In his infinite wisdom, the king has made a rule. A law, if you will. None of common blood may ascend to so noble a realm as knighthood. 'Tis to help us keep to our right place, you'll be understanding."

Ari looked to Sir Cadwel to deny the minstrel's proclamation. The knight scowled but said nothing. Ari's shoulders slumped in disappointment.

"So it's all for nothing," Ari said, dejectedly casting his practice sword to the ground. "That I got to be your page and you're teaching me. It doesn't mean a thing." He lowered his head, willing the tears he felt to stay in his eyes and not slide down his face.

"Now, now, me lad, I wouldn't say 'tis all for naught." Larke put aside his polishing. "These skills will serve ye well in life. You could be a weapons master and train the sons of young nobles, or perhaps you could be a steward or a soldier."

Ari sighed. He stooped to retrieve his padded stick, still not looking up, and headed to their packs to stow it. Glancing back at them, he saw Cadwel turn his formidable scowl on the bard. Larke jumped up to follow Ari.

"Look here!" the bard exclaimed with flourish, gesturing to the cooking pot that hung over the fire. "I've made us a fine pot of porridge while you two were busily beating on each other with sticks."

"They aren't sticks," Ari muttered to the ground. "They're practice swords."

"Cheer up, me lad," Larke said. "Fetch us some bowls, and then we shall see if the mighty lord—" The knight's eyes took on an even darker cast as he glowered at Larke. "Err, that is to say, mighty knight, remembers his squire days well enough to teach you to mend, as I see the legs on those breeches ye wear need letting down, and the coat on yon knight's tabard's come loose."

"His squire days? Me mend?" Ari asked, retrieving the bowls.

"Aye, me lad." Larke nodded seriously. "All good squires know the way of a needle and thread."

"He's telling me true?" Ari asked.

Sir Cadwel shot Larke another hard look but smiled at Ari. "Indeed."

"Why, I remember, in his younger days, when he did apprentice to old Sir Specton." Larke chuckled, waving the cooking spoon at the knight. "He used to stay up all hours, fingers bleeding for all the times he did miss his mark, trying his hardest to mend the hems of his lord's garments. Least, till he met a lass who didn't mind seeing to it for him."

"You remember? How do you—" Sir Cadwel began, his voice sounding younger than usual, astonishment coloring his tone.

"That is to say," Larke interrupted, looking strangely frantic. "Me father told me such tales about you, sir."

"And just who was your father?" Cadwel said, his eyes narrowing.

"You mean I have to sew?" Ari asked, rising up on his toes and trying to regain their attention.

"Aye, me lad," Larke said, turning to Ari. "Only don't let the lasses know. It would shatter their image of so mighty a warrior to know those great callused hands have done a woman's work, and thus break their hearts."

Predictably, at the mention of his greatness, Sir Cadwel's face darkened. He grabbed the now full bowl Ari was distractedly holding out to Larke and stomped off toward the tent.

"When you're done babbling with that lute strummer, boy, come get my tabard, and let the jongleur teach you to sew. He gossips so well, he must be apt at other womanly occupations." The knight let the tent flap fall closed behind him.

Ari scowled at Larke, not sure exactly why he was in trouble, but moderately sure it was Larke's fault. The bard winked at him but said nothing.

Chapter Four

In unspoken accord, the three stopped as they crested the hill overlooking Poromont. The capital of Lggothland sprawled across the flatland, stretching from the base of the hill on which they stood, all the way to the ocean. Ari gaped at the city in awe. It gleamed with such bright whiteness in the afternoon sun that it hurt the eyes to look upon. Thick walls surrounded a central castle, and another set ringed the city, but buildings spilled over and beyond them in great abundance. The city looked like a giant beached sea creature. Its thick center had tentacles of buildings branching off around the many roads that breached the city walls, and its long white docks reached out into the water. Ari's eyes followed one of those lengths of white-painted wood into the vastness of the sea, and he realized he was looking at the ocean for the first time. The ocean, which went on forever until the end of the world and then poured out in a great waterfall, continuously fed by the melting of the huge glaciers to the north. He'd heard tales of the great icecaps and of the ocean and her ways. He shuddered, thinking of the dangers of the sea hidden by the serene beauty it adopted near the shore.

"This is a day which had to come," said Sir Cadwel, sighing. "Fetch me my helmet and shield, boy," he said without taking his eyes from the city.

Ari jumped to comply. Maybe in Poromont, he would learn what made the knight so miserable.

"Well now." Larke's expression was unreadable. "This be where we temporarily part ways."

"You're leaving?" Ari said, pausing as he unwrapped the great blue feathers that went in the top of Sir Cadwel's helm.

"Don't question a blessing, boy," Sir Cadwel said.

Larke cast the knight an amused glance, his face regaining its typical mobility. "But alas, yes, me lad," Larke said with exaggerated sorrow, swiping his broad-brimmed hat from his head with flourish. "For in yon castle is a heart I broke so soundly, I dare not return. Though it was the purest of love that the lady did give me, I found other loves too strong, and so I left her. I fear to look on me again would cause her a pain so great, she may faint away and come to some harm, so I dare not approach yon city too closely. 'Tis but to spare her that I take this upon myself." He ended with the hat clutched over his heart and his head bowed.

Ari laughed.

"I should have expected as much," Sir Cadwel said with a snort of contempt. "Be off with you, knave, and do not fear that we shall mention you to any ladies of the court, for I would sooner claim companionship with your late namesake, notorious scoundrel that he was, than with thee, for he at least blazed with something resembling talent to redeem him."

Larke, grinning at Sir Cadwel, bowing to him, and the knight awarded Larke with what might have been the slightest of smiles. Ari looked back and forth between them in surprise. He'd never heard Sir Cadwel speak in a courtly manner before. He didn't realize the rough old knight knew how. Perhaps even more surprising, Ari was moderately sure the knight was making fun. Ari had occasion to hear many traveling players in his time, and although he knew he was by no means an expert, he was relatively sure Larke possessed a great amount of talent with instrument and song, and that Sir Cadwel enjoyed Larke's singing and playing even if he wouldn't admit it.

"Now." Larke took Ari firmly by the shoulders. "Make sure you bow low to the king, and lower to the queen. Treat everyone with respect, but do not believe they're any better than you. A title doesn't measure a man's worth. Only his actions can do that. Keep your head up, your mouth shut, and your gaze steady. Behave, and do not leave Sir Cadwel's side. I don't want you talking to strangers."

With that strangely succinct advice, Larke stepped back, gave another florid bow, and swung round. His long legs carried him quickly away in the direction they had come. Ari stared after him, blinking.

"You're crushing the feathers," Sir Cadwel said, his light and unconcerned tone at odds with the look of resignation on his face.

As they continued to get ready, Sir Cadwel moved with a slow deliberateness that was almost dreamlike, and Ari felt his anxiety build. What would happen in the city that made Sir Cadwel so reluctant to go there? Ari couldn't even enjoy putting on the blue and brown tabard Sir Cadwel gave him to wear, his mind fumbling through the possibilities.

Once all was ready, they descended the long, gentle slope the roadway took down the hill into Poromont. At the bottom, buildings reached out to engulf them. The buildings on the outskirts were squat and unassuming, but the farther into the city they traveled, the taller the buildings got, and the more substantial. At first, they were made of wood, but deeper into the city, they were brick. As Sir Cadwel and Ari approached the great castle walls, everything was made of huge blocks of gray stone, except they could only see it was gray because there were chips, since every brick, timber, and stone in the capital was painted white. Ari wondered where they got all the paint and how they made everyone do it.

White was not the only thing striking about the Poromont. There were also the paved streets. Dirt road gave way to brick which gave way to flagstone. Ari found the neat hard-packed earth of the King's Way impressive, but to see people using great big stones just to walk on was incredible.

And what people they were! Ari kept his head up and tried to keep his mouth closed, but he was having trouble remembering that he was just as good as these people. Ari had never been anything approaching concerned with what he wore or how he looked, but the people around him made him keenly aware that the only clothes to his name were a pair of thin, patched, brown breeches that were darker at the bottom where the newly let out fabric hadn't seen as much wear. The lacing on his once-white shirt was broken, so he couldn't close it all the way to the top. The newly awarded blue and brown tabard didn't fit well, only emphasizing the shoddy nature of the old clothes he wore underneath.

He only hoped Sir Cadwel wasn't as embarrassed by him as he was by himself. The knight rode in full amour and accoutrements. He sat perfectly straight in the saddle, and Goldwin, whether by instinct or training, walked forward at a stately but unrelenting pace. People drew back out of the knight's way or risked being slowly trampled by the blue-and-silver-festooned destrier. This became less likely as they traveled, for news spread from the outskirts of the city quickly, and soon the road to the castle was lined with people. Young girls threw late-blooming flowers. Women blushed and whispered behind their hands. Men hoisted tankards that somehow began to spill from the taverns, and they told each other tales of Sir Cadwel's great deeds in a contest that seemed mostly about who could talk the loudest.

Trailing in Sir Cadwel's wake, Ari and the packhorse were small and, he hoped, relatively unnoticed. Ari found himself wondering if this was the reason Sir Cadwel didn't like to come see the king. Ari didn't know if having to undergo this much attention was horrible enough to drive a man to drinking, but it did seem rather undesirable. Then again, Sir Cadwel must be accustomed to it. He was the most famous knight in the kingdom and had been for over twenty years.

Ari pictured the young and brash Sir Cadwel to which Larke sometimes alluded, and he could imagine the knight preening before the crowd. The Sir Cadwel in Ari's mind wore a broad smile and accepted flowers from beautiful ladies with lace-coifed heads and downcast eyes. Ari added himself to that scene, longing for those days before he was born, when there were great deeds to be done and Sir Cadwel was the one who did them. For good measure, Ari made himself taller and riding his own horse instead of trailing behind on foot, so that maybe the occasional young lady would want to give Sir Cadwel's protégé a flower as well. He smiled to himself.

Caught up in picturing exactly what such a young lady might look like, Ari would have walked right into Goldwin's rump if the packhorse hadn't balked at the idea. Ari looked up to see the castle walls looming over him. Sir Cadwel had halted at the gate, though it stood open.

"What knight does approach the castle of our king so boldly and under arms?" a soldier in the king's livery called down from atop the wall.

"I, Sir Cadwel, chosen knight and champion of King Ennentine, do approach," Sir Cadwel said.

"Chosen knight and champion of King Ennentine, Lord of the Northlands and Duke of Sorga," the man on top of the wall amended.

Ari couldn't see Sir Cadwel's face, but the man on the wall turned pale under the knight's gaze. "Ah, enter the castle of your king, my lord."

At no signal Ari could see, Goldwin moved forward. Inside the courtyard, the gleaming white castle towered above them. Flocks of brightly clad men and women decorated the enormous front steps, culminating in the forms of the king and queen, also clad in blue and silver. They stood just outside the open ornate double doors which led into the castle, each door large enough for a carriage to pass. King Ennentine was tall and wore his silver beard trimmed short. He looked to be ten or more years Sir Cadwel's senior, but his shoulders showed only a slight stoop, and his waist was trim enough that well-tailored garments hid any paunch age may have added.

Queen Parrella was as regal as Ari could have imagined. She was nearly as tall as her lord, a height which exceeded any other woman Ari knew, and she looked to be the king's junior by as many years as Ari had been alive. That her hair was no longer purely golden didn't diminish it in any way, as the silver strands seemed only to enhance the overall effect that she was sculpted and gilded instead of real. There was not the slightest hint of submission in her stature. Ari would have been quite terrified of her but for the warm smile that turned up her lips.

Sir Cadwel halted Goldwin at the base of the steps, and Ari jumped forward. Feeling so many eyes notice him, Ari's face turned bright red as he assisted his lord to dismount. He retrieved the reins of the pack animal and Goldwin and tried discreetly to look about for the stables. A groom in gray castle livery appeared and expressionlessly took the horses from him. Sir Cadwel mounted the steps, leaving Ari standing alone at the bottom as the animals were led away.

Sir Cadwel removed his helmet when he reached the top. Pinning it to his left side, he swung his right arm out in a courtly bow. "Your majesties," he said, staring fixedly ahead at the space between them.

"Our knight," King Ennentine said, inclining his head. "It grieves us that you have been so long absent from our side, and yet it grieves us all the more for our meeting to come to pass for so sorrowful a duty."

Ari could feel the strain emanating from Sir Cadwel as the king opened his mouth to continue.

"Perhaps our knight would care to rest himself after so long a journey," Queen Parrella said, placing a hand on her husband's arm. "For the hour to dine is almost upon us, and he has been long in the saddle and on the road."

Casting her a quick look, King Ennentine nodded. "Until dinner, then," he said, offering his arm to Queen Parrella.

Sir Cadwel stood rigid as they turned and entering the castle. A steward appeared at Sir Cadwel's elbow, gesturing for him to follow with a bow, but the knight stayed as he was, jaw clenched, seeming unaware of the man. The crowd of nobles started to twitter, some of them moving tentatively toward the knight as if they might speak to him. Ari sprang up the steps.

"Sir," he said in a low voice. "Sir Cadwel, it's time to go in."

Ari put a hand under the knight's elbow and propelled him forward. Ari had enough experience in dealing with an uncooperative Sir Cadwel to know how best to handle him, and it was much easier when he was actually walking on his own. The steward gave Ari a startled look but didn't hesitate to lead them away.

The balding steward in blue and silver led them across the grand foyer and through one of the many side doors. Ari tried to take in the marble inlaid floor and the tapestries which hung on the walls as they hurried through, but he concentrated most on keeping Sir Cadwel moving, not wanting any of the flock of nobles to intercept them.

The steward led them up a broad staircase, which rose to a wide hallway with ornate wooden doors. At the seventh door down, the man stopped, producing a silver key. He unlocked the door and followed them inside. After holding out the key to Sir Cadwel for a moment, he turned and handed it to Ari, bowing. Ari noticed that, although the door was locked, their saddlebags were already inside.

"Dinner will commence at dusk in the grand dining hall," the steward said. "Will that be all, my lord?" he asked Sir Cadwel, letting silence hang for a moment before backing out the door.

"Wait," Ari said, clutching the key in his hand. "Um, please wait," he amended when the steward looked down his nose at him. "We'll need—" Frantically, Ari cast his mind about. What did he need to get Sir Cadwel ready for dinner? "Water and clean clothes," Ari said. All of theirs were dusty, and he was not sure that even clean, they would be good enough to face a hall full of people like the ones on the steps. "That is, are there clothes we could have to wear? I don't mean to keep them," he added, as the man was still staring at him disapprovingly.

"Of course, young master—" the man paused, inviting a name.

"I am Ari, Aridian, that is, and I'm not a master of anything," Ari said, not wanting the steward to think Ari pretended to be more than he was. As an afterthought, he transferred the key to his other hand and held out his right to clasp.

"I will see to it you have everything you need," the steward said, ignoring the hand. "Someone will be up to assist you immediately."

Ari let his hand drop as the man turned away. Feeling that somehow he had already made too many mistakes, he closed the door to the room.

Ari looked about in confusion, wondering what he should do next. The room they stood in, the sitting room, boasted six arched windows bedecked with heavy brocade drapes, two couches, a fireplace, and many rugs, chairs, and wall hangings. All of it looked much too nice for Ari to touch. A doorway led to a room Ari deduced, based on the giant four-poster bed, was for sleeping. Ari couldn't see if there were any more rooms beyond that.

Deciding the most important thing was to get Sir Cadwel into a presentable state, he led his still-unresponsive master to the center of the room and began stripping off his armor. Ari nearly dropped Sir Cadwel's breastplate on his foot when part of the wall alongside the fireplace opened and a young man came through, carrying a steaming bucket of water. The man nodded to Ari, then proceeded through the doorway leading to the sleeping chamber. More young men came behind the first. Ari could only assume there was a tub back there somewhere. By the time bucket-baring young men in the king's livery stopped appearing through the small door, Ari had Sir Cadwel's metal casing off.

Ari led the scowling knight into the next room, which was filled mostly with the bed and a fireplace, and found there was not only a tub but a whole room dedicated to bathing. The bathing room was as large as the sleeping chamber and boasted yet another fireplace, which was lit. He walked Sir Cadwel up to the steaming tub.

"Were you planning on undressing me and sponging me off too, boy?" the knight growled, shaking Ari's hand from his arm.

"If I have to!" Ari shot back recklessly, brushing his too-long hair out of his eyes to glare at the knight.

"Well, you don't," Sir Cadwel said. "I'm not some soft-handed lordling."

"People keep calling you my lord," Ari said without thinking. He jumped back, curling his arms about his head protectively as Sir Cadwel raised his hand. The knight never struck him, but Ari knew it was perfectly acceptable for him to do so.

"Leave me!" Sir Cadwel snarled, advancing on him.

Ari scurried backward and out the door. Closing it quickly behind him, he stood trembling on the other side, wondering why he said such a thing. After a long silence, he heard quiet splashing as the knight entered the tub.

"You need to get cleaned up too, you know, to attend him at dinner," a voice said from the sitting room doorway. "You must be really brave," the voice continued, coming from a boy several years younger than Ari, with dark hair and eyes. "I sure would never dare say anything to Sir Cadwel at all, least not something to make him so angry."

"I'm Ari." Ari stepped forward and offered his hand. He started to snatch it back, remembering how the steward sneered at him, but the boy took it and shook vigorously.

"I'm Peine," he said, still enthusiastically shaking. "They sent me up to help you. They sent me cause I'm the youngest page and somehow you made the master steward angry with you. Are you really good at that? Making people angry with you?" he said, looking impressed.

"I guess so," Ari said.

"I'll be the lowest page for a while," Peine said, "because my dad isn't a very big land holder and I'm the youngest of three sons and I have Whey blood in me too." He let go of Ari's hand to pat his dark hair. The boy's lack of rancor as he said these things buoyed Ari's spirits. "So what do you need?"

"I need, that is—" Ari looked around the room in bewilderment.

"You need help," Peine said.

"Exactly," Ari said, grinning.

"You and Sir Cadwel have to get ready for dinner and you have only—" He screwed up his face, thinking. "One hour and a half of one left."

"But I don't know what I need to do to get us ready!" Ari said, throwing his arms up in frustration.

"You need to get cleaned up so you can attend him at dinner, and you both need nice clothes to wear," Peine said.

Ari stared at him. He was right, of course, but having it stated for him didn't seem to be getting Ari anywhere. He opened his mouth to say so.

"Come on." Peine grabbed Ari's sleeve and started pulling him toward the door.

"But Sir Cadwel—" Ari said, gesturing at the bathing room, inside which the knight was now splashing vigorously.

"He's a knight. He'll want to bathe and shave himself anyhow," Peine said, dragging Ari along. "Knights aren't like lords. I'd rather be a knight's page than a castle page any day, but I'm too small."

"Shave him?" Ari croaked. Sir Cadwel shaved himself every morning, except for his thick mustache. Ari didn't even want to imagine his own shaky hands holding a razor anywhere near the knight's face.

"You could use a shave too," Peine said, looking up at Ari critically as they entered through the servants' door beside the sitting room fireplace. When closed, it blended into the woodwork so perfectly as to be invisible. Ari didn't see how Peine had made it open. "I'll help you clean up all that armor after dinner," Peine added as they walked through.

Ari raised one hand to his face, feeling the lack of smoothness there. "He won't wear his armor to dinner? I have to shave?" Ari asked as they descended a dimly lit stairwell.

"No, no armor at dinner." Peine laughed. "We can get you cleaned and dressed right quick, and then we can lay out his things and see what he needs for me to fetch, and you can dress him, because I have to tend a lord at dinner too." The boy nodded as he spoke, as if agreeing with his own plan.

They reached a narrow hall. From the side they had come down descended many staircases, and the other side of the hall was lined with rooms piled with various items or devoted to specific domestic tasks. Servants bustled about from doorway to doorway in well-ordered chaos. Ari gulped, glad Peine was there to guide him.

Entering one of the many doors, Peine pushed Ari down at a long table, shoving things out of the way to make room for the bowl of water, mirror, and other accoutrements the Wheylian boy produced. Ari eyed the block of soap, thick horsehair brush, and thin blade with trepidation.

"First, you get the soap wet and rub it with the brush and get your face all sudsy," Peine said.

"I know," Ari said, coloring slightly. Taking a deep breath, he proceeded, until his face wore a veritable beard of white.

"And now you shave it all off," Peine said with what Ari felt was an unrealistic amount of confidence in his ability to do so. He picked up the very sharp-looking, shiny piece of metal.

"How's this?" A long, handsome man in the king's personal livery leaned against the doorframe. "Sir Cadwel's new page, I wouldn't doubt. I see they've saddled you with this scamp." The man grinned, taking any perceived sting from his words. Peine grinned back.

"And I'm teaching him how to shave," Peine said, puffing out his chest in pride.

"A sheep leading a goat up a mountain." The man laughed. He limped into the room, and Ari tried not to stare at his obviously ruined right leg. "I don't know what sage advice you've gotten so far, young man, but I'll add to it that you should start under your chin for practice. People can't see a cut down there as well, and shave with the grain, not away from it. That won't seem to matter as much now when your beard is new, but later, it will be good advice for you. And lad, try to leave your nose on your face."

With one last assessing stare and a wink, he sauntered away, obviously at ease with his limp.

"That was the king's personal valet, Sir Endar," Peine whispered as the man disappeared. "He's just about the most important man in the castle."

"He isn't the master steward," Ari said. "I thought the master steward would take care of the king."

"No, the steward's in charge of all of us pages," Peine said. "I wish Sir Endar was in charge of all of us. He's much nicer. Of course, the master steward always says he'd be a kinder man if he didn't have to deal with us pages."

Ari wasn't sure of that, having met him, but he kept his opinion to himself and peered into the little mirror, gingerly touching the razor to the skin under his chin and immediately cutting himself. Ignoring this unpromising start, he switched to a new location and tried again. In short order, he was shaved, finding it not as hard as he feared and much easier once his hands stopped their initial shaking. All in all, he didn't think he'd embarrass Sir Cadwel too much at dinner.

***

After much running about and watching Peine yell at everyone as if he were in charge, all the while dodging kicks and swats, Ari arrived back at Sir Cadwel's rooms cleaned, shaven, and dressed in blue and brown.

"Silver is for more important people than us," Peine said when he gave Ari the clothes, although Ari didn't ask and had no thought he would be dressed in silver anyhow.

The two barely finished laying out Sir Cadwel's things before the knight emerged from the bathing room. He had on the clean britches Ari had placed there for him. Ari hadn't dared enter the room but reached in and grabbed the dirty clothing off the stool by the door, leaving clean ones in exchange. Ari didn't look up as Sir Cadwel approached, instead busying himself fussing over the clothes laid out on the bed. Peine silenced his continuous stream of advice for how Ari should act at the banquet with a squawk and backed out of the room, bowing.

"Don't go," Ari said, but the boy was already gone. "I needed him to show us the way to the grand dining hall," Ari muttered.

"I know the way," Sir Cadwel said. "I see you finally admitted you need to start shaving. Not too bad a first attempt."

"But I—" Ari looked up, startled that the knight noticed. Sir Cadwel clasped him briefly on the shoulder before turning to the clothes on the bed. Ari relaxed, knowing the apology for what it was and glad everything was all right again.

It didn't take long to ready Sir Cadwel for dinner, and soon they descended the wide staircase and walked down the hallway leading back to the grand foyer. Ari had more of an opportunity to look about this time, gaping up at the vaulted ceiling soaring several stories above him, painted to look like the spring sky. Just in time, he remembered to look down, almost missing it when Sir Cadwel turned and entered another hallway.

Ari felt better as they walked to the great dining hall. He knew Larke would tell him that clothes didn't make a man, or some such thing, but he wasn't sure it was true. Ari knew for a fact that he was the same as he'd been that morning, but now that he was dressed properly to be Sir Cadwel's page, it was almost as if he was a new person. Not to him, but to the people in the castle. Now, instead of getting condescending or offended looks, he was completely ignored, like a good servant should be. Peine told him that a good servant was never noticed, only a bad one, and Ari intended to take that to heart. He didn't want to do anything to disgrace Sir Cadwel.

As he trailed Sir Cadwel down another marble-floored hallway, it occurred to Ari to wonder how long they would be at the castle. A long time? When Sir Cadwel left, surely he meant to take Ari with him? Until now, there had only ever been talk of journeying to the capital, but Ari was Sir Cadwel's page, and that didn't last for just one journey, did it? He was old for a page already, though, and Sir Cadwel said he wouldn't be able to be a knight. What would he do if Sir Cadwel didn't want him anymore? He didn't want to go back to his uncle's inn. How did one become a sword trainer? Should he join the king's army? Ari chewed on his lower lip, his mind filled with new worry.

The grand dining hall certainly was just that. It was huge and ornate, and the long table that filled it could seat a hundred people, and it did. After Sir Cadwel was announced, all eyes turning to look at him, the steward directed them to the head of the table, where Sir Cadwel would sit to the right of the king. To the king's left sat his queen, looking even more lovely in the soft lamp light, and to her left, two chairs stood empty. Ari worked hard not to shrink into himself as they started down the endless table. He told himself that no one was staring at him. All those eyes were on Sir Cadwel, who certainly could handle them.

A third of the way along the table, a man's profile caught at the edge of Ari's vision and a jolt of pure fear stopped him in his tracks. His mouth went dry. He managed to turn his head, taking in the angular profile of a pale-skinned man who sat talking quietly to his neighbor. Ari didn't know him. He'd never seen him before in his life, but he was so scared of that profile that he couldn't move. In front of him, Sir Cadwel drew away, oblivious, and Ari wanted to call out, to bring the knight back to ward off the immobilizing terror that seized him.

"Psst." A boney elbow jabbed Ari, and he was propelled forward. It was Peine, standing behind a chair in which a very old man sat. The old man appeared to be asleep. "Get on, Ari," Peine said in a vehement whisper.

Ari straightened his shoulders and turned forward, hurrying to catch up to Sir Cadwel. He didn't understand. He was sure he didn't know the man who struck such fear into him. How could he? Yet just thinking about looking back filled him with terror. Thinking about the man at all was a strain. It would be better if he didn't think about him, Ari realized. Once he decided that, a great relief washed over him. He felt his body and mind relax, and his attention moved on. Sir Cadwel was rapidly approaching the head of the table, and Ari had to be there to help with his chair.

"Your majesties." Sir Cadwel bowed as Ari hurried up to stand behind the knight's chair.

"Our champion," King Ennentine said, nodding.

"Dearest Cadwel." Queen Parrella smiled up at him. "Won't you be seated in your proper place at my husband's side?"

Ari could see the tension in his lord, but the knight could do nothing but comply. Bowing once more, he moved to sit, Ari swiftly pulling out the large wooden chair.

"That's a strong young man you have there," Queen Parrella said. "Most of the pages have troubles with these chairs."

"More so than he looks, my lady," Sir Cadwel said.

"Wherever did you come by so handsome and able-looking a page?" she inquired as talk resumed around the table, the spectacle of the knight and the monarchs meeting ended.

"Bought him from an innkeep in Sallsburry, my lady."

"So he's not to be a knight, then?" She sighed, smiling slightly. "That will break the young ladies' hearts."

Sir Cadwel grunted in reply as Ari looked about, trying to see what the other servants were doing. All along the walls of the room were long, thin tables laden with food and drink. One set of servants kept those tables full, while the lords and ladies were all served by their own personal retainers. Ari moved to the sideboard to retrieve a platter of meat to offer Sir Cadwel as the queen gave up her attempts at cheerful conversation. She looked a bit helplessly at her husband, as if to say, *I tried.*

"Cadwel, if any man deserves his family lands, you do," King Ennentine said. Sir Cadwel scowled into his plate. "I fully intend to award you your titles before the evening is over. It is, after all, merely a formality."

"What if I refuse to accept them?" Sir Cadwel growled in a low voice.

The tray in Ari's hands was surprisingly hot, but he could tell Sir Cadwel wouldn't welcome the offer of meat. He wasn't sure if he should wait for the knight to notice him or put it back.

"Then I will order you to," King Ennentine said, his face set.

"If you force me to take them, I'll refuse to swear allegiance of Sorga to the crown," Sir Cadwel said.

Around them, people leaned forward, trying to hear.

"But as my champion, you are already sworn to the crown," the king said with growing ire. "Surely you would not forsake that vow?"

"I could not, your majesty," Sir Cadwel said, his voice pained.

"Sir Cadwel." Queen Parrella leaned across her husband to rest a hand on his arm. "It all happened so long ago. Can you not give yourself the blessing of forgiveness everyone else has? The forgiveness you would give any other man, were it he in your stead?"

"Never," Sir Cadwel said vehemently, looking down at the hand on his arm. "I cannot forgive myself, and all of those I might seek forgiveness from have preceded me to the afterlife. In time, I will meet them there and beg of them on my knees to give me the punishment I deserve."

All other talk ceased in the room as the knight's savage tone cut across it.

"He forsakes his family's lands?" a querulous voice blurted out from the other end of the table.

"But there will be war!" another man said, standing.

"The king should award someone else the lands!" someone called out.

Voices erupted about the room. Men stood and started to argue. There was a crash as a wineglass toppled. A woman cried out.

"None of you powder-coated lordlings shall touch my family lands," Sir Cadwel roared, rising. "I'd sooner give them to this boy!"

Ari tried to look inconspicuous as all eyes turned to him. His hands were getting very hot under the platter he held, but he didn't dare move.

"Then there will be war to see who can take them from him!" said a man in fur-trimmed green.

"No one would dare," Sir Cadwel said, the menace in his tone silencing the room.

King Ennentine stood, and all turned to him. Ari thought he could feel his hands blistering. He wondered if he could put the evil silver platter back yet.

"Is there no way I can convince you to accept your family titles?" the king asked.

Sir Cadwel turned toward the king, his gaze on the marble floor. His massive shoulders bespoke the tension he felt, straining against the confines of his doublet. "Prove to me I am worthy to be lord of the lands that my brother ruled, and my father before him," Sir Cadwel said, raising his head. "Do this, and I will gladly take them, steward them, and keep them for my king, as my family has done since time untold."

The king mulled this over, looking to his wife for help. Around the table, people still stood. The air in the room was taut with tension.

"A quest, then," Queen Parrella said, rising to stand at her husband's side. Sir Cadwel turned to her. Her earnest blue eyes and silver dress gleamed in the lamp light. No one in the room stirred, and Ari forgot his hands were being scalded by hot metal. "You see beside me, our knight, two empty chairs." The sorrow that throbbed in the queen's voice brought tears to Ari's eyes. "One is the chair of the Princess Clorra, betrothed of my son, who lies at this very moment in the royal wing, dying. Naught can be found to cure her, or even slow the wasting sickness that doth leach away her life. We have bent all our resources to the task, only to fall short. For this trouble, a knight can offer no remedy, but the second chair is for my son, Parrentine, my one and only child, who ran off on a fool's quest, seeking some last way to save her." The queen reached out her hand to Sir Cadwel, who took it in his large callused ones. "I fear that in the rash madness which has overtaken him, he will come to great harm. Reason has fled him, and he races toward disaster. Bring him back to me, Sir Cadwel. Find him, keep him safe, and bring him back to his people." She closed her eyes, squeezing back tears.

Knocking his chair aside, Sir Cadwel sank to his knees beside the table, the queen's hand still clasped in his own. "I will find him, my lady. This I swear to you," he said in his great, booming voice. Ari wanted to cheer.

"So you are charged, our knight," King Ennentine said. "Bring us back our son, well and whole, and your shame shall be washed clean by the healing of Lggothland, for a country without an heir is broken indeed. Your task fulfilled, we shall award you with your family lands. Until this deed be done, they are under the protection of the crown."

"So I am charged, so it shall be, or my life be given pursuing it," Sir Cadwel said, releasing the queen's hand and rising to bow. Straightening, he turned and strode stone-faced from the hall. Ari deposited the platter into the surprised hands of a nearby servant, who yelped at the heat and all but threw it onto the side table, and ran after Sir Cadwel.

***

"There hasn't been that much excitement in the great hall since the prince stormed off!" Peine exclaimed as he backed through the narrow servant's door.

"Shhh," Ari hissed.

Sir Cadwel had paced the room for over an hour after they quit the dining hall, and had only just retired.

"Sorry," the boy whispered in a voice that was not so much quieter as more exaggerated.

Ari lost any worry for the comfort of the knight, however, when he saw what Peine was burdened with. He jumped up to help the Wheylian boy with the tray.

"I told the steward you and Sir Cadwel wanted food, since he didn't stay at dinner at all," Peine said as they set the overburdened tray on a small table by the couch. "I even got him a sweet. We don't get to have them, cause even if there are extra, the ladies have them with tea the next day."

"He's asleep." Ari stared at the heavily laden tray, his mouth watering.

"You shouldn't let it go to waste," Peine said with a straight face.

Despite being cold, the food was delicious. Ari ate half of it without pause before he realized Peine was watching him silently, a hungry look on his face.

"Haven't you eaten?" Ari asked, his attempt at politeness marred by his full mouth.

"Some," Peine said, but his face betrayed his yearning.

"Have some." Ari gestured, swallowing. "I surely can't eat it all myself."

They ate in silence until only the little pink frosted sweet was left. Ari eyed it with longing. He'd never seen anything so decadent looking. Sometimes, his aunt made pastries. Puffy, flaky things filled with hot, sweetened berries, which Ari could never seem to eat enough of, but this delicate miniature cake with white lace-like trim promised a spectacular deliciousness afore unknown.

"We should split it," he said, looking at Peine. It was a very small cake.

"Nah." Peine shrugged, apparently not as impressed with the cake as Ari was. He grinned. "I got them to give me three for Sir Cadwel," he said with a giggle. "So you best eat that one."

Ari didn't need to be told twice. He stuffed the little cake in his mouth. The creamy pink frosting melted, while the white lace parts crunched as he chewed.

"You're so lucky you get to go with Sir Cadwel to find Prince Parrentine. It must be a great thing to be his page," Peine said.

Ari swallowed his cake. "Yes, but—" He shot a guilty look at the sleeping chamber door, lowering his voice. "Why won't Sir Cadwel take his family lands?" By now, Ari had surmised that the reason Sir Cadwel was so touchy about being called a lord was because he didn't want to be one, which meant he didn't want to accept his family lands from the king. Right now, he was a knight, but once he officially accepted them, he'd also be a lord. Lord of Sorga and the Northlands, which seemed to be how everyone thought of him already. Since everyone already thought it, Ari couldn't imagine why Sir Cadwel would be so opposed to the king declaring it officially. He looked at Peine expectantly.

"You don't know about—" Peine looked fearfully toward where the knight slept as if Sir Cadwel might come smashing through the door at any moment. "What happened after the Great War?"

"I know that everyone fought for years and years, and everyone knows Sir Cadwel's bravery and skill won the war for the king." Ari couldn't help sounding a bit proud. He was Sir Cadwel's page, after all.

"But after that," Peine said.

"I guess after that, everyone went home," Ari said, unsure.

"You don't know about the Lord of the Northlands?" Peine whispered.

"I thought that was Sir Cadwel." Ari frowned. He was sure people called Sir Cadwel that, although Ari rather felt everyone should know better than to refer to the knight as a lord by now, seeing how it made him make his most terrible face, and any sane man would want to avoid having that face turned on him.

"Only cause Sir Cadwel killed him," Peine said, nodding toward the sleeping room.

"Sir Cadwel killed the Lord of the Northlands?" Ari asked. He didn't know why that surprised him. It occurred to him that the man sleeping in the next room, who he sometimes aggravated so much, and who he traveled with for months, had most likely killed a great, great many people. Not by accident in jousts, or to save maidens, but on purpose, in war.

"Sir Cadwel's father was Duke of Sorga, and the Lord of the Northlands killed him, and Sir Cadwel's mom, his sisters, his wife, and knocked his older brother down the stairs, and he was asleep for all these years since and never woke up, but Sir Cadwel wouldn't take the dukedom, and he gave the Northlands to his brother too, even though his brother was asleep." Peine paused to take a deep breath. Ari blinked, trying to keep up. "But this past spring, his brother died, which makes Sir Cadwel the duke now. He's been in charge as regent all this time already anyhow."

"Why did the old Lord of the Northlands do all that?" Ari said, shocked. "Why didn't Sir Cadwel stop him?"

"Well." Peine frowned, thinking. "I think it was a little while after the war, and the Lord of the Northlands was on the other side, against the king, and Sir Cadwel killed both his sons in some battle somewhere. I think," the boy added, looking a bit confused.

"But how did this Northland lord get into the castle and kill so many people if Sir Cadwel was there? He's the greatest knight ever!" Ari's voice rose in indignation.

"It is time for sleep," came a grating cold voice from the sleeping chamber doorway.

Ari froze. Peine gave a frightened squeak and darted from the room. The sleeping chamber door closed with a muffled clunk. Ari curled into a guilty ball on the couch and spent a long time trying to fall asleep.

Once he was finally asleep, things didn't noticeably improve. His dreams were troubled by the profile of the dark-haired man he'd seen at dinner. Ari didn't know why, but he feared that man more strongly than he'd before realized fear could be felt. In his dreams he ran, but the man was much swifter than he was, and Ari didn't have much of a head start. Trees grew up ahead of him, and Ari saw something glow luminously. He knew if he could just reach it, he would be safe, but the dark-haired man was closing in. Ari awoke to find Sir Cadwel looking down at him.

"Troubled dreams, boy?" the knight said. "Sure sign of a guilty conscience." Ari blushed. "It's almost noon. I was hoping you would have us packed by this time," Sir Cadwel said, turning to walk into the sleeping chamber. "Get yourself up and moving, boy.

I've been all morning talking with the king and queen, and I think I know where the prince went."

Ari stifled a groan as he unfolded himself from around the pillow he was clutching. Every muscle in his body ached. He stretched, noticing that the sleeves on the blue shirt Peine gave him were actually long enough, unlike those on his old white tunic. He wondered if he was allowed to keep it.

Chapter Five

Sir Cadwel once again dressed in full accoutrement. At their departure, there were a great number of nobles adorning the castle walls and steps, and flowery well-wishes from the king and queen, the latter looking tired and anxious. Then, amidst a blaring fanfare, Ari helped Sir Cadwel mount, and the knight reared his horse dramatically and wheeled away. They passed through city streets thronged with women who wept and threw flowers, as all knew of the prince's tragic devotion to his princess. The citizens of Poromont firmly believed Sir Cadwel would set everything right.

"Where are we going?" Ari dared to ask once they left the city behind.

"West," Sir Cadwel said.

"But this road goes back north," Ari said before he could stop himself.

"But it will intersect a road that goes west," Sir Cadwel growled. He nudged Goldwin into a faster pace, making Ari and the reluctant packhorse have to jog to keep up.

"It warms me heart to hear the gentle banter of my dear travel companions once more," a merry voice rang out from behind them.

Sir Cadwel muttered several choice curses, but Ari swung about happily. Riding up behind them came the lengthy form of the minstrel Larke.

"Look, me lad!" the brightly clad man exclaimed joyfully. "I have a present here for ye!" He shook the reins of a second horse, which he led behind him.

"For me?" Ari's gasped.

"Well, I fell to thinking," Larke said, holding out the reins to Ari. "In all the truly great ballads, the heroes gallop about, you see, and since I am wanting to ensure the greatness of this quest, I decided it behooved me to acquire mounts, that we might embark on some galloping."

"For me?" Ari blurted again, too surprised to take the proffered reins.

"Acquire?" Sir Cadwel asked, eyeing the minstrel suspiciously.

Larke winked at him, causing the knight's scowl to deepen. "Yes, for you, me lad!" Larke said, taking Ari's free hand and placing the reins firmly into it.

"This is the best horse I ever had!" Ari said.

Sir Cadwel gave a bark of laughter. "The only other horse you've ever had was in the cooking pot at your uncle's inn, boy." The knight turned Goldwin north, urging the charger forward.

"Thank you so much," Ari said, looking up at Larke in astonishment.

"Think nothing of it, me lad," Larke said, looking embarrassed. "As I said, 'tis only to ensure the greatness of my ballad, after all."

Ari's face split into a giant smile. Handing Larke the pack animal's reins, he struggled into the saddle. After a few minutes of fumbling, he got the reins in order, the stirrups somewhat the correct length,, and the packhorse's reins lengthened to tie to the back of his saddle. He noticed that the saddle wasn't new, but he surely didn't mind a used saddle. Once everything was situated properly, he looked about. For all his time working in his uncle's stable, Ari had never sat on a horse, and the world looked very far down from atop the roan. He felt a little dizzy.

"Are you two accompanying me on this journey, or should I be seeking out a new lazy boy and mewling peacock to fill my days with joy as I travel?" Sir Cadwel called back.

Despite the knight's sarcasm, Ari could tell Sir Cadwel was in a much better mood than he'd been before the bard had arrived. Gently, Ari nudged his horse forward, and to his relief, the animal complied. Ari grinned at Larke as if he had just mastered the most difficult skill known to man. "What's his name?" Ari asked.

"Stew," Larke said impassively.

Sir Cadwel's laughter rang back down the road.

***

Later, once Sir Cadwel deemed the horses had done enough work for one day, they set up camp in a grassy field alongside the road. Larke set about making a fire and Sir Cadwel began marking off a practice area. Ari removed Sir Cadwel's tent and the rest of their gear form the packhorse and started brushing Stew.

"So where do ye mean to search for this wayward prince?" Larke asked.

"We'll try first the convent in Celiton," Sir Cadwel said.

"A convent?" Ari said, his tone worried. Most of the nobility of Lggothland embraced the more civilized religion of the mainland, but the majority of the peasantry, like the people of Ari's village, still subscribed to the naturalistic theology of their Wheylian neighbors. "I heard they lock away all the prettiest girls there, and if they catch any men around, they kill them."

"Worry not, me lad!" Larke brandished the stick he was using to stir up their campfire. "I be sure the mighty Sir Cadwel can vanquish dozens of berserk nuns!"

"It is where many nobles choose to send their daughters for schooling, and strictly speaking, no men are allowed," Sir Cadwel said, ignoring the bard, who was now dancing about the fire, swinging his smoldering stick. "The nunnery in Celiton has an extensive library, however, and they do make exceptions for people needing to consult their books for scholarly reasons."

"So if you look at the girls, they won't kill you?" Ari asked.

"Oh yes, if you look at the girls, they will kill you," Sir Cadwel said without a trace of a smile on his face. "Now put that brush down. Just because you spent the night going soft in the city doesn't mean you've gotten out of learning how to handle a sword properly. If we went into battle now, I would die of shame as the enemy watched you stab yourself in the foot."

Ari groaned, brushing his hair out of his eyes. After his first day riding a horse, the last thing he wanted was more sore muscles and bruises from being beaten on with a practice sword, but sword training was one of his greatest joys in life, and he wasn't going to let anyone say he ever shirked it.

***

The next evening, they stopped at an inn, as it was raining and the fall air had turned a bit chilly. Ari watched in apprehension as Sir Cadwel ordered an ale, but the knight drank only two with his dinner and retired early, gesturing for Ari to stay seated when he would have risen to attend him. So it was that Ari found himself alone at a table with Larke, who was not playing this night as another minstrel had already started before they entered the inn. He wasn't bad, but Ari privately thought that if the people in the common room knew what talent they were giving up, they would boo him off the stage.

"So do tell, me lad, how was the capital?" Larke asked after a long pull of ale.

Ari thought it might be nice to try ale, but Sir Cadwel kept all the money and ordered all the food, and Ari didn't know how the knight would react if he asked for some. Ari's uncle beat him the one time he tried to filch some from the inn while growing up. Ari sighed. It was probably smarter to steer away from anything that might make Sir Cadwel consider drinking more.

"It's really quite big, and everything is white," Ari said.

"I know that, me lad." The bard smiled. "I have been there, after all. How fare the king and the queen?"

"Well, they seemed good," Ari said, not sure what Larke wanted to know about them. He wondered if he could safely bring up the topic of Sir Cadwel and the Lord of the Northlands. He glanced up the narrow flight of steps leading out of the common room. Surely, even Sir Cadwel couldn't hear him from all the way up in their room.

"Was the queen as lovely as ever?" Larke asked a bit wistfully, contemplating the brown liquid in his cup.

"She's very beautiful," Ari said. "We went to dinner in the great dining hall."

"Do tell," Larke said with a smile, his melancholy gone as quickly as it had come.

Ari began to recount all that Sir Cadwel had said at the head table, hoping to work the conversation around to his question of how the knight's family was murdered and why Sir Cadwel didn't prevent it.

"Sir Cadwel suggested he give you all his holdings," Larke said, frowning.

"It isn't like he can, really," Ari said. "I'm not a noble or anything." Ari couldn't quite hide the sullenness in his voice as they touched upon why he would never be a real knight.

"The king could make ye one," Larke said.

"He could?" Ari's eyes opened wide.

"Of course. He is the king, after all."

"Would he?" Ari asked.

"I suppose he might," Larke said, leaning forward in a conspiratorial way. "Kings are known to do that from time to time when people do the kingdom a great service."

"Really?" Ari felt suddenly buoyed by hope. He could be a knight!

"You already have a horse," Larke said.

Ari scowled. "Don't make fun," he muttered, his dreams once again dashed away as he realized Larke was toying with him.

"Truly, me lad, it can be done," Larke said. He jumped to his feet. "I will sing ye a ballad of just such a time!" he said. The round man on the low stage to one side of the room looked up from where he was about to launch into another song. "Just one, for me lad here."

Not giving the man time to answer, Larke swung his lute into place and began to play. Soon all talk ceased, and everyone's eyes were on Larke as he sang a ballad of love, death, and triumph. When he was through, the room filled with applause, and the throng of people shouted for more. Ari slouched in his chair. Any chance he had of talking with Larke was gone. People never let Larke stop singing till they all fell asleep where they sat or stumbled home. Across the room, the other player tapped his finger on the table slightly off beat and looked on sullenly.

***

Several evenings later found them on a low hilltop looking across empty grassland at the nunnery of Celiton, foreboding even from a distance.

"Mayhap I will await you here." Larke eyed the three-story stone building dubiously. There were no windows that Ari could see, and only one small, but very stout, wooden door. "I can be watching the horses."

"I doubt they'd let you in anyhow," Sir Cadwel said, looking the red-and-yellow-clad bard up and down. Dismounting, he handed Larke Goldwin's reins. "Come along, boy," he said and set off down the trail.

Ari hesitated slightly in handing over Stew's reins, worried it would insult Larke to serve as a stable hand for a page and still not at all certain he wanted to go into the nunnery, but Larke smiled at him encouragingly. Ari relinquished Stew and hurried to catch up with Sir Cadwel's long strides.

Even with the morning sunlight bright on its walls, the convent didn't manage to look cheerful. It was built of dark stone, and the tar-covered roof dripped long black streaks down the sides. Sir Cadwel stopped before the thick oak door and knocked hard with his gauntleted hand. A narrow wooden panel slid open, and two drooping hazel eyes peered out.

"What purpose have you here?" a woman's voice asked coldly.

"I am Sir Cadwel, champion to the king, and I have come seeking knowledge of the location of his highness, Prince Parrentine," the knight said.

"And who is that?" the woman asked, looking at Ari.

"That is my page, ma'am." The knight showed no ire, so Ari assumed such distrust was customary.

"The prince was here, but he left some time ago," the woman said, and the wooden panel started to slide shut.

"Did he perchance use the library?" Sir Cadwel asked, raising his voice slightly. "If by chance he did, we would like to see what books he read from."

"He spent some time in the library," she conceded grudgingly. "I'll take you to the Mother Superior," she said after a pause.

The eyes disappeared as the wooden panel slid back into place, and Ari could hear the rattling of chains and removing of a wooden beam beyond. After several moments, the door swung open to reveal a large woman in black robes. She wore a hood that was lined in white. Ari had seen women like her come to his town. They met with the village women and talked with them, but he didn't think they ever got on very well.

"You are a knight, but what of this young man?" She looked Ari up and down coldly. "Is he a heathen?"

"I will vouch for the purity of his soul," Sir Cadwel said, starting to show a bit of his usual asperity.

Ari wasn't sure what a heathen was, but the woman's tone implied it wasn't a good thing to be. He was, however, relatively sure his soul was fine, so he decided not to worry about it until he could ask Larke.

"This way," she said, sounding displeased.

She turned and led them down a long hall, at the end of which Ari was surprised to see sunlight. As they walked along, he realized that while the outer walls of the building were windowless and dark, inside everything was painted white, and in the center was a large courtyard with many windows opening onto it. He could see twenty-odd girls playing there. They looked to range from around age five to older than him. Off to one side, sitting under a tree alone and watching the others play, was a girl with long, shiny black hair. She glanced up, meeting his gaze with startlingly blue eyes. Blushing, he looked away.

"Here." The woman stopped before a door centered on the hallway that circumnavigated the courtyard. She knocked once and led them in. "The king's champion to see you, Mother," she said, her voice filled with something approaching reverence.

The woman behind the desk was thin, and Ari thought if she stood, she might be nearly as tall as the queen. Her eyes peered out from a maze of lines. They were cold eyes, and not the least bit forgiving.

"What business has a knight here?" she asked in a barely civil tone.

"I am sent by the king to discover what has become of his son," Sir Cadwel said.

"Certainly you do not think we have him here?" she said.

"Certainly I do not," Sir Cadwel said in a studiously neutral tone. "However, I was told he came here, seeking knowledge from your extensive library. I was hoping to find what knowledge he may have gained so I may ascertain where he planned to go when he quit this place."

The Mother Superior, who Ari did not find very motherly at all, gazed at them with agate eyes for a moment. "Who was on library duty that day?" she inquired of the doorkeeper.

"Siara." In that single word, the doorkeeper managed to convey an all-consuming disapproval.

"I should have known," the Mother Superior said. "Fetch her here, please."

"Yes, Mother." The doorkeeper scurried away.

Ari entertained notions of what might happen if someone ever said, "No, Mother," to pass the time while they waited. Sir Cadwel stood with his eyes forward and one hand resting on the hilt of his sword. When the doorkeeper returned, it was with the black-haired girl Ari noticed earlier. She was even prettier close up. He looked down, blushing.

"Siara." The tall woman behind the desk addressed the girl coldly, her face revealing distaste. "I want you to take Sir Cadwel and his page to the library and help them to find what the prince read. I know you re-shelved the books later that morning, so you must have some idea what he looked at."

"Yes, Mother Superior," the young woman said in a respectful tone, nodding.

"Off with you then, and when they're done in the library, show them the way to the door."

The Mother Superior bent over the papers on her desk, ignoring Sir Cadwel's perfunctory bow. The doorkeeper remained behind as they followed Siara away. She led them back to the central hallway and around the courtyard to the other side of the building. She stopped at a stout door, using both hands to push it open.

Inside were a few tables strewn with books and shelves holding more. The only book Ari had ever seen before was the large ledger his uncle kept behind the bar at the inn, where people would make their mark. The innkeep would keep track of how much money they owed him and cross their name off when it was all paid. Ari hadn't ever looked closely at that book, although trying to more than likely would have gotten him yelled at. These books were quite different, however. They appeared to come in any size, from ones that would fit into the palm of his hands to ones that needed their own stand to hold them up so you could turn the pages. Most delightful, though, was that many of these books had pictures. Some had only a few at the top of the page, more designs than pictures, but some had full pages of inked-out illustration, occasionally even with color applied.

Siara led them to one of the tables. "Stay here. I'll bring you the books the prince may have seen," she said, moving off through the shelves with assurance.

Book after book piled up as she came and went. Sir Cadwel delved into some but set others aside after glancing at the titles. Ari was relieved to find his master had no expectation of his page's assistance, because Ari had no idea how to read. Although, he supposed he could pick out some words, like Sallsburry High Inn, because he had seen them so often in his life.

"This is the last of the ones that I re-shelved the morning the prince left," the girl Siara said impassively as she placed another leatherbound volume on the large oak table where Ari and Sir Cadwel sat opposite each other.

Sir Cadwel read the title with a frown.

"Surely this is not all," Sir Cadwel said, scrutinizing the girl. She gazed back with calm blue eyes, so startling in contrast with her dark Wheylian hair. "Come, child, I know you're keeping things from me," he continued with a gentleness that surprised Ari.

Ari had a sudden vision of what a wonderful father Sir Cadwel would have made to daughters and thought it was sad that the knight had never remarried.

"You have to take me with you," Siara blurted, causing Ari to start. "I can guide you to him, but I won't stay here!" Her voice was low but vehement, and she clenched her hands together tightly.

"That's preposterous," Sir Cadwel said, but his tone was soft.

"I'm the only one who knows where he went," Siara said with a stubborn lift of her chin. "I'm seventeen. That's old enough to make my own choices by the laws of both my mother's people and my father's." She locked eyes with Sir Cadwel's boldly, but Ari could see her fingers digging into the backs of her hands where she clenched them before her.

"But surely your parents wish you to remain here," Sir Cadwel said, his face kind.

A slow blush rose in Siara's cheeks, but she didn't look away. "You know why most of these girls are here," she practically spat at him. "I'm no different. My family has no use for me."

"Child, you know we cannot just spirit away noblemen's daughters from convents." Sir Cadwel kept his voice kind. "Why do you not tell us what you know? It's the prince's life we seek to protect."

Ari could tell this swayed her. He saw worry flash across her face, and she lowered her eyes, but then her visage shifted again to become firm and bold. Her gaze fixed once more on Sir Cadwel.

"And well you should seek to protect it, but losing his life is the least of the dangers where he journeys," she said. "Yet here you sit, choosing to argue with me, when my health and location are of so little consequence to the realm."

"It's simply out of the question." Sir Cadwel shook his head. "The Mother Superior would never permit it."

"I was not planning on consulting her," Siara said primly.

"The king's champion cannot go about stealing away young girls!" Sir Cadwel's voice rose slightly in volume, and Ari looked around nervously.

"You wouldn't be!" Siara whispered heatedly. Ari supposed it must have been nice to be a girl so you could argue with people and know they wouldn't beat you for impertinence. "I will quit this place. I'll leave here tonight whether you take me with you or not!" She clenched her hands together even more tightly. Ari saw she was shaking, but he didn't know if it was due to anger or fear. He would be afraid if he were arguing with Sir Cadwel. He realized he was holding his breath and let it out slowly, looking back and forth between the girl and the knight. Sir Cadwel's face was impassive. "I have a note already written."

"I could go to the Mother Superior and tell her all of this," Sir Cadwel said, half-rising from his chair.

"Do what you must." The girl's shoulders sagged, and her hands fell open at her sides. "They can treat me no worse than they already do."

"Child." Sir Cadwel took her small hands in his. "This is for the life of the prince and the good of the realm. Surely you bear your prince enough love to want to help me find him and keep him safe in the madness that has overtaken him?"

The girl's face flushed bright red, then went pale, although white was scarcely lighter than her natural skin tone. Ari got the idea that she did indeed love her prince enough to want to help him. He wondered if Sir Cadwel realized that.

"Please take me from here," Siara said. "Let me help you find him."

"I cannot." Sir Cadwel's tone remained gentle. "I also cannot condone you running away."

"Don't tell them," she said, looking up at Sir Cadwel, where he loomed over her.

"Tell me where he went," he said.

Siara bit her lip, throwing him a look very near hatred. She wrenched her hands from his and headed toward a rack of hanging parchments, gesturing for them to follow. She swung out a map of Wheylia, pointing to a cave in the mountains. "He went there." Her voice was cold.

Sir Cadwel took the edges of the map from her and studied it carefully, gesturing for Ari to do the same. "He would have gone this way, I think," Sir Cadwel said, pointing to a barely discernible trail.

"Doesn't that go through all those mountains?" Ari asked. "I mean, wouldn't it be faster to take this big road and then go up here?" He ran his finger down the only large road marked in

Wheylia, and up a shorter path that cut into the same mountain range from the opposite side.

"More than likely," Sir Cadwel said, "but I don't think in his present state of mind he would take a longer route in the hope of speed. I believe he would instead take the most direct route from here. It grows late, so perhaps we should camp for the night and think on which track it would be best to take. There's even the chance that cock's tail of a minstrel will have something useful to say about this. Thank you, child," Sir Cadwel said at last, letting the map drop and nodding to Siara.

She scowled at him, turning to lead the way out of the library without a word. Ari noticed that her shoulders were no longer slumped.

***

Larke did agree that Prince Parrentine would have taken the most direct route, despite the additional hardships of the steep road up into the Mountains of Whey. What the knight and minstrel did not agree on, however, was which path they should take to reach the prince. Ari sat by the campfire, listening to them argue. They made camp in the dark. Larke hadn't set up the tent while they were away, not knowing their plans, although the bard had taken the liberty of setting a fire and cooking for them. Ari hit his hand with a rock while trying to place the tent stakes in the fading light and it hurt abominably. That, coupled with his companions wrangling, was putting a pall over the evening. He likely wouldn't even get to practice his sword work.

"My duty is to keep the prince safe, and that is best served by following the road we suspect him to be on," Sir Cadwel said loudly, trying to drown Larke out.

"And I say he is perfectly safe on that trail, so we should take the more expedient route and head him off before he can reach the top," was Larke's exasperated reply.

Ari noticed Larke dropped his normal baroque as the argument grew more heated. He wondered if it was on purpose or not.

"You know he's safe in the mountains alone? Well, now that I know you know, I must concede." Sir Cadwel's tone was heavy with scorn.

"He is safe," Larke repeated.

"How can you be sure? What would I tell the king? My lord, this horse's arse assured me your son would come to no harm on the mountain pass. The blame is his."

"I know is how I know!" Larke cried. Scowling, the bard stalked away from the fire.

Sir Cadwel didn't offer to spar, and Ari didn't think it was a good idea to ask when Sir Cadwel was in such a dark mood. Besides, his hand was sore. Moving slowly, as if Sir Cadwel was some sort of a bear or a bull, Ari went to the fire to get more food. In Larke's favor, he made very good food.

"Look what I found off in the darkness, watching us," Larke said lightly, striding back into camp, firmly holding the arm of a small person.

Stopping before the fire, Siara threw back the hood of her cloak. She looked a bit frightened, but she stared at them defiantly. Sir Cadwel cursed.

"How did you get here?" Sir Cadwel asked in a tight voice that spoke more eloquently than words of how close to outright rage he was.

"Well, first I watched which way you went, and then once I got closer, the firelight and the yelling guided me." She faced him squarely, her chin tilted up in challenge.

"Don't be impertinent, girl," Sir Cadwel growled. "We're taking you back this instant."

"No, you are escorting me to my homeland," Siara said. "I'm going to Wheylia, with your guidance and protection or without, and if anything horrid should happen to me when I go alone, it can be on the conscience of the mighty Sir Cadwel."

"Absolutely not." Sir Cadwel said. "We can't be traipsing about the countryside with an unattended woman amongst us."

"Fine," Siara said. "I'll just travel along behind you. I'm seventeen. I'm free to leave the convent if I choose."

She stood before him with fists clenched at her sides, glaring at him. Sir Cadwel stared back, his scowl deepening. Ari saw the knight's hand twitch toward the hilt of his sword. With a low growl, Sir Cadwel turned and stomped off to his tent.

Siara looked after him in triumph for a moment before turning to set her pack near the fire. Giving Ari and Larke each a challenging look, she curled around her small bundle of possessions and pretended to sleep. Ari might have imagined it, but it seemed to him, right before she closed her eyes, that she looked at Larke with something close to fear. He wondered if the bard had scared her out there in the dark.

***

The next morning, as they readied to travel, Sir Cadwel came over to where Ari was saddling Stew. "You'll have to take Siara up with you," he said.

"What?" Ari looked over where the girl was gathering up her things. "Can't she ride the packhorse?"

"Then who will carry all of our supplies?" Sir Cadwel asked.

"We could divide them up between the other horses," Ari said. He realized his mistake immediately, as the knight glanced at Goldwin and then back, scowling. The great warhorse managed to look offended as he nickered at Ari.

"Get her up on that excuse of a horse of yours and ride behind her, boy," Sir Cadwel said in his tone that meant he was done discussing the issue. "Never knew a lad so against riding with a pretty girl," he added as he turned, causing Ari to blush. He hoped Siara was too far away to hear.

"What do ye mean, excuse of a horse?" Larke called from where he bestrode his pale gray mount. "Stew is a fine animal!"

"Stew?" Siara giggled, coming over to stand by Ari and his horse.

Ari scowled at her. He might have known she'd be trouble, with her startling eyes and her pretty face. Whey's had uniformly brown eyes, and he found her blue ones disconcerting. Plus, pretty girls always thought they deserved better. He'd seen that at his uncle's inn. "If you don't like his name, you don't have to ride on him," he said.

"Maybe it's short for Stewart," Siara said, smiling at Stew. She tentatively patted the horse's nose. Stew batted his eyelashes at her. Ari turned his scowl on the besotted horse, but Stew was unrepentant.

"Have you ridden much?" Ari asked, lengthening the stirrup. He was tall enough he could mount without having to adjust it, but he rather expected Siara would have more difficulty. For that matter, he wasn't exactly sure how someone even got on a horse with a dress on. He looked Siara up and down speculatively.

"When I was very small, with my father," she said, her smile fading. "Before my mother died and he sent me to live in the convent."

"Well, um, put your foot in here and pull on the pommel," he said, not knowing what to say to that. "No, not those! Those are the reins. The knobby thing on the saddle."

She pulled, and Ari pushed, being very careful not to note what he was pushing on, and soon Siara was seated on top of the horse.

"Oh," she gasped, looking down. She gripped the saddle horn tightly.

"If you are done, page, perhaps I could claim some trifling moment of your attention?" Sir Cadwel asked, raising one shaggy eyebrow.

Ari started to protest that it was the knight's idea in the first place that he put Siara up there, but the glint in Sir Cadwel's eyes told Ari he was being baited. Goldwin stood quietly while Sir Cadwel hauled himself up and Air reset the stirrup. Goldwin was a tall horse, but Ari was sure Sir Cadwel could have mounted unaided if only he wouldn't wear so much armor. At first, Ari had thought all the armor grand, but since he was the one who had to help take it off and put it on and had to keep it clean, he was beginning to resent it always being used. As far as he could tell, it was just for appearances, because no one had yet challenged them, and the land had been at peace since before Ari was even born.

They rode that day through open grasslands, stopping once for lunch and once to gather wood for the fire that night when the edge of a small forest drew near the road. Ari wandered off into the trees, collecting sticks, Siara trailing along behind him. They gathered wood in silence, although Ari was very conscious of her following him, and returned to where they tied the horses.

"Why does Larke keep looking at your hand all the time?" Siara whispered, as they tied their bundles of kindling to the packhorse's saddle.

"My hand?" Ari looked at his hand. The bruise that covered it the night before was barely visible. "I guess cause I hurt it last night. Why are you so nervous about him?"

"I'm not," she said, looking away. "That bruise looks a week old," she added in a slightly peevish tone.

"No, it's from last night, and yes, you are." Ari finished knotting his bundle and started on hers, taking the ropes she was ineffectually trying to tie into a bow away from her.

"I know how to tie a rope!" Siara said.

"Right, if you want it to come untied and all the wood to fall off, you do," he said. He glanced over to find her glaring at him. "Look," he said, "You need to knot it like this but with a loop here, so if you pull on this one, it all comes undone, but if no one pulls on it, it's really strong."

"That does look better than how I was doing it," she said almost graciously, bending near to watch. "Because he was glowing," she whispered.

"What?" Ari asked.

"Shhh," she hissed. "He was glowing." Her whispered words came out in a rush. "Larke was, last night before he saw me, and then he put his hand on my forehead and told me to forget I saw him, and I almost did, but I didn't."

"Did they drop you on your head a lot when you were young?" Ari asked.

"I'm telling the truth!" she said. "Just you look sometime. Look really close."

Ari met her intense gaze evenly. He knew she wasn't telling the truth. Larke definitely did not glow. Obviously, she was covering up the real reason the minstrel made her nervous. Then it came to him. "You like him!" he said, taunting. "You think he's dashing!"

"Shh! I most certainly do not!" Siara grabbed his arm, her eyes intent on his. "Just really look sometime, and I do not like him."

With that, she turned and marched back to Stew, waiting for Ari to assist her in mounting. Ari grinned, sure he had found the true cause of her unease. Still, as he turned to help Sir Cadwel mount, he caught a glimpse of Larke regarding him, a worried expression on the bard's face. But when Ari turned to look full on, Larke appeared to be in deep contemplation of one of his lute strings.

***

Travel over the next several days brought them into rolling hills, and the mountainous land of the Wheys came fuzzily into sight far in the distance. Ari didn't believe anything Siara said about Larke glowing, but he found it was unexpectedly difficult to test. For one thing, the bard always rode beside them, and staring really hard at someone who was next to you was too obvious. Especially when that someone was often looking in your direction as an endless stream of stories and songs flew from his lips. Even when the trail narrowed, Ari was always forced to take Stew forward first, because Larke would bow in his saddle, saying, "Ladies first." Ari particularly hated when Larke did that. Not because he couldn't check for mysterious glowing, but because he didn't know if the bard meant Siara or if Larke was secretly teasing him, suggesting he was a girl.

Adding Siara didn't change how far the horses could carry them each day without rest, and the days were getting a bit shorter, but there was plenty of time in the evenings for practice. Ari was not an overly brash young man, but he felt he was getting rather good with his practice sword, and it seemed to him he impressed Sir Cadwel greatly with the speed at which he learned. At first, it was hard to practice with Siara there, because her large blue eyes seemed perpetually fixed on him as he darted about, stripped to his breeches and covered with sweat, being beaten on by Sir Cadwel. She even clapped whenever he scored a hit, much to his embarrassment.

Still, the travel was pleasant. As they ascended the narrow trail they believed the prince had taken into the mountains, Ari realized he had never been truly happy like this before. He was journeying through places that until then were only strange words dropped from the lips of seasoned travelers passing through the inn. Places he'd only dreamed of seeing. He had his very own horse. He was learning swordsmanship from the greatest knight that had ever lived. Larke, the finest minstrel Ari knew, filled their days with tales of valor and with song. It was even nice to have Siara around, although she made him a bit nervous all the time. Life was perfect.

Chapter Six

It was two days after Ari had this revelation that they found the prince's horse.

"'Tis well past dead," Larke murmured sadly from where he knelt by the charger's head.

"I make it a week at the most." Sir Cadwel hadn't bothered to dismount, and Goldwin shied away from his one-time comrade. The knight circled his restless steed. "It isn't like Parrentine to treat his horse thus."

It was hard to tell, but Ari thought it must have been a very fine horse. Whip marks showed it had been ridden hard, and now the body was all puffy and covered with bugs. Ari tried not to inhale the smell. Of the prince, they saw no sign.

"This does not bode well," Sir Cadwel said, his voice rumbling with some deep emotion Ari couldn't label.

"We'll find the prince well, if not sound," Larke said as he remounted.

"Parrentine isn't far," Siara said, her gaze fixed on the trail ahead. "We should hurry."

"And how do you know that?" Sir Cadwel asked, rounding on her.

"I just know," she said, locking gazes with Sir Cadwel. "I do."

Ari gave Sir Cadwel a helpless shrug. Just because she was on his horse didn't mean he knew anything more about her than the knight did.

"This is just fine," Sir Cadwel said. "Now I'm traveling with two would-be seers."

"If his royal highness turned back, we would have seen him," Larke said. "Whether ye believe us or no, there is not yet a reason to be turning aside."

Sir Cadwel glared at him. Ari didn't think Sir Cadwel wanted to turn back. He thought the knight just liked to be the one who made the decisions.

"Do we press on?" Ari interceded, trying to end the face-off. It was colder in the mountains, even though it was still early in the fall, and Ari was keen to find a suitable spot to make camp so he could build a fire. The light cloak he slept in didn't keep out the chill that crept into the air as the sun drew low.

Sir Cadwel shot him a scowl but turned forward in his saddle and urged Goldwin up the trail. That night, Ari was privileged to suffer quite a few bruises, Sir Cadwel stating that Ari needed no more coddling during sword practice. Ari didn't really mind, because it seemed as if every time Sir Cadwel increased the severity of his training, Ari found himself able to increase his skill accordingly. He even forgot about the cold, finding it no longer troubled him.

What did trouble Ari were his dreams. That night, they were worse than they had been for quite some time. In them, that cold dead face whose profile he was so sure he saw at the king's great table loomed over him. The face was so white, it should have reflected the light of the moon, but instead, it sucked all of the luminescence into itself and still managed to be draped in shadow.

That face promised him pain and death and suffering. Ari felt an endless scream rising from deep within him.

Then the Lady was there. Ari knew he knew her, this delicate and ancient woman, although he could not recall from where, and behind her came Larke. Both glowed as if moonlight poured out of them, and the light they cast could not be absorbed by the evil menacing Ari. The man from the king's table fled before it. Ari sighed, drifting down into a deep and dreamless sleep, the face of the Lady firmly between him and the dark.

***

The next morning, Sir Cadwel sent Ari and Siara out to gather wood, the early light filtering at a steep angle through the trees. They had enough for the day, but Sir Cadwel was worried trees would become sparse once they reached the rocky top of the mountains, which would be soon, and wanted to carry extra.

"Well?" Siara asked in the quiet voice that meant they were discussing something she didn't want Larke or Sir Cadwel to know about.

"Well what?" he said, ducking under a low branch.

"Did you look at Larke? Look how I asked you to look?" she said, coming to stand in front of him.

"Why would I look at Larke?" he asked in confusion, shaking his head. His hair was getting much too long, he realized. He needed to find a way to cut it or tie it back.

"Because of the conversation we had!" she whispered intently.

Ari wished she didn't feel the need to whisper at him all the time. It was an unnatural way of speaking, and he was quite sure they were alone. "We had?" he asked, thinking. "You mean about how you fancy Larke?"

"That is not what it was about!" she said in her most vehement whispering yell, scowling at him.

"That's what I remember us talking about." He shrugged, rubbing his forehead.

She pushed his hand away, replacing it with her soft, cool one. "Someone has been messing about in there," she murmured, her face taking on an abstract look.

"Hey now." Ari ducked away. "What are you on about?" He rubbed his forehead with both hands. It felt tight inside.

"He's using magic of some sort to keep you from noticing there's something odd about him," she said. "Just like he tried to do with me."

"Larke?" Ari stared at her. "I've known Larke a lot longer than I've known you," he said. *A lot longer,* his brain murmured in agreement. He went back to rubbing his forehead. All this talk of magic was making it hurt.

"Well, he is!" she said.

"How would you know?" Ari said irritably. She needed to stop talking so they could get back with the firewood. If they used too much of the day up now, they would never make it to the top of the mountain before dark. He started to push past her but noticed her face was all red, her gaze fixed on nothing. "What's wrong?" he almost groaned the words. He knew he didn't really want to know what was wrong, but he couldn't keep from asking. He couldn't just leave her standing there all scared-looking.

"I think—" She flushed a deeper red. "That is, I know, just because I do. I think maybe—" She was staring very hard at the ground. "I've read a lot of books about it, you know, about my mother's people, and some of the women, they have powers. The witches of Whey, your people call us." The flashing eyes she raised to meet his informed him of how she felt about being called a witch, even indirectly. "And then, the other day, I made a jumping rope move," she said, her voice very quiet now. "I was so angry with some of the other girls for teasing me, and I made it trip them. I saw it lurch up and tangle in their feet as they ran." She swallowed and looked away, and Ari realized she was trying not to cry. "I don't want to be a witch, Ari. Everyone hates me already for being half Whey."

"Siara." He patted her on the back awkwardly, not bothering to try and sort any meaning from her tumbling words. "Don't worry. I don't even care if you're half Whey. It's fine. I mean, you're fine."

"I know I am!" she said. "I don't need you to tell me that I'm fine." Scowling, she retrieved her bundle of sticks and stomped off back toward the camp, leaving Ari looking after her in confusion.

***

The sun hung low on the horizon as they crested a steep hill some thirty-six days after Ari had met Sir Cadwel in the yard of his uncle's inn. Oddly, the rise they ascended was flat on the top, looking not so much smoothly worn as cleaved off, as if some great being had taken offense with this particular peak and dismantled it. To both their north and south, tall, jagged mountains framed them in, but to the west and to the east, from whence they came, the crags dropped away, allowing endless views of the world below. On the south side of the plateau, set into one of the higher peaks, a cave gaped at them. In front of that cave stood three bent and haggard old women, cloaked and veiled in black. In front of them knelt Parrentine, crown prince of the realm. He was dressed in black as well, but a black that was dull and torn by hard travel, and tears stole down his cheeks as he beseeched the old women.

"Parrentine!" Sir Cadwel roared, greatsword leaping from its sheath, but the gaunt face the prince turned to them broke into a radiant smile.

Against his chest where she sat before him in the saddle, Ari felt Siara's body tense, and she made a small sound that might have been a sob. He tightened his arms around her.

"Sir Cadwel," the prince croaked. "I have wonderful news." He rose and stumbled to them, falling against Goldwin.

With desperate speed, Siara was free of Ari's arms, sliding down his horse, and at the prince's side. Ari caught Larke's look of surprise, which changed rapidly to understanding. The minstrel shook his head sadly.

“We need a fire and food,” Siara said, bracing the prince against her. Ari, Larke, and Sir Cadwel stared down at her. “Now!” she said, and Ari found himself dismounting and moving to the packhorse to unbundle their things.

“Siara, you cannot love him,” Larke said softly, coming to stand by her. His face was etched with concern. He lay a hand on her shoulder. Siara glared up at him. Sighing, Larke dropped his arm and came over to retrieve their cooking utensils, shaking his head.

“Is it permissible to set camp here?” Sir Cadwel said, turning to face the three dark-cloaked figures, only to find them vanished. His eyes darted about the flat mountaintop, lingering on the cave.

“Maybe it would be warmer inside the cave,” Siara said in her normal tone.

“I do not think we should go in there,” Larke said.

“Aye,” Sir Cadwel said. “That cave belongs to the wise women of Whey. It is forbidden us.”

“Cadwel,” Prince Parrentine called from where he was wedged between Siara and Goldwin. “I found it. I found the cure!”

“I am happy for you, my lord,” Sir Cadwel said. His face was very grave, and Ari could see years of sorrow and disappointment etched there.

“So am I, Cadwel,” the prince murmured as Sir Cadwel took him from Siara and helped him to a blanket Ari spread out. “So am I.”

The prince didn’t wake again that night. They erected Sir Cadwel’s tent and put Parrentine in it. Siara sat by his side, ready to offer him water whenever he woke. It was obvious Parrentine had neither eaten nor drank in some time. As night deepened, Sir Cadwel unrolled his bedding by the fire with Ari and Larke, though there was probably room in the tent for two. Ari thought the knight looked at home in front of the fire.

***

The next morning found them sitting about on the barren plateau, waiting for Parrentine to wake. Brushing his hair out of his eyes, Ari stared into the tent where Siara tended the sleeping prince. Parrentine was more than likely blond, but his hair hung stringy and dull around his head. Ari knew the prince was a man of only twenty-one, but even asleep, his face bore so many lines as to make him look much older. His frame was gaunt, thinner even than Larke.

Ari shook his head. He was not sure what he had expected. He'd heard only good about Prince Parrentine, yet he harbored a certain angst toward the man who had ridden that exquisite horse to death. Now, looking at the condition Parrentine was in, Ari had to concede that at least the prince had asked no more from the animal than he had from himself.

Ari wondered if love was really as desirable a thing as everyone always said, if it could drive a person to such a state of desperation.

They spent the day waiting, but still Parrentine slumbered. Ari found himself dozing, and it was evening again before he knew it. There was no sword practice, as Siara commanded them not to disturb the prince's sleep. Sir Cadwel agreed, saying the hilltop was a holy place for the Wheys, who might not look kindly on even the play-acting of a gentleman's way of delivering death.

Ari sighed, gazing up at the darkening sky. Hearing a movement on the other side of the fire, he looked to see Larke rise and walk off into the falling night. He got up and followed the bard, bored with watching Siara watch the prince.

"Larke," he said, coming up behind him where he stood at the edge of a steep slope down the mountain.

"Ari," Larke said. "May I be of some service to you, me lad?" Larke bowed with his usual flourish, perhaps to ward off the melancholy that seemed determined to lay its weight upon them.

"It's just something Siara said," Ari said. He hadn't realized he meant to talk to Larke about it, but now that the bard asked, it seemed like a good idea.

"From the mouths of fanciful girls." Larke smiled.

"Pardon?" Ari was confused.

"Nothing, lad. Just a saying." Larke regarded him kindly. "What was it you wished to know about what young Lady Siara has to say?"

"It's just—" Ari felt foolish. How could he accuse Larke of glowing to his face? "She says she can do magic," he said instead.

Larke chuckled. "'Tis a common thing for young women to believe, me lad. Especially those of her heritage." He turned back to the sunset. Ari felt better immediately. Of course Siara was just being a silly girl. She couldn't move jumping ropes with her mind at all. "She most likely has a mind full of imaginings from all her time spent in the library."

"She said she read all about it in books!" Ari said.

"Well, there's no real harm in it, lad. She'll outgrow these ideas." Larke cast him a reassuring smile.

Ari stood quietly, mulling things over. He was pleased with the bard's easy dismissal of Siara's magical powers. That made a lot more sense than Larke glowing.

"I should go stir the fire," Ari said, meaning to leave Larke to his evening contemplations, but before he turned to go, a stray thought came to him. "Who is the Lady?" he blurted. He could see the muscles in Larke's shoulders tense.

"Your pardon, me lad?" the bard asked without looking.

"I don't know," Ari said, flushing. "I just heard it somewhere."

"There are many ladies in this world, me lad," Larke said. "Once we are back to the capital, maychance you shall meet one or two." The bard turned his back on the setting sun. With one arm companionably over Ari's shoulder, Larke guided him toward the camp. "If we burn yon knight's dinner, he'll have at us both with that wooden sword he uses on you."

Ari nodded as they walked back to the fire. Any thought for what they spoke of scattered from his mind. He didn't try and retrieve the fragments, as they surely couldn't be as important as not burning Sir Cadwel's food.

***

Ari was enjoying the brisk mountain breeze that blew across their campsite as the sun rose the next morning. He sat with Sir Cadwel, Larke, and Siara around their small cooking fire. Larke was telling them a particularly ridiculous story about a bear and a plum tree, but Ari could see it wasn't doing much to distract Siara, who didn't even seem aware of the rest of them as she sat gazing at the tent.

"Cadwel," Prince Parrentine called from inside, interrupting Larke's tale.

Ari was surprised at how thin Parrentine's voice sounded. He could hear the prince moving about inside the tent.

"Yes, your highness?" Sir Cadwel rose from where he sat beside their morning fire, handing Ari his half-eaten bowl of porridge. Siara moved quickly to fill a bowl for Parrentine, following the knight into the tent.

"Your highness, you're too weak," Ari could hear her protesting. The prince brushed aside the tent flap and stepped out into the early morning light. He was gaunt and pale, but he stood without swaying. He took the bowl of food Siara was trying to force on him.

"I know you," Parrentine said with a frown. Siara blushed. "You're the girl from the convent. The one who helped me. Thank you." He smiled at her, consuming the contents of the bowl in three bites.

"You're welcome, your highness," she said, looking down.

"Cadwel." Parrentine pulled his shoulders back, standing tall. He thrust the empty bowl at Siara. "When do we leave? I must get back. I must see Lord Ferringul. The wise women told me he is the one who can keep this strange illness from taking Clorra's life."

"That path will lead only to sorrow, prince of Lggothland."

They all turned to see a tall, white-robed woman standing on the mountain above the cave entrance. She had a thick plait of long gray hair, but her face was agelessly unlined.

"Queen Reudi," the prince said with a low bow. Hurriedly, Ari followed suit, noticing Sir Cadwel and Larke bowed immediately. Ari shot a quick glance at Larke, who mouthed, *The queen of Wheylia.* Ari took a half step back as he rose from his bow. Everyone knew the High Priestess of Whey was a powerful sorceress.

"Why do you say this?" Parrentine said, his tone hostile. "Do you wish to curse my bride and me?"

"I could dream of no curse more great than that which you already unwittingly pursue," Queen Reudi said. "I beg you to turn from its falsehood."

"Falsehood?" the prince said. "It is my sole hope. This girl of your people set me on the course, and your own wise women steered me to the resolution. Do you say they lie?"

He cast Siara a look filled with anger, under which she grew wan and swayed slightly on her feet.

"My granddaughter," Queen Reudi said, her own face paling as her eyes fell on Siara. "What is this you have done? A priestess's heart is once given, and given once only."

"Granddaughter?" Sir Cadwel exclaimed.

"Once given?" Siara asked at the same time, biting her lip.

"What treachery is this?" Parrentine roared over them both.

Ari stared at them in confusion.

"Granddaughter?" Siara repeated quietly into the silence that followed the prince's outburst. She raised a shaky hand to her forehead.

"Did you set this girl in waiting to lead me false, witch?" Prince Parrentine said, striding toward the base of the ledge on which Queen Reudi stood.

"Were it in my power, my granddaughter ne'er would have laid eyes on you, Prince of Lggothland," Queen Reudi said in a cold voice. "Heed me or not. I came only to absolve my people of their guilt in this, not to persuade you."

"Guilt for what?" the prince yelled. His hand went to his belt, but he found no sword there, for they relieved him of it as he slept. Nor, apparently, could he see any way to ascend the cliff face. He stood, staring up at Queen Reudi in impotent rage.

"You are not yourself, your highness," she said, drawing the hood of her white robe up around her face. All became still. Ari was sure if he very much wanted to, he would be able to move, but he didn't want to at all. The priestess's voice boomed across the hilltop, at once both abstract and compassionate. "One tear I shall shed for you, prince of Lggothland, should you continue on this course," she said. She looked past Parrentine to the others. "Daughter of my youngest daughter, I lament the path set before you." Siara looked dazed. "Most noble of knights." Her eyes fell on Sir Cadwel. "You come closer to the man you long should have been. Do not let yourself descend again into the depths of a sorrow so long past." The eyes of Lady Reudi, sorceress queen of Whey, turned on Ari. "He who was born, and born again, and then once more," she intoned, "our vision cannot cross so many lives." Ari stared at her. He realized she was fading, becoming transparent. He could see the mountains through her, the far away snowy tips bright in the morning sun. "Larkesong." The voice was softer now, and warmer, Ari thought. The name stood alone, the tone of it filled with greeting, caring, and worry, and then she was gone. Sunlight streamed in to fill the spot where she stood. For a moment, it seemed as though they still could not move.

"Larkesong?" Sir Cadwel said, breaking the spell.

"What is the meaning of this?" Parrentine strode to Siara, taking her roughly by the arm.

"She must have confused the family resemblance," Larke said lightly, but Sir Cadwel turned to Parrentine.

"I don't know what she meant." Siara's voice pleaded with the prince, tears beginning to slide down her cheeks. "I told you not to come here," she added, not looking away from his hard gaze.

"Parrentine." Sir Cadwel placed a hand on the prince's arm. "Queen Reudi was correct. You are not yourself. Let her go."

"Why did you tell me not to come here?" Parrentine said, ignoring the knight. He gave Siara a little shake. Ari could see the prince's fingers bit deeply into the flesh of her arm.

"I don't know why," she whispered, looking up at him with pain in her deep blue eyes. "I just, I remember feeling something horrible about that book, the book that sent you here."

"Which book?" Sir Cadwel said. "None of the books you showed me told anything. We had your word and a map to guide us."

"I didn't show it to you," Siara said. "It's kept in the secret room of the library."

"A dark book, then," Sir Cadwel said. "You should not have shown it to anyone."

"He insisted," she said, looking down.

The prince scowled, his grip on Siara's arm tightening further. In turn, Sir Cadwel strengthened his own grip on Parrentine's forearm.

"Parrentine," Sir Cadwel growled.

Abruptly, the prince released Siara, sending her reeling backward. Ari jumped forward to keep her from falling.

"Let us quit this place." Parrentine bowed his head, his frame once again etched with weariness.

Siara's face immediately took on a look of concern, and she shook off Ari's supporting hands, moving to start packing up their belongings, rubbing her arm where Parrentine had held it.

Sir Cadwel strode to her, placing a gentle hand on her shoulder. "You need go no further with us, child." His voice was kind. "We have brought you safely here to your people. Indeed, if you are a Princess of Whey, here is where you belong."

"I have to go with you," Siara cried with startling desperation.

"Leave her here," Parrentine said. "Let us be done with her treachery."

"No," Siara gasped, all color leaving her face.

"She must accompany us," Larke said in his most serious tone. "I will watch over her."

"On your head, then," Sir Cadwel said, his brow creasing with annoyance. "We've no time to waste arguing on this forsaken hilltop. We've already lost half the morning."

"She rides with me," Parrentine said. "Where I can best guard against any mischief she plans." Parrentine looked at Larke challengingly, but the bard bowed and backed away. "Which of these sorry beasts am I to bestride?"

"You will take my page's horse," Sir Cadwel said with a look to Ari that brooked no argument.

Reluctantly, Ari saddled Stew and led him to the prince. The roan nickered, and Ari stoked his nose comfortingly as the prince mounted. He could see the misery in Siara's eyes as he handed her up to sit before Parrentine, but she looked away from the encouraging smile he tried to give her.

Ari patted Stew one more time before pulling himself up behind Larke on the bard's light gray horse. Riding behind someone's saddle was the least agreeable way of traveling Ari had encountered so far. He found it far worse even than walking in the dust with the packhorse, but it didn't bother him half so much as watching the way the prince handled Stew, with quick jerks of the reins and a strip of leather for lashing. After a while, Ari sighed and averted his gaze, looking instead for good campsites as they rode, though it was much too early still.

***

They didn't stop until nearly dark, although Parrentine would have pushed them further if Sir Cadwel hadn't insisted on behalf of the horses. Ari rather thought the prince couldn't go much further either, and he desperately wanted to tend to Stew and reassure him that he was a good horse and he wouldn't have to carry Parrentine for long. They set up camp in silence before gathering around the fire Larke made to cook their dinner.

"Am I really her granddaughter?" Siara asked tentatively as they started their supper. She was filling a bowl of food for the prince.

"You need not feign innocence with us, girl," Parrentine said, jerking the bowl from her hands as she turned to him. She didn't meet his angry gaze.

"Queen Reudi wouldn't lie," Larke said, as if the prince hadn't spoken. "To the best of my knowledge, the High Priestess of Whey bore three daughters and a son. The middle and youngest girls she sent out into the world to marry nobly, to forge understanding and alliance between peoples. The middle disappeared across the southern seas, not yet to be seen in these lands again, and the youngest, mother to ye, bore but one daughter and died some few years later. Her eldest daughter and heir, I have heard it told, has borne ye two girl cousins, making you twice safe from the throne. You are the youngest Princess of Whey."

Larke delivered this all in a mild tone, the sudden frankness he'd used when giving Ari advice outside the capital coming back, all but erasing his usual flamboyant way of speaking. Siara stood motionless, her mouth agape, holding a ladle in one hand and an empty bowl in the other.

"Let me be helping ye with that," Larke said. Taking bowl and ladle from her, he dished her out some porridge. "Just sit right down here and eat. You've had a tiring day, lass," he said, steering her to a spot away from the prince and pushing the bowl into her hands. From somewhere about his person, he produced a spoon.

Siara sat, staring up at Larke.

Ari knew how she felt. He was staring at Larke too, and at Siara, and then back at Larke. "If she's their princess, why did they let her leave with us?" he said.

Siara looked at him and blushed.

"I wouldn't be telling ye, me lad," Larke said, shrugging. "You can be sure Queen Reudi has her reasons."

"It's those reasons which build worry in me," Parrentine said.

They all ate quietly after that. Ari noticed Siara casting occasional furtive glances at Parrentine, and as soon as the prince was done eating, she jumped up to relieve him of his spoon and bowl, but no one spoke of much more that night.

***

Several evenings later, while they were out gathering wood, Ari decided he couldn't stand watching Siara let the prince treat her so poorly anymore. She never laughed since they found Parrentine, and she almost never talked to Ari, because she was always with the prince, waiting for him to tell her what to do. Once they were out of earshot of the others, he stopped gathering wood and turned to her. "Why do you let him treat you as if you're a servant?"

"You let Sir Cadwel treat you the same way," she said, not meeting his eyes.

"That's different." He picked up another piece of wood. "I am Sir Cadwel's servant. He bought me from my uncle."

"He bought you?" She stared at him in horror.

"Well, basically." Ari shrugged. What took place between the knight and his uncle was an accepted part of peasant life. "He gave my uncle five gold crowns to compensate for depriving him of my services, and then I swore to serve Sir Cadwel."

"That's monstrous." Siara's blue eyes flashed.

"It's the same thing as when a girl gets married and her family sends along a dowry." He shrugged, pushing hair out of his eyes with his free hand. "Well, almost the same thing. My uncle got paid for me 'cause I'm a boy. If I were a girl, he would have had to pay Cadwel to take me."

"That is not what a dowry is about," she said. She hefted her pile of firewood into his arms, none too gently, and dusted off her hands on the front of her skirt. "A dowry is to help the young couple start a new life together."

"Whatever a dowry is for, it doesn't have anything to do with why you let Parrentine treat you like a servant," Ari said.

"Prince Parrentine is crown prince of the realm." She emphasized the word prince in reprimand of his leaving it out. "Are we not all his servants?"

"You aren't." Ari stopped walking to keep her from taking refuge from their conversation by returning within earshot of the others. "You're a Whey and a princess." He tried to keep the awe out of his voice.

"I don't feel much like a princess." She looked down at her travel-stained gray convent dress with a bitter little smile. "Not much like one at all." With that, she deliberately turned her back on him and walked toward the fire in the fading light. Ari scowled, watching her inevitable course to the prince's side, followed by Parrentine's brisk commands. Her eyes on the ground, Siara hurried away from him to do his bidding.

"There you are, boy." Sir Cadwel rose as Ari entered the clearing. "Stow that firewood. We've been lax in your training."

"Training?" Parrentine laughed, crushing Ari's happiness that he might get to practice. "You presume to train this peasant in the noble art of war?"

Sir Cadwel was not facing the prince, so Parrentine couldn't see the knight's eyes roll heavenward in silent supplication, but Ari did.

"This lad has more potential than I've seen in any noble's son in the past thirty years," Sir Cadwel said, keeping his tone level. Ari winced, as Sir Cadwel's time frame deliberately included Parrentine, who was by all accounts an extremely apt swordsman. Of course, Parrentine was also supposed to be, by all accounts, a kind and likable man. “And I have come to think of him as the son I never had,” Sir Cadwel said in a tone that brooked no rejoinder. Ari smiled, a thrill going through him at Sir Cadwel’s words.

Siara and Larke both went quite still. Ari could see Parrentine clench and unclench his fists. Even the crown prince dared not gainsay Sir Cadwel.

“Let me test him, then,” Parrentine said. He smiled maliciously at Ari.

“Your highness,” Sir Cadwel said, “you are still weak from your recent ordeal.”

“I’m sure I’m fit enough for this,” Parrentine said, casting Ari an appraising glance.

Ari set down the firewood and self-consciously pushed jagged bangs out of his eyes. He thought how he must look to Parrentine. He had switched back to his once white shirt, with its missing lace, and his patched, too-short, brown breaches, coming to barely below his knees, with his none-too-clean, thin legs sticking out beneath. The arms on the shirt were much too short as well, but that he could hide by rolling them up. Ari knew he was strong, but he also knew he was growing fast, and he looked spindly and awkward, sticking out of his clothes. His finer set, from the capital, was carefully packed away in his saddlebag.

“What do you use to beat on him with, Cadwel?” Parrentine asked. “I notice he has no weapon of his own.” Parrentine, on the other hand, did wear a sword, having recovered his before leaving the mountain top.

Ari looked to his mentor for direction. He realized that he very much did want to test himself against the prince, but he would never dare touch Parrentine without Sir Cadwel’s permission.

“Fetch the padded swords, boy,” Sir Cadwel said, not looking away from Parrentine.

Parrentine awarded Sir Cadwel a superior smile, then removed his shirt and began bending this way and that in some sort of stretching routine Ari had never seen before. Suddenly realizing how vastly outmatched he was, Ari cast Sir Cadwel a worried look. Sir Cadwel winked at him.

Within a short time, Ari and the prince stood in the center of a square Larke scuffed into the dirt. A torch stood at each corner for light, although Parrentine insisted that the little bit of day left was more than enough for him to best a half-grown peasant boy. Sir Cadwel merely smiled and set out the torches. Ari, becoming more nervous with each passing moment in the face of the prince's reputation and self-confidence, hoped he wouldn't embarrass his mentor too badly.

"On my count, gentlemen," Sir Cadwel said from outside the square. "Three touches to the body wins. A foot outside the marked area adds to your tally. One, two, go!"

Before the signal left Sir Cadwel's mouth, Parrentine was upon Ari. Ari brought his padded stick up quickly to deflect the blow, dodging away. He could see Parrentine's surprise when his attack didn't land. With a scowl, the prince came after him, weapon swinging high, then low, then high again, Ari matching him block for blow. Now that Parrentine's shirt was off, Ari could see better than ever how thin the prince was. Thinner than was healthy. A quick insight told Ari that Parrentine couldn't keep up the pace he set for long.

They danced about the square, the prince attacking and Ari backing away and away, defending himself only. Parrentine was quick, Ari was swift to note, and more of a fencer than Sir Cadwel. The knight, accustomed to wielding his great broadsword in killing blows against other armor-clad opponents, tended to save his swings and attack more with his body while waiting for an opening. Ari soon realized that the lightning speed with which the prince preferred to ply his weapon left Parrentine little time to think or to change. Once the prince entered into a line of attack, he almost had to finish it. It quickly became easy for Ari to predict and head off each sequence. He could see the mounting frustration on Parrentine's face.

Ari knew the prince's stamina must be flagging, while he was hardly even sweating as yet. Being on the defensive, even against such a furious flurry of attacks, took much less energy, and Ari had more energy to spare. As the prince entered into a set of movements he had already tried once, this time starting from the opposite direction, Ari decided it was time to attempt to score a hit. Instead of parrying the high blow when it came, Ari dropped low to the ground under it, his own weapon snapping out to strike Parrentine's hand where it gripped the hilt of his practice sword. With a shout of pain, the prince dropped his weapon. Quicker than thought, Ari was back on his feet, slapping his sword across his opponent's chest three times in rapid succession.

"That's three!" Sir Cadwel roared.

With an inarticulate growl, Parrentine drew the sword he wore sheathed at his side, lunging at Ari. Ari heard Siara gasp, and Sir Cadwel and Larke call out in protest, but his eyes stayed glued on the prince.

"So you think you can best me with one little trick, cur," Parrentine said, his breath coming in ragged gasps. Lunging forward, the prince made a great overhand swing at Ari's head. Ari brought his practice sword up, only to have it cut clean in two. He felt Parrentine's blade graze his skull even as he grabbed the free half of his practice sword before it could hit the ground. As he sprung backward, he saw Larke and Sir Cadwel surge into the marked-off square.

"Stay out of this, Cadwel," Parrentine snarled over his shoulder at the knight. "Defy me, and I will have your titles and lands stripped and your family name abolished from the books of history. And as for you, minstrel, one hand on my person will sign your death warrant."

Ari waved them back. They paused, exchanging a look which Ari didn't dare glance away from Parrentine to assess. Ari didn't think he needed help yet, and Parrentine's threats might very well have substance. Ari was suddenly glad for his too-long hair, as it appeared to be absorbing enough blood to keep his eyes clear. So far. Across the square from him, Siara stood with her hands clenched to her mouth, her eyes open wide in fear. Not waiting to see what Sir Cadwel and Larke would do, Ari launched an attack on the prince, his two short pieces of wood aimed primarily at his opponent's head and gut.

Ari knew he took Parrentine by surprise, but the prince was quick to recover. Parrentine found some reserve of strength, and his hand on his own blade was much more sure than it had been on the awkward practice sword. Ari took the offensive and was careful to parry only with glancing blows. Just enough to give himself time to dance aside. He'd learned his lesson; his practice blade could not withstand a direct hit from Parrentine's superior weapon.

Out of the corner of his eye, Ari saw Sir Cadwel and Larke stand down, watching the whirl of his twin sticks with awe. Ari forced his arms to move faster and faster, slipping past Parrentine's defenses to strike blow after blow. Soon the prince's face was covered with welts, and one eye began to swell shut. In a final burst of speed, Ari led Parrentine to raise his sword in a desperate attempt to ward off another blow to his head, then jabbed the hilted remnant of his practice sword hard into the prince's stomach, doubling him over. Parrentine fell gasping to the ground.

"Oh!" Siara cried, running toward them. For a brief moment, Ari thought she would hug him, but instead, she fell to her knees, taking the prince's head into her lap. She shot Ari a seething glance. "How could you!" Tears streamed down her cheeks as she stroked the prince's face. "Bring me cool water and a cloth!"

Ari stared down at her for a moment, too weary now the fight was over to care about her attitude. Sticky blood ran down the side of his face and neck. He turned, wending his way through the trees to the stream running not far from their campsite. Falling to his knees on the bank, Ari considered his lack of a bucket, then dunked his head under the cold water for a moment.

"I hope he didn't break a leg in this darkness." Sir Cadwel's voice was gruff with emotion, but what emotion, Ari couldn't tell. "Boy, where are you?" the knight called from nearby.

Ari dunked his head in the stream again, wondering how he could possibly get all the blood out of his shirt. He was disreputable-looking enough already without a great big rusty stain.

"Methinks I hear something." Larke's voice carried to him.

The light of a torch drew near. Sir Cadwel had Ari's good set of clothes and a small jar Ari had often seen in the knight's pack but didn't know the purpose of. Larke held a torch and a bucket.

"There you are, boy." Sir Cadwel stooped down beside him, reaching out to catch one of Ari's ears and turn his head this way and that in the torchlight to scrutinize his wound. Ari was surprised to see the knight grinning. "You've been holding out on me, lad. Where did you learn to use two short swords like that?"

"I didn't. I mean, just now I did," Ari said. He was exhausted now. Just talking seemed to be an effort. His head throbbed in time with the beating of his heart.

"That 'twas a display of swordsmanship worthy of a ballad, m'lad!" Larke commended him, dunking his bucket into the water.

"Brought something to put on your head, and your other shirt," Sir Cadwel said, his face fit to split in half with his grin. "Probably have to use that old shirt of yours for a bandage. Let's get you cleaned up." The knight seemed obscenely jovial, by Ari's pain-clouded perception.

"I best get this water back to their highnesses before the lovely Princess Siara has me head on a stick." Larke smiled down at Ari. "'Twas a fine duel, me lad. Very fine. I'll be leavin' you two the torch."

"Don't you need it to find your own way back? We can fashion a new one." Sir Cadwel began to fish about himself for a bit of wood.

"Yer eyes grow old as the rest of you, me friend. I can see the path clear to the lights of yon campsite." The minstrel stuck the torch into the soft earth on the bank of the stream and headed back.

"There's something passing odd about that one," Sir Cadwel said.

His vision slightly blurred, Ari looked after Larke. For a moment, he thought he could see a luminous glow surrounding the bard, but then Larke was too far into the trees for Ari to follow.

"He's right about one thing, though," Sir Cadwel said as he ripped a line down the side of Ari's blood-soaked shirt and shucked it off him to tear into strips. "That was some of the finest swordsmanship I've ever seen."

"You still beat me," Ari said, beginning to forget the pain in his head in the glow of his hero's praise.

"Aye, but I cheat." Ari blinked up at him in confusion. "I have decades of cunning on my side." Ari managed a weak laugh, and the two set about dressing his wound.

Chapter Seven

Travel after that was not pleasant for Ari, but not because of his head. The next day, he felt almost as good as new. Sir Cadwel examined his wound, stared at it in surprise, said he would have to purchase more of the ointment if it was that good, and didn't even re-bandage it. Larke pointed out that scalp wounds often bled more than they had a right to. The knight agreed, but his expression remained thoughtful.

Parrentine insisted he could ride. He barely spoke to Sir Cadwel and didn't acknowledge that Ari existed at all.

Not that I have anything to say to him, Ari thought.

The prince's face was very swollen, and one eye wouldn't open. He seemed to have trouble standing upright or mounting a horse. Siara still rode in front of him in the saddle, now taking the reins herself as he slumped against her back. She cast frequent and hostile glances at Ari, which he pretended to ignore, but which hurt him nonetheless. In the evenings, she and Parrentine had very little to do with the others, and Ari and Sir Cadwel had to go far from the camp to practice, lest they work under constant glowers of ire.

One benefit of the ill-conceived duel, however, was that now Sir Cadwel had Ari cut many branches of different size and length, so that they could begin to explore different types of weapons and fighting. Ari was amazed at the seemingly unending knowledge the knight possessed about how to destroy one's opponent. While they sparred, Sir Cadwel also began teaching Ari about the art of warfare, which was something far beyond the art of fighting. It seemed Sir Cadwel wasn't content that Ari should be able to defend himself, but rather desired Ari to learn how to wage war as well. Ari never imagined it was all so complicated. There were battlements and siege engines and battering rams and food wagons and the terrain and the weather and uncountable strategies for attacking and defending and even retreating. Sir Cadwel knew about all of it, and more. Ari's spirits were bright on those days when he and the knight could practice in the evenings.

That was not most days, however. The prince was often displeased with suggested campsites, asking Siara, as if they couldn't hear him ask her, to tell them various reasons that the sites were unsuitable, thus often forcing them to travel until well into the night. Ari worried about the horses, taking extra time to fuss over them, but only the pack animal seemed to be suffering. Ari knew Parrentine was trying to ruin his practices, and probably also trying to make Ari's work of setting up camp a lot more difficult because it was now often done in the dark. Ari found, however, that he could see quite well even in very little light, but he didn't let them know that. Sometimes, he would pretend to hurt himself, trying to set up the tent in the dark, figuring if Parrentine thought his strategy was working, he wouldn't seek more ways to torment Ari. Ari reasoned that he could see so well because all his time in the woods at night was paying off. City folk were too accustomed to having lots of lights around.

More depressing than anything Parrentine could dream up to torment him, however, was the rain. It was getting on into autumn, and it rained almost daily. That meant that if you were traveling, you were wet. All the time. Wet clothes, wet blankets, wet everything. And they were coming out of the mountains of Wheylia, far from any roads well enough traveled to boast daily inns like the King's Way did. When they did chance by an inn, Parrentine would declare it unfit for himself and Princess Siara, and they would pass it by. It was all well for him, of course, because he at least got to sleep inside the tent every night. Ari resolved that someday, when he had money of his own, he would buy himself a tent.

Not even Larke could lift their spirits when it rained, for his lute had to be tightly wrapped in an oiled cloth in such weather, and the prince pronounced his stories inappropriate for a young lady of breeding. Somehow, the dimming of the bard's unflagging optimism annoyed Ari the most. Fortunately, Sir Cadwel took the prince's temper with a sort of weary disdain, not letting it drive him back into the dark mood he'd been submersed in when he and Ari had first become companions.

***

When they passed by the road to the convent, Ari gave silent thanks, since this meant they were no more than five days out from the capital, where he and Sir Cadwel could be well rid of the prince. Ari's relief was amplified a few days later when they stopped at the last inn outside the great city of Poromont. This time, Parrentine insisted, wishing them to make themselves presentable before appearing in the capital.

As they journeyed, Siara had taken great pains to mend the prince's clothes by firelight. Parrentine's wounds were healed quite well, and he shaved and washed his hair, which was indeed a dark blond under all of the dirt. When morning came, however, he found something new to complain about. The prince, it seemed, did not find Stew a suitable enough mount. Instead, he set his eyes on Sir Cadwel's destrier.

"Goldwin has been mine for more years than you've seen on this earth, your highness, and no one else has ever bestrode him."

They stood in the stable yard behind the inn, arguing in low voices, lest the commoners hear the disputes of their betters.

"I refuse to ride before the populace on this sack of bones." Parrentine yanked on the reins he held, causing Stew to pull away in fear. Ari wondered if he dared go relieve the scarlet-faced prince of his horse. He looked back and forth between Parrentine and Sir Cadwel uncertainly.

"Parrentine." Sir Cadwel kept his tone almost reasonable. "I know you've been under a great strain these many days, but you can't have lost your senses altogether."

"A great strain?" Parrentine let loose a shaky laugh. "How can you even speak to me of it? You have no idea what it's like to have the one thing you love most being relentlessly taken from you!"

Ari blinked, surprised even the distraught prince would accuse Sir Cadwel of not knowing sorrow.

"Parrentine," Sir Cadwel growled.

"You will not address me with such familiarity, cad," the prince said.

Ari could see Larke just inside the stable door, listening. The bard looked over his shoulder and nodded, and his gray horse came forward, stopping to let Larke lift the reins lightly in one hand.

"And you will address me as sir, princeling, before I take you over my knee as I should have done years ago."

Larke and the gray moved forward.

"Do I have to teach you proper deference to your betters, sir?" The prince slurred Sir Cadwel's honorific insultingly, his hand going to the hilt of his sword.

"I could duel you," Sir Cadwel said. "Or I could let my page take care of you for me."

Parrentine's face turned, if possible, more red, with blotches of white where his bruises were recently healed. Ari winced, trying to stay small in hopes that the prince wouldn't notice him. With a look of complete innocence on his face, Larke walked his horse between the two. The animal seemed somehow taller and more sleek-looking than usual, and in the diffuse sunlight of the rain-swept day, its pale gray coat glowed a delicate and rare silver, instead of its usual drab.

"I will take this horse," Parrentine said, shooting Sir Cadwel a triumphant glare.

"My lord?" Larke stammered in what Ari knew was feigned surprise.

"I'm taking this horse," the prince said, looking down his nose at the bard.

"Yes, yes, of course, my lord, er, your majesty," Larke said, bowing and backing away, the reins held out before him. "I would be honored, my lord."

Ari saw Sir Cadwel roll his eyes, but the prince's back was to the knight now. Parrentine took the gray's reins, walking around him to admire him. Ari slipped up to lead Stew and Goldwin away.

"Yes, this one will do nicely," he heard the prince murmuring.

Ari led his and Sir Cadwel's mounts into the stable to brush their coats into a shine before they headed to the capital, making sure to reassure Stew that he truly was a good horse. After a few moments, Larke entered, his horse in tow.

"Must get 'im good an' shiny for the young master, I must," the bard said, affecting terrified glances back toward the courtyard.

Ari laughed. "You got there just in time," Ari said, sobering. Larke winked at him. "Aren't you worried Parrentine will beat him?" Ari asked, nodding at the gray. Stew bore marks from the prince's riding style already.

"He won't be beating this horse. Stew's been kind to be so tolerant. Mind you, if he really hurt Stew, things would go differently," Larke said. "But you wanted to take a care for the princess, didn't you, boy?" the bard asked Stew, offering him an apple. "And that arse didn't use his crop so often as all that." Larke turned back to his own horse, offering him an apple as well.

"Thank you for agreeing to take him," the bard added in a soft voice to the horse.

Ari shook his head at Larke's peculiarities. "Everyone always said the prince was a good man," Ari said, brushing Stew.

"The prince is a young man," Larke said, producing a brush of his own from somewhere in his packs with a flourish. "And a young man who's always been perfect and good and loved."

"He doesn't seem perfect, good, or very lovable to me," Ari said a bit sullenly.

"Well, ye never know, me lad, how someone whose life has been so filled with all the wonders of perfection will bear up in the face of adversity." Larke shot him a smile over the gray's back. "Don't ye be too quick to judge yer prince, even though he's been a disappointment thus far."

Ari considered that, wondering if he could take Larke's advice. He had already judged Parrentine, after all. Could he un-judge someone? "You aren't coming with us into the capital, are you?" he asked.

"That I'm not, me lad, but never fear. I'll find ye again." Larke regarded him patiently, his face showing he knew there was more than just Parrentine's behavior or Larke's travel plans on Ari's mind.

"I don't understand why Siara likes him so much is all," Ari said. "He's so mean to her, but she lets him be, and she doesn't even talk to me anymore. It isn't my fault he wanted to fight me."

"Ah, so that be where this is going." Larke chuckled. "Who e'er knows the heart of a woman, me lad?"

"I don't like her," Ari said, in case Larke was getting the wrong idea.

"Course ye don't," Larke agreed solemnly.

Ari blushed and went back to brushing Stew.

Chapter Eight

Larke didn't accompany them when they left the inn yard. Instead of growing warmer as the sun rose higher, the day seemed to cool, and a fog swept in to join the morning rain. It bleached all color from Larke as he stood at the gate and waved silently to them, leaving him looking insubstantial as a dream. Ari waved back and suppressed a sigh. Sighing wasn't what men who were about to complete a quest given to them by the king and queen did. Ari knew Sir Cadwel would never sigh on a morning like this. Indeed, the knight rode tall and stern before them, leading the way.

Siara once again sat in front of Ari on Stew. Stew seemed happy to have him back, prancing a bit ridiculously as they rode down the hill toward the city. Siara didn't smile or talk with him like she used to, and she found a large, dark blue cloak to shroud herself in, since the prince declared her appearance wholly unsuitable.

As they drew near Poromont, a large group of armored and festooned knights rode out to meet them, forming up in an honor guard on each side. Sir Cadwel cast a look over his shoulder at Parrentine. Ari could read that look. His mentor didn't know Parrentine sent ahead to the city and warned of their impending arrival. Parrentine looked smug as he straightened in his saddle, urging Larke's horse forward to the front of their little group.

When they entered the city gates, knight escort in tow, they were enveloped by a lavish reception. What they rode through was almost a parade, with the knights on either side and soldiers in their silver-and-blue dress uniforms falling in to both the front and rear. People lined the streets, cheering, but this time, Ari hardly noticed them. He was entranced by the knights, their many-colored pinions snapping in the breeze. He wondered how a knight first received a coat of arms, if he was the first in his line to the honor. If the king made you a knight, would he choose one for you, or did you have to choose? Looking at all the splendidly dressed knights, Ari was glad he had taken extra care with Sir Cadwel's armor that morning.

Ari tried to ride tall in his saddle, despite his reluctant companion. His malaise at leaving Larke alone and behind was gone. His inner trepidation that something about their quest was faulty momentarily fled in the face of the cheers from the crowd and the gleaming metal armor and bright surcoats of the knights of the realm. He was page to the greatest knight that had ever been, and they returned triumphant.

Once again, the king and queen awaited them on the castle steps. This time, there was even less in the way of ceremony, for Queen Parrella rushed down the steps to embrace her son, hurrying them all inside and away from the crowd of nobles to hear what news they had. Soon, they were closeted in a quiet room furnished with low couches and tables made of dark wood and green leather. There was a massive fireplace, to which Sir Cadwel and the king both moved. Not knowing if he was necessarily included, Ari stood off to the side behind a couch, looking about the room at the weapons and animal heads decorating the walls. Siara stood near him, obviously as uncertain as he was.

"I knew you would find him," the queen said once they were alone, her tall form alighting on the end of a couch near the fireplace. "Thank you, Sir Cadwel."

"I'm so close, Mother," Parrentine said. He perched on the edge of a footstool in front of her, taking her hands. "How is she? I must find Lord Ferringul at once." He made as if to rise, but the queen pulled him back by his hands.

"Lord who? But why?" she asked, smiling at her son.

"I spoke to the wise women of Whey, Mother." He pulled his hands away, standing. "He can tell you," he added, waving a hand at Sir Cadwel. "I have no time to waste on this!" With a scowl, the prince quit the room. His mother looked after him in dismay. Siara moved as if to follow him, but he slammed the chamber door in his wake.

"He's worse," the king said. "I entreat you, tell us all you know, Cadwel, and who is this you have with you? Come, child, sit down." The king gestured Siara to the couches, but she remained hovering uncertainly by the door.

"Your Majesties, I am remiss," Sir Cadwel said, sweeping an arm out toward Siara. "May I present Princess Siara, the youngest princess of the house of Whey."

Sir Cadwel executed a smooth bow. The king inclined his head, but not before Ari saw his surprise. Siara curtsied, coming hesitantly forward and lowering her hood. In their reactions, Ari once again saw her as the alluring young woman he'd glimpsed across the courtyard in the convent, with her smooth white skin, lustrous black hair and shockingly blue eyes.

"It was the princess who aided us in finding your son in the mountains of Wheylia," Sir Cadwel said.

"My dear child." The queen smiled, rising to take Siara's hands. "You must come to the feast tonight. You will be a guest of honor."

"I—" Siara looked around. The king smiled kindly down at her from where he stood. "I do not have suitable attire, your majesty. I have only this." She touched the front of her plain gray dress self-consciously.

"Nonsense," the queen said, drawing Siara toward the door. "We shall have you ready in no time at all. Come along with me. I daresay you could use some pampering. If I know my son, the journey offered little rest. So kind of you to come all this way back with him." The queen's voice faded as she led Siara out of the room.

"So, Cadwel, what is afoot?" the king asked.

"Your son found a book in the nunnery, telling him of the wise women," Sir Cadwel said, smoothing his mustache as he spoke. "The princess helped him search." Sir Cadwel gave the king a meaningful half-smile. King Ennentine raised his eyebrows, catching the knight's meaning.

"Now is that not an interesting turn of events?" the king said. "Is it true what they say, that they can only love once?"

"I have no idea, your majesty." Sir Cadwel shrugged, as best as a man could in armor. "Mayhap that is why Queen Reudi let the girl stay with us. The long and short of it, however, is that we went to Wheylia, found your son, got a warning from Queen Reudi not to follow the advice of her own wise women, and came back here."

"Doesn't sound very eventful," the king said, sounding slightly disappointed. "What was their advice? Did she say why not follow it?"

"They advised your son that a Lord Ferringul holds some key to saving Princess Clorra. What key, they said not, and of it Queen Reudi would say only that seeking Lord Ferringul would lead Parrentine to sorrow," Sir Cadwel said.

"Ferringul is a minor noble with the court. He has a title, but no lands behind it. I believe he serves in the commerce ministry. Parrentine should have little difficulty finding him, and I don't suppose we could dissuade him from it, even if we had reason to heed Queen Reudi's advice. What Ferringul could possibly offer to help Princess Clorra is beyond me." The king's mouth pressed into a frown. "Typical Wheylian gibberish," he said, and Ari was glad Siara wasn't there to hear him. "Her warning could mean anything from an unhappy marriage if the princess is made well, to war, to anything in between."

Both men pondered this in silence for a moment.

"I see the fall tourney is about to commence," Sir Cadwel said.

"I wouldn't doubt that you can still win, my friend, but it's time for us to let younger men seek glory," the king said with a laugh.

"I was thinking of the boy." Sir Cadwel gestured to Ari.

Ari fought not to blush as King Ennentine turned to scrutinize him. Not knowing where to look, Ari fixing his eyes with great concentration on a large boar head glaring at him from the other side of the room. Peine told him good servants didn't listen to what their betters were discussing.

"I thought you said him peasant-born," King Ennentine said, lowering his voice.

"An orphan, sire, of unknown lineage. I shall have him as my legatee," Sir Cadwel replied very firmly.

Ari peeked at them out of the corner of his eye. Knight and king locked eyes with each other. Ari wasn't sure exactly what they were discussing, because he had no idea what a legatee was, and he wasn't quite sure what lineage meant, but he truly would like to be in a tourney like a real knight. He realized he was holding his breath.

"If you would only remarry," the king said, but stopped at the sight of Sir Cadwel's features darkening. "Pending my approval of his performance in the tourney then," Ennentine said.

"Pending, but you'll not be disappointed," Sir Cadwel said, the shadow lifting from his features. Like two horse traders, they shook on it. "Thank you, sire." Sir Cadwel bowed with exaggerated formality.

"Knave," King Ennentine said, grinning. "Get out of here. Parrella will have my hide if you're not presentable in time for the banquet. I'll inform the steward myself of your need for an extra chair."

Sir Cadwel bowed, a broad grin on his face. Gesturing to Ari, who quickly made a less elegant version of the knight's obeisance, he strode from the room, Ari hurrying after. Behind them, Ari heard the king chuckle, and the breath he'd been holding exploded from his lungs as the door to the room closed on his heels.

They made their way back through the foyer, Sir Cadwel's frosty glance dissuading the crowd of nobles lingering there from speaking to him. The castle was alive with people and noise. Ari didn't notice the first time they were there how quiet it was, but now he realized everyone had been subdued before, on edge with worry for the crown's only heir. Ari might not like Prince Parrentine that much, but he was probably better than war. Ari tried to make himself inconspicuous as he followed the path Sir Cadwel opened in the throng of gossiping courtiers. He wished he could take Sir Cadwel into the servants' corridors that ran straight and uncluttered behind the brocade-bedecked walls.

"You came back!" A high-pitched voice rang out as Ari and Sir Cadwel entered the rooms they shared on their first visit to the capital. Peine rushed forward, skidding to a halt to bow to Sir Cadwel, and then grabbed Ari by the arm and tugged him toward the adjoining chamber. "We have to get you cleaned up!"

"What are you talking about?" Ari tried to reclaim his arm. "I have to help Sir Cadwel get ready for the banquet." He forced Peine to halt.

"Naw, that's his job," Peine said, nodding with his chin at a young man standing off to the side of the room. Ari hadn't even noticed him there.

"But—" Ari said.

"Go with him," Sir Cadwel said, pointing toward the sleeping room door.

"I have to help with your armor," Ari said, pulling his arm from Peine's grasp.

"I dare say this one can handle it." Sir Cadwel fixed the page with a dark glance. "If he isn't quick enough about it, I can always beat him," he added, winking at Ari. Sir Cadwel gestured the trembling young man over.

Ari watched, feeling oddly bereft, as the other young man began assisting Sir Cadwel. He swallowed, running a hand through his hair.

"Come on." Peine tugged at his arm again, and this time, Ari let himself be dragged into the other room.

"Why does Sir Cadwel need a different page?" Ari said once they passed through the plush sleeping chamber and into the bathing room.

"Cause you're going to be at the head table," Peine said. "The master steward just came down and told us, and I volunteered to come help you get ready. I told him you'd want me. We had to run the whole way to beat you to your chambers. There was no warning at all. You're lucky I was around, or they would have sent someone else."

"I was at the head table last time," Ari said. If Sir Cadwel had a new castle page to help him, did that mean Ari wasn't needed anymore?

"No, I mean, you're going to sit at the head table. With the king and the queen and the prince!" Peine bounced from foot to foot in excitement, all the while trying to unlace Ari's shirt.

"I can do that," Ari said, batting Peine's hands away. "Why am I going to sit at the table with the prince?" Ari didn't overly care for that idea. He wondered if the prince would tell his mother and father that Ari had beaten him. *They beheaded you for that, didn't they?* His hands stopped moving as he pondered beheading, and Peine once again took up the unlacing.

"Because you're a hero!" Peine said, pausing to look at Ari in exasperation. "You and Sir Cadwel rescued the prince."

"They don't behead heroes," Ari said.

"What?" Peine asked, looking confused.

"Nothing." Ari brushed Peine away again, removing his shirt. "Are you really going to stand here and watch me take a bath?"

"I should bathe you," Peine said, frowning.

Ari's mouth fell open. He shut it and shook his head vigorously.

"I could just stay here and we can talk. I won't look. I can give you a towel when you're done," Peine said. "I don't have anything else to do. Just get you ready for dinner and then at dinner, I get to serve you and Sir Cadwel." Peine puffed his chest out, his face proud.

Ari decided to keep to himself his thoughts on the dubiousness of it being an honor to serve him.

"Did you really bring back a Princess of Whey with you? I heard she's beautiful." Peine's face practically glowed, and Ari remembered Peine was half Wheylian himself.

"Yeah, she's pretty," Ari said, pulling off his boots. "She's in love with the prince, though," he added, his voice taking on a sullen pitch. "Turn away."

"She is?" Peine's face went pale with shock, but he turned his back on Ari. "How could she let that happen?"

"People just fall in love with other people, I guess," Ari said with a shrug, remembering his older cousin Mactus and his fiancée. Ari shucked off the rest of his clothes, sticking one finger in the steaming tub tentatively. He had never been submerged in a big tub of water before.

"Sure people do," Peine said, "but not her." The vehemence in the boy's voice caused Ari to look at him.

"I know he's engaged, but it can't be that bad." Ari tried to cheer Peine up. "I mean, she'll cry and all, but then she'll get over it and find someone else."

"You don't understand," Peine said, turning to face him.

Ari jumped into the bath, embarrassed to be standing there naked. He almost jumped back out again. Was it possible to have a bath so hot that you could cook yourself like a stew?

"She's a princess of Whey," Peine said, as if that explained everything. He didn't seem to notice Ari's sweat-covered brow or clenched teeth.

"Could I have that bucket of cold water?" Ari asked in as normal a voice as he could muster.

"She shouldn't have been allowed to do that," Peine said, absently picking up the bucket and dumping it all in. "Oh, did you want it all?" he asked, looking abashed at the empty bucket.

"Yes," Ari said vehemently. He was getting used to the water now. He noticed that all of him that was under the water line was a bright red, and he hoped he wouldn't stay that way too long. His clothes should cover most of it, but bright red hands would surely be noticeable at dinner. "I still don't understand why you're so upset about it."

Ari reached for the dipper to dump water over his head. He wondered which of the containers by the tub had normal soap in it. He recalled from last time that some appeared to have scented rocks in them, and he didn't fancy rubbing rocks all over his already red skin.

"She's a princess of Whey." Peine said each word with exaggerated slowness, enunciating carefully.

Ari gave him a blank look, shaking his head to emphasize his bafflement.

"They can only love once," Peine finally clarified. "And if they can't be with the man they love, they usually die. It's the bargain they struck to end the Second Wheylian War. Women get magic, but men get unwavering loyalty. Don't you know anything?"

Ari stared at him. The dipper slipped from his hand and banged him on the kneecap. "Just once?" he blurted. "And she'll die if he doesn't love her back?"

"Yes," Peine said with a solemn nod.

Ari sat unmoving for several moments, then went back to bathing, a worried frown on his face. "She's only half Whey," he said to no one in particular.

When Ari got out of the bath, quickly wrapping himself in the towel Peine handed him, he found there was a range of doublets, hose, and shirts set out for him to choose from, and he was exceedingly glad for Peine's experienced advice. Peine told him that once his size was taken, he was to have several outfits, at Sir Cadwel's request. This made Ari nervous. He had hoped they wouldn't stay in the capital with the prince for long, and he knew clothes took time to make, but it went a long way in reassuring the worries he was nurturing over Sir Cadwel receiving the assistance of another page.

As Ari followed Sir Cadwel into the dining hall, he was ashamed to find the same feeling of weakness that had come over him on his last visit returned, only this time it intensified as they neared the end of the table, where the prince and a man Ari didn't know sat. The other man, who wore all black and was quite thin, turned to meet Ari's eyes, and Ari would have fallen over if Peine wasn't behind him.

"I know," Peine whispered, prodding Ari forward. "Lord Ferringul always looks so evil."

Ari nodded, forcing himself to keep moving. He knew a lot of people were looking at them. Mostly at Sir Cadwel, of course, but at him too, and he would not embarrass his mentor by fainting like some silly girl. Besides, the white-skinned man turned back to the prince. Parrentine was speaking to him animatedly, laughing and gesturing, a glass of wine in one hand.

"My lord," Peine said, struggling to pull out Sir Cadwel's chair for him. Out of his armor, the knight wore only his highly polished ornamental breastplate that evening. The rest of his clothes were in blue and silver, the colors of his king. Ari wore blue. He seated himself before Peine was done assisting Sir Cadwel, and the boy made a face at him.

"Their Royal Majesties, King Ennentine and Queen Parrella, accompanied by her Highness Princess Siara of Wheylia," the steward boomed, and everyone rose. This time, Peine didn't seem to mind Ari getting his own chair as the boy jumped forward to grab Sir Cadwel's.

If Lord Ferringul made Ari's blood run cold and his knees weak, the sight of Siara all dressed up heated his blood back up again, although she had a similar effect on his knees. She wore a midnight blue gown, the perfect color to accent her eyes, with her hair wound about and curled down and bedecked with strands of pearls. Even that first glimpse of her sitting in the sunshine in the convent courtyard didn't compare to how she looked now. He'd certainly never seen her in a low cut gown like this before. The sleeveless dress swept down from her bosom and hugged her slender waist tightly. Ari had never realized how dainty she was when she wore her rough-spun gray wool. He was appalled that they'd asked this lovely creature to carry around armloads of dirt-covered wood and to sleep on the ground.

He smiled at her as she approached, but her eyes were fixed on Parrentine. The prince didn't even look at her. With a little sigh, she turned to scan the others. Ari could tell the exact moment she set eyes on the prince's companion, Lord Ferringul. Her cheeks went pale, and her step at the queen's side faltered. She sent Ari a quick look, which he returned, trying to convey to her that he felt there was something terribly wrong about this Lord Ferringul as well. She bit her lower lip.

The queen kept Siara at her side, seating the girl to the left of where their majesties sat together at the head of the table. This didn't put her next to Parrentine, as the prince insisted on an empty seat between himself and Siara. "The seat I reserve for my beloved," he said haughtily. Not wishing to make a scene, his mother complied, but the look on her face told Ari that Parrentine had not had the last word on the matter. This left Sir Cadwel sitting opposite Siara, to the king's right, and Ari sitting opposite the missing princess. He didn't mind at all, as a missing princess was by his estimation much better company than Parrentine. Besides, it put him farther away from Lord Ferringul.

Just thinking the man's name made Ari shiver, and he studiously avoided looking in that direction, although sometimes he was positive he could feel Lord Ferringul scrutinizing him.

The room was abuzz with gossip, but Ari did his best not to speak to anyone. As it was, he had to devote most of his concentration to using all of the cutlery spread about his plate correctly, and to getting the small, squishy, slimy fish globs that were served to him out of their shells. It seemed an awful lot of work for slimy fish globs. He was very thankful to Peine for the boy's continuous string of whispered advice.

Near the end of the evening, the king stood, commanding all attention. "It is to my joy and the joy of my queen that I am able to congratulate our champion on the success of his quest." Parrentine scowled, squishing the small pastry on his plate flat with a fork. "And we hereby declare that at the closing of the fall tourney, Sir Cadwel will be awarded his family lands of Sorga, and the position of Protector of the Northlands. Our champion!" The king lifted his glass to Sir Cadwel, who returned the salute and bowed his head to his king. The throng of nobles cheered and, around the table, toasts were raised.

As the assemblage grew quieter, the queen too stood, gesturing for Siara to rise beside her. "And it is to all of our joy that I may present to the court Princess Siara, granddaughter to Queen Reudi of Wheylia. May her presence among us fill this castle with light and happiness."

Siara blushed as she curtsied, and again those gathered raised their glasses, calling out welcome. As the new murmur died down, the king gestured for the royal pages to help him and his queen to be seated once more, but Parrentine sprang to his feet, swaying.

"I, too, have a toast!" he said, wine sloshing from his too-full glass as he swung it toward his table companion. "To Lord Ferringul! Though he himself was unaware that an ancient family remedy holds the key to my Clorra's life, he assures me upon examining her this afternoon that the means to save her are at his disposal. Let all show him honor and respect, for he is the savior of my sweet Clorra!"

This news was met with the appropriate applause and much muted whispering. If Parrentine noticed the reaction of the court was not as favorable to his toast, he didn't let it show. He downed his glass of wine, waving a page in for more.

Not soon enough after that for Ari, the meal ended, and he was allowed to quit the hall. He went alone, leaving Peine behind to attend to Sir Cadwel, who was in deep conversation with the king.

Ari crossed the grand foyer, the vaulted painted ceiling and tall marble columns seeming larger than ever now that it was empty of any but himself and a few guards standing against the walls. They nodded to him as he passed, so he nodded back. He walked down the hallway leading to the guest wing and up the steps. At the top, he began counting doors to make sure he went to the right room, contemplating all the while that it would be easier if they would just number them like at his uncle's inn.

He was halfway to Sir Cadwel's suite when the air around him turned cold. His knees weakened, forcing him to halt lest they buckle. Ari felt a tremor work its way through him, his mind so filled with fear he could hardly think well enough to label it as such. From what Ari thought to be an empty corridor, Lord Ferringul materialized in front of him. Dark eyes set in a pale face looked down the bridge of a thin nose at Ari.

"How is it you live, boy?" Lord Ferringul asked. His smooth voice stole into Ari's ears and worked its way into his brain, bringing more fear with it but sapping any will to flee.

Ari looked up at him mutely, and as their eyes met, Lord Ferringul flinched back. A remote part of Ari's brain, so walled in that neither his own will nor the fear could penetrate it, noted that flinch, but the rest of his mind was unresponsive. His heart flickered in his chest, as if unsure if it should beat or stop.

"What have they made of you?" Ferringul said, taking a half step back.

Ari stood unmoving, unable to summon the will to overthrow the numbness gripping him. He felt a line of sweat work its way down his forehead. Lord Ferringul leaned closer, his breath strangely cold on Ari's face.

"You don't know, do you?" Lord Ferringul whispered. "You don't know what they have done to you any more than I do. They've taken your memories of it and along with them your memories of me." Lord Ferringul issued a low chuckle. "I think they call that irony."

Ari stared at him.

"I've never seen one like you," Lord Ferringul said. "You're dangerous, but it could be you are useful to me." His tone was thoughtful. He straightened, and somewhere inside, Ari was relieved to have that cold breath off his face. "We, you and I, shall look into this more at my leisure, boy." Ari's vision began to dim around the edges. "For now, you will say nothing about me to anyone. Nothing." The soft voice faded away, sending the word echoing around in Ari's head even as darkness closed in.

Ari slumped to the floor. He shook his head to clear his vision, coming to his hands and knees on the cool marble. Arms shaking, he pulled himself up the wall.

Why was he sitting on the floor? Was he sitting on the floor? No, of course not. He was counting rooms.

He shook his head again and started walking. He realized he'd somehow lost count of the rooms, but after only one startled valet, he arrived at the room he shared with Sir Cadwel. He was exhausted, so he forwent any preparations and sank down onto the sofa. He was asleep in moments. His sleep was deep and free of dreams, except for the delicate face of an old lady, which stood fixed in his mind's eye, a wall against what might lie beyond.

Chapter Nine

Ari awoke the next morning to Sir Cadwel shaking him by the shoulder. "I think he would have slept all day," the knight said to a grinning Peine. Ari blinked up at them. He had the oddest feeling that Larke was there, murmuring to him, as he realized the bard often did. He glanced around the room, noting a light brown bird on the windowsill, and sat up. The bard was nowhere to be seen.

"It can't be that late," he said, rubbing the back of his neck.

"Were we on the road, we'd be riding long since," Sir Cadwel said, managing his face into stern lines. Peine, however, kept grinning.

"Come on, I'll help you get ready," the boy piped in, tugging on Ari's arm.

"Ready for what?" Ari asked, looking back and forth between them suspiciously.

"Training," Sir Cadwel said.

"I've been training," Ari said, pretending as if he were going to go back to sleep.

"I get to come help," Peine said, yanking Ari's arm so hard, he was forced to sit up again. The wren on the windowsill gave a chirp and flew away. Ari peered after it, trying to recapture what he'd been thinking when he woke.

"I've never seen such a lazy boy in my life," Sir Cadwel said in mock anger. "I guess I'll have to find a new lad to train."

"I'm up! I'm almost ready!" Ari cried, dashing into the sleeping room, dragging a startled Peine behind him.

It didn't take long before they were riding across the courtyard, Ari and Peine on Stew. The boy clung to Ari's waist determinedly, having never ridden before. As they left the castle grounds, Ari saw a practice area full of knights and pages, all slashing and hacking and riding at each other in grave concentration.

"Why aren't we practicing with them?" Ari wondered aloud.

"Because they're a bunch of worthless fools who have never known the taste of battle and live only to prance about in bright-colored hose in front of the ladies before being unhorsed by real knights like me," Sir Cadwel said from where he rode beside them. Goldwin snorted in agreement.

Peine leaned away from the giant warhorse. The destrier cocked an ear at the boy as if he knew the fear his massive frame and sharp teeth were invoking. They left the city and set off up the King's Way.

"Where will we practice, then?" Ari said. "Is Stew good enough for me to ride for the tourney?" Ari asked, regretting it immediately when Stew let out a reproachful, whistling huff.

"Stew will do better than ye think, I wager," a familiar voice said, practically in Ari's ear.

Ari jumped. He hadn't seen or even heard Larke ride up.

"Not you again," Sir Cadwel said, his tone cheerful in spite of his words.

"Oh, me greatest hero!" Larke said with a bow that was in no way diminished by being made from the saddle. His gray pranced beneath him. "How can the lad practice with wont of musical accompaniment?" Larke asked innocently, strumming a few chords of a well-known tavern song.

"With greater concentration?" Sir Cadwel said.

"How did you find us?" Ari was still staring at the bard in disbelief.

"Fate!" Larke said with another expansive bow. "Me horse asked me to meet him here today, and by the chances of fate, here ye are." This was delivered with a grin, and Peine giggled, but Ari wasn't sure Larke was joking. "So ye have snuck off to train up yer secret weapon away from the prying eyes of the castle, ah?" Larke asked, riding up next to Sir Cadwel.

The knight shrugged. "Secret or no, Ari will beat them all," he said, his tone so matter of fact that Ari blinked in surprise. Then he blushed, quite sure he was undeserving of his mentor's faith.

"I'll do my best, sir," he said, immediately filled with worry that he was going to let Sir Cadwel down.

"If Sir Cadwel says you'll win, you'll will, 'cause he ought to be able to tell," Peine said.

Ari shrugged, not so easily reassured.

"And what have we here?" Larke said, peering down at the boy.

"I'm Peine," he said. "I'm Sir Cadwel's and Ari's valet." He lifted his chin proudly.

"Excellent," Larke said. "These two ruffians need someone ta polish 'em up before they be allowed in decent company."

Sir Cadwel rolled his eyes. "This ought to do," he said, turning from the road and riding back into the woods. Soon enough, they came to a large, round clearing, as if the knight had known it would be there, which Ari supposed he probably had. "We're going to need a lot of saplings," Sir Cadwel said. "So let's get to chopping."

Under Sir Cadwel's direction, they cut several lances and practice swords of various lengths, and the knight unstrapped two old, dented shields from his saddle. Peine helped Ari and Sir Cadwel don the padded practice armor they'd brought along, and the beating commenced. They stayed all day, Sir Cadwel running Ari through drills in all types of weapons, both using them and defending against them with other types of weapons, or the same type. They also did some jousting, although not much that first day. Sir Cadwel said he didn't want Ari to hurt himself falling off his horse, so they should practice only a few passes, and then they would rehash it several times that evening so Ari would better know what he was doing. Through it all, Larke played them songs and told stories, often lamenting their hard work and telling them they would do better for more resting.

"Five days seems little time to train the lad up to be a fine jouster," Larke said as Peine and Ari packed up their things in the fading light. For some reason, Ari had the odd notion that the bard was reassuring himself.

"He'll do well enough," Sir Cadwel said. "He's the finest natural swordsman I've ever come across. The boy was made to be a knight."

Ari's breath caught, and he stopped shoving padded armor into their saddlebags. Was Sir Cadwel saying he would be a knight? Was that what a legatee was?

"Still, ye can't hope the lad to win after five short lessons, even so great and mighty a tutor as ye are," Larke said, sounding worried.

"He'll do well enough," Sir Cadwel repeated.

Ari went back to stuffing the bags, proud Sir Cadwel thought so highly of him, but with fear clutching at his gut. What would be well enough, and what if he didn't? What if he let Sir Cadwel down and missed his chance to be a real knight?

"Are you coming back to the city with us?" Peine asked Larke. "You're really good. I bet the nobles of the court would love to hear you play, and there's the grand ball to commence the tourney."

"Oh no, me lad," Larke said, shaking his head. "As I told me fine companions, there be a lass in the capital whose heart I have no wish to further break, and I fear my meager skills would fade into the background were I in the fine company of the king's musicians. Tomorrow will be soon enough for ye to be seeing the likes of me."

"Or too soon," Sir Cadwel said as he pulled himself onto his horse. "Let's get back before they close the gates. I don't fancy having to spend the night in this glade."

They arrived back at the castle too late in the evening to dine in the great hall, much to Ari's relief. He had no wish to sit opposite either a teary-eyed Siara or the prince and his new companion. Also, he had forgotten what it was like to practice a new weapon with Sir Cadwel. New weapons were always the worst, and he felt bruised all over. Tired and hungry, he scarfed down what Peine brought up to them and then curled up on the couch to sleep, not even minding that someone aside from himself had the honor of assisting Sir Cadwel in his evening ablutions.

***

The next morning, they set out almost before it was light, with Sir Cadwel awarding the guards a menacing scowl as they worked to open the massive castle gates fast enough to suit him. Once again, Peine rode behind Ari, but the boy had already lost his fear of riding on Stew and that day spent the ride looking about the city and pointing things out to Ari as they passed.

When they reached the clearing, they found Larke seated in so near the same position as when they had left him that Ari thought he must have stayed that way all night, a supposition perpetuated by the dew that glistened on the bard's clothes. Larke sat with one hand outstretched, a delicate brown bird alighting on his index finger. The bird was singing to him, but as they approached, it broke off and turned to look at them. Larke nodded, and with a last chirp, it flew away.

"Yes, something passing odd," Ari heard Sir Cadwel mutter to himself.

"Wow," Peine said. "How did you do that? Can you teach me? Will it come back?" The boy slithered off Stew's back before the brown even halted. He ran up to Larke. "Hey," Peine said, "You're all wet."

"I must have dozed off," Larke said, rising to stretch.

"Dozed off?" Sir Cadwel's voice was filled with skepticism.

"Dozed off," Larke said with a nod. "An' how are ye this fine morning, Ari?" he asked, turning his attention to patting Stew on the nose. His gray walked toward them, and Ari started. He hadn't noticed the animal was in the clearing.

"I'm well, thank you, Larke," Ari said, sliding down off his horse. Stew walked over to Larke's mount, ducking his head almost as if in greeting.

"Ye look well, lad," Larke said, amusement coloring his voice.

"If you two are through chatting," Sir Cadwel said, dismounting. He walked Goldwin to a tree and loosely wrapped his reins around a low branch.

Ari went to the packs and started retrieving their padded armor. "I don't have any armor," he said, pausing.

"How could you forget to bring yours?" Sir Cadwel asked with a scowl.

"No, I mean, for the tourney. I don't have any real armor." Ari felt his heart sink. How could they not have thought of that? How could he be in a tourney for knights when he didn't have any armor?

"Oh, that," Sir Cadwel said. "Don't worry over that. We'll go to the armory and outfit you. In fact, we'll do that tomorrow morning. You could use a few days' practice in it."

"I'll have my own armor?" Ari grinned. His own armor. Like a real knight!

"Well, you won't be able to keep it. Someday, you'll have to have your own made to fit," Sir Cadwel said. "We'll borrow it. You're right, though. I'll see what can be done about getting you a chain shirt or something. Did they measure you for clothes yet?"

Ari blinked at him in confusion. He recalled Peine saying something about his having clothes made up.

"You see, sir," Peine said from where he was trying to drag practice padding from one of Stew's packs. "They were to measure him yesterday, but no one could find him, on account of us all being out here all day."

"I know where we were." Sir Cadwel scowled, including them all in his angry glance indiscriminately. "I guess we best go back early this afternoon, to get some of these things taken care of," he said. "For now, let's get started. We're dueling today, boy. You're quite good with the broadsword, but let's see how you do with something a bit quicker. Get out the foils."

"Ah, dueling," Larke said, gesturing flamboyantly with an imaginary foil, apparently forgetting the real one he wore at his side. "T'occupation of choice for all powdered nobles' sons. The women will swoon for ye."

"Yes, women love duels," Peine said as Ari and Sir Cadwel made ready, apparently not aware Larke was poking fun. "I wonder if Princess Siara does? They say the queen wants the prince to marry her," he said, causing Ari to scowl as he donned his practice armor. Peine handed him a foil, still going on about the idea of Siara and Parrentine together.

"On your guard," Sir Cadwel said, and they faced off, the knight moving in, his weight on the balls of his feet. That was quite different from Sir Cadwel's stance when he wielded his greatsword, Ari noted, trying to mimic his mentor's light movements. Sir Cadwel pressed him, the knight's thin blade whipping about. Ari tried to stay focused on it and ignore Peine's endless string of chatter. Not that the boy needed anyone to listen for him to keep talking.

"And they're going to honor Lord Ferringul at the ball." Peine's chatter broke through Ari's concentration. "Because Princess Clorra is better now. Not sick anymore at all. A curse was laid on her by an evil warlock, and that's what made her so sick to begin with, and Lord Ferringul discovered it and cured it, so that's why he's to be honored. And I heard Lord Ferringul knows who did it, and the king said that whoever wins the tourney will have to go and fight him," Peine's said. "Fight the warlock, that is. Do you think it will be you, Ari? Can I come too?" At the very first mention of Lord Ferringul, Ari froze, receiving a whip-like slap on his sword hand that caused him to drop his blade in spite of the heavy leather glove he wore.

"How do you expect to win if you can't concentrate?" Sir Cadwel said, disgusted.

"But did you hear what he said?" Ari shook his hand, trying to alleviate the pain that filled it. "About Lo . . . Lor . . ." Ari couldn't get the name out.

"I don't care if he just told you the queen is standing behind you naked!" Sir Cadwel roared. Ari's face went red. "If you can't keep your mind on the fighting, odds are you won't keep your head on your shoulders! Now pick up that sword and let's start over."

Ari forced himself to concentrate. Before he even realized the time, Peine was offering them lunch, of which Larke happily partook. Over lunch, Sir Cadwel quizzed Peine about what he had said earlier, but now that he was free to, Ari found he didn't have any desire to speak about Lord Ferringul. He wasn't sure why he didn't want to, because he had the nagging notion in the back of his mind that there was something he ought to tell them about the man. He decided to wait to tell them until he could recall what it was he was supposed to tell. This logical conclusion comforted him, and he let his mind leave the subject.

After lunch, they packed up. Sir Cadwel decided Ari needed armor that very afternoon, so they could work with lances the next day. He gave Peine a list of other items to acquire as they rode back, after once again bidding farewell to Larke. Ari looked over his shoulder, glimpsing through the trees the bard sitting at the edge of the clearing, just like when they'd found him that morning.

***

The armory was vast. Now Ari knew why Sir Cadwel wasn't worried about the armor. There were racks of breastplates. Rooms full of swords. Great chests were opened to reveal they brimmed with gauntlets. Ari and Sir Cadwel sorted through it all, picking out what fit Ari and what was in the best shape. Sir Cadwel, of course, ordered Ari to have all of his borrowed armor cleaned and fitted with new leather straps by morning, giving Ari the excuse he needed to once again not attend dinner in the great hall.

"Why does the king have so much armor just sitting around like that?" Ari asked as they carried it back to their rooms.

"For times of war," Sir Cadwel said. He glanced at Ari, whose face must have betrayed his lack of understanding, and elaborated. "We were at war for a long time, boy. I was born into war. The king and queen were born into war. I spent the first half of my life in the saddle, riding from one bloody field to the next. We needed a lot more armor back then."

Ari tried to imagine what it was like. He'd been born into peace. His cousins didn't have to leave to go fight for the king. His uncle wasn't killed in some far-off battle. Nobody had ever burned their town to the ground because they were on the wrong side of an imaginary line some nobles drew. Ari knew a lot about battles from listening to Sir Cadwel, but he knew he didn't really understand what it was like to be at war.

He remembered how on the road, in his darker spells, Sir Cadwel would talk of danger and enemies and always being ready to fight. Ari was glad he didn't have to live that way. Being a hero sounded like a good idea until you realized how many bad things had to happen to set the stage for it.

When they arrived back at the room, a tailor was waiting to take Ari's measurements, and Sir Cadwel and Peine left for the great hall. Ari wished he could keep Peine there to give him advice about being measured, but he knew how much his friend enjoyed serving Sir Cadwel in front of the rest of the pages, standing at the head of the table right alongside the king's and queen's own servants. After the tailor left, Ari sat down to clean and mend his new borrowed armor, a task he would have found happier if his mind wasn't on war, the image of all those racks and racks of weapons stored in the bowels of the castle haunting him.

***

Ari was almost done refitting the armor when a castle page arrived.

"Her royal highness, the Princess Siara, commands your presence immediately," the page said in what Ari felt was an unnecessarily loud voice, since he was standing right there.

Ari bristled a bit at the wording, but looking at the page, who obviously thought quite a bit of himself, he decided Siara probably hadn't even phrased it that way. Besides, he hadn't seen her in days.

The page escorted him back along the corridor and down to the main foyer. Ari's new boots clicked on the marble floor as they crossed to the steps leading up into the royal wing. He felt like the whole castle must be able to hear him walking around.

I should have asked that man who came in and measured me for some shoes, he thought. His old ones were falling apart. Sir Cadwel always wore boots, though, so maybe that was what knights did. The guards at the base of the broad staircase leading to the royal wing stood stern and unmoving, ignoring Ari's polite nod.

The differences between the two wings were subtle but distinct. They were the external architectural mirror of each other, framing an interior garden, but the royal wing had brighter tapestries, more guards, and fewer doors lining the hall. It was in general more ornate than the wing Ari stayed in, with decorative columns and delicate patterns inlaid in the marble floor.

When they reached the door to Siara's room, the page knocked. From the room opposite, Ari could hear the throaty laugh of a woman, and with a fearful certainty, he knew Lord Ferringul was in that room. A shiver ran down the back of his neck, and he glanced over his shoulder at the closed door.

"Princess Clorra's room," the page said, observing Ari's look.

Ari nodded, not trusting his voice while under the chilling influence of knowing Lord Ferringul was so near. He realized Siara must be forced to see the man often, both at dinner and by chance when walking in the hall. Ari shuddered, glad he wasn't royal and didn't have to stay on this side of the castle.

The page raised his hand to knock again, but before he could, the door was opened by an impeccably dressed maid. The page gave a short half bow.

"Page Aridian to answer the summons of Princess Siara," the castle page announced. The maid nodded, stepping back so Ari could enter.

"Please, be seated," she said, gesturing at couches centered in a ridiculously large sitting room. It was double the size of Sir Cadwel's. There was a tall harp in one corner that he found intriguing, but no one played it. He seated himself as far back in the room as he could, facing the door. The page took up his place to one side of the hallway door, and the maid left through a smaller one to Ari's right, presumably to announce him.

Siara entered a moment later, looking lovely. The queen had given her closets full of gowns, mostly in various shades of blue to offset her perfect skin and underscore her striking eyes. Her dark hair was coiled and curled and full of pearls again. Looking at her filled Ari with an odd desire to sigh hopelessly. He stood when she entered but didn't sit again, because instead of coming to alight opposite him, she began to pace, one hand indecorously holding her full skirts out of the way.

"Thank you for coming to see me," she said without looking at him. "I know you must be busy getting ready for the tournament."

Ari nodded.

"Are you hungry? I noticed you weren't at dinner." She bit at a nail on her free hand.

"No, thank you," Ari said, rather wanting to sit down, but not sure if he ought to when she wasn't. Siara stopped pacing and scowled at him, as if by refusing food, he had insulted her.

"You asked me here," Ari said.

"Yes," she said, removing the nail from her mouth and replacing it with her bottom lip.

"You wanted to talk to me about something?" he said, shifting his weight from foot to foot.

"Yes." She nodded. She opened her mouth and shut it several times.

"You can't?" Ari asked, a note of excitement in his voice. "I have something I want to talk about, but I can't either." He got the words out as fast as he could.

"You do?" she asked, startled.

He opened his mouth to say more, but he couldn't get himself to speak.

"About a person?" she said, and he could see she struggled to get the words out.

"Yes," Ari said. They stood facing each other, both wanting to speak, but unable to.

"Well, at least we have that sorted out," Siara said, grimacing.

"Is it true you can only ever love one man?" Ari blurted. He felt his face go red and looked down at his boots.

"Yes," she said, her voice filled with anger.

Ari winced. "I'm sorry." He knew it was a wholly inappropriate question.

"Why?" she said, her tone savage. "You're not the one who sent my mother away from our people to die and let me be stuffed into a convent, not knowing who I was or what dangers lay in my heritage."

Ari looked up in surprise. He expected her to be angry at his question, or angry at him for intruding in her life. He hadn't realized she would be angry with her grandmother. He tried to rearrange his thoughts on the subject. "They probably had a reason."

"A reason? Such as?" she said, glaring up at him. Now she was angry at him, he could tell.

"I don't know," he said, trying not to notice how close she was standing.

"I can't imagine why you would want to defend them," she said, folding her arms across her chest in an unladylike fashion and scowling up at him.

Ari blinked. She made a good point. "But that's not what you wanted to talk about," he said, realizing he had derailed the conversation, almost against his own will.

"No," she said, her anger changing back to nervousness.

"Someday, we really ought to make ourselves talk about . . ." Ari tried to say *him*, but found even that wouldn't come out.

"Yes," she said. "I'm very tired," she added.

Indeed, she had gone pale and even seemed to shake a little. Ari realized he was tired as well. He wasn't even sure if he would be able to finish with the last few straps on his armor that night. Maybe Peine would be back from assisting Sir Cadwel at dinner and he could enlist his friend's aid.

"I should probably go," he said, crossing the room to the door. "Siara," he added, looking back, "if I can ever help with anything, just say."

She inclined her head, her blue eyes wide. "Thank you for coming to talk with me," she murmured as the page opened the door for him. Ari nodded, managing a smile.

As Siara's door closed behind him, his eyes fixed on the identical one across the hall. For a brief second, he knew there was evil behind that door, but he shook his head and the feeling was gone. Almost stumbling as he went, Ari found his body and thoughts moving quickly away, propelled by a force much greater than himself.

***

Three more days of practice did seem to help, but Ari hardly felt ready for the tourney the next day as he stood awkwardly beside Sir Cadwel along an outer edge of the grand ballroom. His new clothes were not ready, so Peine outfitted him in an array of borrowed finery. None of it fit quite right, but Peine assured him it all looked fine. Ari wished his friend was allowed to attend the ball, but apparently, unlike at dinner, the only servants in the ballroom were the few considered practiced enough to weave their way through throngs of people while carrying trays of drinks. Ari didn't know what the drinks were, because the one time a tray of the small crystal glasses drew near, Sir Cadwel scowled it away again.

"We only have to stay until the king and queen arrive, lad," Sir Cadwel rumbled beside him. "It's the polite thing to do."

The knight wore no armor and didn't even have a knife about his person. He looked continually pained by his blue hose, tall soft leather boots and stiff silver embroidered doublet. Peine had tried with all his might to get Sir Cadwel to wear a large floppy blue hat with fluffy gray feathers, only to have the knight end the argument by ripping it from the boy's hands and throwing it on the fire. Sir Cadwel had driven his point home by offering to send Peine in after it.

Ari stifled a sigh. He was wearing one of the hats and he hated it. It meant nothing to him that all the other men were wearing the silly things. Sir Cadwel wasn't.

Ari scanned the room. There was crystal and light everywhere, and the music was fascinating. It wasn't fun, like the music Larke usually played or that which was played in taverns. It was involved and hard to follow or anticipate. In the center of the room, nobles walked in slow patterns about the dance floor in time to the beat. Ari tried to stay small near Sir Cadwel and hoped no one would strike upon the unimaginable idea of asking him to dance.

The herald stepped onto the landing at one end of the room, and the music and dancing stopped. The crowd parted to form a walkway from the bottom of the steps to the raised dais on which two thrones sat with three ornate chairs placed on each side of them. The double doors at the top of the steps opened and Siara entered on the arm of an older noble Ari didn't know.

"Her highness, Princess Siara of Wheylia, accompanied by Ambassador Keila of Wheylia," the herald announced in his strident voice.

Siara wore pale blue, and she seemed pale inside it. The gown had large tufts of fabric on the arms and shoulders and an elaborate skirt, and to Ari, it looked as if it was swallowing up the delicate princess. He tried to smile reassuringly at her, but her eyes were locked straight ahead. She and the Wheylian ambassador strode stiffly to the dais, where they stopped before two of the ornate chairs and turned to face the entrance. Siara flinched slightly, and Ari looked back to see Lord Ferringul at the top of the steps.

"Lord Ferringul of Western Clempt, savior of Princess Clorra, and royal guest of honor of Prince Parrentine."

Every step Lord Ferringul took down the stairs stabbed fear into Ari's heart. He would have run if he hadn't felt Sir Cadwel's appraising gaze on him. Instead, Ari squared his shoulders and clenched his jaw. He felt the keen desire for some sort of weapon and scrutinized a crystal candlestick speculatively.

"Her highness, Princess Clorra of Hapland, accompanied by Ambassador Kroost of Hapland," the herald boomed.

Clorra stood still atop the steps, surveying the crowd through narrow eyes. In contrast to Siara, the Hapland princess wore a slim gown, not currently in fashion, that clung indiscreetly to her figure. The effect was far from alluring to Ari, because the princess was too thin and too wan after being ill for so long. She had lovely yellow hair, though, which trailed loosely down her back to her waist and sparked a brief memory in Ari of the girl he'd met at the farmstead on the way to the capital. The similarity went no further, for while that girl had been conniving, there had still been an innocence about her that Clorra utterly lacked. Ari didn't know how to interpret what he saw in Princess Clorra's eyes, but it wasn't innocence. There was a heaviness there, a full acquaintance with types of pain and longing Ari knew nothing of, that made him look away. He cast his eyes down until at last she stopped ignoring her bristling escort and descended the steps. As they passed, Ari was glad the bulky Hapland Ambassador was between him and this strange princess.

"His royal highness, Prince Parrentine," the herald announced, catching Ari's attention. Parrentine was already halfway down the steps, hurrying after his fiancée. The prince looked to be recovering from his desperate journey well, but his manners were still missing. He hurried through the room to Clorra's side, ignoring the nobles. Ari glanced up at Sir Cadwel, whose lips were pressed into a thin line of disapproval, hoping the knight would soon signal their departure.

"Their majesties, King Ennentine and Queen Parrella," the herald announced at last, his voice ringing off the vaulted ceiling.

The king and queen looked stately, as always, and descended the steps slowly. They smiled and nodded to the nobles as they passed. They took their place before their throne, and the assemblage bowed to them. As the royal couple sat, the music started up again. Siara and her escort took their seats. To the right of the king, a muted argument broke out as Parrentine tried to send Ambassador Kroost to sit beside the queen with Siara and the Wheylian ambassador, leaving Clorra to sit between Lord Ferringul and himself. Ari felt Sir Cadwel tense next to him and saw the king frown.

A throaty laugh filled the hall, and the music faltered. "All this fuss over me?" Princess Clorra's voice was low, but it carried through the now still room. "But it matters not, for I will require no chair tonight. Is this not a ball? Come, Parrentine, dance with me."

Parrentine proffered his arm, shouldering the Hapland Ambassador away. Clorra laughed again as she strode beside the prince to the center of the dance floor, nobles melting out of their path.

"Music!" Parrentine ordered, and the musicians picked back up where they'd left off.

There was a moment of tense immobility, and then other dancers joined them and talk resumed about the room. Ari watched in pained fascination as Clorra writhed about, not at all in time with the music. Parrentine held one of her hands, and this seemed to be the only thing anchoring her from complete abandon. The prince looked unconcerned with how strange her behavior was, letting her drag him around the floor with a happy smile cutting across his face.

Ari felt Sir Cadwel shift and looked up to see his mentor and the king exchange a worried glance. Sir Cadwel nodded at his liege. His eyes shifted to Siara's miserable face for a moment, then came to rest on Ari. "I think we've seen enough here," Sir Cadwel said and led Ari out.

Chapter Ten

The first day of the tournament dawned clear and cool. Ari woke up feeling like he hadn't gotten in enough practice to have any hope of winning, so he decided just to try very hard not to embarrass himself. Also, the city was abuzz with the news Parrentine had entered the tourney, filling Ari with the new worry that he might have to face the prince in combat again. The king decreed that the winner of the tourney should accompany Sir Cadwel on a quest to confront the evil warlock who had cursed Princess Clorra, and Parrentine wanted it to be him. If Ari beat Parrentine in front of everyone and kept him from being able to accompany Sir Cadwel, he doubted the prince would ever forgive him.

The tourney was held on the castle grounds. Many different squares and rectangles were roped off and set with colored flags to denote the events to take place in them. Bright tents of knights, nobles, smiths, and other artisans surrounded the flagged-off areas. Men and women walked about with baskets of sweets or salteds for sale. Outside of the castle, all of the city inns were full, and outside the city walls was another city of tents. These were more often brown than the gaily striped ones of the gentry and select artisans permitted to camp within the castle grounds themselves, but the atmosphere there was just as festive.

Ari learned there would be no jousting until the final day, so he hoped he and Sir Cadwel might still have time to practice some more. All unproven combatants, like Ari, had to compete in varying competitions just to show themselves worthy of the joust. The joust would take place at noon on the seventh day. Already established knights had but to wait and watch while the younger men fought to see who would have the honor of facing them.

The opening event was the broadsword and shield. It was fought afoot in full armor. The first man to take three blows to his trunk lost, and they fought with dulled swords. Stabbing was not permitted. Each man faced three opponents and therefore would score between zero and three points for the day.

As Ari watched the first few rounds, which he hadn't drawn a spot in, his hopes rose. Most of the men seemed very slow and clumsy, compared to Sir Cadwel. Ari saw the king's words were not idle when he acknowledged Sir Cadwel could surely still win against the youths competing in the tourney. Ari didn't want to get too hopeful, but he saw he had a distinct advantage, having trained with a man so accomplished in his art, and to make things better, Ari didn't draw Parrentine for that event.

Ari's first opponent was formidable-looking, being much taller and broader than Ari, despite how he'd grown since spring. Ari soon found, however, that the older boy was slow, and he didn't know how to use his longer arms to his advantage. Quicker than his opponent could follow, Ari dipped in under his sword arm and scored a hit, then ducked round behind him before he could bring his weapon back in close enough to his body to strike. Ari's opponent turned around, seeking him, and Ari darted to the side once more, this time striking above the other young man's shield, which he forgot to keep up as he spun. The crowd cheered, but Ari was too focused to take much note. Quickly, he slipped in a third blow, right across the confused young man's exposed stomach, and the match was ended.

Ari won all three of his matches that day. He did let in one hit, much to his disgust. Someone in the audience mentioned Lord Ferringul rather loudly, causing Ari to freeze for a moment. Sir Cadwel was so angry with him that in the evening, when everyone else went to the feast, they practiced with the shield and broadsword for hours, with Peine standing to the side, talking about Lord Ferringul until the poor boy's throat went hoarse.

Peine told them at length about the fight Prince Parrentine and Lord Ferringul had with the ambassador from Princess Clorra's homeland, Lord Kroost. It seemed her father's representative and her ladies in waiting hadn't deemed it appropriate for their princess to be locked in a room alone with the strange Lord Ferringul. Apparently, Parrentine had ordered them physically restrained and locked them in the Hapland diplomat's chambers. Peine said King Ennentine and his advisors had been up all night, writing a formal apology to the Hapland ambassador to try and dissuade him from sending for the Hapland fleet to forcibly take the princess home.

Ari at first took a lot of hits. He was distracted not only by the mention of Lord Ferringul, but the content of Peine's discourse also interested him. Fortunately, after a few short hours and countless bruises, Ari managed to find his concentration.

"How does that name unman you so, boy?" Sir Cadwel said, halting their sparring.

"I don't know," Ari said. He could tell by the deepening of the knight's scowl that his answer wasn't satisfactory.

"I know Lord Ferringul is disconcerting," Sir Cadwel said. Ari wondered what disconcerting meant, but he didn't think it was the time to ask. "But the way you act, you'd think he killed your parents or something."

"My parents—" Ari went still. The practice sword he held began to slip from his hand. "Aren't who he killed."

Sir Cadwel opened his mouth to continue with the lecture.

"Ho there, laddie," a mirthful voice interrupted. "Ye all but lost yer weapon." Larke was there, his warm hand brushing Ari's ice-cold one as he caught up the hilt of the practice sword.

Ari rounded on the bard in anger. He almost remembered something, and Larke's voice had a way of filling up his mind so as to make him lose what he was thinking about.

"I thought we were to be spared you while in the capital," Sir Cadwel groaned.

"But how could I resist watching t'lad?" Larke asked. "Anyhow, I be in disguise!"

Indeed, Larke wore a large gray cloak, which covered him from head to toe. With the heavy cowl drawn up, it was hard in the half-light at the end of the day to see his face beneath it.

"Oh yes, you don't stand out dressed like that in this weather at all." Sir Cadwel shook his head. "Collect your sword, Ari. We won't get any more done now this vagabond has shown up."

"I had to come," Larke said, leaning toward the knight as if confiding. "I couldn't be deprived for one more day from basking in the glow of yer greatness. Oh, noblest of knights, please forgive the frailties of a common man!"

Sir Cadwel shook his head, clearly disgusted. "Peine, come help me get this padding off," he ordered the Wheylian boy, and they headed toward the castle.

"Larke, why am I so afraid of . . . of . . ." Ari tried to ask.

"'Tis best if ye don't think on that for now, me lad," Larke said, his tone persuasive. His blue eyes looked out from the depths of his hood to lock with Ari's.

"Yes, you're right," Ari said in an almost dreamy tone. "I need to concentrate on winning the tourney so I can be a real knight."

"Yes, that's it, me lad," Larke said.

Ari smiled, happy to have that settled, and turned to follow Peine and Sir Cadwel back into the castle.

***

The following day, they fought with flails and shields. Ari collected three new points, as did the prince, but they never drew each other, a coincidence that was beginning to make Ari suspicious. He didn't know who was more likely to have suggested it, Sir Cadwel or Parrentine, but he had an inkling one of them was making sure he and the prince didn't meet on the tourney field.

On the third day, when dueling was to take place, Ari waited to walk Stew from his spot in the picket to the well until he saw Parrentine's page set off toward the tourney master's tent. Ari's route happened to take him right behind the tent, just as Parrentine's page entered. He knew eavesdropping was bad, but he very much wanted to know if not drawing Parrentine was a coincidence. Ari felt he had a right to know, since it concerned him, but it wasn't likely anyone would tell him. Pretending to notice something in Stew's gait, he bent down to examine a hoof, pressing himself between Stew and the back of the tent.

"Remember," the now familiar haughty voice of Parrentine's page was saying. "His highness does not want to duel that peasant boy Sir Cadwel is trying to pawn off on us as a knight."

"I admit, at first, I agreed with the prince, but Sir Cadwel believes the orphan's blood may be noble," the aged voice of the tourney master answered. Ari wondered at that, for Sir Cadwel knew Ari was his Uncle Jocep's nephew. "In the old days," the tourney master said, "skill such as his spoke for itself. A man's worth was proven on the body of his foes. Sir Cadwel is within his right."

"These aren't the old days, old man," growled the prince's page. "And it would be a sad thing if, after a lifetime of being known for your impeccable integrity, it came out you have long taken bribes."

"Sir!" exclaimed the master, and Ari could hear his chair scrape back as he stood. "I have never taken a bribe."

"I can have twenty witnesses by morning ready to swear you have," the page said. "Just see they aren't matched up, old man. It isn't worth it to you not to."

Ari listened to the hard thud of the page's boot heels on the packed earth as he strode from the tent. Ari could picture the page's arrogant walk. He heard the old man in the tent sigh and settle back into his chair.

Ari stood, patting Stew's neck absently and thinking. He wasn't angry. He was almost amused. He hadn't realized he was that scary to Parrentine. The prince must realize that eventually they may have to face one another. He and Ari were matched evenly for points. They would obviously be entering the jousting together, unless one of them did very poorly that day in fencing or the following day in archery. Certainly, Parrentine couldn't hope Ari to fail on the fifth day. It would be asking a lot for Sir Cadwel's page to be horrible enough at ring-jousting or skewering swinging scarecrows to disqualify himself from the final joust. Ari shrugged. It wasn't really his concern. When it came time, Parrentine would have to face him or forfeit.

The dueling didn't go as well as Ari would have hoped. He managed to win all of his matches, but he was plagued by ill luck. Some of the straps on his padding snapped, despite being brand new. Somehow, his gloves and the leather grip on his foil had been oiled, making it all rather slippery. One of his boot heels even fell off during his final match. Although he won, he was tagged at least once in each fight, and the crowd began to murmur maybe it was wrong for an orphan of unknown heritage to compete in a nobles' sport.

Even Siara's normally impassive face showed concern. Each day, she watched the tourney from the raised box where she sat with the king and queen. A seat was also provided for Princess Clorra, but she never attended. Ari had heard she was present each night at the evening feast, but he didn't see her because he always found a reason not to go. Other nobles watched from boxes as well, and they ranged down the castle wall, festooned with colorful banners. Common people had bleachers to sit in, although many set picnics on the ground or climbed the few trees within the grounds.

"I think tonight we'll take all of your equipment up to our room and check it over," Sir Cadwel told Ari when he rejoined the knight and Peine after his final match of the day.

Peine groaned. "But we'll just have to carry it all back down tomorrow," he said.

"Why, so you will," Sir Cadwel said.

He bent low over the chest where they stored Ari's equipment at night, gesturing for Ari to join him. Leaning close, Ari saw Sir Cadwel pointing to some odd scrape marks around the lock hole on the chest.

"Someone opened it?" Ari whispered, aware that the walls around them were of thin canvas, not aged stone.

"Opened it and had their way with the contents," Sir Cadwel said, scowling.

"I think I know who," Ari said. He wanted to tell Sir Cadwel about Parrentine's page and the tourney master, but he couldn't work out how to do it without revealing his unchivalrous eavesdropping.

"I daresay we both do," Sir Cadwel said.

"They threatened the tourney master they would tell everyone he takes bribes if he matched us," Ari said, hoping Sir Cadwel wouldn't ask how he knew.

"Better you don't humiliate Parrentine in front of everyone, anyhow," Sir Cadwel said with a grin. "I'll let the tourney master know there's no reason to fight them on it. No practicing tonight, lads," he continued in normal tones, straightening. "Just drag all this upstairs and check it proper."

"I think that's a very good idea," Siara said, ducking into their tent. "His equipment was falling off him today." She was discreetly followed by a maid and a castle page. "I was worried for him. Maybe I can help? I planned to watch your practice."

"Why would you do that?" Ari asked, surprised.

Siara glanced at who was around, Ari, Sir Cadwel, Peine, and her two servants. She crossed to Ari, rising up on her tiptoes to bring her mouth closer to his ear.

"I don't think I can stand sitting across from her for another meal," she murmured. "There's something amiss there."

"Now, lass," Sir Cadwel said, putting a hand on her shoulder. "Jealousy never solved a thing. You must try to get on with the princess. Who knows but you could become quick friends." Ari didn't know if the knight's ears were that keen or if he had simply guessed the source of Siara's disquiet.

"You're right, of course," Siara said pleasantly, taking a step back from Ari and smiling at Sir Cadwel. "All the same, mayhap we can become friends tomorrow, and tonight I can busy myself with helping Ari."

She might have been smiling at Sir Cadwel, but when her gaze met Ari's again, he saw in it a dreadful seriousness. He remembered with a chill that feeling of evil when he stood outside Princess Clorra's room and the deep throaty laugh he'd heard that had sounded so terribly inappropriate.

"Not that it's my place to decide," Sir Cadwel said. He gave Siara's shoulder a last little pat. "I'm sure an evening away from the great hall and all the noise and commotion there would do anyone more good than not."

Agreed, they set to carrying Ari's equipment up to the room. Peine recommended they take the servants' entrance, as it was quicker and it was in poor taste to drag armor and weapons through the grand foyer. Sir Cadwel agreed but, Ari felt, more because it was discreet than out of a sense of decorum. Thus, the Princess Siara and her two servants, the king's champion, Ari, and Peine found themselves with armloads of clanking metal in the dim back passages of the castle. All of them had been in these passages before, barring the princess, and Ari could see by her wide eyes the experience was educational for her.

Siara did help him with his armor, and they found several more pieces had been tampered with. She didn't ask why the armor was in such poor condition, and Ari didn't want to ruin an otherwise happy evening by bringing up the prince. Besides, he had only suspicions of who had ordered his things tampered with, not proof.

Of Princess Clorra, Siara mentioned only that to affect her cure, Lord Ferringul, whom Siara referred to as the prince's new friend, had stayed sequestered completely alone with her in her room for three days. Not even the prince or her maids had been allowed in. At the end of the three days, they'd found her cured but not the same. Siara didn't know exactly what they meant by not the same, because no one dared talk about it. To Siara, Clorra seemed a bit wild-eyed and pale, refusing to eat all but the most choice morsels at dinner, and laughing inappropriately but talking almost not at all. Ferringul was in constant attendance to her. It was there their conversation ended, as if it were all they could do to have almost mentioned Lord Ferringul twice.

***

Archery did not go well. Ari rose early to check his bow, strings, and each individual arrow, in spite of having slept next to them all night, but out of all the things Sir Cadwel had taught him, Ari was worst at archery. In hand-to-hand combat of any type, he excelled, but he didn't have a knack for shooting long. He was not a complete disaster at it; he earned the one point he needed to make sure he would be included in the pre-joust, but he was keenly aware of how poorly he did and that his shooting didn't go far to reassure the populace and the king after his ill-omened fencing the day before.

Ari thought he was even worse than usual with a bow, but he couldn't in good conscience blame it on anyone but himself. Oddly, he did look up before the final round and find Larke staring intently at him from under the low hood of his cowl. When he met

Larke's gaze, the bard flushed, looking away. Ari rallied to do better that round than in the other two, locking down his place.

The pre-joust lasted for two days, as everyone who qualified from the ranks of the unproven participated in it, as well as all those men who had qualified for jousting at any point in the past. Only ten men would enter the final joust, and the fifth and sixth days were filled with tests of skill to determine which ten. When it wasn't his turn, Ari watched other knights skewer rings and scarecrows. He wondered if they took ten men to the final joust to save time, or just so they risked having only ten men completely disabled. Ari decided not to dwell too much on that second possibility.

He felt a certain amount of indifference as Parrentine captured four of the five colored rings. Then it was his turn. He climbed the steps to mount, and he and Stew rode toward their first line of colorful circles. Ari lowered his lance and tapped Stew with his heels. Unlike the knights, he didn't wear spurs. Stew knew when Ari wanted him to run.

He approached the yellow ring confidently, but just as he was about to slide his lance through it, it lurched, seeming to jump away from him. Ari blinked in confusion, but no one seemed to have noticed. People were cheering and people were booing, and he was quite sure he could hear Sir Cadwel cursing even from across field, but what he did not hear was anyone yelling out that the ring had jumped.

He didn't have time to think about it for long, because the red ring rapidly approached. This ring too seemed to jump away from his lance, but this time, he was ready for it and caught it anyhow. More people cheered than booed.

The orange ring jumped left and the green right. The final ring, the purple, seemed to try to dive. Ari caught them all except the first yellow one. He was ready for their tricks now.

As he racked the fifth ring onto his lance and Stew began to make the turn that would keep them from colliding with the bleachers, Ari once again looked up and saw Larke. The bard's face was intent, and for a brief instant, Ari felt that concentration was directed not at him succeeding, but rather at the opposite. He frowned at his companion. Larke noticed his gaze and managed a weak smile. Ari wheeled Stew around tightly and headed back, a stiff breeze in his face.

A woman's scream cut through the crisp autumn air, nearly startling Ari from his horse. Across from him, in the royal box, Queen Parrella stood, one long arm extended as she pointed at Ari and screamed. Everyone seemed as stunned as Ari, for no one moved as her voice trailed off and her arm fell. She crumpled into a heap on the painted wooden floor of the royal box. King Ennentine and Siara nearly fell from their chairs to kneel at her side. Fearfully, Ari looked around him, then behind. Was the queen screaming at him?

"Apprehend that man!" the king roared, pointing over Ari's head.

Ari turned just in time to see Larke, struggling to get his fallen hood in place, slither between the bleacher seats and onto the ground. He landed running. Guards poured after his retreating form.

A recess was called while the queen was attended to. After a while, the king's men came back, reporting that the cloaked man had eluded them. Predictably, King Ennentine sent for Sir Cadwel, who waved for Ari to accompany him.

"Cadwel," the king said. He gestured for Sir Cadwel to step aside with him. Ari stayed near the edge of the platform. On the other side, the queen reclined, a damp scarf on her brow. Siara held her hand.

"How fares the queen, your majesty?" Sir Cadwel asked.

"She just had a bit of a shock," the king said, his eyes on his wife. "That man . . . he looked, well, I would wager half my kingdom that he was the bard Larkesong."

"That would be impossible, your majesty. That man looked to have no more years than thirty, and Larkesong would be older now than I," Sir Cadwel said. "Perhaps it was a long lost son of the man?"

Beside the queen, Ari saw Siara open her mouth to interject something, and he gave her a hard look. If Sir Cadwel didn't want to mention that he knew the man who had made the queen scream, Ari was sure he had his reasons. Siara glared at him but held her piece, bowing her head instead to the task of re-wetting the gauzy cloth on the queen's brow.

"That is a fine explanation." King Ennentine sounded pleased. "And my poor wife reacted as she did because she believed she saw a ghost."

"Undoubtedly," Sir Cadwel said.

Ari knew Sir Cadwel well enough to know the knight was being tactful more than he was being honest, but fortunately, the king seemed too preoccupied to notice.

"Well, we should resume the tourney," King Ennentine said. "Resume the tourney," he called loudly, turning to face the rail. A cheer went up from the crowd at the announcement, and another for Queen Parrella as she re-took her seat beside the king.

"Why did seeing Larke make the queen scream and faint?" Ari whispered to Sir Cadwel as they descended the dais.

"Because she thought he was the famous minstrel of her youth, Larkesong," Sir Cadwel said.

"Wouldn't she be more inclined to think it was his son? Does she believe in ghosts? It all seems a bit odd to me," Ari said.

"It was the heat of the day. The queen thought she saw a ghost. Ghosts scare people, and she got scared," Sir Cadwel said with a tone of finality.

Ari dared to scowl at his back, but he knew that here and now, he would get no more answer than that. Next time he saw Larke, he would confront him about it. If he saw Larke again. The bard had been running awfully fast. Ari had to admit that Larke had forewarned them there was a lady in the city he didn't wish to upset with the sight of himself. Ari just never imagined Larke meant the queen.

A little excitement must have been what Ari needed, because after that, he stopped imagining that things were jumping out of the way of his lance. Over the next two days, he performed superbly, and the crowd was once again behind him. Ari didn't really care what the crowd thought, except that if they liked him, it looked better to the king, and Ari knew it was up to the king whether or not he got to be a real knight someday. Ari did better on the two trial days than anyone else, including Parrentine, although the prince also gained the top ten.

***

The night before the final joust, Ari lay awake on the couch in Sir Cadwel's sitting room, his armor neatly piled on the floor next to him. He knew he should sleep, but sleep eluded him. Sir Cadwel said he'd done well enough already to prove to any man that he was worthy of being a knight, but Ari found himself daring to dream he might actually win the tournament.

With a sigh, he rose and walked to the window. The autumn air was quite cool, and he wore only light cloth breeches, but he didn't feel cold. As usual since he'd taken up with Sir Cadwel, he could see almost as clearly in the dark as he could have in the light, and also as usual, his brain slid away from wondering how that was.

It's a lot lighter in the city in general, he told himself.

Ari gazed out over the castle towers. Some were pointy and tiled with red clay shingles. Some were flat with battlements around the top and trap doors to let men up.

He thought about his aunt and uncle and cousins. His older cousin, Mactus, must be married by now. Jare would probably be thinner and more nasty, what with having to actually do work now that Ari was gone. It would be really splendid if they could see him in the joust the next day, or if they could have seen him the past few days. Well, except for at archery and fencing. He realized he missed them. He wondered if they missed him, and not just for the work he always did as his share of keeping up the inn. Maybe if he ever managed to get any money, he should give his uncle some. He'd raised Ari, after all, and he always needed money for the inn. Someday, that inn would be Mac's, and Ari liked his older cousin.

A movement caught his eye, and he lowered his gaze from the tower tops to the row of balconies across the courtyard. The rooms in the wing where he and Sir Cadwel stayed had large windows, but the royal suites across the inner courtyard had balconies, and onto one stepped Princess Clorra, completely naked.

At first, Ari was too awestruck by her pristine white skin and waist-length blond hair to notice the gauntness of her or the way she skulked. Then Lord Ferringul stepped onto the balcony behind her. Ari moved back into the shadows of the drapes beside the window. He couldn't hear what the two said, but suddenly, Lord Ferringul struck her across the face, and she seemed almost to hiss at him. Her teeth gleamed white and sharp in the pale light of the moon. Ferringul took her roughly by the arm and led her back inside.

Ari stood very still for a while, making sure they didn't reappear. He moved slowly back to the couch. He would never fall asleep now, he realized gloomily, picturing himself falling off his horse the next day, not because he was hit with another knight's lance, but because he fell asleep waiting for the charge. The image of the two on the balcony pressed against the inside of his eyelids. Now he did feel cold and pulled a blanket off the back of the couch. Almost unbidden, the soothing vision of the dark-eyed old woman that so often appeared in his dreams rose up to fill his mind, and he thankfully drifted to sleep.

***

The day of the joust dawned as clear and cool as only the most perfect of fall days could. Ari watched the sun rise as he inspected, cleaned, and set out Sir Cadwel's clothes and ceremonial armor and then did the same for his own more modest accoutrements. As he was finishing, Peine entered and the boy's chattering began. Seeing that Ari had already dealt with Sir Cadwel's armor, Peine headed through the sleeping room to begin setting out the knight's shaving kit and other morning needs.

Alone again, Ari went to the large window and gazed out. Nothing drew his eyes down from their inspection of the castle ramparts that morning. High above, King Ennentine's silver and blue flag, black stallion rearing high, snapped from the tower tops. As Ari observed how the banner-festooned white stones of the castle stood out against the clear blue sky, he wondered if it was all a dream.

It would make sense of everything. It would explain how Ari had played in the woods one spring night, only to find it fall when he'd returned to his uncle's inn the next morning, having somehow missed his own birthday and his older cousin's engagement. It would explain why that loss of time didn't bother him like it should and why, when he tried to think about it, his thoughts inevitably slipped away.

It definitely explained how he had somehow managed to end up as Sir Cadwel's page and why he seemed to be so fast and so strong that after a few lessons with a weapon, he could best most men, and even had the speed and dexterity to learn and adapt as a fight commenced.

His eyes fell to the balcony that must belong to the room across from Siara's. It didn't explain Princess Clorra, or why Siara didn't like him, or why the prince had turned out to be somewhat of an ass. Ari liked to think if he were dreaming up his perfect world, he'd have done a better job than that.

Ari squared his shoulders. No, it wasn't a dream, and today, he had to be his best. He couldn't allow any distractions or silly mistakes. He had to make Sir Cadwel proud. This was his chance to be a real knight.

He checked every bit of his armor again as he put it on, carefully adjusting the straps. He checked his borrowed broadsword too, although if he did well enough, he wouldn't need to use it. His lances and Stew's armor were below, and he paced back and forth by the chamber door while he waited for Sir Cadwel to be ready.

"Feeling well this morning?" Sir Cadwel asked as Peine trailed him out of the adjoining chamber.

"I'm ready," Ari said, opening the chamber door.

"I see that," Sir Cadwel said, sounding amused. Ari flushed, stepping back to wait for the knight to precede him. "You needn't have put all your armor on yet, you know. Would be easier to navigate the steps without it." Sir Cadwel was the perfect knight in his decorative breastplate and long, blue cape with a brown hawk on the back, the symbol of Sorga. Ari wondered why Sir Cadwel had chosen to wear his own colors that day instead of the silver hawk on blue that was the conglomeration of his house's symbol with the colors of the crown. As king's champion, Sir Cadwel was the only man in the kingdom allowed to merge the crown's colors with his own coat of arms. He carried a parchment-wrapped parcel under one arm, and it looked as though he'd even combed his mustache. "Let's go down to the stables and see to that horse of yours," Sir Cadwel said, leading the way.

***

Crowds were gathered, despite the early hour. It seemed as though everyone wanted to get a head start on the day's revelries. Ale was already being served alongside meats that had cooked all night. Ari's stomach growled, but he ignored it. He would surely be nervous soon, and it would be best to leave his stomach empty.

Stew was in high spirits. He was proving to be a wonderful jousting horse. Peine braided blue ribbon into his tail and mane, which made Stew preen all the more. Watching Peine work, Ari could have sworn Stew had actually grown larger to accommodate his new role.

When the time came, Sir Cadwel assisted Ari onto his prancing mount himself.

"You settle down and pay heed to what you're about," Sir Cadwel said to the excited horse, holding Stew by the bridle and looking him in the eye. The knight looked up at Ari. "Tomorrow, I'm going north to find the villain, Lord Mrakenson, who cursed Princess Clorra. Even if the king hadn't ordered it, those are my lands, so it is my responsibility. I want you to know that however you do today, you have done well, and better than well, in this tourney. Win or lose, I would like you by my side when I ride north."

Ari nodded. The opening trumpets sounded, saving him from having to answer around the sudden tightness in his throat. Sir Cadwel stepped back and gave Stew a slap on the rump to send him toward the jousting field. Ari looked around in wonder at the cheering people, many waving sticks covered in ribbons and bells. Far from being worried by the clamor, Stew walked with his head up and his neck arched, his feet lifting high with each step. Ari shook his head, trying to focus amid the cornucopia of color and noise, and patted Stew on the neck.

His first opponent was Sir Collen, a man twice Ari's age whose arrogance did little to hide his nervousness. Like most, he observed Ari's swordsmanship and watched him skewer target after target. Peine said the rumor was Sir Cadwel had imparted to Ari the great secret that had made the knight the best alive. Since no man would willingly challenge the king's champion, being his protégé lent Ari a certain amount of presence.

On the first pass, Sir Collen used a trick Ari hadn't seen before, practically dismounting mid-pass to keep well away from Ari's lance, while still managing to smash his own on Ari's shield. The point seemed to bolster Sir Collen's confidence until he made the mistake of trying the same trick again. Ari ducked down behind Stew as well, copying Sir Collen's trick, and leveled his lance across Stew's chest, smashing it on his opponent's shield and throwing him to the ground, for the steep angle at which Sir Collen held his body offered little purchase in the saddle. After that, the man took a more conventional approach, and splinters flew as Ari's lance crashed into Sir Collen's shield once more, sending the knight clattering to the hoof-churned soil.

Ten competitors qualified for the joust on the seventh day of the tourney. Those ten matched off in pairs, taking five passes each, with a point awarded for a successful hit to the shield, and three for unhorsing your opponent. The eight with the most points continued, and from that round, the six best, the fourth, and so on until there were but two left.

Ari wasn't sure if he was relieved or chagrined when Parrentine got eliminated in the second round without having ever drawn him. Most of the knights left were older men, and while it seemed to Ari in some of the earlier rounds that Parrentine's opponents may have let him win, these men apparently felt it was wiser to please the current king than to pander to a future lord. If Ari's feelings about the prince's disqualification were ambivalent, Parrentine's were painfully obvious. The prince stormed from the tourney field, cursing them all. Ari saw Sir Cadwel and the king exchange disapproving looks, but he noticed the queen merely seemed relieved. All knew she didn't wish her only child to travel north to fight this foul being who had cursed Princess Clorra.

Ari hadn't been keeping track of the rounds, preferring to concentrate on each man as he faced him, so it came as somewhat of a surprise to him when he was announced as the winner. The announcement was drowned by the roar of the crowd even as it was made. Ari sat atop Stew, blinking in confusion. Stew, far from confused, pranced back and forth in front of the bleachers before heading to the royal box. Two servants were there with wooden steps to help Ari dismount, and Peine was trying to get him to give over his helmet. Ari climbed down and handed his friend his helmet, relieved to have it off. Ari stood where he was, dazed by the idea he could have won. Peine shoved him toward the platform on which the king, queen, and Siara stood.

As Ari reached the bottom of the steps, Sir Cadwel joined him, and the king descended halfway to meet them. Ennentine held out his hand, and a page placed the royal sword of his house in it. Ari creaked to his knees in front of the king. Bowing his head, he resisted the urge to ask someone if he had really won, just to be sure.

"Page Aridian," King Ennentine boomed, his voice carrying across the field. "It is my honor to proclaim you champion of our annual fall tourney, and our servant in the quest for righteous vengeance on the person of the Lord Mrakenson in the event that our envoy, whom you shall accompany forthwith, finds him guilty indeed of the charge of treason against the crown. As you are young to be a knight, we shall your conduct watch in this. When, on the dawn of your seventeenth year, you have finished your trial of servitude to your betters, we command you present yourself once more to us that we may, at our discretion, finish that which was today begun and promote you to your rightful place as a true servant of our realm and myself, your king."

Ari stared at the ground in confusion, trying to sort out what the king had said.

"Rise, page Aridian, that we may bestow on your brow a brotherly kiss and forthwith attend to other matters that press us on this day." The king reached down and clasped Ari's forearm.

With more strength than Ari expected, Ennentine helped him to his feet. The king leaned forward and bestowed the symbolic kiss to Ari's forehead, his lips not actually touching Ari's sweat-stained brow. The onlookers clapped and cheered. The king turned toward the people, pulling Ari around to face them, and they waved at the crowd of revelers. Ennentine gestured for silence, and Sir Cadwel stepped forward. Ari, not knowing if he should stay, backed down the stair to give his mentor room.

"Sir Cadwel, our champion," the king said, turning to the knight. "Kneel, my friend."

Ari watched, a bit light-headed, as his mentor knelt in front of the king, an act which Sir Cadwel accomplished with much greater ease than Ari had. Of course, the armor Sir Cadwel wore was ceremonial and didn't include the more cumbersome parts that covered the joints. Peine, who now held Sir Cadwel's brown-wrapped parcel, appeared at Ari's side.

"It is the honor of the crown to confirm upon you," King Ennentine said, his sword held over Sir Cadwel's left shoulder, "the title of Duke of Sorga and the title of Lord Protector of the Northlands, as well as the position of envoy to Lord Mrakenson." The sword moved to Sir Cadwel's right shoulder, then back to the left. "May you and yours be strong, true, just, and loyal. May you steward over your lands with honor in the name of your king. So swear you to the crown."

"So swear I to the crown," Sir Cadwel said, the pledge uttered loud and true.

Another great cheer went up from the crowd. Sir Cadwel creaked to his feet. "There is one more honor to bestow this day," he said in his gravelly voice.

The king stepped back. Sir Cadwel gestured to Peine, who began to unwrap the parchment-covered bundle, his face nearly split in half by his smile. Ari felt dizzy inside his hot armor, his mind struggling to comprehend that he, Aridian, had won the king's tourney. The crowd was a surging mass of color and noise around him, and even Siara and the king and queen seemed barely real. Ari shrugged, trying to ease the way his armor dug into his left shoulder. He wished they hadn't all picked this time to be eloquent. He needed to take off his heavy plate and dunk his head in Stew's watering trough to clear it enough to think.

"As duke and lord, I will need an heir," Sir Cadwel said. More than a few of the noblewomen present leaned forward, taking a revived interest in what went on below. "But as all know, I will take none to wife in replacement of mine lost." The knight's voice turned harsh, and Ari saw in his face that familiar look of pain.

"Therefore, I choose to name the orphan Aridian heir to my lands, my possessions, my titles, and all of the responsibilities that accompany these things." The knight was forced to shout the last words to be heard over the sudden babble of the crowd.

He held out his hand, and Peine gave him a blue cloak adorned with a brown hawk. Sir Cadwel stepped down and pinned the cloak on Ari, who stood staring at him in complete disbelief.

"Kneel," Sir Cadwel growled at him, and Ari instantly obeyed, bruising his knees as he all but threw himself onto the ground in front of his hero. "I dub thee my heir," Sir Cadwel intoned, touching his sword once to Ari's left shoulder and once to his right. "Rise, son," Sir Cadwel said, reaching down to lift a stunned Ari to his feet and clasped him in a rough embrace.

The crowd was deafening. Many of those not noble-born were cheering wildly, as Ari had become a hero to them in the past seven days. One of their own risen to greatness. In the tiers occupied by the nobles, however, there was much muttering and angry words. The king moved back up to stand beside his wife, both with impartial smiles on impassive faces. Ari stood there staring at Sir Cadwel, unable to think, let alone speak.

"Come, lad," Sir Cadwel said. "Wave to the crowd once more, and then we best get you out of that armor and into some finery. There'll be no excusing you from dinner this night."

Ari waved again, renewing the exuberance of the crowd. Then, with a grinning Peine beside them, Sir Cadwel, Duke of Sorga, Lord Protector of the Northlands, and king's champion, and the orphan Aridian, his page and heir, quit the field.

Chapter Eleven

"But I don't understand," Ari said to Sir Cadwel as Peine helped him remove his armor. "You can't just make me noble." He was fighting between shock, confusion, joy, and the return of the idea that it was all a dream.

"You would be amazed at what I can do when I so choose," Sir Cadwel said, a crooked grin on his face. "Besides, you're an orphan, so who's to say what blood flows in your veins?"

"But you know my aunt and uncle are just innkeeps," Ari said.

"And exactly which of them is related to your parents?" Sir Cadwel said. "Was it your aunt's sister who bore you, or are you the son of your uncle's brother? Or perhaps his sister's child?"

Ari stared at him in amazement. In all his fifteen years, that question had never come up. It was always *your mother and father*. Neither his aunt nor uncle ever spoke of his parents as brother or sister. In fact, they were rarely mentioned, which Ari never wondered much about, as he certainly didn't recall any other life, and if his uncle hadn't told him, and his cousin Jare continuously reminded him, he wouldn't have known he wasn't the child of the two who raised him.

"As I suspected," Sir Cadwel said, watching Ari struggle with the idea. "You don't know, and I would wager that why you don't know is because you share as much blood with those at the inn as I do with Peine here. Now get washed up," he said, gesturing Ari into the bathing room. Ari struggled with the idea while he finished undressing after making Peine turn away.

"Peine," Ari said, deciding for the time being that he needed to know more about his new life and worry less about his old one. He settled himself slowly into the steaming water. "Tell me about when Sir Cadwel's family was murdered. I want to know what happened."

"I told you, it was end of the Great War," Peine said in a whisper. He moved to the bathing room door, peeking out before shutting it firmly.

"How long ago was that?" Ari asked.

"Don't they teach you anything where you're from?" Peine said.

"Teach me? People tell stories in the tavern, if that's what you mean."

Peine shook his head. Ari could tell from his friend's disappointed look that storytelling in the tavern was not what Peine meant. "Let me start at the beginning." He screwed his face up, thinking. "Twenty-five years ago, when the king and queen got married, that ended the hundred years of war," Peine said. Ari listened closely, forgetting he was supposed to be getting clean for dinner. "The Lord of the Northlands didn't want King Ennentine to be king, but he agreed because he lost the war. One of the reasons he lost was because Sir Cadwel arranged for King Ennentine to marry Queen Parrella, and another was because Sir Cadwel killed both of the Lord of the Northland's sons." Peine paused here, probably trying to put the details of the conglomeration of history and gossip he had heard all his young life into order.

"I think the queen was in love with someone else, though, but she married the king anyhow, for the good of the land." Ari raised an eyebrow at this, wondering if it was really acceptable for them to talk about the king and queen this way, but he didn't interrupt. "So, the Lord of the Northlands was very angry, especially at Sir Cadwel."

"Why especially at Sir Cadwel?" Ari asked. "I mean, why not at King Ennentine and Queen Parrella?"

"I just said," Peine said. "Because Sir Cadwel killed his sons."

Ari nodded. He supposed it made sense to hate the man who killed yours sons more than the one who became your king.

"So everyone came here for the wedding." Peine pointed to the stone floor of the bathing room. "Except Sir Cadwel's wife couldn't come because she was too pregnant, so she stayed in Sorga, and I guess his brother must have stayed too because then the Lord of the Northlands led his men to Sorga and made a siege, and I know Sir Cadwel's brother was there."

Ari found himself gripping the scrub brush tightly, even though he had yet to see Sorga and of course had never known Sir Cadwel's family. He reminded himself it all happened long before he was born, but the image of Sir Cadwel's pain-filled face rose up in his mind's eye. He clenched the brush till his knuckles turned white.

"A messenger came to Sir Cadwel and told him about the siege," Peine said. "There were lots of knights and soldiers here, of course, and they went with Sir Cadwel, but by the time they got all the way to Sorga, the Lord of the Northlands was in the castle, and they were fighting inside." Peine stopped for a moment, looking at Ari with solemn eyes. "So they say by the time Sir Cadwel got there, his wife and the baby were already dead, and his brother was already unconscious." Ari stared at Peine, aghast. "So they took back the castle, and they say Sir Cadwel killed the Lord of the Northlands with his bare hands, not with a sword or anything." Peine sounded awed, and he looked over his shoulder toward the door that led to the sleeping room a bit fearfully.

"I think he could have," Ari said, following the boy's gaze. "But his brother didn't die."

"No. He never woke up again, though," Peine said. "Never in twenty-five years, but Sir Cadwel wouldn't take his titles, and he made the king give his brother the Northlands too, even though the king wanted to give them to Sir Cadwel, since he killed the lord and all his heirs, but now his brother finally died, so he had to come here to be made Duke of Sorga and Lord Protector of the Northlands."

Ari stared at the stone wall across from him, considering this information. "And then Sir Cadwel made me his heir."

"Yes," Peine said, brightening. "Isn't that truly splendid?"

Ari didn't answer him. He went back to bathing, his mind grappling with understanding his new heritage.

***

Dinner that night was not as arduous as Ari anticipated, or at least not in the way he anticipated. This was mostly because the three people he preferred to avoid didn't attend. The prince locked himself in his room in anger over not being allowed to go north with Ari and Sir Cadwel, a decision which lightened Ari's worries over the journey considerably. Peine told him that Parrentine refused food or visitors completely, and the king placed a guard on his door at all times in case the prince needed anything. Why Princess Clorra was not at dinner confused Ari. He knew she was recovered from the wasting sickness which threatened to take her life, but now something else seemed to be wrong with her, and people wouldn't talk about what. Siara told him she could hear Clorra screeching in her room at all hours of the day and night, and the princess didn't sound weak or ill. Whatever was wrong with her, it kept Lord Ferringul by her side, to Ari's relief. He didn't relish the idea of spending an evening across the table from the strange lord.

What form his troubles for the evening did take was completely unexpected to Ari. While the young men of the court were off arguing with anyone who would listen about their distant but superior claims to the Dukedom of Sorga or to the Northlands, all the unattached women of the court who long hoped to capture Sir Cadwel switched targets. After all, if marrying an old man who would soon leave you alone with all his wealth was good, marrying a naive young one who would be putty in your hands was almost as much so. In consequence, for the second time in his life, Ari found himself the focus of the attention of women. Ari didn't find the situation at all comfortable, because if his first experience with them had taught him anything, it was that you couldn't trust them. If you did, you would end up with Sir Cadwel laughing at you.

Ari didn't know what to make of the women at all, but he truly was amazed by them, albeit not in the way they obviously hoped he would be. They walked boldly up the head of the table to where he sat on Sir Cadwel's right. They wore gowns so low cut he was embarrassed to look anywhere but at their faces. They told him ridiculous stories about their good upbringing and their skills while whispering about the horrors of their rivals. Little did they know, he couldn't manage to keep any of their names straight, so their efforts to poison him against their compatriots were in vain, even if he was inclined to believe them, which he was not.

Worst of all, Siara and Sir Cadwel carried on an exceedingly happy conversation revolving around making fun of him. When a woman would approach him, they would switch to the weather, but once she was gone, they would give glib reviews of his performance.

"And I said his face couldn't get any redder," Siara said, as another lace-clad, flowery-smelling woman walked away.

"I thought not myself after that one in green," Sir Cadwel said. "I think they actually fell out of her dress when she bent over to whisper in his ear. Probably why she left so fast."

"Well, that or his breath," Siara said.

"Do you think his breath would stop her?" Sir Cadwel said. "We're speaking of a lot of lands and titles."

"Have you ever smelled his breath? I think it would stop a dragon."

"I always assumed that smell came from his horse," Sir Cadwel said, looking at Ari speculatively. Beyond him, the king and queen smiled.

So it went the entire evening, until finally Siara seemed to tire of the game, and Sir Cadwel said they shouldn't stay much later as they would have to rise early to start preparations for the journey north. He hoped to leave before noon. Conversation became more serious then, with the queen saying they needn't leave so quickly and Siara looking quiet and sad.

When Ari finally climbed into bed, he was feeling very much abused and looking forward to the quiet of the open road, where at least no one was charging at him with a lance, throwing bosoms in his face, or critiquing his social etiquette. The only good thing he heard all dinner was the king suggesting he ought to have his own tent.

It had been a long day, and he was quickly asleep.

***

Ari awoke a bit late the next morning because Sir Cadwel had said to let him sleep himself out. Peine had already managed to finagle his way into accompanying them. He was to share Ari's new tent as well. Peine had, it appeared, convinced the lot of them Ari needed his own valet now that he was heir to a dukedom.

By the ninth hour of the day, the three were ready to depart, but found they couldn't leave until noon. The king and queen prepared a public goodbye and, to Ari's embarrassment, a parade to escort them from the city. Thus Ari found himself wandering without purpose around a small garden tucked away in the middle of an unused courtyard. He had stumbled upon it while trying to take the long way back from checking Stew over a final time. Stew looked well, seemingly still in high spirits from his performance the day before, and not a bit tired or sore.

He was in the garden when Siara found him, her two ladies in waiting trailing behind. When they saw Ari, the younger of the two, who looked to be about fourteen, blushed brightly, while the older gave him a slightly challenging look. He was moderately sure he had encountered both the night before, and fervently hoped they didn't try to speak to him as he couldn't remember their names. To his relief, Siara told them to wait, approaching Ari alone. She gestured for Ari to turn his back slightly to the two who watched, but she didn't bother moving too far away. They would never be allowed out of sight of the ladies, their purpose being to ensure the princess was never left unattended, especially in the presence of a man.

"I've been searching for you all morning," she said.

As usual, since the queen had taken an interest in her, Siara wore a blue dress, and her hair was curled and shone from hours of brushing. Ari noticed she smelled good too.

"I've been busy," he said. She looked around the empty little garden, raising an eyebrow in skepticism. "I mean, I was busy until now."

"Ari," she said and stopped.

Looking more closely, he noticed that despite the artful application of face paint and the obviously elaborate care taken in her appearance, Siara was pale and tired, and she chewed her bottom lip.

"I'm sorry we're leaving you here," he said, reaching to take her hand. He said it partly because he meant it and partly because he thought maybe it was what she wanted to hear. He supposed if he were being left there, he would be quite upset.

"It isn't that." She took his other hand and looked up at him seriously. "I don't mind it here. It's better than the nunnery, after all. Besides, I don't think I have a choice since he is here."

The last she said so bitterly that Ari blinked down at her in surprise. He knew she resented not being warned she could only love once, but he thought she liked Parrentine. He was handsome and a prince. Of course, he was also in love with another woman, to whom he was engaged. And, as far as Ari could tell, Parrentine was a little crazy. Ari looked away from her, not wanting her to see the pity in his eyes. He reprimanded himself for ever thinking about how unfair it was that he couldn't have a chance with Siara. Her situation was a hundred times worse.

"Ari," she said, ignorant to his inner turmoil. "I don't want you to go to the Northlands to challenge Lord Mrakenson."

"But," he protested, taken off guard. "I have to. I won the joust. I'm Sir Cadwel's page. And he cursed Princess Clorra. He must be made to set things right or take proper punishment." He looked down at her tense face in sudden suspicion. "You don't want us to stop this Lord Mrakenson. You hope he makes her sick again," he said.

"Ari!" she gasped, dropping his hands. "What an awful thing to say! I came looking for you because I'm afraid for you, you addle-brained, ungrateful, worthless son of a . . ."

"I'm sorry, I'm sorry!" he interrupted her, taking back her hands. "Siara, I'm sorry. I didn't mean it." In spite of his assurance, he didn't quite believe her. How could she want Princess Clorra to be well? Peine said Wheylian women waste away and die if they can't be with the man they love. He reminded himself, as he often did, that Siara was only half Whey.

"Ari," she tried for a third time, taking a deep breath. "I just want you to think about on whose word it is you're going. There's no good can come of this. There's no hope you are being sent in good faith."

He looked down at her serious blue eyes and nodded. He realized his own brain had been trying to tell him the same thing, but for some reason he couldn't bring himself to really think about it. Sometimes, when he was half asleep, or if he woke from quickly fading dreams, he thought he remembered something. He didn't know what, but it made everything clear, except once he was awake, it was gone. One of these days, he was going to take the time to sort through all of it.

"Thank you," he said after a moment, not knowing what else to say. "I do have to go, though, Siara. I see what you're saying, I really do, but this is my first mission for the crown, and I can't not go because I'm afraid of things I can't even put to voice." He willed her to understand, and meeting her eyes, he knew she did. She squeezed his hands.

"Just—" She sighed. "Be careful, Ari."

He nodded. Biting her lower lip again, she let go of his hands, turning to walk back to her ladies, who instantly flanked her and began a babble of whispers, casting curious glances back at Ari. Siara appeared to ignore them, walking slowly from the garden. Ari watched her go before heading back to the room he and Sir Cadwel shared.

Chapter Twelve

It seemed they had not been on the road long, after what Ari felt was a ridiculous and embarrassing amount of fuss over their departure, when Larke joined them. He rode up from somewhere behind them, the sound of his lute drifting forward. Even though he couldn't see it from where he rode, Ari could picture the grimace on Sir Cadwel's face. He smiled. Peine, riding on a chubby little horse the king gave him that he'd dubbed Charger, twisted around to see who approached, almost falling off in the process.

"I heard you eluded the king's guards," Sir Cadwel said once the bard drew abreast.

"Of course, had I done wrong, I would be the first to turn myself in." Larke strummed a dramatic chord. "But I'm sure 'twas all a misunderstanding."

"When you said you didn't want to distress a lady," Sir Cadwel said. "It didn't occur to me you might mean the queen. Tell me, is there any reason I shouldn't run you through this instant?"

"Noble Sir!" Larke said. "What could a lowly minstrel such as myself have ever done to the queen?"

"Why did the sight of you upset her so?" Sir Cadwel said.

Ari held his breath.

"I can but assume she thought she saw Larkesong," Larke said, shrugging. "I'm told I bear a passing similarity to the man."

"You do at that," Sir Cadwel said. "But that doesn't explain why you ran or why she was so upset. I still don't trust you, bard."

"I ran on account of they were chasing me," Larke said with a grin.

Sir Cadwel grunted.

"I won the joust, Larke," Ari said, his excitement with winning returning now it seemed Sir Cadwel wouldn't kill Larke today.

"Well done, me lad, well done," Larke said, but the chord he struck sounded ominous to Ari. "I did not doubt but ye would."

"I suppose we're stuck with you again?" Sir Cadwel muttered.

"Stuck? Stuck!" Larke sputtered. "Why, can it be stuck, when with me ye have the finest travel music acquirable by man?"

"I'm going too," Peine said, full of pride. "I'm Lord Aridian's valet."

"Are ye now?" Larke asked, his voice amused. "Lord Aridian's valet! What a grand thing, lad." With that, the bard launched into rousing ballad.

Ari shot Larke a grin, glad to have him back.

***

It wouldn't take them the twenty-odd days it took to get from Sallsburry to the capital in the end of summer, but Sir Cadwel estimated it would take nearly a score. It was a much different road for Ari heading north, riding on his own horse, not walking in the dust with a pack animal. He didn't even have to lead the packhorse, because now that was Peine's job. They also didn't stay at any inns, although Sir Cadwel and Larke both agreed they might have an early winter, and once the snow started falling, it would be better to sleep indoors given the chance.

For now, though, they set camp each night. Ari and Sir Cadwel kept up on their sword practice, and Larke cooked and sang. Peine helped with all of the chores, from brushing down the horses to stirring the food for Larke. Ari was happy again. Even the frost on the ground each morning when he crawled out of his tent seemed wonderful. Instead of being cold, as Larke complained daily that it was, Ari felt it invigorated him. The trees along the King's Way were bedecked in many-colored leaves, the sky was blue and clear, and Ari didn't spend much time thinking about where they were going or why.

When they passed by the little road leading up to the farmstead where they had stopped on their way south, Ari couldn't help but wonder how the pretty blonde girl fared. He was relieved, however, when Sir Cadwel made no move to turn off the Way. Unfortunately, the knight too recalled that evening, surprisingly well for a man who had imbibed that much blackberry wine, and he thought it only fitting to regale Larke and Peine with the tale.

"What were you doing before you went into the barn?" Peine asked when Sir Cadwel was done.

"Sitting on some bags of grain," Ari muttered, blushing.

"Sitting on some bags of grain?" Larke said, inordinately amused. "Ye know, me friend," the bard said, turning to Sir Cadwel. "Those vast tale-telling talents of yours be wasted on the life of a knight."

"No, no," Sir Cadwel said. "A story that great needs no skill of telling."

"It's true, 'tis a fine tale," Larke said. He shot Ari a devilish grin. "A tale so fine, it seems in me humble opinion, must needs be set to music."

Ari groaned. Peine giggled. Ari shot him a quelling glance. "Traitor," he muttered. Stew shook his mane, and Ari was convinced even his horse was laughing at him.

"A ballad!" Sir Cadwel said. "What a fine idea. I think that's the best idea I've heard in months. Nay, years!"

"It isn't really that funny," Ari said, his patience with their amusement starting to run thin.

"Did I not tell ye, lad," the minstrel said, "one day you would be a great knight, and songs would be written of your valiant deeds? It seems this fine day is already upon us." To Ari's horror, Larke removed his lute from his back and began tuning it, muttering potential lyrics to himself. He caught Ari's distressed look and grinned. "Oh yes, a fine ballad indeed," Larke said, running his fingers over the strings. Ari groaned.

***

Ari felt a thrill of excitement when they turned off the King's Way onto the smaller road leading to Sallsburry. They didn't have to pass through his former home to reach Sorga, but out of the few larger roads bisecting the country, one was as good as the next, making it only slightly out of their way. Both Ari and Sir Cadwel thought it would be good of them to stop and let Ari's aunt and uncle know how he was faring.

They reached Sallsburry in the afternoon a few days later, and Ari felt an odd sense of disjointedness as they rode into town. On one hand, here was all he had known until that summer. On the other, Sallsburry looked small after some of the other towns he had seen, and certainly after the capital. Ari always thought of it more based on all the people who were in it, not noticing it had but one main street, and not very many side streets, and you could see from one side of the town to the other.

If it was a bit early for stopping, no one mentioned it as they rode into the inn's courtyard through the open gate. Ari heard a muted call from inside, and in a moment, his cousin Jare stumbled out into the yard as if pushed. Jare looked a bit thinner than Ari recalled, but he seemed just as surly as he stepped up to help Sir Cadwel dismount.

"Welcome to the Sallsburry High Inn," Jare mumbled, reaching for Goldwin's reins.

"I'll get him, Jare," Ari said, jumping down from Stew. He was surprised to notice he was now taller than his cousin.

Jare's jaw dropped, and he took one stumbling step backward. "Ari?" he croaked, and Ari almost laughed. He'd never seen anyone quite so much resemble a frog before.

"No, lad," Sir Cadwel said. "I keep telling you; now you're a duke and my heir, you can't be tending to horses and the like. Your valet and this boy can see to it. You and I are going inside."

Ari looked at his mentor in surprise, for that wasn't the type of thing Sir Cadwel was always telling him at all. Sir Cadwel winked at him, gesturing for them to enter the inn, leaving Jare slack-jawed and mute in their wake.

"Jare will never forget that," Ari said to the knight under his breath. "Now things will never be the same between us again."

"Good," Sir Cadwel said firmly, gesturing to the innkeep, who was already hurrying over.

"My lords," Ari's uncle said. "How may our humble inn . . . Ari?" His uncle's face registered shock at seeing him, but shock quickly gave way to pleasure. "Ari, boy!" His uncle shook his head in amazement. "Just look at you! You look a lord."

"He is a lord," Sir Cadwel said firmly.

"Is a lord?"

"Is a lord," Sir Cadwel said. "He is heir to the Dukedom of Sorga and the Protectorate of the Northlands."

Ari groaned inwardly. Why was Sir Cadwel ramming that down their throats? How could things be like they were if he did that? How could things ever be right?

"Well," his uncle said, seeming to be at a loss for words. He looked back and forth between Ari and Sir Cadwel.

"May we have a table and something to eat? There are four of us," Sir Cadwel said, his voice finally taking on a more gentle tone.

"Yes, yes, of course," Ari's Uncle said. "Sit anywhere you like." He gestured toward the small common room. "My, my," Ari heard him murmuring to himself as he hurried into the kitchen. Ari could make out excited conversation and his aunt's squeal, and the next thing he knew, she and his older cousin Mactus came running out.

Mac slapped him on the shoulder, and his aunt kept hugging him, and she was crying, although why, Ari wasn't sure, because she sounded happy.

". . . was the only one who saw you, so we all thought he dreamt it," she was saying, but they were all talking at once, so he couldn't hear the rest. Then nothing would do but for Ari to tell them about the castle and the mission to save the prince, and the joust. Somehow, while he was telling it, the inn got full. Jare came in, then Mac's new wife, as well as other people he had known his whole life. Larke, Peine, and Sir Cadwel took a table to one side, talking quietly and observing him.

It was all so different. Everyone was shorter, and everything was smaller, and he realized his clothes, which had seemed so modest at the castle, were very rich here, and everyone had a slight country accent. He found himself leaving most of what happened out of the story, realizing they wouldn't understand a lot of it, and having the odd feeling it wouldn't be right to speak of the prince's failings to these people. They looked up to the royal family, to knights and nobles. They paid their taxes and were happy in the certainty that good and just people watched over them and the country they lived in. Of Siara, he said absolutely nothing.

Glancing up once from all their questions, he saw Sir Cadwel watching him. His mentor's face was very serious, and he seemed to be taking in every word Ari said. Ari gave him what he hoped was a reassuring smile and went back to talking.

Just about the time Ari thought he would never need to bother to speak again, as he must have done all the talking one person could do in their life, Larke moved to stand by the hearth. Placing one foot up on a chair, he unslung his lute and began to play. At first, no one noticed, but in a few short moments, they all stopped speaking to listen, and Ari found he could duck away. He took the bard's vacated seat next to Sir Cadwel, his back to the inn wall.

The music Larke played was stirring, the song old and stately. People began to drift back to their normal tasks.

"That was almost as bad as all those women in court," Ari said, leaning against the wall.

"You handled yourself well," Sir Cadwel said.

"I don't see why you had to tell them all everything like that," Ari said. "I would have broken it to them before we left."

"You aren't the boy you were when you left here. They needed to know it, and so did you."

Ari frowned, thinking that over, and Sir Cadwel sent Peine to see about reminding someone they had asked for food.

***

The next morning, Ari, knowing Jare wouldn't be up yet, saddled Goldwin and Stew while Peine saw to the packhorse and Charger. Larke, as always, cared for his own mount. Ari had long ago stopped wondering about the peculiar relationship Larke had with his horse, asking it to come out of the stall instead of leading it out and the like, but he noticed Peine regarded the bard as if he were a bit mad.

As they led the horses from the stable, Ari's aunt and uncle came to the inn door. His uncle gestured to him, coming out to meet Ari halfway across the yard. The innkeep looked back over his shoulder at his wife, and she gave him an encouraging nod.

"Ari," his uncle said, his worried tone and his fidgeting oddly reminding Ari of the last time he had seen Siara.

"Yes, Uncle?" Ari asked, smiling to put his uncle at ease.

"That's just it," the innkeeper said. His eyes kept sliding away from Ari's. He gestured for Ari to lean close. "There's something we feel you ought to know, boy."

Ari nodded encouragingly, wondering what could have his uncle so worked up.

"Your aunt and I thought you should know, that is," his uncle said. He looked back at his wife once more, and she gestured for him to get on. Ari heard Sir Cadwel call for someone to settle accounts. Giving her husband one last hard look, his aunt hurried back into the inn.

"You see, Ari," he uncle said. "You aren't our nephew."

"Pardon?" Ari asked, rather sure he'd heard wrong.

"Your mother and father, they came here the year you were born, and they set up a farm, but we didn't know them." The innkeeper looked up at him, lines of worry twisting his face. "We don't even know where they came from. Your mother was already with child when they arrived, you know, but for all that, she worked right beside your father, building the house and garden and taking care of that one cow they had."

"You didn't even know them?" Ari said, peering at the innkeep intently, as if something in his face would change the words leaving his mouth.

"They kept to themselves a lot," he said. "They didn't come to town much, and then one day, at the end of spring, came this old lady. If there wasn't noble blood in her veins, let the gods strike me down for ignorance. She didn't say who she was, mind you, and we didn't very well ask. She had you, and she said those what lived at the farm were dead, and she told us not to go there and not to say you came from there neither."

Ari stared at the innkeep as if he were mad.

"Now, she gave us you and said to keep you." Again, he looked at Ari almost fearfully. "We just did as she said. We didn't mean harm by it. I haven't even thought on it for years now. You—" The innkeep faltered. "You're like a son to us. We did what seemed right by you, we did."

"That's fine," Ari said after a few moments, realizing the innkeep was waiting for an answer. "Um, thank you for telling me." In a daze, he walked over and mounted Stew. How could they not be related to him? All these years, he was their nephew, and now he wasn't? He wasn't anything to anyone at all? It was bad enough growing up without parents, but now he had no one. He slumped in his saddle, his eyes tracing and retracing the limbs of the old apple tree leaning against the inn yard fence as his mind traced back over his memories, recolored now, each one suspect for different meanings than previously thought.

Sir Cadwel came out of the inn, and in a short time, they set off. Ari didn't react to the innkeeper and his wife waving. The knight waved at them and reined Goldwin in slightly to come abreast Ari, who rode staring at the back of Stew's head.

"How did you like going home?" Sir Cadwel asked conversationally, peering at him. "Ari?" he said a few moments later when Ari gave no indication of having heard him.

"You were right," Ari said softly, struggling not to choke on the words. "Not a drop of blood between us."

Sir Cadwel raised his eyebrows, regarding his heir speculatively. Behind them, Larke began to sing, and on they rode to Sorga.

Chapter Thirteen

Ari thought all day about what his uncle had said, but his thoughts didn't seem to be getting anywhere. He was so surprised he hadn't even asked his uncle any of the questions churning in his mind. What were their names? Where were they from? Did they have any other family? Eventually, he couldn't stand thinking about it anymore, and his mind went back to a different problem as he followed Larke out of their camp to gather firewood.

"Larke," Ari said as he and the bard meandered through scrawny trees bright with fall foliage. "Was Larkesong really as great a bard as they say?"

"Well, me lad," the bard said after a pause. "He was a passing fine musician, to be sure, but it isn't just the ability to play that makes a bard great, or to sing, or even to tell a story, though in all those things, he did excel. What Larkesong also had, in excess, was the fortune of living in a time full of momentous deeds. So great were the deeds, a toneless old man with half a tongue could have told them and been considered great himself, just for getting to do the telling."

"Do you play as well as he did?" Ari asked, bending down to add to his armload of branches.

"Oh, I may, lad, I may." The bard sounded amused.

"So you've heard him?" Ari asked.

"I have indeed," Larke said, stopping to peer at him in the increasing gloom. He quirked an eyebrow at Ari. "Why all the questions, lad?"

"I'm trying to find out if he was the type of man a queen would fall in love with," Ari said.

"And why is that?" Larke asked, both eyebrows raised now.

"Well, Peine said the queen was in love with someone else and didn't want to marry the king, so I started thinking about the way the queen fainted that day."

"I see, so ye thought if indeed he were my father, or at least some close acquaintance of mine, I could set yer mind to rest, as it were," the bard said.

"Something like that, yes." Ari shrugged.

"And did ye think it may be none of our business, the private doings of the queen?" Larke asked.

"Well, that is," Ari stammered, blushing. Of course, it really wasn't any of his business, except he wanted to know.

"Let me put yer mind to rest then, lad, as ye be wanting," the bard said. "Goodness knows yer imagination will create infinite more scandal than the truth."

Ari blinked in surprise but didn't say anything, lest Larke change his mind. Any story from Larke was good, but one about the queen and the man who might be the minstrel's father ought to be great.

"The queen, in her flowering youth, very well was in love with Larkesong, as were many of the sweet young virgins o'the time, but the queen's love ran deeper and more true than most." Larke smiled sadly. "When Larkesong found out this terrible thing, for terrible it could be when the marriage of the king and queen is what held the nation from war, he left, and she in time learned to love her husband, which is a fine thing."

"That's it?" Ari said after Larke was silent for a moment.

"Aye, me lad, 'tis," Larke said, already gathering sticks once more.

"That's not a very interesting story," Ari said.

"Sometimes, lad, we must do what is right, even if it is not interesting, nor much fun, nor at all spectacular seeming," Larke said, "and even if we know no one will ever thank us for it or sing songs about it, noble as it may have been."

"Did Larkesong love her?"

"There's only one man who 'ere lived knows the answer to that question, lad," Larke said, his face unreadable. "We best be getting back. 'Tis past dark, and yon great knight may worry. Plus, his old eyes need the firelight for seein' in the dark."

They returned to camp, Larke whistling a slow, sad ballad, the words to which Ari didn't know. He trailed after the bard, not at all satisfied with the way their conversation had gone. A small, slightly selfish part of his brain had created the hope Parrentine was not the son of the king at all, and therefore not really a prince and not fit to rule the kingdom Ari wanted to serve. Ari also hoped if Parrentine wasn't who Siara thought he was, her love for him might somehow not count. Ari sighed, tossing the idea out. It really would have been a bad thing for Lggothland anyhow.

***

Ari rose early, dressing quickly in the predawn light. That day, after many long days of travel, they would reach Sorga, and Ari's fingers shook with anticipation as he laced his boots. He would see for the first time the place he was to call home. Not just him, but the woman he would someday marry, and their children, and their children's children. He was part of the nobility now. He was responsible for the lives and wellbeing of many other people. Ari intended to discharge that trust with honor and fairness, and to leave behind a legacy of heirs who would do likewise.

He looked up at the mountains looming over the plain on which they camped. For days now, almost since they had reached the coast and turned north, the mountains had been expanding on the horizon. At first, they were only snowy peaks, and Ari mistook them for low-lying clouds, but then their brown trunks rose into view, and he saw them for what they really were. Still, he didn't fully grasp their immensity, for each day, they continued to grow. That day, he would see the base of the great northern range, and he would see Sorga.

He took a deep breath, looking about for more tasks he might complete to speed them on their way.

"A bit anxious, me lad?" Larke's melodious voice floated out of the morning half-light.

The bard appeared silently and began stoking the coals from the evening before. Not for the first time, Ari wondered where it was Larke slept at night. He had no tent. He would curl up in a rough blanket near the fire when they all went to bed, but if you awoke at odd hours or very early, he was always gone. Ari frowned at him. "Will you be going into Sorga with us?" he asked, remembering Larke's tendency to disappear when they went to Poromont.

"If yon good knight invites me," Larke said, nodding toward Sir Cadwel's tent as the knight emerged, stretching.

"Invite you?" Sir Cadwel scowled, the rising sun angling onto his face, marking the lines of age and sorrow darkly against his sun-worn skin. "Do I look daft?"

"'Tis as I feared!" Larke said, raising the wooden spoon he was using to stir the porridge before him in supplication. "He still bears no love for this talentless husk o' a minstrel!"

"Still," Sir Cadwel said, ignoring the bard. "You seem fond of the man, and we'll need someone to entertain at your welcome dinner."

"Yes!" the brightly clad bard crowed. "I will sing the grand ballad I've been composing, commemorating our young lord's first brush with noble love!"

Ari groaned. Sir Cadwel chuckled, moving to the fire to peer into the pot Larke had been stirring.

“What’s Larke going to sing?” Peine asked, poking his head out of the tent.

Ari was pleased at how well his friend adapted to traveling. At first, Peine was worried about insects, dirt, animals, and noises in the night. Ari thought it was funny, because when he first went to the castle, he had trouble sleeping, knowing he was surrounded by so many other people so very close, yet Peine felt the absence of those people keenly and was worried with so few people, there was too much nature around to be safe.

“I thought I would sing—” Larke spun his lute from his shoulder, striking a dramatic chord. “Oh, once was a lad so tall, so true, and he met a lass so pretty, it’s true, but she had her heart, so dark, so cruel, set on his fortune, oh yes, it’s true . . .”

“Is the porridge ready?” Ari said loudly, cutting over the song. They grinned at him, but Larke stopped playing and went back to stirring, flipping his lute over his shoulder.

***

It took them most of the day to reach Sorga, but the sun had not yet set when they arrived. The mountain, its massive feet finally visible, looked as if it had been set down on the plain, instead of growing gently up from it as Ari always assumed a mountain would. A piece of the mountain opened its arms to embrace the castle of Sorga, and a massive wall was built between those arms. Ari approached the battlements feeling awed, his eyes held extra wide and unblinking as he tried to take in every detail. The rocks making up the wall were gray, but they glowed rose in the evening light. Each was as tall as a man, and Ari couldn’t imagine how they were put into place. The wall they formed was higher by far than those surrounding Poromont, rising up against the backdrop of an immense peak. They were unadorned, with no colorful buntings like at the capital. Flying high from the tall central tower of the keep within waved a single blue, brown hawk-adorned, flag. As they neared, someone must have seen them, because a trumpet sounded, and the heavy wooden gates began slowly to open.

Ari wasn't sure exactly what he had expected, but unlike at the capital, there was no city sprawling between the outer gates and the castle. On their journey, they had passed many small towns beholden to Sir Cadwel, but here there was nothing. No buildings crowded within the outer walls. No streets lined with shops wound their way to the castle. They rode through the imposing metal-wrapped gates, which swung open to engulf them, and into a vast cobblestone yard.

Sir Cadwel didn't wait for the gates to open fully, but spurred his horse forward once there was sufficient space for Goldwin to pass through. The rest of them followed, Ari and Peine twisting about, trying to see everything.

Inside the outer wall, across the cobblestone yard, was a second wall, enclosing a castle built into the cliff face. Indeed, now that he looked, Ari could see there were windows cut into the cliff face, as if some of the castle was carved out of the mountain itself. Goldwin's hooves clattered on the stones as he crossed to the smaller set of gates. Guards stood smartly on top of the outer battlement and on the inner ones around the castle. They all wore brown and blue.

The smaller castle gates opened, revealing more cobblestones and green grass dotted with fruit trees. To Ari, it looked like the most lovely and inviting place on earth. It was an oasis tucked inside a castle, pressed against a vast forbidding mountain, surrounded by a gray courtyard, all encased in the massive shell of the outer walls. It was as if Sorga's inner courtyard was a precious gem, hidden by many layers of block and lock.

As soon as the inner gates were open wide enough, two great shaggy hounds bounded up, charging right at Goldwin. At the last moment, they split, circling round the destrier and coming back to flank him as they passed through the inner gates. So tall were they, their backs were of a height with Sir Cadwel's knees. The knight reached down and touched each on the head briefly in greeting.

As they entered the courtyard, people hurried down the castle steps. Grooms appeared to take their horses, and the two dogs jumped around them as if they were small puppies instead of giant, gnarled old hounds. It looked to Ari as if the entire population of the keep was pouring out into the sunny courtyard with its dotting of fall-colored fruit trees.

"I have an announcement," Sir Cadwel boomed over the chaos greeting their arrival. Although a groom stood at the head of each horse, Sir Cadwel kept to the saddle, and the others followed suit, waiting for him to dismount. "Tonight, there will be a feast!" the knight said, and the noise started all over again as everyone began to cheer.

"Ye would think they'd want to know why." Ari could barely hear Larke over the commotion. The giant hounds began to bark.

"Quiet!" Sir Cadwel roared, silencing everyone but the dogs, who were running in a circle around Goldwin, barking. The horse effected aloof indifference. "Canid, Raven," Sir Cadwel said. "That means you too! Now," he continued, as the dogs came to sit in silent obedience on either side of Goldwin. "Today is a momentous day. In the capital, as you know, the fall tourney was held. This year, the prize was taken by the youngest in history to win it. So young, in fact, he is not yet of age to accept the duty of knighthood. This young man, whose skill in combat I state to be almost the equal of my own, is my page, Aridian of Sallsburry."

This announcement was met with more cheering, and Ari fought not to blush as all the eyes of the castle followed Sir Cadwel's gesture to him. Nearby, he knew Peine was beaming with pride. As his valet, Peine considered Ari a bit of a personal possession.

"I didn't know I was the youngest ever to win the tourney," Ari said.

"Oh, yes," Peine said cheerfully. "Didn't anyone tell you?"

Ari started to scowl but remembered all the eyes on him and thought better of it, pinning a smile firmly in place.

“There is more,” Sir Cadwel said in his immense voice. This time, silence came quickly, with people exchanging curious glances with each other. “As he is an orphan and not yet of age, I have adopted Lord Aridian and pronounced him my heir.”

Ari tried to maintain his smile in view of the shock that caused. There were some cheers, and there was a lot of talking. Noise once again filled the courtyard, but this time, Sir Cadwel let it continue, seemingly completely relaxed where he bestrode his charger.

“I think you should have given them time to get to know me before you told them,” Ari said, moving Stew nearer to Goldwin.

“Nonsense,” Sir Cadwel said, actually looking amused as he gazed around at his people. Ari thought most of the talk sounded surprised, and somewhat pleased, even. At least he hoped that was how it sounded.

“What is the meaning of this?” a woman’s voice shrieked.

Ari looked around the courtyard, finally identifying the noise as having come from a small, round woman dressed in a nun’s cassock. She was pushing her way through the crowd toward them, dragging a petulant-looking young man with her.

“Lyla,” Sir Cadwel said, his voice so cold Ari turned to look at him in surprise.

The woman continued to charge up to them, stopping only when she was close enough that Canid and Raven let out low growls. She cast the hounds a disdainful look but didn’t move any nearer. “What is the meaning of this?” she said again, in that shrill, haughty voice.

“I fail to understand the question,” Sir Cadwel said, gazing down at her with undisguised loathing.

“My Deken is heir to Sorga!” she screeched. “My son!” She emphasized this by shaking the arm of the foppish young man standing beside her. Somewhere in the crowd, someone snickered.

“You tire me with your mendacity, Lyla,” Sir Cadwel said.

Ari was not sure who the woman was, although he could see she wore the garb of the church, but he counted her the greatest fool he'd ever met for not giving way to that tone.

"You cannot take Lordship of Sorga from its rightful heir, and you cannot supplant my son with this worthless vagabond boy you have found," she said, her round face turning pink with the fervor of her speech.

"You and I shall have words on this later," Sir Cadwel snarled, his anger barely contained. "For now, I think you and that spawn of yours should go to your chambers. It's obvious you are distressed."

Sir Cadwel gestured, and two guards appeared, taking Lyla and her unresisting son by the arms and leading them away. The young man went without complaint, although the look he gave the guards was haughty, but Lyla screeched and struggled.

"Tonight, a feast!" Sir Cadwel said, dismounting.

The cheering was renewed. A groom moved to helped Peine down. Not waiting for assistance, Ari dismounted.

They followed Sir Cadwel through the crowd, which parted before him. Ari found himself shaking hands, looking into smiling faces he knew he wouldn't be able to remember after just one meeting, and being told names he feared it would take him years to learn. He was relieved to notice the faces and voices were happy and kind at least.

Then they were up the steps and into the keep, Sir Cadwel's long strides leading them across the hall to a small sitting room. Ari was amused to see it bore a great similarity to the king's. The furniture was leather, and there were weapons and stuffed, dead animals mounted around the room. Raven and Canid bound through the door, sprawling in front of the crackling fireplace. A steward followed them in with five small glasses and a crystal decanter filled with a dark yellow, thick-looking liquid. All but Peine seated themselves as the steward walked around with the tray. Ari took a glass and sipped tentatively, Peine taking up position near the door in case he was needed. The yellow liquid was sweet, but it burned when it touched the back of Ari's throat. He swallowed it anyhow, not knowing what else to do. Once it was in his stomach, warmness seemed to radiate out from it.

"I know 'tis not truly my concern, but do tell," Larke said to Sir Cadwel in his most wheedling tone, accepting a glass of liquor from the steward. "Who was that brave woman?"

"I suppose I should have thought to mention Lyla before we arrived," Sir Cadwel said, scowling. "She's grown more bold than I would have expected." He turned to the steward. "Natan, what has the demented cow been up to?"

"Her usual, my lord," the steward said. To Ari's surprise, Natan took one of the remaining two glasses from the tray and sat down opposite Ari, putting his feet up on the footstool between them and lounging back on the couch. The steward seemed totally at ease, unaware he wasn't behaving as a servant ought. He was a tall man, about Sir Cadwel's age, and although Ari wasn't an expert, Natan appeared to be uncommonly handsome. "Bullying, badgering, pleading, and bribing people into her line of thought. You being summoned to accept your brother's titles didn't upset her, of course. She viewed that as a minor setback. You had no heirs or plans to marry, after all." Natan gave Ari a nod and a smile. "This, on the other hand, seems to be very traumatic to her. It's a pity she didn't happen to drop dead from shock."

Sir Cadwel chuckled, leaning back on the couch. Larke and Ari exchanged confused looks. Peine frowned, his eyes going from the seated steward to the remaining glass of liquor and back again.

"So nothing to really worry about," Sir Cadwel said.

"Not really, my lord," Natan said, sipping his drink. "She's gotten a bit out of control with you away, ordering clothes for herself and that toad of a son of hers, but now you're back, I'm sure you can set it all to right."

"Ah, about that." Sir Cadwel set his glass on a short table which stood against the arm of the couch. "I'm not actually staying for long."

"My lord?" Natan said, sitting up straight, his tone full of worry and reproach.

"Well, you see—" Sir Cadwel said, and Ari looked at him in surprise. Sir Cadwel actually seemed abashed. "There's another mission for the king. I was planning to leave the day after tomorrow. It's a mission of grave importance."

"The day after tomorrow? But my lord," Natan said. "You have a lot to see to here, and not just Lyla."

"Mayhap we ought to stay here a while so as ye can catch up on things," Larke said in a low voice.

"Natan will see to it all for me," Sir Cadwel said with a shrug. "He always does."

The handsome man scowled, quaffing his glass of liquor. "If that is all, my lord," he said, reaching for the tray and rising.

"Oh, sit down," Sir Cadwel said.

"Some of us have work to do," Natan said. He looked down his elegant nose at the knight. "Some of us don't get to spend all of our time gallivanting around, rescuing royalty and slaying villains."

"Natan," Sir Cadwel said. "Do we have to do this right now?"

"Of course not, my lord," the steward said, collecting the cordial glasses, empty or not, and heading toward the door. "We can talk about it later. In private."

Sir Cadwel scowled as the door slammed. Larke raised one eyebrow, looking at the knight questioningly.

"Did that be Sir Natan?" Larke said.

"Yes," Sir Cadwel said, still eying the closed door in irritation.

"So this is where he got to," Larke said, chuckling.

"Was that who?" Ari said, annoyed at being left out. He didn't know who this Lyla was, and he didn't know who this steward was, and he was feeling decidedly adrift in what was supposed to be his home. His one and only home now that he wasn't anyone's nephew or cousin anymore.

"Sir Natan," Larke said, as if that made everything clear. Ari gave him a blank look. "Do ye recall the ballad about the great and handsome knight who won the heart of every lady, 'til so many did love him that he was forced the leave the knighthood behind and go to a far, far away land to escape them and their distraught men folk?"

Ari nodded, turning to look at the closed door. "That is the knight?" he asked, excited to meet someone out of a ballad.

"Well, no," Larke said, earning himself a scowl. "I think that ballad be totally fictitious. Natan was actually discharged in great shame by our ever-wise king for the irresponsible deflowering o' too many young noble women, this includin' the king's niece, or so I be told. Not the best subject for ballads, that."

Ari choked, turning red. He wasn't sure if people were allowed to say deflower aloud.

"Shouldn't the king have killed him?" Peine said.

"Well, he was a passing fine knight in all other ways, and 'twas not as if the ladies he befriended were ever unwillin'," the bard said. "So our great and noble king stripped the amorous Natan of his knighthood and banished him far, far away, to the most remote, cold, and inhospitable ends of all the land . . . Sorga, apparently."

"You can strip someone of knighthood?" Ari said, feeling nervous. Someday Parrentine would be king, and Ari was not on the prince's good side.

"'Tis a rare thing to do, me lad," Larke said, but it didn't make Ari feel any better.

"Who is Lyla, and why did she say her son is lord of Sorga?" Ari asked. He felt he had a right to know, and he wanted to take his mind off potential unknighting. Besides, he would have to manage to become a knight in the first place before he had to worry about being unknighted.

"She's the nun who first took care of my brother while he was unconscious," Sir Cadwel said, sighing. "She bore that toad, and she fabricated some story about my brother coming to and taking advantage of her, thus making the brat his heir."

Now it was time for Ari to look at Sir Cadwel with eyebrows raised in shock. "And you just let her live here and tell people this?" he asked, incredulous.

"I have no way to prove her false, but she has no way to prove herself true," Sir Cadwel said with a shrug. "So we have a stalemate. Besides, I would rather her here where I can keep an eye on her than wandering around somewhere, causing mischief."

"You could have her head cut off," Peine said.

"Don't think I haven't thought about it," Sir Cadwel said with a wolfish grin.

"Can ye e'er know for sure her story is one of falsehood?" Larke dared to ask, receiving a flat stare in return.

"I hardly think a man like my brother would wake for the only time in twenty-five years just to hop onto the nun at his bedside and ride her like a sailor with a two pence trollop," the knight growled. "Besides, why wouldn't she call to the guards outside the room when he woke? Why would he wake only once and never again? Why doesn't the brat look anything like him? Why wouldn't he send for me when he woke up?"

Larke nodded, declining to challenge the idea any further. Ari decided he agreed with Sir Cadwel, and not just because it was him or the toad. He really couldn't see his mentor's brother behaving in that fashion, even though he'd never met the man, and he didn't know why the round woman wouldn't have called the guards. Besides, she seemed like a person who would lie.

"By the way," Natan said, sticking his head through the doorway. "A bird came from the capital a few days ago."

"Well?" Sir Cadwel asked after they locked eyes for several moments. Ari looked back and forth between the two, trying to decide if it was a game or not.

"It had a letter," the steward said, affecting a ridiculous amount of pride in presenting the information. Sir Cadwel growled. "From a Princess of Whey, of all people," Natan added after a moment.

"Do I get to read it?" Sir Cadwel asked.

"I thought you were too busy with questing to tend to all these trifling little details involved in running a dukedom," Natan said.

Sir Cadwel rose, snatched an axe off the wall and threw it at him. It landed in the door near Natan's head with a thud.

"Now, now, no need to make threats," Natan said, eying the axe where it quivered a few inches from his face.

"It wasn't a threat. I missed," Sir Cadwel said, reaching for another weapon.

"Of course you did," Natan said. "Getting old and all. I'll just fetch that letter for you."

As the door closed, a second axe entered the wood almost on top of the first. Peine looked back and forth between Sir Cadwel and the closed door with wide eyes. In a few moments, Natan returned, holding a silver tray with a sealed scroll on it. With exaggerated formality, he presented it to Sir Cadwel. The knight read it quickly, passing it to Ari, who began trying to sound out the words. After watching him for a few moments, Larke took it from him with a quick glance at Sir Cadwel for permission.

"We truly will have to teach you to read a bit, me lad," the bard said before turning his attention to the letter. "Dear Sir Cadwel, Duke of Sorga, Lord Protector of the Great Northern Lands, Knight of the Realm, and Champion of his Majesty King Ennentine of Lggothland and her Majesty Queen Parrella." Larke took a breath, rolling his eyes.

"You could have skipped that part," Sir Cadwel said.

"Don't like being reminded of all of your responsibilities?" Natan said.

Sir Cadwel scowled.

"Ahem." Larke cleared his throat. "My lord, I'm afraid something is greatly amiss here. I know you and the young Lord

Aridian are on a quest set you by the king, but I did not know to whom else I might turn. The situation is of the greatest delicacy. My lord, Princess Clorra is in a very bad way. I know you are aware of her recent illness and miraculous recovery, but what you may not be aware of is that she has now, at the sending of this letter, murdered four people. I do not, I'm afraid, have proof of this, but rumors abound, and none of the servants will enter her room any longer. When you see her about the castle, she is very strange, hissing at people as if she were some sort of great cat or laughing inappropriately. The instrument of her 'recovery' is in constant attendance to her, not letting others near, but even he seems unable to control her wild temper. My lord, I do not know what it is you may be able to do to aid this situation, but I feel it may be important to the very security of the kingdom for you to be in attendance to the king and queen at this time. In addition, I am leery of the quest you and young Lord Aridian have undertaken, in view of its source and timing. I know I hold no power over you, but I beseech you to leave the north and come back to us, for all of our sakes." Larke paused. "It is signed Siara, Princess of Whey."

"She called me young," Ari blurted, scowling. She was only two years older than he was, after all. The others turned to him in surprise. "Well, she did. Twice," he said, wiggling back further into the leather couch.

"I think you should go back," Larke said.

"You?" Sir Cadwel laughed. "I'm afraid neither your thoughts nor Princess Siara's orders hold weight to the king."

"Still," Larke said. "The lovely Princess Siara wouldn't be writing this unless the situation be quite dire."

"The Princess of Whey is a woman in love," Sir Cadwel said. "Her words, when on the subject of Princess Clorra, are to be interpreted with that firmly in mind."

"I think she might be telling the truth," Ari said, leaning forward again.

"Then I ask you, does it matter?" Sir Cadwel pinned him with a hard look. "We were given a charge by the king. What would you say to him when we return? The Princess of Whey wrote us a letter, so we abandoned the quest you gave us?"

"I didn't think about it that way," Ari mumbled, embarrassed. Yet he knew Siara was right. He knew there was more danger to the king being in his own castle with Lord Ferringul about than from the minor lord they were sent to question. "I just—" he said, locking eyes with Sir Cadwel. "I just think she's right. I feel it."

"Not this again," Sir Cadwel said with a groan. "You've spent too much time with Princess Siara and this bard."

"Perhaps the lad's instincts be good," Larke said.

Natan and Peine watched in silence.

"I'm telling you, none of the rest of it matters," Sir Cadwel said firmly, walking to the door. "We are charged a task by the king, and only the king can release us from it. I'm off to clean the travel dust from myself and ready for the feast. I suggest you all do the same."

"The lord of the keep has spoken," Natan said with a quick grin after the door closed behind Sir Cadwel.

Ari nodded, rising. As he and Peine followed the steward out, Ari cast one last look back into the room. Larke sat on the edge of the couch, bony elbows on his knees, his face filled with worry.

***

Entering the great hall, Ari immediately realized feasts in Sorga were very different from the ones at the capital. Instead of one long table, this room was filled with many small ones, the majority of which were unadorned by cloth and utensil-free. The walls were the same plain gray stone inside the castle as out, and large beams of dark wood reached up the sides and criss-crossed the ceiling. There were few tapestries and only one banner, the brown hawk on blue. Instead of elegant chandeliers, there were heavy candles everywhere, long trails of light gray wax giving mute testament to how many years they and their predecessors had stood in the exact same places.

There appeared to be little in the way of formality, although Sir Cadwel did sit at the largest table, centered under the banner of Sorga. His chair was more massive than the other chairs about the table, but it certainly was not a throne. At most of the tables, there were benches.

As Ari and Peine crossed the hall to where the knight sat, Ari observed soldiers and maids and grooms. It seemed as if everyone in the castle ate in the same hall together, and the room was filled with talk and noise. Everyone was eating and laughing as if they were in their own homes, not paying any heed that their lord may be watching.

Of course, this is their home, and mine, Ari realized.

The informality and obvious camaraderie made him smile. Here was a place a person could live, not like that stuffy castle in Poromont. Ari watched as Natan crossed to the side table where food was set and filled two plates. When he returned to the table, the chief steward took a seat next to Sir Cadwel instead of standing behind him, waiting to serve him as he would have to do at the capital. Under the table, the great hounds lounged attentively at Sir Cadwel's feet, hoping for scraps.

It wasn't until Ari passed the table nearest the head table, where Lyla and her son Deken sat alone, glaring at him, that his eyes moved to take in the other people sitting with Sir Cadwel. He paused, not sure if he was supposed to sit with these people, but Peine gave him a shove forward. He came to a stop opposite Sir Cadwel.

A crisp, white cloth covered the head table, and there were more utensils, rather resembling the mysterious montage one would find surrounding his plate in the king's hall. On either side of Sir Cadwel's chair were three others, and one on each end of the table. There were no chairs opposite Sir Cadwel, presumably so the nobility would be facing the room.

Natan sat on Sir Cadwel's left. Next to him sat Larke, his thin frame and garish clothes made more prominent by comparison to Natan's athletic build and crisp black attire. The seat next to Larke and the one on that end of the table both stood empty. In the chair at the other end of the table perched an elegant, ancient woman. Her hair was as bright as snow in the winter sun and lay in a long braid down her back. Her hands on her utensils were small and wrinkled, and she was impeccably dressed in an ancient, high-necked black gown.

Yet it was the person sitting next to her who was the cause of Ari's trepidation. Beside the ancient woman, in an unadorned green dress, sat a girl about Ari's age. She had pale skin, green eyes, and red hair. Ari didn't know anyone with red hair, so he didn't have a very good basis of comparison, but her hair seemed very bright. It was almost as red as an apple, and it lay scattered about her head and shoulders, falling down her back. Some attempt had been made to put pins in it to hold it back from her face, but the frizzy mass seemed to want to reach out and jump into her mouth or onto her fork. Even as Ari watched, she fished about in her sleeves for a ribbon. She was in the process of tying the unruly mass back when she looked up and noticed him. At his end of the table, Larke began to hum the tune to which he put his song about Ari and the farmer's daughter. Sir Cadwel looked up from where he and Natan were talking.

"Ari," Sir Cadwel said, smiling. "This is my mother-in-law, the Lady Enra." Ari did his best impression of someone who knew how to bow. The old woman nodded, eyes gone pale with age fixing on him, although Ari wondered if she could still see. "And this is my grandniece, on my wife's side, Lady Ispiria." The knight cleared his throat, looking uncomfortable as he always did at any mention of his wife. Ari bowed again, then straightened and stood, looking at Sir Cadwel, not sure what he should do.

"Come, seat yourself," Sir Cadwel said, gesturing to the chair on his right. "Peine too. We don't stand on formality here, and I really can't stand people hovering about behind me, waiting to serve me."

"Which works out well, as I have no intention of doing it," Natan said.

Ari walked around the table and pulled out the chair, helping Peine with the one next to it when the small boy had trouble. Peine sat between him and the red-haired girl. Ari could feel her eyes on him, so he made sure not to look at her.

As dinner progressed, Ari found himself completely unable to talk to Ispiria. He would look at her, and then his mouth wouldn't work, and his brain wouldn't think of anything to say, even if he practiced something to say before looking at her. Instead, he would find himself watching her lips or her hair. Even though she tied it back with a green ribbon, it seemed continuously to escape, twisting until its ends landed in her food or her mouth or her eyes.

Fortunately, Peine could talk to anyone, and he was sitting between them. Ari tried to keep his mouth full, so he wouldn't seem rude by not talking. That way, if she did ask him something, he could look over and smile, and Peine would answer for him. This meant he ate a lot more than was his custom, and by the end of the meal, he felt a bit ill.

To add to his discomfiture, Sir Cadwel was talking with Natan in a low voice on his other side, filling him in on what was transpiring in the capital. Each time Lord Ferringul's name was mentioned, Ari had to concentrate on not choking on his food, and he would miss what Peine and Ispiria were talking about. Eventually, it was time to leave the great hall, and Ari hurried back to his rooms, pondering not for the first time why it might be that the mere mention of Lord Ferringul made him feel ill, until his mind, as usual, slid away from the pondering.

***

"She's awful pretty," Peine said at they readied for bed.

Ari was given a suite of rooms, much larger than they had shared at the capital. There was a sitting room with two sleeping rooms off it, each with its own dressing room, bathing room and servants' quarters. One of those sets of rooms, not the one Peine told Ari he should use, boasted a fifth room, which Peine said was for the babies. Ari didn't dare dwell on that idea. A small dining room and a study finished the massive suite. Each of the rooms, even the servants', had a fireplace. All the rooms had a strange, empty feel, as if no one had used them for a very long time. Ari had no idea what he was supposed to do with so many rooms, but Peine was delighted.

The rooms were at the end of the wing, with Sir Cadwel's the next on the outer wall and the Lady Enra's on the inner, overlooking the courtyard. Natan's were the rooms just past Sir Cadwel's. Peine somehow already found out Ispiria was to have the rooms next to her great-grandmother's, but not until she was seventeen. For two more years, she would share the old woman's rooms. Ari was sure there must be something odd about him having the largest suite, but he knew better than to ask Sir Cadwel directly. If he found himself alone with Natan, he would ask the steward.

"Wasn't she?" Peine repeated, and Ari realized he asked the question several times already.

"Who?"

Peine rolled his eyes. "Lady Ispiria."

"Oh, yes." Ari could feel his cheeks redden.

"She's at least as pretty as Princess Siara or Princess Clorra, and she isn't even a princess!" Peine seemed to feel something was wrong with that, as if a girl's station dictated her level of beauty.

"I don't think Princess Clorra is that pretty," Ari said.

"Well, she was very pretty before she got sick. Lady Ispiria isn't really pretty in the same way, though," Peine said after a moment of thought.

"How do you mean?" Ari asked, forgetting he was embarrassed.

"Well, she's more wild, isn't she?"

“She is?” With ease, Ari brought an image of the girl up in his mind, scrutinizing her for signs of wildness.

“Her dress is so plain, and she tied her crazy hair back right at the table.” Peine lowered his voice. “I bet she doesn’t even ride sidesaddle, and you know what they say girls who don’t ride sidesaddle are like.”

Ari opened his mouth to ask what riding sidesaddle could have to do with anything, when a knock came at the door. Peine jumped to answer.

“Free at last!” Larke strode into the room.

“I thought they were going to make you play all night,” Ari said.

“Not many bards make the journey this far north, I daresay,” Larke said. “Look here, me lads, the noble Sir Cadwel has by some mischance overlooked setting aside a place for me to sleep, so if it would be not much trouble to you, I came to thinking I could be the Lord Aridian’s personal minstrel, and therefore maychance be allowed to stay here?”

“We would be honored,” Peine said, while Ari was still trying to sort out exactly what it was Larke asked.

“Many thanks, me lads.” Larke gave them a bow, proceeding to drape himself across the length of the largest couch and snore loudly. Ari didn’t think anybody could really fall asleep that fast, but he looked at Peine and shrugged, returning to his own preparations for bed.

***

Larke was gone when they awoke, though the hour was by no means late. Ari took little note of the bard’s absence, distracted as he was by trying to recall what he had dreamt the night before. He knew it had something to do with Lord Ferringul, which made him very nervous, but he couldn’t seem to remember more.

“I’ve been having so many odd dreams lately,” he said, lacing his shirt.

"Rich food before bed," Peine said, looking up from polishing Ari's boots. Ari tried to prevent Peine from cleaning his boots, even going so far as to hide them, but Peine always found them again.

"Does that make you dream?" Ari recalled his aunt, or rather the woman he had always thought of as his aunt, saying that from time to time when the innkeeper overindulged.

"Sure." Peine nodded, holding the boots up to scrutinize them. "Come here and I'll put them on."

"I can put on my own boots," Ari said, grabbing them.

Peine stuck out his tongue.

Despite Peine's explanation, Ari was still worrying at the dream when they left their quarters. As distracted as he was, he didn't notice Lady Ispiria leaving her grandmother's rooms. Peine grabbed the back of Ari's shirt, stopping him from walking into her.

"Good morning," she said with a dazzling smile. "Going to break your fast?"

"Umm," Ari said intelligently.

"Good morning!" Peine said, stepping up to stand beside Ari. "Yes, we're going to breakfast. Won't you join us?"

"I would be delighted to," she said, turning her smile on Peine, which was fortunate, as it returned Ari's ability to walk. They headed down the hall to the wide wooden staircase.

Ispiria was wearing a light blue gown, which reminded him of Siara, but aside from that, Ari saw little similarity. Ispiria was much taller, and she had a confidence to her which Siara lacked. Siara was quiet and contained while in the presence of most people, and perhaps a bit acidic in private, but this girl had an air of unconscious self-possession. It was as if she didn't even think to consider what other people might be thinking of her. She wore a braid this morning, but it was by no means a neat one, and her red hair was a complete contrast to Siara's shiny and organized black locks. Ispiria also walked very fast, practically flying down the steps.

"If we get there early enough, there will still be sweets," she said, turning to grin up the steps at him.

He caught himself on the banister as he almost tripped. Fortunately, she had already turned away. Head high, Ari ignored Peine's giggle and followed her.

The hall was empty compared to the previous evening. The first meal of the day was obviously not a formal one. Ari wasn't sure how this compared with the capital, as he always ate breakfast in their rooms there, if he ate it at all. As he watched, people drifted up to a buffet and in and out of the room. The head table was empty, which he supposed was reasonable as Sir Cadwel still hadn't retired by the time Larke had knocked on their door. Of the bard, there was nothing to be seen.

They acquired plates of dried fruit and pastries, passing over the remains of the previous night's meat, taking seats at the empty end of a long table. By unspoken accord, they did not sit at the head table. To Ari's relief, there didn't appear to be any utensils involved in breakfast at all.

"Have you traveled with my uncle a long time?" Ispiria asked as they sat.

"Not very long." Ari shook his head. "Just since the end of summer."

"That long? The whole fall?" She sounded impressed. "He really must like you. I mean, of course he must, to name you his heir. His last page came crying back here a couple weeks after they left, telling tales of drunkenness and rage. We were all so angry with him, to leave Uncle Cadwel alone when everyone knows how upset he's been since his brother died. He was never very cheery, but he rarely drank before then, and that idiot left him all alone. Of course, it's good he did, because now we have you." She smiled at him.

"Oh no," Ari said, suddenly realizing if Sir Cadwel was Ispiria's uncle, she and her someday husband would have become rulers in Sorga when Sir Cadwel died. "I'm taking your place. As lord here. Err, lady," he stammered. What if she hated him forever? He hadn't known she even existed when he'd agreed. She would have to understand.

"No, you aren't." She laughed. "It doesn't work that way."

"But you're the last person in the family."

"Not in Sir Cadwel's family. He is," she said, shaking her head. "I don't know what distant relative might have managed to lay claim here someday, but he likely would chuck me out for a start. Really, it's kind of Sir Cadwel to keep my grandmother and me to begin with."

"I don't think any man would chuck you out." Ari turned bright red the moment the words left his mouth, so he bent low over his plate.

"That's a nice thing to say, but I daresay even if a man found me not displeasing to have about, his womenfolk wouldn't appreciate me. What I really wanted to tell you, though, is you're amazing."

Ari was glad he had already swallowed.

"Such a change in my uncle!" she said, not seeming to notice Ari was trying to choke on air. "In all my life, he has never been so happy. It's so very good to see. Thank you, Lord Aridian."

She reached across the table and captured one of his hands. He couldn't help but look up into those warm green eyes. Under the cover of the table, Peine nudged him in the ribs. He struggled to find something to say.

"Thank you," he said. He opened his mouth to say more, although he had no idea what, when a shadow fell across him. They all turned to find Deken standing at the end of the table.

"What is the meaning of this?" the self-styled heir of Sorga said. "How dare you lay hand on her? She is mine!"

"I am not yours," Ispiria said, her tone showing clear exasperation. She squeezed Ari's hand tighter in her own, whether consciously or not, he didn't know.

"You will be when I'm lord of Sorga," Deken said.

Ari raised an eyebrow at this, but Deken wasn't looking at him.

"You will never be lord of anything!" Ispiria spat at him.

At the same time, Peine rather loudly inserted, "Be careful who you say that in front of!"

"Why?" Deken sneered. "Because of this child?" His mocking gaze fell on Ari.

"You can't talk to Lord Aridian that way," Peine said, rising.

"He obviously can't do anything about it." Deken regarded Ari with deliberate insolence. "He can't even talk. He has to have a girl and some Wheylian scum speak for him."

"That is enough," Ari said coldly, pulling his hand from Ispiria's grasp to rise. He was surprised to find himself of a height with Deken, who must have ranked him in age by three years. "There will be no slander in this house."

"This house is mine, and I will prove it upon your body," Deken said, drawing himself up in an attempt to look down his nose at Ari.

"Accepted," Ari said in as casual a tone as he could.

"You'll duel me?"

"Will anything else settle this?"

"Nothing!" Deken said.

"Then we may as well get it over with, but when we're done, I would really appreciate it if you would stop being such an ass." Ari kept his voice deliberately mild.

"I think when we are done, it is I who will be telling you what to do," Deken said.

"If you say so." Ari shrugged. "I believe normally the challenged sets the details, but since I'm new here, I'll leave it to your discretion."

"Noon, at Rock Bay, with foils," Deken said, his eyes bright with guile.

"All right," Ari said, sitting back down.

"You best be careful," Peine said, still glaring at Deken. "Ari won the king's autumn tourney."

"I'm not some court fop, currying for Sir Cadwel's favor. I won't let him beat me," Deken said.

"Can't this wait until noon?" Ari said, worried soon his forced bravado would be betrayed by hands that shook so much he was hiding them under the table. "I'm trying to eat."

Deken scowled and skulked away, a poorly disguised look of cunning glee on his face.

"Don't trust him." Ispiria glared at Deken's back. "When we were children, he used to ask to play with my toys and then throw them off the highest tower so they would smash to bits."

"My Lady." Ari did his best imitation of Larke. "Today at noon, I will right that wrong!"

Ispiria laughed, and Ari bent over his plate again, blushing.

***

Ari's first challenge was his lack of a foil, something Ispiria said they could remedy in the armory.

"Are you sure I should just take one?" he asked her.

The room she led Peine and him to was hewn deep into the side of the mountain. Windowless, it required them to first fetch a lantern from the kitchen, where everyone stopped working to stare at Ari until they lit it and left. With their eyes upon him, he was sure they somehow already knew about his impending duel. He just wished he could tell who they wanted to win.

"You're Uncle Cadwel's heir, so all these foils belong to you now," Ispiria said. She reached out and dusted off the handle of one. "Which one do you want?"

"Any one will do, I guess," Ari said uncertainly. He took the closest one off the rack. The cavern they were in was not as large as the king's armory, but it was by no means small. Ari tried to imagine all the men it would take to wield all these weapons and what it would be like when they turned to him and asked him what to do. He shuddered, intimidated by the responsibility.

Taking a step away from Peine and Ispiria, he swung the blade back and forth a few times, finding the balance to be off. The hilt was too heavy, probably due to the silly ornamentations on it. He put it back and scanned the rest, choosing a more serviceable-looking foil. A few swings told him it was much better.

"I should clean it before we go," he said. Ispiria was watching him, and Peine was wandering around with the lantern, opening dusty chests. "What do we do now?"

"You should ready yourself," Ispiria said. "I'll go tell the grooms we're going to need our horses."

"Is the bay far?" Ari asked, wondering why Deken would choose such a secluded spot. Maybe so if he lost he could later deny it?

"It's not too far, but you wouldn't want to walk," she said. "You look very brave with that sword."

"Uh." He flushed, unsure how to respond to that. Behind her he saw Peine roll his eyes. "Thank you."

"I'll see you at the eleventh hour in the courtyard," she said, turning to go.

"Wait," Ari said. "Are you sure you should go? It might be dangerous."

"You'll protect me." Ispiria smiled. "And besides, how else will you find it?"

Before he could answer that, she spun away in a swirl of red hair, leaving Ari to contemplate how he would even find his way back up out of the weapons cellar.

***

Whoever had named Rock Bay was not an imaginative person, Ari observed. They left their horses at the top of the steep, boulder-strewn hill leading down to the ocean. The water in the north was dark and churning, and it put him in mind of forlorn ladies who lost their lovers and wandered into the sea to die. The water at the capital was blue and sparkling, inviting. Ari realized if Deken turned out to be a better swordsman than he expected, Ari might never get to see that bright blue water again. Not that anyone was meant to die in a duel for honor, but it did happen.

"Why would he choose here?" Ari said, scrambling over a large rock. "The footing is horrendous. You can't even see four feet in any direction." Ari pushed down on the hilt of the foil at his belt, lifting the tip behind him until it was almost horizontal to the ground to keep it from dragging on the rocks they climbed over.

"Maybe he thinks if you should stumble, he shall win," Ispiria said.

"Maybe he has no intention of dueling you at all," a gleeful voice said.

From all around them, men were jumping out from behind boulders. To his right, Ari saw Peine throw himself to the ground with a yelp of surprise. Ari started to draw his sword, but a quick look at the other men's broad blades assured him the foil would be of little use. He dropped down and grabbed a rock instead, casting about for something longer, like a stick. To his left, Ispiria put her back to a boulder, a rock in each hand.

"I should have known you'd come with him," Deken said. "It's too bad for—"

Ari didn't let Deken continue. With all his strength, he hurtled his rock, striking the usurper a blow to the head that sent Deken tumbling off his vantage point to lie motionless on the ground. Ari ducked down to grab another rock, but the ring of men didn't charge, gaping at the blood pooling around Deken's head.

They were a montage of castle dwellers. One wore a blacksmith's smock and another a groom's attire. Ari hoped the groom's political leanings hadn't inclined him to be mean to Stew. Several wore guards' uniforms. In total he counted seven, and all of them, save one, were young.

"Look," Ari said, weighing a rock in his hand. "I know you don't know me, but don't you think maybe I'm worth a try before you commit murder?"

"Don't listen to him," snarled the older man. "When my son is lord, you'll all be rewarded beyond your imagining."

"Your son?" Ispiria gasped. "Deken is your son?"

Ari blinked, surprised the truth had come out so easily, aware the older man's admission meant he intended to kill all three of them.

"I would look to that son before making any more promises," Peine said, scrambling to his feet to stand beside Ispiria. He picked up a small rock of his own. The men shifted from foot to foot, looking from Ari to their leader and back.

"Attack them," the man who called Deken his son said. "Now they know your faces, they'll tell Lord Cadwel who you are. Especially her."

To settle the argument, he charged, and some of the others followed. Ari let loose with another rock, shattering it off a boulder behind Deken's father as the older man ducked in anticipation. Ispiria's throw struck a man in the chest, but it didn't slow him for more than a surprised moment.

With no time for another rock, Ari darted forward, taking the nearest attacker off guard. He ducked under the man's sword and came up in front of his face. Ignoring his comical look of shock, Ari slammed his forehead into the man's nose, relieving him of his weapon as he slumped to the ground.

Ari turned, remembering Sir Cadwel's advice that no matter how great the warrior, his companions could become his weakness. Sure enough, two of the men were rushing at Peine and Ispiria. Ispiria drew a knife from somewhere in her clothes, but she still stood little chance against the men's swords.

Ari bounded across the rocks. Setting chivalry and elegance aside, he took the sword's hilt in two hands and slammed the flat of the blade across the men's heads. The one who took the brunt of the blow fell. The other turned to confront Ari.

"Behind you!" Ispiria yelled.

Ari spun, ducking as a sword aimed at his head entered his peripheral vision. He couldn't capitalize on the man's overextension, as he had to engage his weapon to the right, where another blade hurtled toward him. Ari used his crouched position to launch himself between the two men and up, taking a third by surprise. The man tried futilely to bring his sword across his chest to ward off Ari's forward thrust. Ari shuddered as the force of his momentum stabbed his blade through the man's chestplate.

He wrenched the sword out, whirling to confront the others, only to find the last two men and Deken's father holding a struggling Peine and Ispiria. Her knife lay on the ground between them, as did a man she had struck on the head with a rock when he'd turned to attack Ari.

"Put that sword down, boy," Deken's father said. The one who held Peine had the boy's head wrenched back and his sword awkwardly but effectively across Peine's throat. Ispiria's captor was having a harder time of it as she struggled madly in his grip. Deken's father ignored them, his gaze locked on Ari.

Ari bent slowly, laying the sword on the ground at his feet. He lingered a moment, as if hesitant to let it go, his eyes seeking Peine's. Peine met his gaze with eyes that were scared but rational. Ari looked meaningfully from Ispiria to her dropped knife and back again.

"Get back," Deken's father said.

In one fluid motion, Ari stood, his hand leaving the sword hilt and grabbing a rock. Before the assailants could blink, the rock struck the man holding Peine with a crushing force. Peine grabbed up Ispiria's knife and slammed it into the arm of the man who held her.

At the same time, Ari charged Deken's father, snatching up the sword as he ran. In two short strides, the two collided. Almost immediately, Ari realized this opponent was of greater skill than the others. After a few quick blows, Ari backed off, not wanting to let this more experienced fighter dictate the rhythm of the meeting.

The other man came at him quickly, raining down blows. Ari blocked them, finding himself pressed backward. Worried he would trip, Ari forced his arm to move faster, trying to take the offensive. Surprise registered on the man's face.

Ari passed up several opportunities to strike his opponent, looking for the one he wanted. He didn't want to kill him. Killing turned out to be even less pleasant than Ari would have imagined, and he didn't really want to do it more often than he had to. Besides, Sir Cadwel might want to talk to this one.

"You think you can toy with me, boy?" the older man said. "You may be good, but I know all Cadwel's tricks."

With that, he launched into a more ferocious series of attacks, putting Ari back on the defensive for the moment. Ari knew he could take back the attack. The fight was not straining him at all, but Ari didn't mind parrying while Deken's father tired and Ari tried to work out how to subdue him without killing him.

Behind his opponent, Ispiria pinned the remaining conscious assailant to the ground with a sword at his throat. The man clutched his arm where the knife was still lodged. Ispiria watched Ari and Deken's father for a moment before handing the sword to Peine. With exaggerated care to be quiet, she selected a large rock and maneuvered herself behind Ari's attacker.

Deken's father spun, his sword swinging at the girl's unprotected middle, but before he could make her into two, Ari smacked the flat of his blade across the man's head. Deken's father crumpled to the ground. Ispiria lowered the rock, staring at Ari in wonder.

"He really is as good as you say," a voice said from above them. Ari turned to see a small group of men at the top of the hill. Natan, who spoke, sat astride a stunning black horse, a crossbow resting on one knee.

"You should have more faith in me," Sir Cadwel said. He lounged back in Goldwin's saddle. Stew and the dogs stood next to them, looking over the edge at Ari.

"You could have helped," Ari called, annoyed. He looked around at the destruction they had wrought.

"You should check which ones are alive and tie them up," Natan said.

"I don't have any rope." Ari scowled at them. They grinned back.

"You went to an ambush with no rope?" Sir Cadwel affected shock. "Have I taught you nothing, boy? Nothing?"

"Ari!" Peine exclaimed, falling backward as the attacker he was guarding thrust him aside. The man pulled the knife from his arm and dove at Ari. Even as Ari sprang forward, there was a sharp twang and something sped by very close to his ear. A bolt embedded itself in the man's chest.

"Saves on rope," Natan said, hanging the spent crossbow on his saddle.

Ari shook his head. He opened his mouth to protest that he could have disarmed the man, but suddenly, his arms were full of a warm body and red hair.

"You're a hero!" Ispiria said, applying a kiss solidly to his lips.

She gave him another squeeze before rushing away to help Peine. Ari was glad Sir Cadwel had brought men with him, because as they descended the rocky hill to take prisoners and dispose of bodies, he found himself completely unable to move, the memory of the warmth of Ispiria's kiss keeping his mind in utter turmoil.

***

A short search found the men's horses, and the usurpers were bound and helped to mount. The one Ari had run through, the one Natan had shot, and Deken were laid across their saddles. Ari knew when he stabbed the man that his blow would kill, but seeing the limp body, its arms and legs dangling to either side of a confused horse, made Ari feel ill. He rode back to the castle with his thoughts floundering between how easily his sword had stabbed into the man and taken away his life, and how soft and warm Ispiria's lips were.

She kept her horse beside his, her head high and her green eyes fierce. To Ari, her obvious joy in what had transpired seemed a little gruesome, and he kept looking at her out of the corner of his eye to see if she was still smiling. He wondered how she'd feel if she were the one who had run somebody through. Peine was right. Ispiria was a little wild.

He was unprepared for the riot of people in the courtyard or the cheer that arose when he rode in. Stew, perhaps sensing Ari's disquiet, paused as the other horses went by, giving Ari time to compose himself. Inside the courtyard a woman's shriek broke through the celebration.

Ari turned in time to see Lyla collapse into a cassock-covered heap on the paving stones. Those around her stepped back, none moving to help. Sir Cadwel dismounted and made his way to her slumped form, and Ari saw Ispiria slide down from her horse as well, a look of contrition on her face. Looking up, he caught sight of her grandmother on the castle steps, the old woman's milky eyes as hard as stone as they rested on the girl.

"Get her up," Sir Cadwel said, and two of the grooms hurried to obey, suspending a sobbing Lyla between them. "What's wrong, Lyla?" he asked in dulcet tones. "I haven't even told you your son is dead yet."

"Deken is dead?" she gasped. Her eyes went to the boy's father, who sat atop his horse with his hands bound behind him and a noose hung suggestively around his neck.

"Perhaps you screamed because you saw your lover's neck in a noose?" Sir Cadwel said.

"Deken is dead?" she repeated in a small voice. She threw her head back, a high-pitched wail wrenching from her throat. "No," she cried, going limp in the grasp of her captors.

"Take her to her rooms and keep her there," Sir Cadwel ordered the men holding her. Ari heard no sympathy in his mentor's voice.

The other attackers were escorted to the dungeon, and Sir Cadwel ordered everyone back to their tasks. It seemed he still intended they should have a sendoff feast that night, although Ari did overhear Larke suggesting they stay longer while Sir Cadwel dealt with the troubles of the day. A sharp shake of the knight's head was all the answer Larke got.

***

The feast was jubilant. Ari wasn't sure if that was in spite of people being killed or because of it. The dancing started as soon as Larke finished eating, with people pulling the heavy wooden tables to the sides so some could continue to eat and talk while others danced. Larke sang and played as if he hadn't a care in the world, but before the feast, Ari had walked in on the tail end of another argument between the bard and Sir Cadwel about going north in the morning. Ari wasn't sure why, but Larke didn't seem to want them to fulfill the quest the king had set them on.

Ari found himself conflicted over their mission, too. His gut told him they should head back to the capital at all speed, but he could put no logical reason to disobeying his first quest for the king, so his head told him he had to go. His heart, on the other hand, suggested maybe he should forget about being a knight and stay in Sorga. He needed to learn about his new home and the people in it, and one person in particular.

He looked across the room at her now. She was laughing. She almost always seemed to be laughing. He would just have to be sure to get back before the end of the next summer. Nothing could happen with Ispiria until then. Noblewomen usually weren't engaged until the age of sixteen or married before seventeen, so he needn't worry about someone else stealing her before then.

Of course, they could be promised before that. Ari frowned, worrying. He hadn't actually asked if Ispiria was promised to anyone. Should he ask her? What if she didn't think of him that way? What if he asked her and she laughed? He was being silly, anyhow. When he'd first seen Siara, she'd seemed like the most lovely and desirable woman in the world, but once he got to know her, he found out she might be a sorceress, she was in love with Parrentine, and she could be kind of bossy. For all he knew, things would turn out the same with Ispiria, although if she was in love with Prince Parrentine as well, Ari was going to seriously have to consider killing the man.

"Dance with me, Lord Aridian?" a cheerful voice asked, pulling him from his thoughts, only to look up and get lost in Ispiria's green eyes.

"Do I know how?" he asked. She was wearing a plain gown of a sort of pale green material that was a bit shiny. Ari liked it.

"I don't know, my lord, do you?" She smiled at him, and he liked to think it was not a mocking smile.

"I mean—" He shook himself slightly, looking around. "Where's Peine?"

"Over there," she said, her smile widening to a grin. Peine was surrounded by a flock of castle girls. Most of them were taller than he was, although of a similar age from the look of it. Fair-haired heads bent low, listening as the Wheylian boy described the events of the afternoon.

"He's enjoying his newfound fame," Ispiria said.

"It isn't as if we did anything wonderful," Ari said, scowling at the group. "We walked right into a trap, killed people, and came home."

"Ari." Her voice was softer now and her face serious. She came round the table to sit next to him. To his surprise, she took his hand. "You never killed anyone before today?"

He looked away, feeling his throat go tight.

"Walk with me?" she asked, rising again and pulling him up after her. Hand in hand, they left the room, walking out into the empty hall. She didn't pause but led him through a small door to the right of the massive castle gates. They crossed the lawn, dead leaves from the apple trees crackling under their feet. Ari realized it would soon be winter. Winter came early in the north.

Ispiria led him to a set of steps built against the outer wall, and up. From the battlements, he could see over the empty space around the wall, and out over the outer fortifications and onto the rolling grasslands. Looking back, he could also see the castle nestled into the vast cliff face, light spilling out of the windows of the great hall. Ispiria looked around with him, her face pale in the moonlight.

"You had to kill them," she said.

"No, I didn't." He shook his head, turning to face her. "I could have talked more or let them capture us to buy time."

"They ended the talking, not you," she said, squeezing his hand, "and they wouldn't have captured you. They were there to kill you."

"But they would have captured you and Peine," he said. "You two would have been safe at least. The way I did things could have gotten you both killed."

"Don't be silly," she said a bit sharply. "They would have killed Peine, and to me, Deken would have done a lot worse." She let go of his hand, turning to look out over the plains.

"Worse?" Ari was confused. Somehow, he had upset her.

"Worse," she said.

He stood looking at her, not sure if he should apologize or leave or say something else.

She turned to him, considering his confused expression. "Don't you know what happens to women in war?" she asked.

"But that wasn't war," he said, shocked. "I mean, he wouldn't. He wanted to marry you."

"He tried before." Her voice became fierce. "Why do you think I carry a knife? In case I need to trim my nails?"

"He did?" Ari felt an inarticulate rage build in him. He wished Deken were back alive so this time, he could properly enjoy killing him.

"Ari." Ispiria's tone turned soft again. "They were bad people. You had to kill them."

"There's a sort of resistance when your sword hits the armor covering the chest," he told her, struggling to keep his voice even, "but after that, it slides right in. Right into the person. Of course with the rock, I didn't feel anything, but there was that sound." He shuddered. She took his hands in hers again. He stared at his feet. Maybe he was a coward. How could a man be a knight and protect people if he hated killing?

"You wouldn't be a good man if you liked killing," she said. The similarity of her line of thought to his own startled him into looking at her. He noticed again how tall she was, almost his own height. "Ari, I know you're unhappy," she said, "and I don't know what to say to make you feel better."

She sounded so upset by this that he found himself struggling to think of something to say to make her feel better. "I like when you call me Ari." As the words left his mouth, he shut his eyes, cursing his own ineptitude. I like when you call me Ari? What kind of a thing was that to say? Everyone called him Ari. He groaned inwardly.

A moment later, his eyes flew open in surprise as Ispiria slipped her arms around his neck and kissed him. This was not a quick, smacking kiss like she had given him earlier. This kiss was long, soft sometimes but hard others, and seemed to involve a lot of her hands on the back of his neck and in his hair. His eyes fell shut again, his hands of their own accord encircling her and pressing her to him. Then it was over. She pulled away, coming down off her toes. Ari had to work to force his arms to release her. He didn't want them to.

"We should go inside and dance," she said, stepping away from him. She pressed her lips together, looking up at him sheepishly. He was relieved to see her blushing. He could feel the heat in his own face. He opened his mouth to agree but ended up nodding instead.

With a quick smile, she turned and darted down the steps. Ari stood, taking deep breaths of the night air. By the time he collected himself enough to follow her, he thought she would be gone, but as he descended, he saw she was leaning against the wall at the base of the fortification, looking up at the moon. He took her hand, and they both blushed again. Grinning at each other, they headed back inside to dance.

Chapter Fourteen

Ari didn't want to go. He wanted to be a knight, and he wanted to serve his king, but he and Ispiria danced for so many hours and talked for many more, and he did not want to go. There was a pain in him. It clenched his chest. It soured his stomach. It constricted his throat. He knew the only way to cure it was not to leave her.

She walked down the castle steps, a green cloak wrapped tight about her, her unruly hair swirling in the wind. There were dark clouds overhead, foretelling rain or even snow. He stood by Stew, waiting for her.

She kissed him lightly on each cheek, pausing to whisper in his ear, "Promise you will come back."

He nodded, afraid his voice would crack if he spoke.

She pulled a lace square from her sleeve, handing it to him. "My token," she said with a little smile. He held it in his hand, confused.

"You keep it close to your heart, lad," Sir Cadwel said gently, coming up beside him, followed by Natan. The knight clasped Ari's shoulder, giving it a comforting squeeze. "I'll bring him back to you, Little Ria," Sir Cadwel said, reaching out to pat Ispiria on the cheek.

"I know you will, my lord," she said with a brave smile. She hugged Sir Cadwel and then hugged Ari. Squaring her shoulders, she stepped back.

"Don't travel too far each day," Natan said to Sir Cadwel. "They say the mountain air is hard on man and beast."

"I've been into the mountains before." Sir Cadwel adjusted his stirrup.

"But each time you go, you're that much older than the last time," Natan said with a grin. The steward boosted Sir Cadwel into the saddle. "You and this bucket of bones you ride around on."

Goldwin snorted, shaking out his mane.

"Did you want me to wait on you for the hangings?" Natan asked, lowering his voice.

Peine came forward to help Ari mount. Between saying goodbye to Ispiria and Natan's whispered questions about hanging, Ari was too distracted for his usual protest that he was perfectly capable of getting on his own horse.

"No," Sir Cadwel said. He reached down to pat his two great hounds. "Get it done as soon as possible. No reason torturing the woman. Never fun to hang a woman."

"And the bodies? Lyla is insisting her brat be buried by her church."

"If that's her last request, let her have it." Sir Cadwel shrugged. The knight looked about the courtyard at all the people waiting to send them off. "We should have discussed this yesterday."

"You should have delayed your departure to tend to some of the business you have here," Natan said.

"Just do what you think is right," Sir Cadwel said. "You always do, and it always is."

"That's why you keep me around," Natan said. He reached up, and the two men clasped hands briefly in farewell. Natan fell back to stand beside Ispiria.

Peine scrambled onto his horse. After a well-presented argument and much pleading and begging, Sir Cadwel agreed to allow Peine to accompany them. He admitted Peine had shown himself to be a useful sort. Despite Ari's obvious sorrow at leaving Ispiria, Peine smiled from ear to ear as he prepared to journey north with his companions. Ari found it a little annoying.

There were many well wishes, people waving, and sympathetic looks for Ari. The whole castle knew, it seemed, that he and Ispiria were in love. As Sir Cadwel set off, Ari took one last long look at Ispiria before he rode away. He would never have guessed that in his whole life, this would be the hardest thing he ever had to do. He made himself follow the other horses, not looking back until well after the castle was out of sight. He knew if he saw her alone on the wall, watching him go, he would turn around and gallop back, and somehow, he knew, on the wall watching him was where she was.

***

The mood around their campfire that night was somber. It started to hail about noon, shortly after they entered the mountain pass. The hail wasn't large enough to keep them from continuing but was certainly annoying to ride in. Even the horses seemed out of sorts. Larke was in a foul mood because Sir Cadwel insisted on the journey, although the knight had gifted Larke his own tent so he wouldn't complain so much of the cold. Ari was moping over Ispiria. Sir Cadwel was eternally grumpy, and not being in a warm, dry bed exacerbated that condition considerably. They retired early.

Before Ari realized he was asleep, he found himself bolt upright, gasping, his forehead covered with sweat. He pulled aside the flap of the tent he and Peine shared, letting fresh air fall on his face. He noticed Larke's tent was open and the bard was gone. Not odd for Larke, but it still seemed a bitter night for one of the bard's nocturnal wanderings. The hail had stopped, but it was quite cold and rain was falling.

Ari lay back down, letting the tent fall shut. His mind wandered over the dream. Usually, he could recall nothing from his dreams but vague unease, yet this time it was very clear.

He was walking in the woods, as he used to when he lived at the inn. It was a lovely spring night, with apple and pear blossoms everywhere. In the clearing ahead, he saw a strange glow. Crouching down, he crept forward. Luminous figures darted through the clearing too fast to follow, but then one stopped, a hand clutched against his side.

Glowing to outshine the moonlight, the man stumbled to one knee. He was dressed in a long, white shirt, split up the sides, and flowing white breeches. He was wounded in some way, but not badly. He raised his head, seeming almost to sniff the air. He turned and looked directly at Ari.

"Go back to the inn, boy," he called. He smiled, looking rather young, but seemed somehow old. "Danger runs alongside the Aluiens in the forest tonight."

Ari stared at him, mesmerized. He tried to answer, but a cloaked man slunk silently into the clearing behind the Aluien. The cloaked man seemed to pull the darkness over him in an undulating sheet, like a wall of black ants converging on a rotting piece of food. Ari knew he wouldn't have been able to see that being save for the light given off by the glowing one. The shadowy form raised a poison-coated blade.

"Look out!" Ari cried. Looking back on it, he didn't know why he had warned the Aluien. He had no reason to trust one over the other. Maybe he just couldn't stand by and watch someone be struck down from behind.

The bright being threw one glance over his shoulder, then sped off through the woods like a startled deer. Ari was alone, facing the dark form, and it was so much darker now with the light from the other one gone.

The darkness advanced on him. Ari found himself unable to move. It was as if his limbs were heavy, and he couldn't command them. If he was as afraid as he knew he ought to be, he might have had some luck, but his fear seemed to be asleep.

"You should not have done that, boy," the familiar voice of Lord Ferringul hissed from beneath the hood.

A hand closed around Ari's neck, tilting it back. Still, he found himself unable to struggle. Pain shot through him as a blade cut across his throat. He felt his life spilling out, hot and wet. Just as he fell into blackness, he saw a light draw near.

Ari lay in bed, his hand unconsciously rubbing the smooth skin on his throat. He had never had so realistic a dream before. Or had he? It seemed so very familiar, and why was Lord Ferringul in his dream?

"Ari?" Larke's head poked into the tent. "What are you doing up, lad?"

Ari stared at Larke in shock. The bard was glowing. "You, you're—" he stammered.

"The dream again?" Larke said. "I step out for one night—" He shook his head. "It's getting worse."

"What is?" Ari said. He pulled his feet up, away from where Larke filled the entrance to his tent. "Peine," he called.

"Now, lad, there's no reason to involve him in this," Larke said, making an obscure gesture over Peine. The boy, who was stirring, sighed and fell back to sleep.

"Siara was right."

"I'm not supposed to let you remember, lad," Larke told him, his voice sad.

"But why?" Ari said, realizing this had happened before and knowing he couldn't stop Larke. "I think it's important, Larke. I think I need to know."

"I think so too, lad, but it isn't my choice. It's the bargain the Lady struck with the council so they would let you go." With an apologetic shrug, Larke made a gesture. Ari found himself unable to move, his eyes growing heavy. Larke ducked into the tent, his hand coming to rest on Ari's forehead. Ari felt his memories scatter, and with a sigh, he slid into sleep.

***

In the morning, everything blade to branch was made sharp by a thin sheet of ice, but the stream near the trail they followed still flowed clear. Sir Cadwel presented Peine and Ari with warm fur cloaks. It was obvious from the knight's pleased grin that he had set the gifts aside in advance, and the execution of his plan filled him with an almost childlike joy.

"It's an early midwinter present," Sir Cadwel told Ari, handing him the gray fur bundle.

It was wolf fur, carefully stitched together, lined in blue, padded, and hooded. It was marvelous. Far nicer than anything Ari had ever imagined he would own. He smiled, putting it on. It made him look much more like a real knight, he thought. It was so nice, it distracted him from his moping over Ispiria for almost three minutes.

"Will we be up here in the mountains in the winter?" Peine asked, sounding worried.

"No," Sir Cadwel said, shaking out his own great cloak. "If we make good time today, we should be there by tomorrow evening."

"Let me just stow away me tent," Larke said, pulling up the corner stakes. He crawled inside and pulled out the central pole, causing the whole thing to collapse on him. Ari and Peine went over to help while Sir Cadwel watched, chafing at the delay. Once the bard's tent was successfully bundled, a job which he seemed determined to make as difficult as possible, his horse was nowhere to be found.

"Why you don't keep the beast tethered like a normal man would?" Sir Cadwel said as they watched Larke walk from one end of the little clearing to the other, making a strange noise which he said would bring the horse. Ari wasn't very sure it would, as the high-pitched call seemed to be making the other animals a bit nervous.

"What's your horse's name, Larke?" Ari asked, realizing for all the time they had traveled together, he had no idea what Larke called the gray.

"That, me lad, is a secret!" Larke said with a wink and a flourish of his puffed sleeve.

Sir Cadwel rolled his eyes skyward. "Enough time wasted on this. We'll go on and you can hope he finds us by night. You can ride with Peine."

"There he is!" Peine said, pointing. Indeed, the gray walked into the campsite and came to stand by Larke, an innocent look on his face.

"Put that tent on a horse and let us be off," Sir Cadwel growled, mounting Goldwin, who let out an annoyed snort, flicking his tail. The two started up the trail, giving every appearance of not caring whether the rest followed.

***

That morning set the tone for the next two days of travel. Anything and everything that could possibly go wrong for Larke did. He fell asleep and fell off his horse, which ran away, scattering his belongings, making them have to search for them. He saw herbs he simply had to have for their dinner and ran into the woods to collect them. He got tired early and slept late. Thus, they didn't arrive at their destination until midday the day after Sir Cadwel had predicted.

Ari felt an odd sense of foreboding as they rode through a steep valley toward the small castle. It was crouched among the rocks of the mountain, with a sinuous road winding up to it. The windows were narrow and dark, and the gates stood shut. It felt like a place long abandoned, but a thin reed of smoke curled up from somewhere inside the walls.

Yet none of that was what really bothered Ari. It was something more. Something inside him speaking to him. Ari recognized that voice. It was the part of him that anticipated his opponent's next move in a fight. The part of him that hated Lord

Ferringul and feared the throaty laugh of Princess Clorra. The part of him that knew better. That part of him was telling him not to go into the castle.

"I think Larke's right," he blurted.

"What could that fop possibly be right about?" Sir Cadwel asked, turning to scowl at Ari.

"I don't think the owner of that castle has anything to do with Princess Clorra," Ari said, trying not to let his voice betray his nervousness.

"Then our visit should be brief. We will state the charges, and he shall deny them." Sir Cadwel urged his horse up the road. Goldwin snorted but did not shy.

Ari looked from Peine to Larke, seeing in their faces the same reluctance he felt. He turned to stare at Sir Cadwel's back, moving up the road alone. With a sigh, Ari urged Stew forward.

"Ho the castle," Sir Cadwel called. Despite his outward calm, Ari noticed the knight's hand lingered near his sword hilt. "Ho the castle," Sir Cadwel repeated after several moment's silence. His words echoed about the narrow valley. He was about to call again when a thin form moved at the top of the wall.

"Who disturbs the lord of the castle?" a reedy voice called. A pale head adorned with wisps of dirty gray hair bent over the ramparts to squint down at them.

"By proper definition, I am lord of the castle," Sir Cadwel said, his voice reflecting all the annoyance of the past several days.

"Lord Caddon?" the thin voice asked after a moment's consideration. Ari saw Sir Cadwel stiffen.

"Lord Caddon was my father, dead these past twenty-five years," the knight said.

"Ah, his son," the man said. "I did not realize Lord Caddon's rule had passed. Few come to the castle of my master, my lord."

"We shall have audience with your master, Lord Mrakenson," Sir Cadwel said.

"I will seek my lord's mind." The wizened man disappeared behind the wall.

"Seek his mind indeed," Sir Cadwel said, scowling.

"Well, ye know how these mountain folk be." Larke seemed cheered by the idea they might not be let in.

"My father went round to all of their castles in his youth." Sir Cadwel looked around the valley. "I should have taken his example. They need to be reminded they are not autonomous."

Ari didn't see why. How could it matter if they wanted to stay in this wretched valley in this dismal castle and not believe they had a lord or a king to the south? No one else wanted this land or had any use for it, after all.

Ari started as half of the dark wooden gate swung open. Nodding for them to follow, Sir Cadwel rode in. The old man who peered down from the battlements stood waiting on the castle steps. Inside the walls, the castle looked and felt just as abandoned as it had from without. Ari saw no one else around.

"You may leave the animals here," the man said.

"Peine, stay with the horses and have them ready to leave," Sir Cadwel murmured to the boy as they dismounted. "Yell if anyone tries to close that gate."

Peine nodded, his eyes wide and serious. He placed his hand over the hilt of the small knife he had taken to carrying after Rock Bay. Staying astride Charger, he accepted the reins of the other three horses, leading them to stand near the open gate.

"This way," the old man said, entering the keep. He cast Peine an expressionless look. Ari saw the boy shiver.

The hall through which the servant led them was choked with dust. The beams holding up the small castle were made of the same dark wood as the gate. The stone they supported was gray, with a darker vein through it. Light from one torch-bearing sconce barely reached the glow of the next. The wall behind each was stained with centuries of soot. The place smelled of it, and of dust.

At the end of the corridor, their guide pushed open half of a pair of massive double doors. The relief on the outside looked to be bronze, or perhaps an even more precious metal, but years of soot and neglect dulled it past recognition. The door swung silently open and the servant stepped aside, gesturing for them to proceed.

The room they entered was vast and empty. The floor was of gray marble, inlaid with an elaborate design. Ari found it oddly unpleasant and didn't look at it for long. Narrow windows set high in the walls let in little light, and none were near enough to the raised dais across the room to illuminate it. The dais, with its occupant and more smoky torches, was the only thing in the large room. The servant did not follow them in, closing the door softly behind them. Sir Cadwel strode toward the raised platform and the chair atop it. Larke and Ari trailed behind.

As they neared, Ari began to wonder if this was in fact some sick jest, or if the old servant was so mad and senile, he didn't know the truth of it. It seemed to Ari as if the man in the chair was dead. His skin was stretched taut over his bones and was as pale as they were. His eyes were open and unmoving, a milky blue. He was completely bald. Indeed, he had no hair on him that Ari could see. His nails were long, dark, and twisted on the end of thin, gnarled fingers.

"Sir Cadwel. You have come to visit me, as did your father." The voice was soft, almost as if it were a breeze blowing through the hall. Like a cold breeze, it gave Ari goosebumps.

"I'm afraid this is not a social visit."

Ari felt a renewed respect for his mentor, who was so steady and composed in the face of this talking skeleton of a man.

"Not a social visit?" the voice whispered. It sounded amused.

"I have come in the name of the king to confront you with the accusation made by Lord Ferringul, newly befriended of Crown Prince Parrentine, that you, Lord Mrakenson, have treacherously placed a curse on Princess Clorra, betrothed and beloved of Prince

Parrentine." Sir Cadwel delivered the charges firmly. The silence that greeted the end of his speech was absolute.

The form in the chair made a sound Ari could only assume was a laugh. Ari clenched his teeth until the grating noise stopped, holding himself firmly from shuddering.

"What is it you have done, sir knight, to so deeply offend Ferringul that he would send you here?" the whispered voice asked.

Sir Cadwel answered the talking cadaver with a baffled look.

"Or is it not you?" The unblinking eyes shifted slightly, and Ari felt their force as they settled on him. "Ah," he breathed. "It is you."

"Lord Mrakenson," Sir Cadwel spoke loudly. "How do you plead to the charges, my lord?"

"Do not trouble yourself, sir knight," the voice whispered. "My guilt in this matter is not such that you will be forced to slay me this day for your king. No, guilt has nothing to do with your visit here."

"Speak plainly, my lord," Sir Cadwel said, his never vast patience beginning to wear.

"Ferringul has sent me that." A thin hand lifted from the arm of the chair to point at Ari. "That which he fears, he hopes I will destroy for him, but should I? I fear it too, but less, for I fear all things less. Yet dare I pass this chance by before it comes into its own? No, I think I cannot."

The form in the chair rose, a pile of red robes, so dark as to be almost black, shifting about it. Arms outstretched, it spoke in a deep and booming voice. Before they could react, a wall of air slammed into them, knocking them clattering to the floor. Ari's head hit the strange inlay with a loud crack.

"No, this chance I cannot pass, this gift." The skeletal head remained swiveled toward Ari where he lay. Lord Mrakenson seemed to rise above the platform, moving inescapably closer. Behind him came a wall of darkness, as if all the smoke of the place had gathered into a more substantial mass and was advancing to smother Ari. Ari struggled to his knees, shaking his head to try and clear it.

Then a glowing form sprang up between the red-robed cadaver and Ari. The form was tall and familiar and would have been brightly clad, had not its own light bleached the colors from its clothes. It was Larke.

In the white light emanating from the bard, Ari felt his mind open. Memories sprang out, assailing him. That, not the darkness, kept him from rising. He could barely see the room as a dizzying array of images sped past his inner eye. Him in the woods. A glowing being. Lord Ferringul attacking him. Waking underground, but in caves so vast and lovely, there was no pressure of earth above. Then there were those few days of happiness, when he was one with these magical glowing beings, until the illness came. He remembered them talking while he lay in bed. He remembered the Lady.

"Ari!" Sir Cadwel hoisted him to his feet. In the knight's other hand, he held his great sword, the naked blade glinting brightly in the light that shone from Larke.

With Sir Cadwel's help, Ari stumbled back, away from where the light around Larke and the darkness of the keep seemed to clash and wrestle. The dark twisted around bits of the light, squeezing it, but the light wriggled free, regrouping. Lord Mrakenson made a gesture, snarling words of command. Larke stood unmoving and silent, only the lines of sweat trickling down his brow and the concentration in his eyes giving indication of his part in the struggle. For a moment, they seemed evenly matched, neither gaining ground, but then the darkness surged forward, and Larke fell to his knees.

"Run!" Larke cried. Neither of them moved. With what seemed to be great effort, Larke turned to look at them. "Run, Cadwel. You can't fight him today," he said, managing a half smile.

"Larkesong?" Sir Cadwel gasped.

The darkness surged again, and Larke's head wrenched back round to meet Lord Mrakenson's milky blue gaze.

Ari squeezed his eyes shut. He wanted to help Larke, but images from his past hurtled around in his head, scattering thought and intention. Foremost among them was Lord Ferringul's sneering face filling his mind. If only he had known! Lord Ferringul was a killer, something beyond foul, and they had left him there in the castle. Ari opened his eyes and grabbed Sir Cadwel's arm. The knight still contemplated the battle of magic, and Ari could tell from the calculating look on his face that he was trying to decide how best to attack. Around them, light and dark flared, each threatening to consume them.

"We have to get to the capital," Ari said, dragging Sir Cadwel toward the door.

Sir Cadwel opened his mouth to protest.

"We can't help him." Ari hadn't sorted out his memories yet, but of this he was sure. He and Sir Cadwel were no threat to the evil in this castle. Not now. Not with what little knowledge they had between them. "We have to save the king!"

Sir Cadwel nodded, seeming to realize as Ari did that the kingdom was in grave danger. They turned and charged the double door, smashing through it. They ran down the corridor, Ari looking back once. Larke was on his knees, seeming a lonely point of light against a vast bulk of darkness, but as Ari watched, the bard flung his arms wide.

"My Lady!" The words were wrenched from Larke's throat. Ari thought the glow around him intensified, but then they were outside in the pale afternoon light, a wide-eyed Peine clutching the reins of Stew and Goldwin.

"Larke's horse ran away," the boy cried. "What was that noise? Where's Larke?"

Gesturing for Peine to go, they jumped onto their horses and charged the gate, which even now started to close. Ari didn't see who was closing it, but as he leaned low over Stew and dug in his heels, he could feel claws of malice reaching out from inside the castle to pull them back. There was an explosion of white light behind them, and Peine screamed. Their horses darted through the gate. Ari was sure they made it by so little that Stew left some of his tail behind, but they were away, speeding down the trail.

***

They rode through the afternoon and the night. In the morning they led their horses, eating dried meat and hard bread as they went. Their pace had taken them almost back out of the mountains already. Sir Cadwel's eyes were deeply troubled, his expression dark.

"I never leave a companion," he said.

"What happened to Larke?" Peine asked, fear and weariness warring in his tone.

"It wasn't a battle we could fight," Ari said, pleading with himself for it to be true. He didn't want to think he was just too afraid to help Larke. "Lord Ferringul is the true villain here. We must stop whatever it is he plans."

"Lord Ferringul?" Peine asked. He stumbled, fatigue clear in every movement he made.

"Aye." Sir Cadwel sighed. "Our duty to king and country weighs above all else. I should have treated him kinder," he added under his breath.

"My lord," Ari said, lowering his voice. He didn't know what to say to assuage Sir Cadwel's guilt, but he did know they had to make haste back to the capital. "Sir, if we take our horses, they will go day and night without rest, but Peine's can't, and I doubt he can either."

"How do you know this?" Sir Cadwel asked. His voice was curious but gratifyingly lacking in skepticism. The knight looked back at the bedraggled Wheylian boy.

"Goldwin and Stew are—" Ari floundered for the right words. "They're special. They're like Larke's horse."

"I don't know if Goldwin finds the comparison flattering," Sir Cadwel said, and Goldwin snorted.

"I mean, they are of his people," Ari said. Sir Cadwel gave him a long, measuring look.

"And how do you know this?" Sir Cadwel asked again, patting Goldwin on the nose.

"Think about it, sir." Ari worked his way around the idea, not wanting to try and tell Sir Cadwel everything before he got a chance to sort it all out in his head. Plus, there was no time. "How long have you had Goldwin? How long do horses live?"

"I've had him—" Ari watched as a shocked look spread over the knight's face. "How could I never have noticed that before?" He cast Goldwin an incredulous glance, which the horse pretended to ignore.

"Because they put a—" Ari struggled for the right word. "A compulsion on him, I think it's called. It makes people just not think about how old he is."

"And you can see through this?"

"I can now."

"And Stew is the same?"

Ari nodded.

"And why did they give us these steeds?" Sir Cadwel gave Goldwin a suspicious look. The horse huffed at him.

"I think we are marked," Ari said after a moment's thought.

"Marked?" Ari could tell Sir Cadwel didn't like the sound of that.

"To go with them," Ari said. "Instead of dying. We will go with them. Like Larke."

"So he truly is Larkesong. How could I not have seen it? I knew him well."

"I don't exactly know how they do it," Ari said, looking down, waiting while Sir Cadwel considered his words.

"We will have our reckoning with Lord Mrakenson," Sir Cadwel said. "Never doubt it. And someday, you will have to explain this all to me."

"Yes, sir," Ari said, wondering if he could sort it out well enough to do so.

"But for now, we have to get to the capital," the knight said. "Peine," he called, and the boy struggled to catch up. He and his horse were covered with mud, and their heads hung in fatigue.

"Yes, my lord?" Peine tried to straighten his shoulders.

"Peine, can you go alone with a message to Sorga?"

"Yes, sir," Peine said with determination.

"You must send a bird to the king, and only the king," the knight said. "Use my seal. Natan knows where it is."

Sir Cadwel called a brief halt, giving Peine a message for Natan and one for the king, making the boy repeat them back twice. Ari wanted to send word to Ispiria, too. He realized he hadn't thought of her since they had reached the castle, and he was filled with guilt. He wanted to see her, if only for a moment, but he knew his duty lay south with all speed. A message seemed inadequate, and he was embarrassed to have to tell it to Peine. He almost gave up on the idea, but he thought of Ispiria's face when Peine told her he had no message for her, and he squared his shoulders.

"Peine." Ari captured his friend's attention, his face red already at the thought of what he was about to say. "Could you tell Ispiria, please, that is—" He coughed, his gaze darting to Sir Cadwel, who wasn't looking at him. "That is, ask her please, if, when I get back, maybe she would agree to let me ask her if maybe someday we could be, well, promised."

Peine nodded, eyes wide. As soon as Ari managed to get his request out, Sir Cadwel turned back. "Off with you, lad, with haste," the knight said. "Don't kill your horse, rest if you must, but make all speed."

They all mounted. Peine straightened in the saddle, bolstered by the importance of his charge. He left them with a wave, murmuring the messages to himself as he rode. As one, the two men swung their horses about, kicking them into a gallop south.

Chapter Fifteen

Ari had never known such a harrowing ride. They rode all night and all day. They rode in rain and snow and hail and mud. Towns passed by in blurs. They ate in the saddle, and when the horses walked, they slept in the saddle. Days melted together. Nights gave no respite.

Ari, memories of the glowing magical race of Aluiens tumbling about in his mind, now realized he had more strength and stamina than a normal man, but still he could barely keep the pace. What Sir Cadwel lacked in Aluien-given gifts, he made up for with a lifetime of training and skill. The knight seemed made of stone. He drove Ari and the horses tirelessly on.

Ari was tormented by jumbled images of Larke on his knees before skeletal red robes, of Lord Ferringul attacking Ari at night in the forest near his childhood home, and of light-filled caves. Without Larke there to keep them from him, the memories battled for attention in his mind, plaguing him awake or asleep and robbing him of concentration and rest. He could only hope they would sort themselves into some semblance of order.

"Siara was right," he said to himself, only to have memories of saying that very thing to Larke come flooding over him. How many times had he said it? Always Larke had apologized. Always he had said it was not his choice. Whose choice was it? An image came to Ari's mind of a council, a circle of Aluiens, deciding his fate.

His mind was filled with spinning images of the Aluiens, the magical race to which Larke belonged. They were as varied as snowflakes, but in common, they all had an iridescent glow about them. Some looked old, and some young, but he knew they were all far older than they appeared. Larke himself was at least twenty years older than he looked, and Ari thought he was one of the youngest of them.

And there was the Lady. She was small and ancient, with bright brown eyes and neat gray hair. Everyone deferred to her. Even the oldest seemed not to want to argue with her. It was she who saved him when he would have died at Lord Ferringul's hands, she who brought him to live with the Aluiens and made him one of them. When he fell ill from the poison Lord Ferringul's knife unleashed in his veins, it was the Lady who insisted they perform the ritual to heal him, even though it meant making him human again and sending him back into the world. Ari recalled her promise to the council; he would never remember the Aluiens, never betray the secret of them to other men.

It hadn't worked, though, he realized. That's why they had sent Larke. Somehow, Ari was more resistant to their spells than a human should be. He was faster, stronger, and he could see in any light. He was more like an Aluien than a human. Yet he didn't have the glow. He didn't have the mystical substance that filled them with magic . . . the Orlenia.

The memory of it sparked a longing in him so intense he gasped aloud. A pain stabbed through him at the sudden realization of how empty he was. Built only of blood and flesh and bile, he felt clumsy, his mind muddled. He longed to feel the lightness and clarity of Orlenia running through his veins once more.

Why did they not let him remember? It was so very important he remember. Now he knew Lord Ferringul was evil in his mind, not just with his heart. He knew the Aluiens could cure Princess Clorra with the Orlenia as they cured him. But if they gave her Orlenia, would she have to stay with them? Ari would have been able to stay, had Lord Ferringul's knife not borne an Aluien poison. Surely the prince would rather have Clorra stay with them alive than have her die?

He recalled their laws, their vow not to interfere. They watched humans, but they didn't change their lives. Yet they changed Ari's. They gave Sir Cadwel Goldwin. No matter how they might argue they hadn't changed Sir Cadwel, having Goldwin must have helped him. Obviously they did interfere when it suited them, and Ari would get them to help Princess Clorra.

Determination bolstering him, Ari galloped down the road after Sir Cadwel.

***

Sleet fell heavy from the southern sky the day they finally skidded through the gates of Poromont, but it wasn't the oppressive weather that caused them to slow their mounts. A pall enveloped the city. People hurried through the streets with their eyes cast down, except for fearful, darting glances at anyone who drew too near. Even though Sir Cadwel and Ari walked their steaming mounts, everyone scuttled out of their way as if afraid to be trod on. Occasionally, someone would recognize Sir Cadwel under the grime of days spent riding and run up to them, welcoming the king's champion home with desperate hope in their eyes. It was a stark contrast to the city that had greeted them on their previous visits.

Word traveled fast, and by the time they reached the castle, the king was waiting for them on the steps. He wore a forced smile, nodding and waving to the populous. The queen was not in evidence, and Ari felt a chill in the absence of her usual warm greeting. They dismounted, and grooms hurried to take Goldwin and Stew.

"Take extra care with them, lads," Sir Cadwel said. "They just ran the length of the country." He gave the young men an encouraging smile but got serious faces in return.

"Cadwel, Aridian," King Ennentine said, gesturing them inside. "You two are a sight."

"Ennentine," Sir Cadwel said in a low voice. "We need to talk."

"You need to get cleaned up. You're head to toe mud and no doubt cold through." The king looked around. "You return sooner than hoped. One of my riders must have caught you."

"Riders? We've seen none," Sir Cadwel said, halting and taking Ennentine by the arm. "Didn't you get my hawk?"

"We haven't had any birds in some time." The king lowered his voice, though none stood near. "All of ours were killed, and any coming in, we find ripped to pieces. It isn't common knowledge. I don't want to add to the panic."

"What panic?" Sir Cadwel's face was grim.

"Really, Cadwel," King Ennentine said loudly. "You're unrecognizable with dirt. Go make yourself presentable. The steward will send someone up."

Sir Cadwel took in Ennentine's meaningful gaze and nodded. "Come along, lad," he said, preceding Ari through the hall and up the steps, Ennentine watching them go.

Castle staff followed them, wiping up mud. When they got to their rooms, Sir Cadwel deliberately shut them out, not letting anyone in to keep cleaning. He took a chair and wedged it against the door, following suit with the hidden door leading to the servants' hall. Still saying nothing, he went to the bathing room, gesturing for Ari to follow. The bath was empty, as no one could get in to fill it. They stood in the bathing room, waiting. Ari wasn't sure what they were about, but he felt it was best not to speak until Sir Cadwel did.

Ari almost jumped out of his muddy boots when the wall next to where he was dozing slid away. Inside stood a cobweb-bedecked Ennentine, holding a lantern. The king's face was serious.

"Is anyone else here?" their monarch asked, leaning into the room.

"No, but eventually, they'll pound the doors down trying to bring us hot water," Sir Cadwel said. "What's this all about?"

"I sent riders for you, but none have yet returned, and as I said, there are no birds left. Cadwel, something is very wrong in my city." King Ennentine stepped into the room, closing the secret door behind him.

"That's what we came to tell you," Sir Cadwel said.

"Then you know who's behind it?" The king sounded hopeful.

"Lord Ferringul," Ari said harshly, feeling hatred well up at the name. The two men looked at him. His face flushed and he looked down.

"You're sure?" Ennentine asked, surprised. "I haven't even told you our troubles yet."

"What are they, then?" Sir Cadwel asked, holding up a hand to silence Ari as he looked up.

"People have been disappearing, and animals, for that matter." The king looked as tired as Ari felt. "What's worse, shortly after you left, two servants were found dead in Princess Clorra's room. Since then, none of the others will go in, and we have to leave Ferringul with her at all times, or she starts shrieking and trying to escape. We had to have her doors barred because she kept getting out and walking around the castle naked." The king looked embarrassed. "Her father's people are blaming us, of course, but they can't seem to make her behave, so they have no choice but to let Ferringul be with her. My son is half mad with grief and jealousy. My people are coming unhinged. Now you say Ferringul is behind the disappearances?"

“The quest Ferringul sent us on was a trap,” Sir Cadwel said. “I find it no stretch to assume he sent us there to keep us away from Poromont at the least, or have us end up dead at the most. For my part, I’m not sure exactly what is afoot, but something very unnatural is going on, and that man is party to it.”

“Unnatural?” If possible, the king looked more worried than ever. “As in Wheylian unnatural?”

Ari winced, exchanging a look with Sir Cadwel. He hadn’t thought of that. The last thing they wanted to do was implicate the Wheys, the traditional source of any mysticism in Lggothland. They were already on very shaky terms with Princess Clorra’s homeland. They didn’t need their king at war with two neighbors at once.

“As in some sort of magic, I believe,” Sir Cadwel said. “Not Wheylian in nature.”

“What other sort is there?” the king asked. “Was it not the circle of wise women of Whey who sent my son to Ferringul to begin with?”

Most people preferred to ignore the mystical side of the Wheylian culture. Many referred to the High Priestess of Whey as a queen, ignoring her true title. Some didn’t even believe the priestesses of Whey had any true power, although even those people made sure not to cross them. The general rule was, stay away from the Wheys, and you won’t have to find out whether their magic is real or not.

“For that matter,” the king said, anger mounting in his voice, “It was Princess Siara who gave my son the book that convinced him to journey to Wheylia to begin with, and she’s still here in the castle.”

“I don’t think Siara has anything to do with this,” Ari said, worried about the way the conversation was progressing.

“I’m sorry, young Aridian, but your opinion on the matter carries little weight.” The king favored him with a pitying look. “All know you’re besotted with her.”

"I am not," Ari said. "My one true love is Lady Ispiria." Of course, saying that caused Ari to blush again, which didn't bolster his attempt at credibility.

"Ari." Sir Cadwel lifted his gaze skyward in silent supplication before turning back to the king. "Hear what the boy has to say about Lord Ferringul, sire."

They both looked at Ari. He drew a deep breath. He'd never spoken aloud to anyone of what had happened that night in the woods. Sir Cadwel had only Ari's word he knew something about Lord Ferringul. They hadn't the leisure on the journey south to discuss it.

"Go ahead," Sir Cadwel said.

"It was in the spring," Ari said. "I was out walking in the woods at night near Sallsburry, and I saw—" Ari paused. How could he describe it? "I saw this being, a man. He didn't look old, but he seemed old, and he was surrounded by a sort of white glow. He was in a clearing, and he was wounded."

"I have seen such a man with my own eyes, your majesty," Sir Cadwel put in at the king's skeptical look. "A glow emanates from him as light from the moon." Cadwel nodded for Ari to continue.

"He was beautiful," Ari stammered, taken aback by Sir Cadwel's eloquence. "I mean, I know men aren't usually beautiful, but this being was. Then behind him, out of the dark, came Lord Ferringul. He had a knife, the blade covered with foul poison, and he raised it to stab the glowing man in the back, so I called out, and the man ran away."

The king raised an eyebrow but said nothing. He leaned against the wall, listening. Ari suddenly saw the ludicrousness of the situation. He, Aridian, standing with King Ennentine and Sir Cadwel in a bathing room around an empty tub, talking about a bad dream he kept having over and over. He fought back a hysterical laugh, swallowing hard.

"Lord Ferringul looked very angry, and he told me I would regret warning his prey." Ari swallowed again, his throat dry. "For some reason, I couldn't do anything. I couldn't fight or run or scream. And he—" Ari paused again, the memory so clear in his mind, he had to take a moment to get his voice under control. "He grabbed me by the neck with one hand and slid his knife across my throat. That's how he likes to kill, with that sticky black knife. I learned later it's coated in a special poison, so if he strikes an Aluien with it, they'll die as surely as a mortal man would. When he cut me open, and my blood started to pour out, I knew I was dead. That's the last thought I remember, until I woke up with the Aluiens." Ari looked back and forth between the two faces. He knew at once Sir Cadwel believed him, but Sir Cadwel had seen Larke and the red-robed man. The king had not.

"The bodies we found in the princess's room," the king said. "They had their throats slit, with some sort of black paste dried around the wounds. None could name it. Who are these Aluiens of which you speak?"

"We've wasted enough time in talk," Sir Cadwel said. "We can sort the rest out after, but we must kill that man. He is a threat to the crown."

"Come with me," the king said, his voice decisive.

Ennentine led them from the bathing room. On their way through the sitting room, Sir Cadwel removed the chair blocking the servants' entrance. A valet with a bucket fell into the room, water swamping the thickly woven carpet.

"We don't need baths yet," Sir Cadwel said, loosening his sword. "There's more filth to deal with first."

The boy watched wide-eyed from the floor as the king tossed aside the chair blocking the main door. Outside were several guards, looking to be in the midst of arguing something with the head steward. They fell back a pace when they saw the set faces of their king and Sir Cadwel, the latter with a naked blade in his hand.

"Come with me," the king ordered indiscriminately, and the group fell in behind them. Ennentine led them from the guest wing and across the foyer to the royal wing. There they found

Parrentine, pacing back and forth in front of the guarded door to Princess Clorra's chambers.

"Father," the prince exclaimed. Parrentine didn't look well, and Ari found it in his heart to feel sorry for the man. The prince was very thin and pale. He looked as if he'd lost even more muscle mass than when Ari and Sir Cadwel had found him. His hair and eyes were dull, his appearance unkempt.

"Out of the way, son," the king commanded, but his tone held compassion.

"Your majesty," one of the guards at the door said. They were not palace soldiers, but some of the princess's own men. "We cannot let you bring weapons into the presence of the princess. Please put your swords aside."

"We aren't going to use them on her," the king said. "We're going to use them on Lord Ferringul."

"Father!" Parrentine was anguished. "Father, he's the only one who can keep her from her madness."

"I know, Parrentine, but he is the one who caused her madness." The king made to step forward.

"I won't let you!" Parrentine cried, lunging for his father.

"My lord, we must keep your weapon," a Hapland guard said at the same time, reaching for Sir Cadwel's sword.

Obviously quicker than the guards expected, Sir Cadwel dodged out of reach, bringing his blade up defensively. Parrentine grabbed the king. The princess's guards drew their own weapons, advancing on Sir Cadwel. Some of the castle guards rallied to the knight, while others tried to restrain the frantic prince.

Ari knew Lord Ferringul was in the room beyond. He could sense the evil that seemed to pool about the man, seeping round the edges of the door. Feeling that menace sliding away, Ari pulled his strength to him and charged the reinforced chamber door. There was a deafening crash as he smashed through it. Everyone forgot their quarrels as they turned to look. Ari saw Lord Ferringul vanish onto the balcony. He sprinted across the room, but when he burst into the cold gray daylight, his nemesis was nowhere to be found.

"He got away," Ari snarled, clenching and unclenching his fists convulsively. He turned this way and that, looking both above and below the balcony before the total silence behind him caused him to turn around.

No one was looking at him. Their attention was captivated by the woman on the bed. The princess was perfectly groomed. Her long blond hair fell around her shoulders and spilled over her low bodice, where an overabundance of white skin bulged from the top. She reclined on her bed, eating from a crystal bowl what could only be raw flesh. Her pale perfection was marred by a thin trail of blood trickling from the side of her mouth and smudging her fingers. From the back of the crowd, Ari heard a woman shriek, and they all turned to see Siara faint, sliding slowly to the floor.

"Parrentine, my love," Princess Clorra purred, setting aside her meal. She stretched seductively in the immaculate silken sheets. "Come to me."

"Keep back," Sir Cadwel said, holding his sword across the doorway to block the prince as he moved to obey her. The girl on the bed made a hissing sound at the knight. She shifted, revealing that one of her hands and one foot were chained to the bedposts.

"We have to unchain her." Parrentine sobbed.

"Don't be a fool," Sir Cadwel said.

"Take my son away," ordered the king, looking to the head steward.

The man gestured for some of the guards to help, and they all but carried the weakly struggling prince down the hall to his rooms. For a moment, the others stood, watching in silence as the lovely woman on the bed reclaimed her blood-filled bowl of flesh, delicately sliding morsels of it between her bowed lips. Ari shook his head, looking about the clean, airy room, somehow offended at the lack of indication from anything in its well-kept orderliness of how utterly wrong Princess Clorra was.

"It's only a dog, you know," she told them with a coy smile. "He said I couldn't have any more of you to eat yet." She set her mouth into a pretty pout. Her eyes moved to where Siara lay unconscious on the floor outside. "I'd love to eat that dark-haired little virgin. So young and so sweet."

Ari heard someone gag. In the hall, Siara's maids began hurriedly tugging the unconscious princess back into her room. Ari edged around the thing on the bed to stand with the others.

"You," she said, her eyes narrowing as they settled on him. "There's something about you I definitely do not like."

"I don't see much to like about you either," Ari said.

"I could show you a lot to like," she said. Her bloodied hand went to the front of her gown, leaving red trails down the smooth swell of her breasts, and she pulled open her dress.

"Enough," Sir Cadwel said, turning to push everyone back.

"What is the meaning of this?" a voice said. Lord Kroost, the Hapland ambassador, shoved his way forward. "My Lady!" he gasped, reaching the front of the crowd. His face went pale, then red, then pale again. "Shut that door!" he said. They all stepped back and Sir Cadwel complied, pulling the ruined remains of the door together as best he could.

"What have you done to her?" The ambassador was not very tall, but possessed a ringing voice and a forceful build. "My king will hear of this immediately! You two." He pointed to the two Hapland guards. "Don't let them near the princess!"

Kroost stormed down the hall. Sir Cadwel and Ennentine exchanged worried glances. Sir Cadwel turned to Ari.

"I'll tell you everything I can remember," Ari said.

"Get cleaned up, and I'll see you in my study," the king said, his face set in angry lines. "I want to see Princess Siara as well," he said, looking at the women who stood in the doorway to her room, watching the spectacle. They darted inside, hurriedly curtsying as they went. "And you" He gestured to the Hapland guards. "I don't care if you break orders and let my men help you or not, but I want her off that bed and locked up immediately. I don't care if you have to cut the bed apart to do it. I doubt the villain left us the keys. My steward will find a place for her. Kamers," Ennentine said, seeing the master steward returning from Parrentine's room. "Make sure Kroost doesn't send a single word of this to his king until I have time to reason with him, and set a guard on my son's room." Frowning indiscriminately at everyone, the King Ennentine turned and walked away.

***

When Ari and Sir Cadwel reached the study, they found the king, the prince, and Siara waiting for them. Disregarding custom, Siara had no ladies in attendance. She sat alone on one of the deep leather couches, facing the door. She was every bit as lovely as Ari remembered, but seeing her again stirred nothing but friendship within him and worry at the way she watched the gaunt form of the prince pace the room. As was his custom, the king stood by the mantel of the room's great fireplace. Perhaps due to the oppressive weather, the fire sputtered, bleeding acrid smoke into the room.

"If you knew something about Lord Ferringul, why didn't you tell me?" Parrentine cried, not halting his pacing as he spoke. Madness lurked in the prince's gaze.

"Ari couldn't tell you," Siara said, her worried eyes meeting Ari's. "He had a compulsion laid on him. I tried to tell him, but so strong was it he could not even listen to the possibility he was under one."

"That's not true," Ari said, nervous with everyone looking at him. "I mean, I did listen. I went to talk to Larke about it."

Siara answered that with a sardonic smile.

"What is a compulsion, and why are you now free of it?" King Ennentine asked, ignoring Sir Cadwel as the knight interrupted Parrentine's frantic pacing by all but carrying the prince to the couch and sitting him next to Siara.

Not looking at him, Siara took Parrentine's hand in hers and stroked it soothingly. He leaned back against the leather, looking spent. Sir Cadwel sat down opposite them. Ari stayed by the door, unsure in the king's study if he ought to sit or should stand behind his master.

"It's a suggestion, your majesty," Siara said. "A magical suggestion put into a person's mind."

"Princess." The king frowned. "If I may be so tactless, it was you who found my son the book that sent him to Wheylia, and your wise women who bid him seek out Lord Ferringul."

"My grandmother warned him not to do as the wise women said," Siara said, raising her chin defiantly. "And I asked him not to follow the book," she added more softly.

"But you gave him the book," the king said, watching her intently. Siara opened her mouth and shut it again. She looked to Ari for help.

"Siara has a compulsion on her!" Ari exclaimed, recalling he wasn't the only one who couldn't talk about Lord Ferringul. He hadn't thought to wonder why the Wheylian girl would be likewise affected. "She knows something about Lord Ferringul, and he made it so she can't tell us."

"Is this true, child?" Sir Cadwel asked, leaning toward her. Siara nodded. "But you cannot tell us what you know?"

Siara shook her head, biting her lower lip until Ari was worried she would draw blood.

"He came to the nunnery?" Sir Cadwel asked after a few moments' thought. She nodded again. "He put the book there?"

A third time, Siara nodded, letting out a long breath. She awarded the knight a grateful smile.

"That's why I tried to take the book back from you." She turned to Parrentine. "Why I hid the maps and begged you not to go."

"I thought it was because you were in love with me," the prince said, his voice tired. Siara looked away, biting her lip again.

"So," the king said, drawing all eyes back to him. "We've established Ferringul put a book in the library for the purpose of getting my son to seek him out."

Parrentine groaned, pulling his hand from Siara's so he could bury his face in his palms. Small sobbing sounds came from underneath his hands. Siara rubbed his back, murmuring soothingly.

"You couldn't have known," Sir Cadwel said. "Besides, there may yet be something to be done. Let us hear Ari's story."

Parrentine nodded, though he didn't lower his hands from his face. The others turned to Ari where he still stood by the door. Ari shifted his feet uneasily.

"Well." He took a deep breath, turning to the king. "Your majesty already heard the part about how Lord Ferringul attacked me in the woods. I think he must have left me for dead, but the glowing being I saved, the Aluien, it came back, or others like it did. I'm not sure." He shrugged, deciding it didn't matter. "They gave me the Orlenia, the light of the earth, which fills the endless void within all Aluiens, giving them eternal life. They didn't know, and I didn't know, that Lord Ferringul's blade was coated with an incurable poison that affects only them."

Ari dared to glance at the others. Siara looked at him with intense concentration. Sir Cadwel's face was impassive. The prince sat with his chin resting in cupped hands, his haggard visage beginning to show hope. Ari turned back to the king.

"For a few days, I was one of them," he said, "but then I began to sicken, and they realized I was poisoned. I was very ill, but I remember them arguing a great deal. Finally, they came to me and told me they would try to save me. There was some sort of a ceremony, where they took the Orlenia from me." He shuddered. "It was the worst pain. Not a physical pain, but a loss. Like when someone you love dies. As if everything that is good in the world has been wrenched from you."

Ari met Parrentine's eyes, and in that moment he understood his prince. Princess Clorra was Parrentine's Orlenia. She was the spark of goodness and light that made his life worth living. Ari forgave his future king. He forgave him his pettiness over the last months, and his willfulness and his madness, and in that look, Ari could see that Parrentine knew he understood.

Ari cleared his throat. "And then they performed a spell." His eyes stayed with the prince. "That spell forced my body, which they said had not died, but had passed beyond death." Ari shrugged, indicating his lack of understanding of this. "Forced it to make new blood and refill with human life."

When he stopped talking there was silence. Parrentine's eyes were bright with hope. Siara looked away from the prince, and Ari couldn't see her expression. Sir Cadwel still considered him impassively.

"And then?" the king asked.

"And then they hid from me my memories and sent me home," Ari said with another shrug.

"Is there any proof of this?" the king asked, his voice betraying his skepticism.

"I've seen one of these Aluiens, and one of the others like Lord Ferringul," Sir Cadwel said. "I've seen and traveled with the Aluien, although to be sure, I didn't know it until recently."

"Larke," Siara said.

"Larke?" the king asked, frowning.

"The man who caused the queen to faint," Siara said. Ari realized the princess must known nothing of the rumors involving the queen and the minstrel. Had she, she would never have brought him up to the king. "She fainted because he looked so exactly like the man she knew twenty-five years ago. That's because he is."

The king looked to Sir Cadwel, who nodded. Drawing a deep breath, Ennentine turned to face the fire, his back to them. The prince began to fidget, eyes darting between his father and the door to the chamber.

"The queen is not unwell?" Sir Cadwel said after a few moments.

"The queen?" Ennentine turned back. "She is quite well." He gave Sir Cadwel a reassuring smile. "I've sent her to visit her sister. It seemed prudent."

Sir Cadwel nodded.

"So, Larkesong has come back to life, following you about the countryside, in the form of a magical, glowing being?" the king reiterated with a slight twist of his lips.

"I'm afraid so, your majesty," Sir Cadwel said.

"Must have annoyed you to no end," Ennentine said.

Sir Cadwel chuckled. "That he did, my friend, that he did," the knight said. "And no doubt he took great pleasure in it."

"Where is he now, then?" the king asked, looking about as if they might produce him.

"He stayed to battle Lord Mrakenson," Sir Cadwel said, all mirth departing. "It was a dire trap. Were it not for Larkesong, we would both be dead. I do not know if he lived, but he bought us our escape."

Ari looked at the floor, his throat tightening. He was at constant war with himself not to worry about where Larke might be, as there was naught to be done about it and many important matters pressed on them. Now worry leapt higher than ever, like a caged animal waiting for its chance. He was made especially nervous by how well Lord Ferringul's compulsion on Siara stayed, knowing the ones Larke had laid on him failed completely.

The prince looked up. "You mean the bard you traveled with?" he asked.

"The same," Sir Cadwel said.

"But I took his horse." The prince scrubbed at his face with both hands. "And I treated him with no great kindness."

"I'm sure he understood, Parrentine," Sir Cadwel said. "And the horse ran away. It was back to him by sundown, I would wager."

"The real questions are, then," King Ennentine said. "What is our course of action, and what in the gods' name do we tell the Hapland ambassador?"

"We have to take Clorra to these Aluiens," Prince Parrentine said, half-rising. "Ari will show me where they are."

To Ari's surprise, the look Parrentine cast him was pleading, not commanding. "I will," Ari said at once.

"We don't know for sure these creatures can help her, or that they will," the king said.

"Father," Parrentine said. "We have to try!"

"We'll take the ambassador with us," Sir Cadwel said. They stared at him. "It's the only way. He must witness anything we do with her. We don't want a war."

"No," said the king. "We do not want a war, assuming I can stave one off after today. We'll do it your way." He walked over to Sir Cadwel, who stood. They clasped hands. "I'll persuade the ambassador. You make provisions for the journey. You're in charge, Cadwel."

They locked eyes for a moment, before letting their hands drop.

"I'm going with you," Siara said.

"No," Sir Cadwel said.

"Yes, I am," she said.

Ari sighed, deciding he better find a place to sit down.

Chapter Sixteen

When they set out three days later, Siara was indeed with them. The Hapland ambassador, Lord Kroost, insisted Princess Clorra be accompanied by the appropriate number of ladies. He also insisted her presence be kept secret, even though Ari told him there was no way to hide her location from Lord Ferringul. The ambassador said, "I'm not giving up a standard tactical advantage because you have a feeling this man can tell where she is." It was Kroost who insisted Siara accompany them, to provide a plausible excuse for the presence of so many ladies.

The king and Sir Cadwel were suspicious of Lord Kroost's request, and once he left the room, they agreed he wanted Siara there simply as a matter of insurance. Ari wasn't exactly sure what they meant by that, but he decided to hide his ignorance. He didn't mind having Siara along, after all, and he hated to think of the pain it would cause her to be away from Parrentine if she was made to remain behind. He hated to think of the pain it caused her to be with Parrentine as well, but that was unchangeable.

They were headed west and then north, for the entrance to the Aluiens' cave was in the base of the Wheylian Mountains, on the border between Wheylia and Lggothland. In fact, their journey would be along the very same path they had taken into the mountains when they'd trailed the prince. Parrentine cursed Lord Ferringul anew when he saw their route and how close he had come to finding those who may truly have been able to help his beloved, had he only known.

Thus, Siara added to their cover in more ways than one. The official reason for their journey became one of diplomacy. Siara was reportedly escorting the ambassador of Hapland to meet her grandmother, the High Priestess of Whey. The Hapland ambassador confessed, in truth, he would prefer not to meet the High Priestess because a country being ruled by a woman was unnatural. Ari saw how Siara's blue eyes flashed when Lord Kroost made that proclamation.

For some reason Ari couldn't understand, being around Siara made him miss Ispiria all the more. Every time he saw Siara looking lovely, his mind filled with images of wild red curls and the memory of his hand running through them . . . and their kiss. He kept finding himself wondering, how would Ispiria have acted then? What would she be doing, were she here? What was she doing now?

Ari sighed, looking out over the small caravan of coaches they road with. Siara was in a coach with two of her ladies. Another held four other ladies for no reason Ari could discern. A third carried the Hapland ambassador and his aide. The fourth had the window curtains sewn shut and contained Princess Clorra, alone and bound. For now, she was silent, as they had sedated her in order to secure her in the carriage as quietly and unobtrusively as possible.

There were ten guards, five from Lggothland and five from Hapland. They took turns driving the coaches or riding. Ari, Sir Cadwel and the prince all rode. The Hapland ambassador offered Parrentine a place in his coach, but the prince declined. He preferred to ride alongside Princess Clorra's coach.

It took Ari only one day to decide traveling by coach was the most ridiculous idea anyone had ever come up with. The gilded and glorified hay wagons were slow and ponderous. The weather cleared with the cold, but the roads were still rutted from the fall rain, and the carriages had to negotiate them carefully. Ari found himself riding ahead, ostensibly to check their route, then waiting on a hilltop while they slowly meandered by, just so he would have to gallop to catch up again. He was pretty sure he could have gotten off his horse and run to Wheylia faster than the carriages were going to get there.

Then there was camping. Each afternoon, they stopped early to set up camp. This involved a veritable town being built each day. A suitable spot had to be chosen, and latrines set up, and campfires. Not just one campfire and one latrine. The soldiers needed their own fire, tents, and latrine, while the nobles needed two sets: one for the ladies and one for the men. Princess Clorra was by far the least trouble of them all, as she remained locked in her carriage, refusing to eat what they brought her. She did have an obnoxious habit of screaming at random moments, but Ari quickly accustomed himself to it.

Ari sat on a hill, watching the coaches wait while the soldiers filled in a deep rut in the road they were afraid might break off wheels, pondering their pace. It took them more or less twenty days to ride ahorse from the capital to the border of Wheylia, and they were hurrying. At the rate the carriages were moving, it would take them almost twice as long, and winter was upon them. So far, the skies were a clear crisp blue, and the cold breeze was inoffensive enough, but that wouldn't last. He rode down to talk to Sir Cadwel.

"My lord," Ari said. Noting the knight's far-off expression, he paused. "Is all well?"

"Aye, lad," Sir Cadwel said with a half smile. "I was just thinking on how much that cock's tail of a minstrel would be annoying me right now, were he here."

They looked down in silence.

"I hate leaving a companion behind," the knight said after a moment. "Never knowing what became of him."

"We'll find out," Ari promised impulsively. "When we're done with this, we'll find out."

Sir Cadwel gave him another small smile but offered no opinion. "You wanted to speak to me?"

"It's just, I was thinking about our pace and how far we have to go," Ari said. Sir Cadwel nodded at him.

"I know," the knight said. "We'll speak with Kroost about it tonight."

Sir Cadwel turned his eyes forward again, but Ari knew it was not the road in front of him he saw. They rode side by side, both absently patting their destriers on the neck.

***

"Kroost, we have to talk," Sir Cadwel said, entering the ambassador's tent.

"What about, sir knight?" The stocky man looked up from his camp table where his dinner was set. His aide hovered nearby.

"Our pace," Sir Cadwel said.

He and Ari had already supped. They stood near the entrance of the tent, a house-sized structure. Ari wasn't sure why the giant tents were necessary. They could eat by the fire. All one needed a tent for was sleeping, assuming one needed a tent at all.

"We've been making excellent time," the ambassador said.

"Yes, excellent time for a bunch of one-legged octogenarians on a picnic." Sir Cadwel said so affably it took the ambassador a moment to realize what was said.

"I beg your pardon, sir?" Lord Kroost set down his dinner utensils.

"My lord," the knight said. "If we maintain this pace, we won't reach our destination until the winter solstice, and even if the snows hold off long enough for us to get there, we'll never manage to get back."

"I understand that, sir." Kroost pushed thick, gray hair back from his forehead. "But there's no help for it."

"No help?" Sir Cadwel cast a look over his shoulder at Ari, rolling his eyes heavenward. "There is plenty of help."

"What do you suggest we do?" the ambassador asked. "This is the speed at which coaches travel."

"What I suggest is we rid ourselves of the coaches, my lord," Sir Cadwel said.

"Unthinkable." Lord Kroost shook his head vigorously, as if by the gesture he could better convince them of the solidity of his stance. "What would we do with the princess? Where would we get horses for all of the ladies to ride?"

"My lord?" a soft voice spoke from outside the tent. Ari and Sir Cadwel stepped aside, revealing one of Princess Clorra's ladies.

"Yes?" Kroost asked, favoring Ari and Sir Cadwel with a slight scowl. "Come in, girl."

"Lady Arline, my lord," the girl said with a curtsy, entering the tent.

"Yes, yes, I know, Arline." The ambassador's scowl deepened. "I just couldn't see who it was in the dark. What is it you require?"

"It's about the princess, my lord," the girl said, her eyes darting toward the two men standing in the tent and back to the ambassador.

"They can hear," Kroost said, leaning back in his chair.

"She grows weak quickly, my lord," the girl said. "She'll eat nothing we bring her. She's even given up trying to bite us. I think she does not have the strength left."

"She is not getting flesh, and that's the end of it," Kroost said, absently scowling down at the rabbit on his plate. "She'll have only vegetables and grain."

The girl opened her mouth to speak again.

"That is final," Lord Kroost said.

"Yes, my lord." The girl curtsied and left the tent, her face worried.

“What would we do with the carriages and the women, Cadwel?” the ambassador asked after a moment.

“We have the men escort them back,” the knight said with a shrug. He moved to stand before the table again.

“I beg your pardon, Sir Cadwel.” Kroost peered up from his chair. “But forgive me if I still do not consider this country to be entirely non-hostile. I would prefer to keep my men about me, and not to send my women back alone with your men.”

Ari saw Sir Cadwel’s lips thin in annoyance. “We’re coming soon to a convent, my lord," the knight said. "We could leave the women and the carriages there.”

“And what would we do with the princess?” Kroost said, still scowling.

“She could be bound and cloaked and made to ride with Parrentine,” Sir Cadwel said.

“I’ll not have her traveling unattended with a group of men,” the ambassador said. “If she is ever well again, she will need her reputation intact.”

Ari looked to his mentor for an answer. He knew what Sir Cadwel must have been thinking. What did it matter about the girl’s reputation now? She had more than likely eaten several people. Did the ambassador really think anyone still cared if she was a virgin? Lord Ferringul was sequestered alone with her for days, everything else aside. None of it mattered. Parrentine was obviously willing to marry her despite any of it.

“Princess Siara will accompany us still,” the knight said.

Ari winced. Poor Siara, made to take care of the woman the man she loved was in love with. Could anyone think of a greater torture? Still, she would probably prefer it to being left behind, especially at the convent.

“We’ll have it your way,” the ambassador said, slouching back in his chair with a sigh.

“The encampments have to go as well,” Sir Cadwel said.

“What?” Lord Kroost asked, sitting upright. “Why?”

"We waste hours each day on something that should take us no more time than brushing down a horse," the knight said. "This is no way to travel if you want to get where you're going."

"Fine, fine," Kroost said. He put his elbows on the table, chin in his hands, looking down at his elaborate dinner. He sighed. "Fine. Never let it be said I did not do all there was to do toward the success of this venture."

"We would never say that, my lord," Sir Cadwel said. He turned and strode from the tent with Ari behind him.

***

Traveling with the carriages, it took ten more days to reach the convent. Sir Cadwel and Ambassador Kroost rode down to make the arrangements while the others set up camp. Ari was relieved this would be the last evening they would have to stop with three hours of daylight remaining. He hoped Siara hadn't grown too accustomed to the lavish encampments. He wondered if Ispiria enjoyed camping. Remembering how wild she was after the fight in the bay, she seemed like she would.

When Sir Cadwel and the ambassador returned, they were accompanied by two nuns. All four walked, each man leading his horse. Ari recognized the Mother Superior at once. The other he hadn't seen before.

"This way, Mother," Lord Kroost said, leading the two dark-robed women toward Princess Clorra's tent.

"Siara?" the cantankerous woman exclaimed, catching sight of Siara where she and the other women stood in front of their pavilion, warming themselves by the fire.

"Mother Superior," Siara said.

"Siara, what are you doing with these people? You will come with me this instant," the Mother said. Around the encampment, people stopped what they were doing to watch.

"Mother Superior," Sir Cadwel said. "I forgot you are acquainted with Princess Siara, who accompanies us by order of the king."

The Mother Superior glared at Siara. "Your father has been very worried, your highness," the woman managed eventually, her voice thin with suppressed anger.

"Then you have my permission to write to him and inform him I am now under the care of my grandmother," Siara said, her face impassive. She gave the Mother Superior a slight nod. Turning back to the fire, she dismissed the woman.

"If you would come this way, Mother," Ambassador Kroost said. With a parting scowl at Siara, the woman allowed herself to be led away.

A moment later, she and her assistant came storming back out of Princess Clorra's tent.

"There is no help for that creature," the Mother Superior said. "You would do well to cut off her head and burn the lot of her."

Parrentine put his hand on his sword hilt. Ari wended his way toward the prince, worried he might need to be restrained.

"It's well you have brought these women here," the Mother Superior said as she and her companion hurried from the camp. "They'll need to be cleansed after being in the presence of that thing!"

The last was delivered in a ringing voice, one hand raised in the air, as the two nuns fled toward the convent. They never turned to look back, even when they reached the thick wooden door. The Hapland ambassador sighed, taking refuge in his tent. Parrentine didn't relax until the convent door closed behind them. Ari returned to the fire he and Sir Cadwel shared, wishing Larke was there to do the cooking.

***

In the morning, the ladies, the carriages, and all of the pavilions save one were delivered into the hands of the nuns. At first, Ari felt sorry for the ladies, abandoning them to the care of the Mother Superior, but he garnered from their chatter that they were happy to be done with travel and away from the princess. They seemed to feel travel was no occupation for women, especially of noble birth.

Ari had never heard Siara say anything to that effect, but then, she was different from other girls. Certainly she showed no hesitation at continuing on with them, riding a horse of her own this time.

"Come on, men," Ambassador Kroost called, mounting his newly requisitioned horse with practiced ease. "We'll want to make good time today."

"Yes, General," one of the older soldiers said.

"General?" Sir Cadwel asked, maneuvering Goldwin nearer Kroost.

"How do you think a man like me gains enough favor with his king to be an ambassador, Cadwel?" Kroost said with a slight smile.

"So why all the fuss about tents and carriages?"

"Do you know how many years it took me to earn those tents and carriages?" Kroost said. They both chuckled, turning their horses to lead the men out.

Ari found he liked Kroost much better as a general than an ambassador. Once out of the stuffy air of his carriage, the man opened up. He and Sir Cadwel rode side by side, exchanging war stories, and Ari found himself and Parrentine riding behind, listening. Ari looked over at the prince, where he held his precious cloak-wrapped bundle in front of him, and saw in Parrentine's eyes the same wistful look that must be in his own. What would it have been like to live in times when the world needed heroes?

Parrentine caught Ari's look and smiled. The prince seemed more aware of the world than the last time they had traveled together. Ari found himself wondering what Parrentine was like before his princess had fallen ill. Certainly, the prince appeared happier riding with his arms around his beloved. Clorra was biddable, her will seemingly drained from her, but Ari sensed a manic strength lurking in her docile form.

Kroost's aide, on the other hand, did not adapt well to riding. A court-bred noble's son, he'd never spent much time ahorse, barring the occasional fox hunt, and he wasn't making a good show of it.

By the time the day was through, the whole camp resounded with his moans and complaints. Apparently, Kroost's aide actually did think one could die of pain, and that he would.

Two days later, they left him in a small cluster of houses, barely a town, with two guards. A bit of the old animosity sprang up between Sir Cadwel and Lord Kroost at the negotiation of it, but it was eventually decided to leave him with one soldier from each country. How they were going to get the whining young man back to the capital, Ari didn't know, but he didn't envy the two men who drew the short straws.

Chapter Seventeen

Despite their lighter style of travel, it was snowing by the time they reached the foothills of Whey. There they set up a true encampment as the men were staying behind with the horses while the rest of them climbed the steep trail Ari recalled on foot. It took a lot of effort and checked anger on the parts of Ari and Sir Cadwel to arrange to leave the soldiers behind, but Ari insisted the more people who went up into the hills, the less likely it was the Aluiens would aid them.

As he set out to locate the path, Ari realized he could only remember when he left the lair of the Aluiens, not when he arrived. Eventually, he ended up walking along the edge of the foothills, his back to the mountains, searching for the view that greeted him on his descent. Kroost watched impatiently.

"The lad will find it," Sir Cadwel said.

"You have great faith in him," Kroost said.

"Not unfounded."

Kroost grunted noncommittally, folding his arms across his chest.

Ari did find the thin and worn trail, but not until almost dark. While he knew he would be able to climb it in any light, he realized the others could not. Even with his guidance, the way was too steep if you couldn't see, so they settled in for the night, Kroost setting extra guards in spite of Ari's assurances.

***

That night, the Lady called to Ari. He was not at first sure what had awakened him, but then he heard her voice, a voice that didn't so much compel him to obedience as fill him with the desire not to disappoint. He rose, crawling out of the small tent he used to share with Peine, and followed her voice out of the camp.

Moving almost as a sleepwalker, he slipped between the guards, finding himself shortly at the base of the trail. Quietly, he ascended, taking extra care not to dislodge small stones that might tumble down and make noise below. He rounded a curve to a flatter place, with rocks about it to serve as benches. Not the top, to be sure, but a resting point.

She stood small and erect in the center of the stone platform. The soft, moonlike glow of the Aluiens illuminated her delicate features. Gray hair rested in a bun atop her head, and keen dark eyes regarded him seriously. He felt as if he had known that face all of his life.

"Ari." The Lady smiled. "My Aridian, the Thrice-Born. Who would have dreamed?"

"I don't understand what that means," Ari said.

"It means you have no fate," she said, still smiling. "Each of us, Aluiens and Empty Ones, can look in the eyes of a man and fathom the ever-churning ripples of his fate. We can see when and how he may die and, more importantly to the dark ones, if a man may kill us."

"So they don't know I won't kill them?" Ari asked slowly, fitting the pieces together in his head. The Lady nodded.

"And this fills the Empty Ones with fear. They know not what you may do, nor what they may do to stay you," she said.

"But how could I kill them?" he said. "I can barely move or speak when Lord Ferringul is around."

"You are stronger than you know," she said, "but that is not why I have asked you here."

Ari almost pointed out he had not been asked so much as ordered up the mountain, but he didn't want to interrupt her.

"You should not have brought these men here, Aridian," she said. "It is not our way to be known to the world of men."

"They need your help," he said.

"Men always need help," the Lady said. "We are not enough to help them all. They must learn to help themselves."

"At least let us present our case to the council," Ari said.

"It is not within my power to stop you," the Lady said, her voice sad.

"Yes," Ari said. "It is. You know it is." He looked down at the ground, feeling oddly embarrassed by the admission. Did she not know he couldn't refuse her? There was no way to deny the Lady.

After a few moments' silence, he looked up, but she was gone.

***

Ari felt groggy the next day, and he found himself wondering if he had really spoken to the Lady or if it was a dream. He shook his head, trying to clear it. He pulled his boots on, noticing how dirt-spattered and scuffed they were. Peine was going to kill him when he saw them.

The journey up the hill was slower than Ari would have liked. He recalled the descent taking but half a day, but he hadn't taken into consideration the strain on the others of going up, or the weather, or carrying Princess Clorra between them. The girl had found new strength. Shedding the listlessness of the past few weeks, she struggled with them fiercely, refusing to walk on her own and fighting when Parrentine tried to carry her. In the end, they constructed a litter, binding her to it, and took turns carrying her between them. At points, this made the steep trail almost impassable, but they silently pressed on. None of the five who climbed the hill with her were willing to give up.

Around midday, they reached one of the level areas similar to the one where Ari had met the Lady the night before. Siara insisted they take a short break, telling them all to drink water and handing around travel bread. She and Ari alone were not drenched in sweat under their winter cloaks. Siara because she didn't take turns carrying an end of the litter, but Ari for other reasons. He tried to act as tired as the other men, not wanting to seem different. They ate in silence, leaning against the rounded rocks about the edge of the clearing.

"She's quiet again," Siara said once she was finished with her bread. She was looking at the blanket-wrapped form bound to the litter.

"Have we come halfway, lad?" Sir Cadwel asked Ari, his gaze on the sky. Ari noticed Lord Kroost also scrutinized the clouds above them.

"I don't think so, sir," Ari said, turning his eyes upward as well. The sky was darker than it ought to be at noon, and the wind was picking up.

"We need to make better time," Kroost said, looking at Sir Cadwel.

"Aye," the knight said. "We didn't come here to die on the side of this mountain."

"I could carry her," Ari said.

He'd pondering offering. He knew he was strong enough. Since they'd lost Larke in the Northlands, Ari was acutely aware he was different in small ways. He wished the bard were there to talk to about it. He knew Sir Cadwel knew, but they didn't speak of it.

"If anyone is going to carry her, it will be me," Parrentine said, straightening from where he leaned against a rock and thrusting his shoulders back.

Ari looked at the prince speculatively. Sir Cadwel opened his mouth, but Ari cast the knight a quick look and shook his head. Ari crossed to Parrentine, turning him aside so they could talk with more privacy.

“Your highness,” he said, then paused, meeting the prince’s gaze before continuing. “Parrentine, you aren’t strong enough. You’ve been fasting and not sleeping. You’ve been so unhappy for so many months. I don’t know how you manage to go on walking. I don’t know how you managed to make this trip or the last one. Let me carry her. I swear to you, my prince, I will let no harm come to her while she is in my care.”

Ari dropped to one knee, unsheathing his sword and handing it hilt first to his liege. He didn’t look up, keeping his head bowed, but he hoped fervently Parrentine would agree instead of throwing a fit as he would have the last time they’d traveled together. Not just because they needed to get up the mountain before dark, but for their future together. He knew, or at least he hoped, Parrentine had once been everything a prince and king should be. His people loved him. He was reputed as noble and fair and good. Ari needed him to be all of those things. Ari wanted more than anything in life to be the next king’s champion, and he needed a man to serve who gave the position honor.

Parrentine took the sword from Ari’s hand, reversing it to offer it back. “Arise, Lord Aridian of Sorga,” the prince said quietly.

Ari stood, feeling awkward over his display. His hand met Parrentine’s on the proffered hilt, but the prince held onto it for a moment, looking down at the sword.

“Please, Ari, will you carry her for me?” Parrentine asked quietly. He met Ari’s eyes briefly, and Ari saw the pain there, the anguish. He knew the others were all staring at them. He took his sword and sheathed it.

“It is both my duty and my honor, your highness,” Ari said, giving Parrentine a reassuring smile.

“We really have to get you a better sword,” the prince said as they rejoined the others. “You certainly can’t keep carrying around that old thing. It looks like you found it lying around the castle armory.”

“I just may have,” Ari said with a laugh.

They removed Princess Clorra from her litter, binding her hand and foot. Ari swung her easily into his arms, trying not to look down at the muffled face. She acted as if she was sleeping now, but he didn't trust her. He was glad he was wearing a mail shirt.

Heading up the trail, they sought the Aluiens.

***

By mid-afternoon, it was snowing again. At first, it was a few flakes spiraling about them in the wind, but soon, it developed into a blizzard. The sky went nearly dark as night, and drifts of snow seemed to materialize before them.

"We're close," Ari called back to the others where they struggled behind him. Parrentine leaned on Sir Cadwel for support. In the rear, Siara gave a little cry as she slipped, falling into the snow along the trail. Lord Kroost wordlessly went back and picked her up. Tired as she was, she didn't even protest.

As the last of the feeble daylight left the sky, Ari found the cave he sought, leading them inside out of the wind. It was a large cave, oddly round, but dark and empty. As they stood shivering near the entrance, Ari realized they had brought very little food or water and nothing with which to build a fire. It must have occurred to the others as well.

"I thought you said we weren't here to die in these mountains, Cadwel," Kroost said, looking around the empty cave. He set Siara down.

"Ari?" the knight said. "Where from here, lad? There're enough stray branches in here to give us a bit of heat, but probably not to last the night." As he spoke, Sir Cadwel moved to gather the meager collection of wind-tossed branches scattered about the cave.

"They're here," Ari said, moving to the back of the cave. He still carried Princess Clorra, not daring to set her down. He knew she was awake now. "We just have to get them to show themselves."

"How do we do that?" Parrentine asked, following Ari.

"They'll never let you in with me," the form in his arms hissed.

"They will," he said firmly.

"I can see why he fears you," Clorra said, her voice betraying trepidation. "There is nothing in your eyes. Nothing but danger."

Ari didn't answer, finding it odd this creature in his arms feared looking him in the eye as much as he feared meeting her gaze. The emptiness in her eyes made him queasy. Last time he'd looked into them, he'd almost dropped her.

"Do you know," she said softly. "I've never before in my life been out in the snow? It was never allowed for a single flake to fall unhindered to perish on my skin. I've never swum in the ocean or ridden a horse before this journey. I have never fallen in love."

Now he did look at her, but her eyes were far away. He realized for a moment, he was seeing the girl she was, before Lord Ferringul did this to her, before she became ill. Or maybe she was never this girl either, who wondered why she was not allowed to do the things other girls were allowed to do. If Clorra knew about Siara's anonymous upbringing in the convent, would she envy it? Certainly she would idolize Ispiria's unfettered life.

Their eyes met, and he was forced to look away. Her voice may have been soft, but when she looked on him, it was with a desperate hunger, and he could see her gaze travel down his face to where his lifeblood beat along his neck. He suppressed a shudder.

"But now I can do all those things and more," she purred, snuggling against him. "Now I am free. Free of them all!"

She gave a lurch, twisting in his grasp, trying to break free. Ari squeezed her against him, holding her tight to his chest. He knew she was strong, much stronger than a girl should be, but she was also melancholy. Soon, she gave up, shutting her eyes again in feigned sleep. After a moment, Ari went back to scrutinizing the wall in front of him.

He gazed at the stone intently. He wasn't sure what he was looking for, but he knew there had to be something. From behind him, a glow filled the cave as Sir Cadwel managed to start a fire. Ari realized that beside him, Parrentine was shivering.

"You should go get warm, your highness," Ari said, turning to the prince.

"I suppose you're correct," Parrentine admitted ruefully, but Ari wasn't really listening.

When he turned to look at the prince, he saw something on the wall, but when he turned back, it was gone. Experimentally, he turned his head to the side. Out of the corner of his eye, he could see glowing script flowing across the rock. He turned to face it once more, and it disappeared. He squinted at the wall.

There! When his vision was slightly blurred, he could see it. He scrunched up his face. Yes, the glowing runes were in a circle, and in the center of the circle . . .

He reached out and placed his hand on the glowing ring in the center of the circle. The runes shimmered outward, seeming to draw back the wall as they went. He heard Siara gasp. There, before them, was the lair of the Aluiens.

Chapter Eighteen

The glowing beings stood in a semi-circle beyond the wall, filling a vast cavern, its vaulted ceiling craning away above them, reaching even beyond their light. The Aluiens had obviously been waiting. Ari's eyes swept over them, familiarity washing through him. Some were tall, and some were not. Some were thin, but some were not. They seemed to be of a vast assortment of colorings and builds, men and women. Yet they were united by the pale glow of the Orlenia, and by the universal looks of disquiet marring their usually placid faces.

"Who are you who come before the Aluiens?" the head of the council intoned, stepping forward. His visage wore no greater age than the rest, but about his features, there was a fae-like quality that distinguished him.

"It is I, Aridian, Thrice-Born, and once of your number," Ari said, although surely they must have known who he was.

"Why have you returned here, from whence you were sent forth?" the elder asked, his voice still pulsing with a singsong lilt.

"We seek the aid of the Aluiens," Ari said, not sure how much he was supposed to elaborate during this formal exchange. There was a soft murmuring, and he who gave voice to the council tilted his head, listening to their will.

"You, Aridian, are known to us," the Aluien said. "You may state your case to the council."

"This girl has been taken by the darkness." He held up his burden before him. He was aware his companions arrayed themselves behind him. "When I was ill, you took the light from me." His throat caught as he remembered the pain of having the Orlenia dragged from him. He was forced to clear it before he could continue. "I wish you to take the darkness from this girl and restore her mortal life, as you did me." He was relieved Clorra chose this moment to be silent, perhaps spent for a time by her recent attempt to escape him.

The murmur that rose from the council was much louder this time. Ari could almost sort out individual voices. He looked around for the Lady.

"Even could it be done, why should we do this thing?" the elder asked, holding up his hand to silence the council.

"Because you can," Ari said. "You can right this wrong. We mortals have no way to fight this evil. We cannot conquer it on our own."

"You shall know our will before the mid of night," the elder said, starting to step back into the crowd of Aluiens.

"Wait!" Parrentine came forward. "Please, she is both heart and soul to me. You must help her. I am the crown prince of Lggothland. I offer you anything in my power to give."

The Aluien nodded, but did not speak again. He stepped back. The runes reappeared at the edges of the opening, sparkling across the space as they slid toward the center. The wall reformed behind them.

With a shrug, Sir Cadwel went back to sit by the fire. The others followed, except Lord Kroost, who stood squinting at the wall. Gingerly, he reached out a thick finger to poke it, then lay his hand on it, pushing. “I wouldn’t believe it had I not seen it,” he muttered. “Still don’t believe it!”

“What’s that, Kroost?” Sir Cadwel asked, a slight smile on his face.

“I’ll admit it to you, Cadwel,” Kroost said, coming back to sit by the fire. He craned his neck to look over his shoulder at the wall. “My physicians and I thought this was all a pile of steaming bull patties. Only brought the girl because they convinced me we were out of reasonable options.”

“And what do you think now, Lord Kroost?” Siara asked, her tone sharp.

“Now I don’t know what to think, princess,” Kroost said. “No, not what to think at all. I’ll never be able to explain this to his majesty.” He sighed, staring into their fire.

***

“We must speak with you.”

The companions looked around, a bit startled to see an Aluien standing by their small fire. The glowing being didn’t wait for an answer, but turned and moved to the back of the cave. He touched the wall, and the stone parted. Gesturing for them to follow, he entered the realm of the Aluiens.

They stood slowly, their bodies stiff. Ari lifted Clorra from the floor beside him, where she lay awkwardly with her limbs bound before her. Lord Kroost stretched. He'd been snoring lightly, his head resting on his chest where he sat, but he awoke immediately when the Aluien spoke.

Ari held Princess Clorra tightly in his arms. He thought she truly did sleep now, exhaustion taking its toll on her, but he remained vigilant to her tricks. They followed the Aluien cautiously through the space where the wall had once been.

The home of the Aluiens was a great system of caves. They seemed to favor light, for even though each gave off his own glow, there were strings of light everywhere. They formed patterns on the ceiling and walls, decorating and illuminating. The large chambers were made even more lovely by veins of quartz running through them, capturing and reflecting the light. And everywhere there were Aluiens. Mostly, they read or sat in small groups, talking. Many looked up at Ari as they passed, and he felt he should know them.

Smaller passageways sprawled forth from the vast communal chamber, and it was to one of these their Aluien guide led them. They traveled down a well-lit corridor, doorless rooms branching off on both sides. In those rooms were often Aluiens, the wonders of the world at their fingertips as they worked on inventions and ideas.

They were led to another massive chamber, a library. Ari couldn't fathom the size of it. The shelves seemed to move away from him into eternity. Their guide led them along the right wall to a small, round cave carved into the side of the larger gallery. Here, there was but a single book standing on a pedestal in the center of the room.

"We, the Aluiens, do feel responsible for the fate of this girl," their guild said, his voice musical. "I wish to read to you from the Book of Ages. No mortal has before heard its words."

He stood in front of the book and watched them, perhaps weighing their response to his words. He was thin, but not tall, and he wore the loose, flowing pants and knee-length tunic of the Aluiens. As with all of his race, it was hard to fully ascertain his features, for the white glow of the Orlenia emanated from him. When he did not continue, they looked around at each other, not sure what answer he expected to end his silent scrutiny of them.

"We would be honored, sir," the prince said for the rest of them.

The Aluien nodded, lowering his head to the book. "From The Curse of Tal Mraken," the glowing being intoned. "On a night now burned in history, there was in a clearing an Aluien transporting one he marked beyond life. Into this sacred act came a man ahorse, his throat full of jubilant cries and his hand wielding a cruel weapon of iron. So sudden was his intrusion that he struck down our brother before action could move from thought to fruition, and left both Aluien and his marked charge for dead. Thus, for the first time, the ritual went uncompleted.

"The marked one was brought past life, yet his body was never infused with the light of the Orlenia. He was left an empty vessel.

"Thus, a creature was created who was trapped between two worlds. No longer human, yet not Aluien. As the moon traveled to its nightly pinnacle, this new being arose, driven nearly mad by the emptiness of his form. Having never partaken of the beauty of the Orlenia, he knew no other way than to fill his boundless cravings with the blood and flesh of living things.

"Thus was born the Empty Ones."

The Aluien fell silent. The companions stood in a semicircle around the glowing being, whose head remained bowed. Ari saw Parrentine look at Princess Clorra and clench his fists.

"How could you let this creature live?" the prince sputtered.

"For many years, we did not realize the full extent of this evil. We thought, like us, he would wither and die without the renewal of the Orlenia." The Aluien raised his head, his iridescent eyes meeting the prince's blue ones. "And we do not interfere in the actions of men."

"Actions of men?" Parrentine said, incredulous.

"It was the action of a man that created the Empty One," the Aluien said, unperturbed by the prince's anger.

"Surely," Siara said, stepping between Parrentine and the Aluien, "both men and Aluiens are responsible."

"Many have come to think as you do, princess," the Aluien said. "Many feel we should have put an end to the Empty Ones while they were still few, despite the role humans took in their creation, but others saw the self-destructive nature of the creatures and felt we need not intervene. Most of the creatures go mad with the endless striving against their emptiness and simply perish.

Only those few strong enough to channel their insatiability into other realms survive."

"Other realms?" Sir Cadwel said.

"Flesh and blood do not sustain them any more than other victuals," the Aluien said. "The craving simply reveals their base nature. Others strive to fill the void within with power, or lust, or any number of human vices, but always, it is insatiable."

Siara placed a restraining hand on the prince's arm.

"So you will help us?" Ari said. He wasn't sure what he would do if the Aluiens said no. They'd come here on his word. He'd promised the king and Parrentine the Aluiens would be able to aid them.

"So we will help you," the Aluien said. "But you must gain some understanding before."

"What do we need to understand?" Lord Kroost asked, his narrowed eyes betraying his distrust.

"What you ask of us has never before been done," the Aluien said. "With young Aridian, we removed the Orlenia and returned to him his mortal life, but this girl has never tasted of the Orlenia, nor will we force it to her, her soul being so blackened, the wellspring will not tolerate her. We will attempt to cleanse her and restore her mortality, letting her own life once more well up within her mortal form, but we cannot know what will come of it."

"I see." The ambassador scowled at the glowing creature. Ari was relatively sure Kroost had no idea what the Aluien meant.

"Is there anything else we need to know before we decide?" Sir Cadwel asked, his tone carefully respectful.

"Nothing more needs to be understood," the Aluien said.

"May we go apart to discuss this?" Sir Cadwel asked, looking at the strained faces around him.

"To be alone?" the Aluien said, receiving a nod in reply. "I will show a place to you."

The glowing being walked past them and back through the library. He led them to the large central chamber once more and down another side passage. This one had doors. At one of these, he stopped, opening it to reveal a small room with a round table in the center surrounded by chairs, low couches along the walls.

"You would eat?" the Aluien asked, standing aside to let them into the room.

"I would sleep," Kroost muttered.

"Yes, we would like to eat," Sir Cadwel answered for them.

The Aluien nodded, leaving the room and closing the door behind him. Siara steered an angry Parrentine into a chair. The others seated themselves as well, Ari placing Princess Clorra upright in the heavy wooden chair between himself and the prince, as unobtrusively as possible tying her to it. She hung her head listlessly.

Before they were settled, their guide reappeared with a basket that he silently left on the table. They peeled back the covering cloth with a certain amount of wariness, unsure what the glowing ones might consider to be food. Inside was a veritable picnic. There was fruit, fresh apples and plums, which Ari began to eat immediately, but which Sir Cadwel looked on with a great suspicion that confused Ari until he recalled the snow outside. Under the fruit, they found an incredibly sharp cheese, along with white bread that was crisp on the outside and soft in the middle. There were also two bottles. One contained pure, clear water and the other wine. The wine was a deep and dark red. Confronted with food, Ari realized how hungry he was.

Parrentine poured some water for Clorra, holding it lightly to her lips, but she turned her head away, her gaze flickering with sullen anger. He tried again with fruit, and she took it only to spit it at him, the look on her face an odd mixture of triumph and despondency.

"Clorra," Parrentine pleaded in a low voice, "you must take water at the least. You shall parish from thirst."

"Thirst," she whispered, and Ari fought back the urge to lean closer to hear her, as Parrentine did. "I do thirst. I thirst for your blood!"

With inhuman speed, her head darted at Parrentine. Blood spurted from Parrentine's ear even as Ari reached across to shove the prince away from her. Parrentine let out a startled exclamation, his hand going to his head to stem the bright red flow. Siara jumped from her chair, moving to his side to examine the wound and staunch it with a square of lace-trimmed fabric.

"Clorra!" Parrentine beseeched, ignoring Siara but not hindering her.

"Salty and warm," Princess Clorra purred, her eyes narrowing in triumph. She ran her tongue slowly across her bloodied lips.

Parrentine drew in a ragged, sobbing breath and turned away from her. Siara retrieved some water and set about cleaning his face, her body between the prince and his fiancée. Ari stood and lifted Clorra, chair and all, setting her against the wall behind them. She glared at him, her face sullen once more, but he ignored her. Kroost handed the prince a glass of wine.

"This red is by far the best I've ever tasted," Kroost said, coughing and looking anywhere but at Clorra.

Only he and Parrentine drank any wine. Sir Cadwel would take only bread, water, and cheese, still looking distrustfully at the fruit, even when Siara offered him delicate slices.

"I have to concur with you on the wine," the prince said after a time, his voice forcedly light. "It's higher praise from you, of course, as you are a renowned expert on such matters."

"I wonder if they would consider exporting it," the ambassador said.

Ari winced inwardly.

Sir Cadwel cleared his throat. "So are we all agreed?" the knight asked.

"That depends on what you think we're doing, I suppose," Kroost said.

"I think we're going through with it," Sir Cadwel said, looking around the table. "That's why we came here."

"But when we came here, we didn't know it might not work." Parrentine leaned forward. "Or that they couldn't even tell us what will happen."

"We cannot leave her how she is, Parrentine," Siara said, looking sadly at the cloak-wrapped form tied in the chair behind Ari.

"But are we sure we've exhausted all other possibilities?" Kroost asked, sipping his wine.

"I'm sure," Parrentine said, slouching back in his chair. Ari was reminded of the many months the prince had already spent searching for a cure. Parrentine pushed his plate of food away.

"I don't see that we have a choice," Sir Cadwel said. "But I leave it up to her fiancé and her father's representative."

Parrentine and Ambassador Kroost locked eyes for a moment. Kroost sighed, and both men looked away. The prince gazed at the bundle in the chair, while the ambassador looked at nothing, his eyes and thoughts far away.

"Her father would want us to try," Kroost finally said.

"I want us to try," Parrentine said. "We can't give up."

They all went silent. Ari thought about what it would mean to give up. Would they lock her away until she died? She was slowly dying before any of this began, so in the end, her fate would be no different. Ari thought it would be kinder just to kill her if they didn't try, but he didn't say so aloud. He wondered how many others at the table were thinking the same thing.

The door opened, their Aluien guide standing without.

***

The room where the ceremony was to take place appeared to be a perfect circle. Glowing designs decorated the floor and ceiling, and although drawn onto the rock itself, they seemed somehow to move and undulate, giving Ari the odd sensation the room was spinning. In the center was a stone slab, and to this, they bound

Princess Clorra. Ari and his companions stood against the wall, outside the largest of the glowing circles on the floor. Aluiens entered, robed in white, and arranged themselves to stand inside the different rings. The leader of the council arrived last, moving to stand at Princess Clorra's head. The girl was awake and uncloaked. Her golden hair spilled down the side of the slab to pool on the floor at the council leader's feet. She struggled weakly against the manacles holding her to the stone, hissing at the Aluiens around her.

The Aluiens began to chant, and memories washed over Ari. He'd been on that slab, his body throbbing with the poison speeding through it, filling the sputtering corners of his heart. Glowing faces, pale eyes reflecting his own glow, bent low around him, chanting. Unlike the princess, he had not been bound.

Ari bade himself focused on the present, watching the Aluiens begin to sway, and then to walk. They moved in intricate steps around the slab, chanting. Their delicate, glowing hands wove patterns in the air. Ari remembered it all from within the fever-hazed dream state he'd been in. He remembered the chanting, the swaying, and then . . .

As Ari had when they took the Orlenia from him, Princess Clorra began to scream. Ari grasped Parrentine by the arm. The scream rose, shifting up octaves until it was barely a sound to the human ear, but still it grated on every nerve in Ari's body. He clenched his teeth, one hand firmly restraining his prince from interrupting the ritual.

Beside him, Parrentine gave up struggling, the prince's efforts so feeble in comparison with Ari's strength that Ari barely paid attention to his monarch. The prince fell to his knees, covering his face with his hands. Ari let go of him. On Parrentine's other side, Siara knelt, stroking his hair and murmuring reassuringly.

A darkness coalesced over the writhing girl. Ari recalled it being a light, and he remembered reaching for it, as if he could take it back. The darkness writhed, then seemed almost to dart, trying to dive back down onto the slight form secured to the slab. The Aluiens cried out, bringing their arms forward, hands pointing at the darkness. Without touching it, they seemed to fold it, compress it. One of them brought forth an iron vessel and removed the top. With great effort, the others forced the undulating darkness that came from the princess into the container and secured the lid.

The chanting began anew, and Clorra's passage from consciousness was marked by the blessed absence of her cry. Color blossomed in her pale lips and cheeks. Finally, the girl's eyes opened, and for a moment, Ari could see lucidity stark inside them. Then reason shattered and Clorra's mind seemed to fall from her gaze. Her open eyes stayed empty and fixed on the ceiling.

The Aluiens' arms dropped. The chanting dwindled. Their luminous glows dimmed, the ancient ones helped each other walk from the room, leaving the council leader holding the iron urn. He stood at the head of the table, his face and shoulders bowed.

Two new Aluiens entered, bearing a white linen litter. They gently lifted the staring, sweat-covered girl from the table. She gave no reaction. Ari was amazed at how young she looked, and he realized she couldn't be much older than he was. Parrentine, after all, was only six years his senior.

Ari looked at the prince. Parrentine stood, having struggled to his feet with Siara's aid. The remnants of tears streaked his face. Siara held onto his arm.

"Where are they taking her?" Parrentine asked, his voice coming out in a broken whisper.

"You may follow," the Aluien at the head of the table replied, lifting his face. He looked very tired and very old. "I must dispose of this." He nodded to the rune-covered urn he still held.

"What was that darkness?" Lord Kroost asked, his own voice a bit ragged. "It–" The retired general shuddered. "It looked as if it was trying to get back in."

"The foul stain which clung to her soul," the Aluien said. Looking at their worried faces, he elaborated. "When the flesh dies, the soul returns to the wellspring of life, the Orlenia, deep within the earth. It is from that spring all life is sparked, be it a flower, a bird, or a child. Of all creatures, man has been granted the most freedom in what he does. Given that freedom, he often chooses to do wrong. When the spark of life leaves the mortal body to return to the wellspring, it sheds all evils. All wrongdoings are left behind in the mortal shell. It must be so, or the wellspring would become contaminated with the sins of mortal things, and thus would be the very earth.

"If the evil ones seek to fill the empty void within them by supping of flesh and blood, they are partaking of the deeds done. The infractions, the lies, the thefts or murders, they all reside in the flesh and thus enter the body of the Empty Ones. This is why they become increasingly bitter and foul with time. Man does not know of this but in some ways senses it. This is why the eating of each other is so instinctively taboo. Those who sense it most strongly, the holiest of your people, often forgo flesh, for even many animals have enough freedom to engage in acts of violence or anger."

They stared at him, trying to understand what he said. Siara shuddered.

"You may go to your companion." The glowing being gestured toward the door. "We know not when she will rouse. Our healers attend her."

They looked back and forth between each other, worried expressions on their faces. The old one bowed his head again. At that cue, Ari led the others from the room.

Chapter Nineteen

They headed down the wide corridor, but they were too long in the room and now couldn't find the princess on her litter. As they reached the main chamber of the caves, an Aluien woman approached, about to pass them on some errand of her own. Ari bowed to her, keeping his head low until she addressed him.

"May I be of assistance to you, human?" she asked with a heavy accent which Ari didn't recognize. She had midnight-colored skin, so dark as to be almost blue, especially with the iridescent glow of the Aluiens surrounding it. For the first time, Ari realized there must be more Aluiens in the world, in more places than just here on the border between Lggothland and Wheylia.

"We seek the infirmary, my lady," he said, gesturing to include his companions in the statement.

"You seek the empty child of the ceremony this day," she said. "Follow that passage west until you find a path south. This path will take you to the place you wish."

"Thank you, my lady." Ari bowed, but she had already turned with a distracted smile and started on her way. Ari looked after her white-clad form. She walked with such grace as to seem to float down the hall.

"She has the most beautiful skin I have ever seen," Siara said, envy clear in her voice.

"Women," Sir Cadwel muttered to Kroost. "Never satisfied with what they have."

Kroost chuckled, but Siara ignored them. She took Parrentine by the arm and turned him back around, gesturing to Ari to lead the way.

Unlike the castle infirmary, there was no large room full of cots. Instead, there was a hall with small rooms leading from it. Ari looked down the corridor, trying to distinguish if there were any outward signs of the content of the rooms. He could vaguely recall them carrying him to this hallway as he floated in and out of consciousness on a litter, but although there were not many rooms, he didn't know which one they had placed him in.

He started slowly down the corridor, trying to formulate a plan. He didn't want to open doors at random, disturbing any ill Aluiens there might be. Most of the rooms must be empty, though, as he knew Aluiens were rarely unwell.

Halfway down the corridor, he found himself cocking his head to one side. There was something . . . music? And a familiar voice, he realized, coming from inside the room to his left. With a startled cry, he threw open the door.

"Larke!" Ari exclaimed.

There in the bed, covered in white linen, was Larkesong. He looked pale, and his hair, although cut short, still revealed a recent singeing, but he was sitting up in bed, strumming a little song on his lute. He was surrounded by the light of the Orlenia, but his glow was noticeably dimmer than the others'. It was not, however, more diminished than the glow around those who had performed the ceremony on Princess Clorra.

"Ari, me lad! It's about time ye came to visit!" Larke said, looking up. "A fellow might start to think ye didn't care."

“Larkesong?” Sir Cadwel said, his large frame filling the doorway. It was both a question and a greeting.

“Um, Cadwel, old fellow.” Larke gave Sir Cadwel a sheepish look. “I see ye put two and two together and got something approximating four. I would have told you I was myself, really, I would have. Eventually. Don’t be angry?”

“Of course not,” Sir Cadwel said, and to Ari’s surprise, a broad grin split his face. “I’m just glad to see you well. We can put the little misunderstanding you perpetuated about who you are aside, since you more than likely saved my life. Few are the men who have done that twice!”

“Too good of you to understand, too good,” Larke said. He started to smile but winced, and Ari noticed a large bandage on the side of his jaw facing away from them.

“What happened?” Ari asked, coming forward to lean over the bed to see. Larke was covered in bandages. Behind him, Ari was aware of Sir Cadwel entering and the others squeezing into the room.

“I seem to have gotten myself lit on fire, thrown through the air, and hit my head into a wall,” Larke said, wincing at the memory. “I have to say, as far as experiences go, it wouldn’t be one of my favorites.”

“Did you kill him, then?” Ari’s tone dropped to almost a whisper. “That thing in the castle?”

“Nay, lad.” Larke started to shake his head, but apparently thought better of it. “There’s not that much strength in me. Even the Lady could not kill him, not while he be ensconced in his layer, but she gave him quite a sting.”

“Someone will have to kill him someday,” Ari said, squaring his shoulders. Larke raised his good eyebrow, and Ari heard Sir Cadwel chuckle.

“I see without my cultural guidance, ye have turned him into quite the barbarian,” Larke said to the knight.

“Not I, sir, not I,” Sir Cadwel said.

"We have to find Clorra," Parrentine said from where he stood near the door. He turned from the room, looking up and down the hallway.

"Your highness." Larke inclined his head to the prince, who ignored him. Larke spotted Siara beside Parrentine and smiled. "And Siara, lass! Have you come to wish an old man well on his deathbed?"

"You are neither on your deathbed nor old nor, I think, a man," the princess said coldly. "And I do not wish you well."

"Oh!" Larke threw his unbandaged arm across his face. "I am stung! Wounded! Hurt to the core! Now I shall never rally from my awful wounds, never!"

"Why are you so angry with Larke?" Ari asked, rounding on the girl with a scowl.

"He put a compulsion on me not to be able to speak of Ferringul," she said, her voice hard with anger.

"I am wronged, I say," Larke said. Siara glared at him. "My dear girl," he continued. "I have done no such thing. He placed it there himself. My only crime was in not removing it."

"And why did you not?" Parrentine turned back from his scrutiny of the hallway, apparently more aware of the conversation than Ari thought.

"Because, your highness, in this, I am not free." The bard's voice became sad. "I'm bound by the rules of my people."

"I beg your pardon." Lord Kroost cleared his throat. "But may I assume this is the bard of whom you spoke?"

"Pardon the poor manners of an old warrior." Sir Cadwel stepped to the bedside. "Lord Ambassador Kroost of Hapland, this is Larkesong, minstrel renowned."

The stocky man gave Larke a half bow.

"Renowned, is it?" Larke asked Sir Cadwel, but then his face went serious. He turned to the prince. "Prince Parrentine, I know what you have come here to ask of us. I beg you not to."

"Save your machinations. It is already done," Siara said, obviously still angry.

"Then it is done." Larke sighed. Closing his eyes, he leaned back on the pillow.

"Why didn't you and the Lady want us to come here?" Ari asked. He could see Larke was tired, and realized most of the bard's bravado was just that, a simulation of his usual self, but he wanted to know the answer, and Larke was one of the few Aluiens he felt he could ask.

"The Lady has long studied the Empty Ones, me lad," Larke said, his eyes still closed. The others drew nearer to hear. "She has long disagreed with our people's mantra of seclusion and our complete lack of involvement in the world of man, and what troubles her most greatly are the Empty Ones. Most of our people feel getting too close to man is what caused the creation of their evil from the start, and worry any more tampering will only share out more grief."

Ari nodded, not looking at the others. He didn't understand why then the Lady, of all Aluiens, should wish to stop them. Larke opened his blue eyes, pale now with the light of the Orlenia no longer hidden by illusion.

"She has sought a way to fix our wrong," he said. "To unmake the Empty Ones. That is why sometimes she and her followers venture out at night to capture them. We've even forced the Orlenia to them."

"And?" Ari asked, swallowing against the sudden dryness in his throat.

"And a way can not be found, Aridian," a lovely voice said behind him.

They all turned to see the Lady. The light of the Orlenia radiated strongly from her diminutive frame. Kroost, who was nearest the door, stepped back from her, then covered his surprise with a bow.

"My Lady," Larke said with a faint smile. "Forgive me for not bowing."

"I have asked you many times not to," she said, looking at him fondly. "I did not realize it would take you almost dying for me to achieve my wish. Maybe this will teach you a greater amount of cooperation in the future."

Larke answered with a crooked grin, and the Lady sighed.

"My lady." Parrentine bowed. Even in his distraught state, the prince seemed humbled by the presence of the small woman, but his face showed great strain. "Why do you say there is no way? We saw the darkness leave her."

"So it did," the Lady said, her voice musical. She had the lilt of the Wheys, but it was stronger, her vowels even more round than any Wheys Ari knew. "But the body is wrought different, by its time beyond death. It is as when we took the Orlenia from Aridian. He remains different from other mortals, and so shall your princess remain changed."

Ari looked at the floor, not wanting to see the faces of his companions. He heard someone shift further away and guessed it was Kroost. Ari could feel Parrentine's eyes on him. The Lady moved to the bed and gently set aside Larke's lute. The bard seemed to have drifted to sleep.

"What does this mean for the princess?" Lord Kroost asked, a scowl covering his face.

"We cannot know, but I fear for her."

"But how much can she have changed?" Parrentine asked. He wrung his hands together, looking around as if he wanted to pace. "She wasn't under Ferringul's influence for long. Why did he do this to her?"

"I do not know his will," the Lady said.

"So you have only theories," Kroost said, his tone angry. "And all you can do with them is scare us."

The Lady met the ambassador's eyes, holding them until he looked away.

"I need to see her," Parrentine said. He turned and pushed his way out of the room. Scowling at them all, Siara hurried after, Kroost following.

"I'm sorry, my lady," Ari said awkwardly, feeling embarrassed for his companion's behavior.

"People never receive well an unwanted truth, Aridian."

"I know you," Sir Cadwel said suddenly. He'd been staring at the Lady since the moment she appeared.

"Yes," she said, smiling up at him. "Your friends will need you," she added, looking from Ari to the knight. "And my minstrel needs his rest still."

"Yes, ma'am," Sir Cadwel said, turning immediately and heading to the door. He paused in his step for a moment, seeming to realize how effortlessly he was dismissed, but with a shrug, he continued out of the room.

"Get well soon, Larke," Ari said, squeezing the bard's arm in farewell.

"I will, me lad," Larke said, opening one eye and winking. Then he was back to feigning sleep.

Ari left the room.

In the hallway, an Aluien met them and led them to the room where the princess was. She lay on the white sheets, looking very small and pale, surrounded by Aluiens. She slept peacefully. Parrentine knelt by her bed, holding one delicate hand in his own.

***

"Is there nothing to be done?" Parrentine asked for what Ari was sure was the five-hundredth time in the past four days.

It had been seven days since the Aluiens performed the ritual of unmaking on Princess Clorra. For three days, she slept, but on the fourth, she awakened and started to scream.

"There is nothing more to try," the tired Aluien said. His glow was reduced to a dull glimmer after four sleepless days of trying to help the princess. So diminished was it, Ari could see his eyes had been green when he was human.

"Her mind is gone," a female Aluien said. "The strain of all that has happened to her broke it. She could not reconcile the things she did while an Empty One with her mortal self."

In the background, they could hear the screaming. It would start a low, wrenching moan, then rise in volume and pitch until it spread throughout the complex of the Aluiens, seeming to permeate every room.

"We can't leave her like this," Parrentine beseeched them all. "Can't you take the memories from her? Like you did to Ari."

"We have tried this. There is nothing to be done," the male Aluien said. "We have taken all the memories we can. Even if we could keep them from returning, her mind is broken inside. Perhaps if we had more time . . . if we could keep her alive for more time to study the problem . . ."

The Aluien's voice trailed off. He sounded sad and tired. Ari knew they worked diligently with the princess. He could see the toll it took on them. They were wan and drawn, their movements slow, their glow dimmed.

"She's dying?" Parrentine gasped, stepping forward to take the Aluien by the arm. "But you healed her!"

"We did," the Aluien said. "But she does not have the will to be living. All she will do is scream."

"It would be kindest—" The Aluien woman looked about the room at them, gauging them. "If we would end it for her. This is no way to let her die."

Parrentine's hands fell and he bowed his head. Siara put an arm about him, but he pulled away. Kroost sat staring at the wall, a frown of concentration on his face. Ari exchanged a worried glance with Sir Cadwel, who had taken to tugging on his mustache, which was in dire need of a trim, whenever the screams rose to their highest point.

"You may choose to let her die slowly, of course," the Aluien healer said. "It will only take a sevenday more, if not less. If you do, you must take her from here. We will not be a part of such suffering."

"No." Kroost looked up. His voice was firm. "Clorra is under my care. I have made my decision. Her suffering must be ended. Letting her linger in this state is no way to discharge my duty to her welfare."

Parrentine rounded on him angrily. The two men locked gazes until finally the prince looked down. Out of the corner of his eye, Ari saw Sir Cadwel relax, removing his hand from his sword.

"But first, they will be married," Kroost said.

Siara gasped, swaying. Ari took her by the shoulders to make sure she didn't fall. Parrentine's head snapped up.

"Married?" the prince asked in a strangled voice.

"Yes," Kroost said. "The diplomatic function of your union with Princess Clorra still stands. It is the reason behind the marriage. You deciding you love her was always incidental. I wanted to insist on the wedding months ago, ill or no, but you were running about the country like a mad man."

"But—" The prince stared at him in bewilderment. "I'll marry her, and then you'll kill her?"

"You'll marry her, and then you will kill her," Kroost said. "It would be treason for me to kill her. She will be your wife, your property. You will kill her, and I will explain to my king it was a mercy."

Siara's face paled, and she began to tremble. Ari, afraid she would faint, lifted her up, carrying her to a couch and laying her on it. She looked up at him with desperate eyes.

"Cadwel," the prince croaked, turning to the knight.

"Parrentine." Sir Cadwel stepped between the prince and the ambassador. "I've been your father's closest friend for almost forty years. I've watched you grow from a babe. Believe me when I say I would not put you through unneeded pain." Sir Cadwel cleared his throat, locking eyes with the young man who would someday be king. "But I will tell you what I think your father would tell you were he here. Ambassador Kroost is within his rights to ask this marriage of you. This always was a diplomatic union."

Parrentine looked about. He met Kroost's unbending gaze and Sir Cadwel's sympathetic one. He looked behind him at Ari, who shrugged his ignorance. Parrentine didn't look to Siara, whose blue eyes were locked on his face. The Aluien healers carefully avoided showing judgment.

"I have the contracts with me," Kroost said after a moment. "You need only sign. I will sign for Hapland. I think we will forgo the ceremony."

Once again, Parrentine looked about the room for help. The Aluiens stood unmoving, their faces passive. Sir Cadwel patted the prince on the shoulder, stepping away.

"Get the papers." Parrentine's voice cracked as he spoke, and he cleared his throat. "And quill and ink and wax." The prince began to work his signet ring off his right hand as the Aluien left the room.

***

Sir Cadwel insisted on reading over the lengthy contracts, not quite trusting Kroost not to have altered them since their king approved them. The Ambassador watched over his shoulder, scowling. Parrentine paced the small room, looking at the two older men in increasing annoyance as the day wore on. Aluiens brought them food they did not eat and wine they did not drink, except for Kroost, who took a glass of red.

Ari knew the ambassador plagued the Aluiens, trying to get one of them to agree to export the wine to his country. They asked Ari, whom they preferred of the humans to speak with, what they should do, and he advised them to start ignoring the burly man.

At one point during the long afternoon, Parrentine stopped pacing and went to kneel by Siara where she still lay on the couch, her large blue eyes following him.

"Siara." The prince's voice was thick with emotion, although Ari hadn't seen him cry. "If it were you, in that room screaming, would you want to die?"

"Yes," she said softly, holding his gaze. "If it were me, I would want you to give me the dignity of a clean death."

Parrentine held her gaze for a moment, then returned to his pacing. Ari heard Siara sigh. She closed her eyes, tilting her head back against the cushions.

"Ready," Sir Cadwel said. He stood, offering the chair he vacated to Parrentine.

The prince walked slowly to the table but did not sit. He bent over the document, reaching for the quill and ink the Aluiens provided. He signed methodically. Taking up the wax, he warmed it on a candle, smudging it onto the paper and stamping the crest of Lggothland into it. Ari watched the dark smoke rising from the candle where the red sealing wax dripped on the wick. He could faintly smell honey as it burned.

Parrentine stood silently as Ambassador Kroost signed the parchment, placing the seal of Hapland beside his name. Kroost poured five glasses of wine, handing them around. Siara refused hers. They raised them to their lips in silence, no one having a toast to give. The wine smelled of berries and warmth. Ari almost choked on it as he swallowed. Parrentine emptied his glass, setting it on the table with a jarring clank.

"Ari," the prince said, gesturing for Ari to follow him.

Together, they left the room, their purposeful strides seeming to span the distance to Clorra's sickroom with dreamlike slowness, the corridors they walked elongating around them. Yet Ari almost gasped aloud when her door loomed in front of them. Parrentine stopped, hand on his sword hilt, straining to draw each breath. The screams were at their highest now, mimicking the last call of a great bird of prey struck down in flight as it plummeted unhindered through the sky that was once its refuge.

"Make her ready," Parrentine commanded Ari, his face averted.

"What do you mean me to do?" Ari asked, unsure what was called for.

The look Parrentine turned on him made him wish he hadn't spoken. The prince's eyes were bloodshot pools, punctuated by pupils so large, they smothered the blue of his irises, set in a face of chalk and pain.

"Tie her down," Parrentine said, the words forced through unmoving, blue-tinged lips.

Ari fled into the room.

The princess didn't acknowledge him as he gathered the strewn bed sheets from the floor, twisting them into something resembling rope. Ari worked as fast as his shaking hands allowed, wanting to finish while she was still moaning, spent from her last great shriek. He bound her arms to her sides, her legs flat. There were no bedposts, so he wound the sheets around the bed as a whole. Her thrashing was weak and purposeless, the random flailing of a body seeking to escape its own mind, but he didn't want the spasmodic jerking to cause Parrentine to miss his stroke.

Once he secured her, he paused, looking at last into her mad eyes. He sought something, anything. Her mouth opened wide as her screams mounted. Clenching his teeth, Ari opened the door.

"She's ready." He garbled the words, unsure what to say, but Parrentine didn't appear to be listening. He pushed past Ari into the room. Ari backed awkwardly into the corner, hoping the prince would ask him to leave.

"Clorra." Parrentine's voice cracked and he cleared his throat, inhaling deeply through his nostrils. "Clorra, it's me." He stroked her forehead, but her screaming continued, her wide eyes locked on the ceiling. "Clorra." Parrentine bent over her face, placing himself in her sight. "Clorra!" He began to shake her, banging the bed against the floor, for Ari had bound her tightly. The screams undulated, reverberating sharply as he shook her harder and harder. "Clorra!" Tears streamed down Parrentine's face now. Releasing the bed, he slapped her with enough force to draw blood, but she didn't stop screaming. Her gaze never wavered. The prince raised his hand again, his face molten with rage.

"Parrentine." Ari caught his liege's hand in a strong grasp, halting its decent.

Parrentine turned anger-filled eyes on him. Ari kept his grip firm, watching until rage was replaced once more with sorrow. The prince drew a shaky breath. He opened his mouth, but no words came out. Ari released his arm.

Shaking his head, Parrentine turned away. Ari stared at the prince's back, not looking at the bloodied, screaming, white face on the bed. He resisted the urge to put his fingers in his ears, knowing to give in even that much to the mad horror of it all would end with him sobbing on the floor. Instead, he stood unmoving, his every muscle clenched, waiting. At last, Parrentine drew his sword.

The prince flinched as his eyes took in the livid bruise on Clorra's face, the blood trickling from her eye, nose, and mouth. He raised his sword high in both hands, knuckles white on the hilt.

"I love you," Parrentine whispered, and the sword crashed down through Clorra's thin neck and into the hard wood of the bed. The screaming stopped, the silence so sharp, Ari felt his heart skip a beat. Parrentine's hands fell from the hilt as blood soaked the soft pillows. Leaving his blade where it stuck, he quit the room.

Chapter Twenty

Clorra's body was carried through the caverns amidst the mourning Aluiens and laid on the same slab where they had tried to cure her. There, a blue fire consumed her without smoke or sound, reducing her body to ashes, which the Aluiens helped Parrentine take to the top of the mountain and scatter to the four winds. Parrentine participated mutely, moving as a man asleep.

That night, Ari saw Aluiens come among his companions, lift them, and carry their sleeping forms from the room, but he made no move to stop them. The others were carried out until only he and Sir Cadwel remained. Larke appeared, leaning on a cane.

"Time to wake him, lad." Larke gestured to the knight. Other Aluiens were silently taking the companions' belongings.

"What?" was Sir Cadwel's immediate response to Ari's hand on his shoulder. Ari smiled, trying to convey reassurance he wasn't sure he felt.

"Time to be going, oh vast and mighty warrior," Larke said.

Sir Cadwel sat up, his eyes narrowing. "Did you just call me fat?"

"We all increase with age, oh noblest of knights," Larke said. "But you only in greatness, of course."

Sir Cadwel grunted and stood, looking around. “What’s going on?”

“We’re taking a little trip,” Larke said. “First down the mountain, and then your friends will break camp, mount up, and journey a night’s march from here. In the morning, they will have no memory of where to find us, nor that Aridian does.”

“And me?” Sir Cadwel asked.

“Can you make them forget what happened here?” Ari said.

“We could, me lad, but little good would it do the world.” Larke said. “We have not the skill to create memories, only to suppress them. What would they think when they woke and could not recall what was done? Or shall we take all memory of her, so they shan’t even wonder? Yet too many knew her. It would be impossible.”

Ari sighed, giving up on that vague hope.

“Come,” Larke said. “All is done here.”

***

As the Aluiens approached, the soldiers raised the alarm, but soon all fell into a waking sleep. The companions were set down, and they joined the soldiers in breaking camp. In short order, everything was loaded and everyone was riding south and east. Sir Cadwel and Ari brought up the rear with Larke, whose gray awaited them at the bottom of the trail, along with Goldwin and Stew.

“Larke,” Ari said. “Why couldn’t you just let me remember? Maybe I could have stopped all this.”

“It was the promise the Lady made the council in exchange for saving you. You would lead an ordinary life.” Larke’s eyes scanned the star-filled sky. “The council felt it unwise to try saving you, working a magic we’ve never before attempted, to what consequence we could not know. The creation of the Empty Ones taught us the old rule is true: to mix human and Aluien can lead only to sorrow, and returning your life was a terrible lot of mixing.”

"I don't see why," Ari said after a moment.

"Because you should be dead," Larke said. "Twice over! Anything you do for the rest of your life is the result of our meddling. So in exchange for your life, the Lady promised you would be ordinary, and to be ordinary, you needs must be ignorant as well."

"But Sir Cadwel made me his page."

"Yes!" Larke's voice rang with consternation. "And the council wished to correct the situation, but the Lady argued this would be interfering. To mollify them, she sent me to ensure you end up an unremarkable page in Sorga."

"Correct the situation?" Ari felt a chill. "But then I won the joust and we went to confront Lord Mrakenson. So you really were trying to stop us, losing your horse and all. But you must have known we wouldn't give up."

"I didn't need to stop you," Larke said. "Just delay you. A messenger from the king was so near to hand to call you back. Just another day or two—"

"But we did go in, and I remembered everything, and you weren't there to fix it anymore," Ari said. "But the Lady could have made Sir Cadwel forget too, and me again."

"It had gone too far." Larke shook his head. "This all went too far. Our powers are not so great as that. Were we to take memories from the king as well, and Peine, and all in Sorga who knew of your journey?"

"You could have just killed Lord Ferringul at the start," Ari said.

"Hah! We've tried. In fact, that's half what we were about the night you died. He always eludes us. It's a great game for him, with his poisoned blade at the ready."

Ari looked away. He didn't like being reminded of his own death. His mind wandered until it alighted on his troubles at the tourney. He'd blamed them on Parrentine and his own nervousness. Now he wasn't so sure. He looked over at Larke, but the bard's head was sunk low to his breast, and he snored lightly.

The Aluien council head rode over, his glowing countenance grave. "Aridian, an oath is required of you. You must swear never again to reveal us. We ask you guard our people and our way of life. We ask you hold these others to the secrecy they have pledged. If we are to be known to these mortals, you must be our mortal protector."

"I swear, my lord," Ari stammered, taken aback by the formality of the request. As if his promise was a sign, others rode over to him then, speaking softly to him and reaching out to gently touch his face. As they came to him, he remembered them. He recalled the affection lavished on him when he was briefly among them.

Last came the Lady, bearing a silver medallion wrought with an intricate pattern that seemed to twist and change, defying attempts to fathom it. She told him it would keep Lord Ferringul and any other Empty One from being able to find him, and he was never to remove it. She clasped it round his neck herself, kissing him once on the forehead. And then she was gone, and though he was surrounded by people, Ari felt alone.

***

"Why am I allowed to be awake?" Sir Cadwel asked Larke as they reached their destination. The sleepwalkers dismounted and started making camp. It was about an hour before dawn. Ari set about putting up their tents while the bard and knight spoke nearby.

"You are marked, my friend," Larke said. "Not that I would have chosen it. Can't for the life of me understand what they see in you. Something about the greatest knight to ever live and an unparalleled store of military knowledge. No accounting for taste."

"Marked," Sir Cadwel said. "Explain."

"Certainly they didn't choose you for your verbosity," Larke said. Taking in Sir Cadwel's scowl, the bard continued. "It means on the day you are slated to die, one of us will offer you instead the gift of eternal life as an Aluien. Marked."

"You know when I will die?"

"Actually, the day has come and gone, but it will come again."

Ari glanced up at the silence that followed to see his mentor leveling a hard look at Larke.

"What?" the bard asked innocently. "It isn't a certain thing, when a man will die. When it is close, it is more certain, but when you travel with the Thrice Born, well, who's to say? The one who marked you will sense it, and she will come."

"She?"

"Yes." Larke said. "It is the Lady who marked you. Years ago, when you were young, she saw the greatness in you, the way you would shape the world."

"Shape the world?" Sir Cadwel said. "She should have marked Ennentine, then. I was just a young fool who thought battles were fun."

"Truly?" Larke sounded amused. "Who was it rose up from decades of war and vengeance to ban the barons together? Who was it, knowing himself and what was best for his land, who choose to make Ennentine king when the crown could so readily have been his own? Who was it, through the force of his will, brought peace to lands long made to suffer under the harsh yoke of war?"

"I, but—" Sir Cadwel stammered. The old knight's face showed shock at hearing the deeds of his youth so described. He looked to Ari for help, but Ari shrugged. He was on Larke's side. Ari was sure Sir Cadwel was the greatest knight to ever live.

"Do you know what they already call you in the tomes of history?" Larke asked, obviously enjoying himself. "Cadwel the Uniter. Cadwel Kingmaker. Cadwel—"

"Yes, well," Sir Cadwel interrupted. "I don't read much." He cleared his throat several times. "We best get into our tents. Dawn nears. Your people depart."

The knight held out one rough, scarred hand, and Larke clasped it. With a wave and a wink for Ari, the bard turned and hobbled back to his horse. It seemed to Ari that Goldwin and Stew both dipped their heads to the gray in farewell.

***

The ride back to the capital was long and dreary. Snow made travel more difficult, and an oppressive silence filled their evening camps. There seemed little to say after Clorra's death.

Sorrow and failure weighed heavily on them, and as he looked about him at the cold world, Ari felt a twinge of longing for the glowing caves of the Aluiens. There was peace there, and learning, and pursuits of knowledge only fathomable by the immortal. Ari had been one of them. Almost, he could see himself turning around and going back, leaving the trouble and turmoil of the mortal realm behind.

He scanned the snow-covered hills as the sun cut briefly through the cloud bank. The snowflakes reflected back a multitude of glinting lights, brighter and more dense than the stars on a moonless night. His mind drifted to memories of the ocean's azure waves before speeding northward to linger on Sorga's towering peaks. He could picture them soaring high over the home he'd seen but once, those northern peaks tipped in snow as old as stone.

A slight smile lifted his lips at the image he conjured up in his mind of Sorga's impenetrable walls. Above those walls flew the brown hawk on blue of Sorga, so long synonymous with the role of king's champion, a role Ari aspired to. And atop those walls, in his mind, stood Ispiria, watching each day for them to come home, his best friend Peine at her side. No, he would never abandon this life. He smiled a real smile. It was not time yet to give up the beauties and wonders of this world.

Chapter Twenty-One

They arrived in Poromont just before the end of winter, though the cold lingered and spring was not yet upon them. The celebration of their return was subdued, and the very next morning negotiations began with the goal of settling matters amicably between Lggothland and Hapland. The king of Hapland sent word he required the promise of a union with whatever offspring Parrentine may yet have and those of the crown prince of Hapland's issue, as well as a second marriage between his house and a foremost Lggothland dukedom a generation hence. Ari thought it odd to decide something that would happen so many years from now, but as it didn't concern him, he paid it little heed.

What did concern him was Sir Cadwel. When he was alone, the knight would sit for hours, an undrunk glass of wine in his hand, staring at nothing, and Ari found this even more worrying than the drunken guilt of their first ride south.

Ari knew what troubled the knight. Sir Cadwel felt he had failed. He felt he should have done more, somehow, to save Princess Clorra. Ari didn't know how to relieve him of this worry, so he didn't try, but he kept a careful eye on his mentor. Fortunately, in company, the knight seemed himself, and he insisted on being present at all negotiations with Kroost, speaking animatedly and firmly on behalf of king and country.

It was at the end of these negotiations, when all was decided and pen laid to paper and wine passed round, that Kroost raised the question of just how Parrentine was to beget enough heirs to rule Lggothland and be sent across the sea to fulfill the promise to Hapland.

"What?" Parrentine said, looking up from his glass, his eyes red with lack of sleep.

"I said," Kroost said. "Who's the lucky lass you get to be begetting with?" Ari noticed that ever since Sir Cadwel and Kroost had become friends, the Ambassador didn't seem to feel the need to re-don his facade of polite diplomacy.

Parrentine stared at Kroost, his lips slightly parted, but no sound emerging.

"I suppose we'll have to choose someone," King Ennentine said. "I did wish to avoid having any of the dukedoms think they were favored, but now there's no help for it."

Sir Cadwel put down his glass. "Actually, I think there's a good match for Parrentine that will circumvent that trouble for you, your majesty."

From his customary place against the wall behind Sir Cadwel's chair, Ari couldn't see the knight's face, but he could see Parrentine's as the prince clamped his mouth shut in a thin line, his wine glass hitting the thick wood of the table with a loud clank.

"How can you speak of such a thing?" Parrentine said. "How can you ask me to marry another, and Clorra's ashes barely cold?"

"You better marry another," Kroost said. "My king was promised an offspring of royal blood."

"Of course you must remarry, Parrentine," the king said. "It is your duty to your people."

Parrentine crossed his arms over his chest, looking away.

"So who did you have in mind, Cadwel?" Kroost asked, poorly disguised disdain on his face as he looked at Parrentine.

"I believe the Princess Siara would be a suitable match," Sir Cadwel said after a moment's hesitation.

Ari's heart jumped in his chest at the rightness of Sir Cadwel's suggestion. He should have known Sir Cadwel would look out for Siara. Parrentine's head snapped back around. Ari felt the happiness blooming inside him wither at the anger clear on Parrentine's face.

"My wife has been suggesting to me that very thing, truth be told," the king said with a glance at his son. "And I've noticed over the years that when Parrella sets her mind on something, she usually sees it done."

"I think it's a grand idea," Kroost said, raising his glass in a salute. "Pretty lass, and reinforces the peace you enjoy on your western border."

Parrentine stood up from the table with such abruptness as to overturn his chair. He glared around him at the ring of older men. "Never!" he spat, and stormed from the room.

"He'll come around," Kroost said, looking after the departed prince.

"Yes, in time," King Ennentine agreed.

Sir Cadwel nodded, and Ari got the distinct feeling Parrentine didn't have much of a chance of not marrying Siara. He only hoped that as the prince's heart healed, he'd learn to love his Wheylian bride, for both their sakes.

Three days later, when the weather finally broke and he and Sir Cadwel took to the road once again, it wasn't soon enough for Ari. He was tired of endless hours indoors. He longed for the freedom of travel, with space for him and Stew to ride. He missed Ispiria desperately, and Peine too.

They chose the coastal road north, forgoing the King's Way. The weather was more fierce on the coast, but warmer. They traveled with the forest to their left and were often in sight of the eastern sea, which enthralled Ari. He thought one day, he might try getting on a ship, even though he found the idea a bit scary. He wondered if he could bring Stew.

The only thing Ari didn't like about their trip north was that Sir Cadwel declined sparring. He said the cold of winter was too deep in his bones. Instead, the knight would stare into the fire. Ari wished Larke were there, or Peine. Maybe they would brighten Sir Cadwel's mood.

***

Ari was snapped from sleep by a sense of wrongness. His eyes scanned the inside of his small tent, ears straining. He smelled only wet leaves, sea salt and the lingering smoke of their quenched fire, but a tension filled him that would never allow sleep. He crawled from his bedding, surprised to see Sir Cadwel's tent stood open and vacant. There was in that black hollowness of Sir Cadwel's unoccupied tent a strange finality, as if the dwelling itself knew it had been abandoned.

Ari looked up at the sky, which was empty of any moon. He judged it to be several hours before dawn. In the soft earth in front of Sir Cadwel's tent, he could see footprints. They led to the woods.

Ari followed the trail slowly, as quietly as he could. He felt foolish, sneaking up on the knight. Sir Cadwel was not some child, wandered off. He was probably just seeking a bit of privacy, and the last thing Ari wanted to do was stumble across him and embarrass them both. He would not have gone, except every nerve in his body was twitching. The dark forest around him was hushed, and he shivered.

He crept after the footprints, pushing leafless branches gently out of his way. Inhaling deeply, he took in the smells of spring. The new earth, the lingering scent of rain. For a brief moment, he was potently reminded of the previous spring, when he had snuck from his uncle's inn and stumbled on an Aluien in a glade.

A clearing spread out before him, and he instinctively crouched down. It was not a good time for hiding in the woods. No bushes nor brush were grown up yet, and he didn't want to lie on the muddy ground unless he had to. Out of the corner of his eye, he saw the white of snowdrops, the little flowers half closed and dull in the moonless night.

In the clearing before him knelt Sir Cadwel. The knight's greatsword was jammed blade down into the soft ground in front of him. His head was bowed, and he seemed deep in thought. As Ari watched, Sir Cadwel looked up to the heavens, his expression searching.

Ari was embarrassed he let nameless night-fears drive him to spy on his mentor. He was about to sneak back to camp when he caught sight of a movement across the clearing. His skin went cold. He knew that undulating darkness.

The dark form surged forward, knife swinging down, but Sir Cadwel was on his feet, wrenching his sword from the earth as he sprang away. Ari blinked in surprise. He was good, but he would never know how his mentor could move so fast. Sir Cadwel, who seemed so unaware, reacted before Ari could even call out.

Sheathing his knife, Lord Ferringul drew his sword. It was thinner than the knight's, light and quick. He drew back his lips in a sneer. "I know you've been wanting to kill me, Cadwel," he hissed. "I thought I would give you the chance."

Ferringul lunged forward, his blade snaking out. Sir Cadwel parried easily, despite the weight of his broadsword. The knight dropped low.

"It's time I put you out of my way forever, old man," Ferringul said. "Someone must pay for thwarting me. A few days more and I would have broken her to my will. The perfect puppet queen to gain me the perfect puppet king!"

Sir Cadwel didn't waste his breath talking. Seeing his words in no way affected the knight, Ferringul fell silent as well. The two began raining blows on each other. Their swords rang like crazed church bells in the night.

It looked to Ari as if Sir Cadwel would win. The knight was fast, his skill greater. The small cuts and bruises Lord Ferringul received did not appear to slow him, though, and Ari began to worry. He knew how heavy Sir Cadwel's greatsword was. It was not meant for duels.

Ferringul took a deep slash on his left arm, but he merely smiled. Ari drew a quick, hissing breath, remembering something the Lady said. Lord Ferringul knew. The Empty One looked in Sir Cadwel's eyes, and he knew Sir Cadwel would die this night.

Ari's hand went to his belt, and he almost groaned aloud. He wasn't wearing his belt. He wasn't even wearing shoes. Just light breeches. Why had he not thought to bring his sword? What kind of a warrior was he?

Looking around, he spied a thick branch. He quietly pulled it to him, hefting it experimentally.

In the clearing, Ferringul made an arcane gesture, and Sir Cadwel went still, his eyes dulling. Ferringul smiled. "Enough of this game," he said in a soft, smug voice. "I enjoyed testing myself against you. You truly are as great as they say. Perhaps I will even indulge myself and partake of your flesh once you are dead."

A pale hand reached toward the knight, whose sword drooped listlessly. "Give me that weapon," Ferringul said. Ari recognized the same type of beguiling used on him in the past, both by the Aluiens and Lord Ferringul. He saw Sir Cadwel start to move, reversing the hilt of his blade.

"You cannot have him," Ari yelled, crashing into the clearing.

Ferringul spun about, his face stunned. "I did not sense you near," he said. His eyes took in the medallion on Ari's bare chest. An angry hiss left his mouth. He made another gesture. "You may as well remove that trinket and go back to your tent, boy," Ari's enemy whispered in honey-coated tones. "I will take care of your friend."

"You may as well fight me," Ari said, mimicking the other's dulcet voice. "Or are you afraid of a boy with a stick?" Ari dove forward, not waiting for an answer. His blow was aimed at Ferringul's head, but the creature ducked away, jumping back and swinging at Ari's midsection. Dropping one hand low along the length of the branch, Ari twisted the bottom end up, knocking aside the blow. He felt the damp wood crack.

He parried the next blow on the opposite end of the staff, wincing as it cracked further. He danced back. Ferringul moved to follow, and Ari darted to the left, landing a hard swing on the side of his opponent's head. Ferringul stumbled back slightly.

Ari continued to move left, bringing himself closer to his mentor. The knight stood, sword lowered, staring at nothing. Ari blocked a swing aimed at his head, ducking away as the rotting wood in his right hand crumbled. He jammed the jagged end of the branch into Ferringul's gut. Ferringul folded but didn't pause. His sword came in a wide arc, trying to remove Ari's head from his shoulders.

Dodging to avoid the blow, Ari leaped past Sir Cadwel. Reaching out, he clawed the knight's sword free. The blade fell to the ground. Realizing Ari's goal, Ferringul pressed after him, driving him away from the sword as Ari blocked blow after blow with his increasingly shorter piece of stick.

Dropping the last bit of wood, Ari charged. Ferringul swung his blade in, aiming at Ari's middle. At the last instant, Ari flattened, launching himself to the ground under the blade and sliding past his enemy. He came up behind Ferringul, Sir Cadwel's sword in his hand.

As Lord Ferringul spun to face him, Ari leveled a swing at his neck. Ferringul came about just in time to see the blade coming, but not soon enough to stop it. With shocking ease, Ari felt Sir Cadwel's sword decapitate Lord Ferringul. His head sailed through the air, bouncing off a nearby tree. It came to rest nose down in last year's decomposing leaves as the body collapsed to the earth.

There was very little blood, Ari noticed. Probably a human would have a lot more blood, if his head were cut off. Before Ari's eyes, the remains began to shrivel. They curled in upon themselves, turning black. Ari stepped back, covering his nose at the smell of decay.

"Ari?" Sir Cadwel called.

Ari turned to see the knight looking north, where two glowing forms stood at the edge of the clearing.

"Thrice-Born." The Lady smiled. "You have changed this man's fate."

"You've come for him," Ari whispered. He moved to stand beside Sir Cadwel, naked blade still raised.

"Ari, me lad." Larke raised an eyebrow. "Could ye find it in yer heart to point that sword another way?"

"Sorry," Ari said, reversing the sword and handing it to Sir Cadwel, who placed it point down in the earth and rested both hands on the hilt.

"What happens now?" Sir Cadwel asked. To Ari's surprise, he didn't sound suspicious or angry, merely curious.

"You did not die this night," the Lady said, as if she spoke of the weather. "It seems we came too soon to take you home."

"I hope it doesn't disappoint you," Sir Cadwel said.

"No night is perfect," Larke said.

"Not with you around, it isn't," Sir Cadwel said.

"So he doesn't have to go?" Ari asked, relieved.

"We do not take lives," the Lady said. "We give them back." She turned and looked at the crumpled remains of Lord Ferringul. "You have destroyed a great enemy of our people, Thrice-Born. It seems we are in your debt."

She gestured, and Lord Ferringul's half-decayed body was engulfed in the same blue flame they had used to cremate Clorra. They stood in silent vigil, watching him burn, as if to assure themselves every last bit of Lord Ferringul was gone. As the fire went out, Ari felt a weight lift, and glancing around, he didn't think he was the only one.

No one will bother to scatter his ashes, Ari thought. He doubted even animals would want anything to do with what was left of Ferringul.

"I think more than just the Aluiens are in your debt, boy," Sir Cadwel said, his voice gruff.

"It was a spectacular battle, me lad," Larke said. "In truth worthy of a ballad."

"One, I think, you shall sing only for us," the Lady said.

"Yes," Larke said, but his tone was wistful. "Yes, I know. It is not a tale fit for this world."

"You have done well, Aridian," the Lady said. "May the rest of your journey be in peace."

"Until we meet again, lad, Cadwel," Larke said with a bow to each of them.

Ari realized they were fading, but he couldn't tell if they were disappearing or moving away. "Larke," he called.

"Aye, lad?" came a distant reply.

"Someday, will you sing at my wedding?" There was no answer, but Ari thought he heard a chuckle in the wind stirring the branches on the trees.

"Your wedding?" Sir Cadwel asked, raising an eyebrow.

"Well, that is, I mean—" Ari stammered, blushing.

"I'm sure you both will be very happy," Sir Cadwel said. He clasped Ari briefly on the shoulder, and they turned and walked back to their camp.

ABOUT THE AUTHOR

Summer Hanford grew up on a dairy farm in Upstate New York. After graduating from Marcellus High School, she went on to complete an undergraduate degree in psychology, followed by two years each of graduate and doctoral work in behavioral neurology. Eventually, Summer realized her true passion is writing fantasy novels. She now lives with her husband in the Blue Water region of Michigan, where she writes fulltime. To learn more about Summer and her work, visit www.summerhanford.com.